Account of the Union Meeting

Anatiposi

Anonymous

Account of the Union Meeting

Reprint of the original, first published in 1874.

1st Edition 2023 | ISBN: 978-3-38250-160-0

Anatiposi Verlag is an imprint of Outlook Verlagsgesellschaft mbH.

Verlag (Publisher): Outlook Verlag GmbH, Zeilweg 44, 60439 Frankfurt, Deutschland
Vertretungsberechtigt (Authorized to represent): E. Roepke, Zeilweg 44, 60439 Frankfurt, Deutschland
Druck (Print): Books on Demand GmbH, In de Tarpen 42, 22848 Norderstedt, Deutschland

ACCOUNT

of the

UNION MEETING

for the

PROMOTION OF SCRIPTURAL HOLINESS,

held at

OXFORD

AUGUST 29 to SEPTEMBER 7, 1874.

LONDON:
DALDY, ISBISTER & CO., 56, LUDGATE HILL.

*** This volume is made up of notes made by those who were present at the Oxford Meeting for the Promotion of Scriptural Holiness. It is a matter of much regret that addresses from many valued speakers were not reported, so that the same names recur more frequently than the persons themselves would have desired or permitted had there been a more full report.

From the various dates assigned by different reports to the same addresses, it was found impossible to place them with certainty in the exact meetings in which they were delivered. A few liberties have been taken in filling out the evident but unreported purpose of the speakers, who cannot be held responsible, beyond the general purpose of their addresses, for what is here reported.

The book is sent out in the hope that the same overshadowing presence of the Spirit which made the Oxford Meetings what they were, may accompany the reading of this imperfect and partial report. May many hearts be stirred up by it to seek—*and to find*—the Lord in the fulness of His grace and the energy of His mighty power!

May we also venture the hope that this narrative will lead Christians in many places to gather together to seek the Lord in the fulness of His grace. The circumstances and details of meetings may greatly vary, but He will always open the windows of heaven upon those who bring all their tithes into His storehouse; He will "be found" in living power by those who seek His face; He will manifest Himself to those who keep His commandments, not in the oldness of the letter, but in the newness of love.

Preface.*

God be thanked that He seems now to be calling His Church specially to betake herself to her Sovereign Lord and Head, in order to claim her undoubted heritage of power and blessing. The cry has gone forth afresh, "Awake, awake; put on thy strength, O Zion; put on thy beautiful garments, O Jerusalem, the holy city: for henceforth there shall no more come into thee the uncircumcised and the unclean." And though many do not, and will not, hear the call, and are content to remain as they are, hundreds are hearing it, and, in obedience to the Divine summons, are setting themselves to claim the blessing which the bounty of their God has promised them. Hence meetings of God's people up and down the country, gathered for the express purpose of waiting upon the Lord, and seeking from Him the power to serve Him, with the full surrender of all that they are and have. The

---

* From an Address delivered to the members of the Evangelical Union for the Diocese of Carlisle, at their Annual Conference, held at Kendal, September 29th, 1874, by the Rev. T. D. Harford Battersby, M.A., Vicar of St. John's, Keswick, and Hon. Canon of Carlisle.

meetings at Oxford at the beginning of September last were a notable example of this. It was in itself a remarkable sign of what God had been leading many hearts to, that more than 1,000 people should be willing to leave their homes, and to travel considerable distances, at the summons of one who was a stranger to them, and an American, not to listen to eloquent addresses merely, or to take part in scenes of transient human excitement, but to wait upon God for the attainment of a higher measure of "Scriptural holiness."

And so vivid was the sense of God's presence at these meetings, and so unprecedented the results in the experience of most of those who attended, that the conviction was forced upon them that a new era of blessing was about to dawn upon the Church of God, in which the power of God would afresh be manifested in an extraordinary degree, for the comfort of His people and the confusion of His adversaries.

I had the great privilege of taking part in that ten days' "Union for the promotion of Scriptural holiness," and language fails me to tell of the richness and fulness of the blessing which was poured out upon us during those wondrous gatherings. We were taken out of ourselves; we were led step by step, after deep and close searchings of heart, to such a consecration of ourselves to God, as in the ordinary times of a religious life hardly seemed possible, and we were brought, hundreds of us, clergy and laymen, men and women, to the enjoyment of a peace in trusting Christ for present and future sanctification which exceeded our utmost hopes. These things were testified openly, evening after evening, as the days went on, by clergymen of the Established Church in the presence of many hundreds of Christian people, and so deep and solemn was the impression produced by these testimonies, and by the faithful teaching of those who were chosen to address the assemblies, that persons who had failed in the earlier days to receive the blessing, a blessing which they saw reflected on the very countenances of their more favoured brethren, were stirred up with intenser earnestness to seek for the same benefit, and, I may add, in the great majority of instances, failed not to find it. I can never forget those happy days; the language of the 126th Psalm, I felt then, and I feel still, could alone fully express the emotions of our hearts. "When the Lord turned again the captivity of Zion, we were like them that dream. Then was our mouth filled with laughter, and our tongue with singing: then said they among the heathen, the Lord hath done great things for them. The Lord hath done great things for us; whereof we are glad." And yet there was nothing whatever of fleshly excitement in the meetings; there were no impassioned addresses; no excited prayers; a still, calm, sober, though deeply earnest spirit, seemed to animate both speakers and hearers. We often knelt in silent prayer, and it was then, perhaps, that the presence of the Divine "Comforter" was most felt, and that our souls were most awed under a sense of His Holy, yet gracious operations in our hearts. But I am conscious that my poor words can give but the very faintest impression of what these Oxford meetings were, and yet to those who were not present, it is possible that they may savour of exaggeration; and it will be asked, What were the permanent results? Were the impressions produced at these meetings followed up by any sensible increase of power in service, by mastery over special temptations, or by other equally satisfactory evidences of the abiding presence of the Holy Ghost with those who experienced them?

My answer to this question can only be a very partial one. I have had little opportunity of meeting or conversing with others since, who had the privilege of sharing with me in the blessings of that festal time. But I have seen and heard enough to convince me that the joy and the peace to which so many bore testimony during those happy ten days, were indeed the "fruit of the Spirit," and that just in proportion as there has been faithfulness in guarding the treasure there received, has it been productive of those definite practical results to which I have alluded. It were easy for me to mention those who, to my own knowledge, assert that they discovered a secret of power in service for Christ at these meetings, to which before they were comparatively strangers, and that their Christian life has flowed on mostly since with a sweet calm and inward peace which calls for continual thanksgiving. Others, not present at the meetings themselves, have been stirred up by what they read or heard of the blessing poured out at Oxford, to seek for, and lay claim to the same blessing, and have, to the full measure of their faith, "divided the spoil" with those who were there.

But why should those who believe in that first instalment of the Divine gift, which was poured out at Jerusalem 1800 years ago, doubt the reality of the same Spirit's presence and power at Oxford, where such very similar tokens of His work were manifested? If there was no gift of tongues, there was no lack of that "more excellent gift of charity," binding and cementing all hearts together in the most perfect sense of unity and brotherhood. If there was no great excitement, such as led the dwellers at Jerusalem to ask, "What meaneth this?" there was something in the unexcited flocking together of so many hundreds day by day, and many times a day, to the place of assembly, and in the supernatural calm and joy which shone out in the very features of not a few of them, which prompted the same question, a question which was thus answered by a simple countryman, to one who put it to him at the door of the Corn Exchange, "Don't you know? It is all the Christian folk in all the world, going to be one sect." So truly might it be said once more, in this instance, at least, "The multitude of them that believed were of one heart and of one soul."

I have brought before you these particulars of the meetings at Oxford, because I myself was permitted to be present, and can testify from my own experience of the advantage to be derived from thus meeting together. It may be asked, indeed, what was the peculiarity of these meetings, in distinction from other meetings for religious edification, such as are so common in our day? What was there in the method pursued at these meetings, or in the doctrines propounded, which tended to bring about results so remarkable? In what respect did they differ from our annual conferences, or from other special gatherings, having for their object the spiritual advancement of those who partake in them?

I shall endeavour to answer these questions. In one respect there was no difference between these meetings, and others of a religious character which are commonly attended by Evangelical Christians, in that no new or peculiar doctrines were enforced, and that the Word of God and prayer, with the singing of simple hymns, were the sole instruments employed for securing the desired end.

In another respect, however, there was a difference. There was a definiteness of purpose at these meetings, and a directness of aim in the speakers, which were very remarkable. That purpose was, as expressed in the circular which announced the meetings, "the promotion of Scriptural holiness." The aim of the speakers therefore was to bring about this result by an ordered scheme of teaching out of the Holy Scriptures. There was a gradual progress in the truths brought forth. The promises of a condition of abiding holiness; examples of the manner in which it had been sought and attained; the contrast between such a state, and that of the larger portion of the professing Church at the present day; the satisfaction and peace enjoyed by those who have attained to the one, and the unsatisfied state of soul of those who stop short of it; these, and other kindred topics, were pressed home, with every variety of appeal to the hearts of the hearers, and each person was invited to self-examination as to his and her state; to a renunciation of all idols of the flesh and spirit, and to a willing surrender of all to Christ, with a full trust in Him for the bestowal of the blessing asked. Such was the character of the teaching employed; whilst, besides this, opportunity was given daily for same Spirit's presence and power at Oxford, where such very similar tokens of His work were manifested? If there was no gift of tongues, there was no lack of that "more excellent gift of charity," binding and cementing all hearts together in the most perfect sense of unity and brotherhood. If there was no great excitement, such as led the dwellers at Jerusalem to ask, "What meaneth this?" there was something in the unexcited flocking together of so many hundreds day by day, and many times a day, to the place of assembly, and in the supernatural calm and joy which shone out in the very features of not a few of them, which prompted the same question, a question which was thus answered by a simple countryman, to one who put it to him at the door of the Corn Exchange, "Don't you know? It is all the Christian folk in all the world, going to be one sect." So truly might it be said once more, in this instance, at least, "The multitude of them that believed were of one heart and of one soul."

I have brought before you these particulars of the meetings at Oxford, because I myself was permitted to be present, and can testify from my own experience of the advantage to be derived from thus meeting together. It may be asked, indeed, what was the peculiarity of these meetings, in distinction from other meetings for religious edification, such as are so common in our day? What was there in the method pursued at these meetings, or in the doctrines propounded, which tended to bring about results so remarkable? In what respect did they differ from our annual conferences, or from other special gatherings, having for their object the spiritual advancement of those who partake in them?

I shall endeavour to answer these questions. In one respect there was no difference between these meetings, and others of a religious character which are commonly attended by Evangelical Christians, in that no new or peculiar doctrines were enforced, and that the Word of God and prayer, with the singing of simple hymns, were the sole instruments employed for securing the desired end.

In another respect, however, there was a difference. There was a definiteness of purpose at these meetings, and a directness of aim in the speakers, which were very remarkable. That purpose was, as expressed in the circular which announced the meetings, "the promotion of Scriptural holiness." The aim of the speakers therefore was to bring about this result by an ordered scheme of teaching out of the Holy Scriptures. There was a gradual progress in the truths brought forth. The promises of a condition of abiding holiness; examples of the manner in which it had been sought and attained; the contrast between such a state, and that of the larger portion of the professing Church at the present day; the satisfaction and peace enjoyed by those who have attained to the one, and the unsatisfied state of soul of those who stop short of it; these, and other kindred topics, were pressed home, with every variety of appeal to the hearts of the hearers, and each person was invited to self-examination as to his and her state; to a renunciation of all idols of the flesh and spirit, and to a willing surrender of all to Christ, with a full trust in Him for the bestowal of the blessing asked. Such was the character of the teaching employed; whilst, besides this, opportunity was given daily for clergymen and others, who had come into the enjoyment of that condition of soul which was aimed at, to confess what the Lord had done for them, and bear witness to the results of it in their own experience.

Here, indeed, there was a novel feature introduced, as compared with religious meetings in which English churchmen and clergymen are accustomed to take part, and whilst I am very sensible that exception may be taken to this sort of thing, and I feel that such an element needs to be employed with great caution, yet I am bound to say that the testimonies given at Oxford, with some few exceptions, were of the most solemn and awe-inspiring character, and, at the same time, were most effective in encouraging others to avail themselves of the same grace, which had proved such an abundant source of blessing to the speaker.

It is not necessary doubtless to adhere, in any future meetings which may be held for a similar purpose, to the special mode in which the Oxford meetings were conducted. If those who conduct them be under the guidance of the Spirit of God, He will doubtless show them how they ought to act in each particular case, so as best to subserve the object for which the assemblies are gathered, and the individual peculiarities of those assembled. But, at the same time, it can hardly be doubted that if the same blessed results are aimed at, something of the same method must be employed to produce them. God is a God of order; and, amidst all the varieties in detail which characterise the action of His Spirit for the good of souls, there will be found a general similarity in the modes in which that action is manifested.

Introductory.

THE Oxford Conference was the expression of a widely realized need of a more definite consecration to the Lord and trust in His promises. It was to a great extent a meeting of Christians who, while walking in full unvarying assurance of the forgiveness of sins, were yet feeling a painful deficiency in their own personal experience as to maintained communion with God, and uniform victory over sin. Probably almost every one who came would have the next hour gone to the stake once erected at Oxford for the martyr-confessors, were it still surrounded with burning faggots, rather than have denied their Lord. Many of them were walking in practical devotedness to the service of their Master, and had been the channels of salvation and blessings to others; and yet—there was a sad *yet* in their experience—they had great sorrows pressing upon them, and great needs not yet supplied. Probably there is no greater sorrow in life to those who ardently love their Saviour than the sense of frequently and continuously grieving their dearest Friend. Other sorrows are soothed by the passage of time or by becoming used to them. This only becomes more deep as fresh discoveries of the love of Christ to us are made. They saw Christ as not only "the Way" to reach heaven by, but as a Way to walk in, not sometimes, but always, and yet they often wandered out of this Way and stumbled. They read of the victory, the faith which overcometh the world, and yet they were frequently overcome instead of being "more than conquerors." They sought to walk in the light, and yet were too often in twilight or darkness. The testimonies were before them of hundreds of the most sober and godly Christians, who had long walked in sadness and too frequent failure, but who had now by faith found a new and higher level of experience.

The blessed Master in the midst of all His mission, with a world of sinners around Him, knew that there was something more important to His disciples than work. He understood their weakness; He had mourned over their self-seeking and impetuosity; He knew their need of inward quiet and restfulness of spirit; and He desired to replace the tumultuous energies of nature by His own calm heavenly power. He perceived even in their enthusiasm of service, the danger of their being thrown out of full communion with Himself; He knew, even after He had taught them all things in Moses and the prophets concerning Himself, that they needed to tarry at Jerusalem until they were endued with power from on high; and the call to Oxford seemed to many like the Master's voice to weary and often-failing labourers, "Come ye aside and rest awhile;"—"Wait for the promise of the Father, which ye have heard of Me."

The great power and blessing which had marked special meetings for consecration held during the past year, for two or three days at a time, at Mildmay Park and Hanover Square Rooms, London; at Dublin, Manchester, Nottingham, Leicester, Paris, and other cities, prepared the hearts of many to expect larger and more definite blessing from a more complete separation from ordinary cares, when the up-lifting of the spiritual life at one meeting would not be clouded by urgent duties and social distractions before the next should occur. The privilege anticipated in continuous meetings of spiritual communion and prayer was, that the advance should be maintained from meeting to meeting, and the heart prepared for those larger and more glorious manifestations of the love of God passing knowledge, which result in a permanently higher level of communion and power.

The object, then, of the "Union Meeting at Oxford, for the promotion of Scriptural Holiness," was to lead Christians to acts of more complete consecration to the Lord, and of unlimited trust in His promises, thus preparing the way to "be filled with the Spirit,"—"baptised with the Holy Ghost."

Its origin was in the desire that a number of young University men, who had found partial blessing in some meetings for consecration, held with them at Cambridge during the severe pressure of the term, should have a few days of quiet prayer and meditation upon the Scriptural possibilities of the Christian life, as to maintained communion with the Lord and victory over all known sin. The plan being alluded to in the presence of the generous proprietor of Broadlands Park, he at once said, "My place is at your service if you will accept it." The plan was extended to the invitation of about a hundred persons for six days, July 17–23, all of them to be the guests of the Right Hon. W. Cowper-Temple, at the mansion, or in the neighbouring village of Romsey.

Among those present were Rev. Messrs. Boardman, Douglas, Wilberforce, Hopkins, Thornton, W. Arthur, Fox, the Earl of Chichester, Samuel Morley, Esq., M.P., S. A. Blackwood, Esq.; and from France, Pasteurs Theodore Monod, Baron Hart, Rivier, and others; also M. St. Hilaire.

The time was not so much occupied in teaching, as in seeking to realise, in living, personal apprehension, the truths of the Word already known or taught by those present. The means were the reading of the Scriptures and occasional short addresses, but especially prayer, consecration, acts of faith, silent waiting upon God, and the confining ourselves for the time to topics bearing upon personal experience of grace.

The meetings were mostly held beside the quiet, flowing river, under the shade of some large and beautiful beech-trees. Such was the absorbing interest, that no difficulty was found in gathering the guests at seven o'clock in the coolness of the morning; and it was even an effort to separate when the breakfast hour of nine came. At ten o'clock conversational meetings were held, Bibles in hand, in different places, and at eleven o'clock there was prayer, with singing, and addresses. About one o'clock Mrs. Pearsall Smith held meetings for ladies. The three o'clock conversational meetings were followed by a general gathering at four; and after tea Bible-readings were given, till the regular evening meeting.

So quietly, and with such freedom from excitement, did the current of the meetings flow on, that their continuousness seemed rather to refresh than weary those present. The felt presence and power of God pervaded every meeting, and many stated that the long periods of silent prayer which accompanied the meetings had been to them the most solemn seasons of their spiritual history.

The expression of the feelings of most of those present would be, "My soul is athirst for God, the living God!"—and He did satisfy the longings of His waiting people. Possibilities of faith before not dreamed of, or but dimly seen, became to us glorious, present realities.

We began with the negative side, renunciation of discerned evil, and even of doubtful things which are not of faith, and therefore sin. For some days the company was held under the searching light of God, to see and to remove any obstacles to a divine communion, aught that frustrated the grace of God. We sought to have that which was true in God as to our judicial standing in a risen Christ also true in personal appropriation and experience. Many secret sins, many a scarcely recognised reserve as to *entire* self-renunciation, were here brought up into the light of consciousness, and put away in the presence of the Lord. We desired to make *thorough* work, so as to leave no known evil or self-will unyielded; and we have reason to hope that those present did so, and that we took the position of solemn purpose to renounce instantly everything in which we should find ourselves "otherwise minded," as from time to time "God shall reveal even this unto us."

These days of preparation and solemn waiting were most essential before those which followed. Alas, how many had to acknowledge to God that, while talking of sitting in heavenly places, they had been stumbling in the mire of this world; while clearly teaching a standing in a risen Christ, they had been living more or less after the corrupt flesh! "These things ought not so to be." The cry was loudly sounded in our hearts, "Awake to righteousness"—practical, actual righteousness—"and sin not!"

The provisions in the indwelling Holy Ghost, the exceeding great promises of the Word, the separating power of the cross, the risen Saviour, the life more abundantly, were then set before us in various aspects, and pressed upon us as realities, to be grasped by faith and held with unfaltering grasp.

When many or most were able to say that they took Christ to be their Saviour from not only the guilt but the power and practice of sin, we were led on to see that the Scripture command, "Be *filled* with the Spirit," was our immediate privilege, and that Pentecost was but a sample of what was the gift to the Church in all generations of this "the dispensation of the

Spirit," in which we are living. As we waited and prayed "with one accord," there came upon the company such a sense of the presence and power of God as filled most hearts full—unspeakably full—of the realisation of the Father, Son and Holy Spirit. "The communion of the saints" never meant so much to us before. The great truths we had believed and taught were illuminated as with the sun, and many felt the power of the Spirit for service as never before.

After this, in all the meetings, we were able to fix our minds on Christ Himself, and to dwell on the closer union to which, in His love, He was calling us. Our one aim had been to get "out of self into Christ," and now it seemed no longer any effort to realise how truly we had been made "one" with the Christ in whom we trusted. We were prepared then to take up in a succeeding meeting the reality of Christ as "our life"—the very life of our lives—Himself living in these tabernacles a supernatural life—the great Heart and Head, vitalising and guiding the "members of His body." It was no new teaching, but new, and soul-inspiring, satisfying *realisation* of old lessons, learned in the head, and now experienced in our consciousness. The more we yield ourselves thus to the indwelling Christ, the more He makes us "pure in heart;" and the more here and now "we call on Him out of a pure heart," the more we shall even now "see God," and by beholding the glory of the Lord be "changed into the same image from glory to glory."

In the intervals of the meetings, it was interesting to see groups gathered, in the more secluded places in the woods by the river, on their knees, praying, searching the Scriptures, or speaking earnestly to each other of the all-absorbing subjects of our meetings. Some one had proposed to have reading at the meal-times, so as to concentrate our minds; but no such plan was needed to keep the company, even at times of refreshment, to the one engrossing subject. It was the nearest to the employments of heaven of anything we had ever known, to be so easily and absorbingly occupied with the contemplation and praise of Christ. How earnestly had He waited for this more full response to His own love! Having saved us, He comes as the Heavenly Bridegroom to win our *hearts*. At first we cannot believe this—surely He can hardly mean this! But He has set His heart upon the bride. At length she suddenly sees that it *must* be so, and she yields her heart—her whole heart; the barriers are broken, and she comes to "dwell in love and in God." Then it is easy in *this* love to "bear *all* things," and to "love one another with a pure heart fervently"—to love even the unlovely. As we knelt in silence beneath the trees, it seemed as if He said to the soul, "How much love will you give?" and the heart-answer was, "All! All!" "And service?" "All!" "And how fully will you follow Me?" "Lord, I will follow Thee whithersoever Thou goest!"

There would have been no condemnation had the alabaster box not been broken and poured out, for no such enthusiasm of love could be demanded or acceptable as mere duty. But when done from love, it was to be held in everlasting remembrance. When thus we give to Him, we receive without measure from Him—"good measure, pressed down, running over," "rivers of living water." Service took a new and more sweet aspect than ever before in many hearts, and when, in the final meeting, the thought of "filling up that which is behind of the sufferings of Christ for His body's sake, which is the Church," was brought before us, many were able to ask even to "suffer with Christ," if so be they might thus express their gratitude and love.

Alas! that we can but give in our poor words glimpses of what were only themselves glimpses of the fulness of Jesus. It was the realisation to us of our Lord's word, "I will love him and manifest myself unto him." If a few days of special consecration and trust can open such a soul-inspiring vista of the eternal love of Christ, what must His unveiled presence be?

A letter received from Rev. Theodore Monod, a Paris pasteur, says:—

"The difference between those Broadlands meetings and many others that I have attended is just the difference between a flower and the name of a flower. Christians too often meet only to talk about good and precious things; peace, joy, love, and so on; but there we actually had the very things themselves. I cannot be grateful enough to God for having led me into such a soul-satisfying and Christ-glorifying faith. I think I may say that I got all that I expected, and more. And I begin to suspect that we always get from God everything—provided it be good for us—that we ask for, expecting to get it. Oh for self-forgetting faith—that I may have more, and more, and more of it, and that the Church of Christ may cease to grieve Him, distress herself, and hinder the coming of His kingdom, by disbelieving His Word! My French companions have all derived much benefit from the Conference. God be praised for His work! Never mind the world, nor the devil, as long as you have the sunshine of Jesus' smile in your heart."

The following beautiful verses, showing the progress of his spiritual life, were written by M. Monod during the meetings at Broadlands, and will be read here with peculiar interest.

THE ALTERED MOTTO.

Oh the bitter shame and sorrow,
  That a time could ever be,
When I let the Saviour's pity
Plead in vain, and proudly answered,
  "All of self, and none of Thee.

Yet He found me; I beheld Him
  Bleeding on the accursed tree,
Heard Him pray, "Forgive them Father!"
And my wistful heart said faintly,
  "Some of self, and some of Thee."

Day by day His tender mercy,
  Healing, helping, full and free,
Sweet and strong, and ah! so patient,
Brought me lower, while I whispered,
  "Less of self, and more of Thee."

> **Higher than the highest heavens,**
> **Deeper than the deepest sea,**
> **Lord, Thy love at last hath conquered;**
> **Grant me now my soul's desire—**
> **"*None of self, and all of Thee.*"**

The power in the Broadlands meeting was such that it was the general exclamation, "We must repeat this meeting on a larger scale, where all who desire, can attend." One of the guests volunteered £500 toward the expenses of such a public meeting, none of which, however, was needed or called for.

The next point was the place. Many were named, and reluctantly put by on account of want of accommodation for large numbers. At length, as we were walking up and down by the side of the beautiful river which runs through the park, Mr. Stevenson Blackwood exclaimed, by a happy inspiration, "*Why not at Oxford?*" "Yes, by all means, Oxford?" was the general response.

Several invitations to hold conversational meetings with undergraduates at Oxford, such as had been held at Cambridge, had been declined during the past season, because there was an unwillingness felt to influence the young men in any way not fully approved by their friend, the Rev. A. M. W. Christopher, Rector of St. Aldate's. Mr. Christopher had felt an honest anxiety lest the current of teaching at the various conversational meetings should not be fully Scriptural. These anxieties, however, had been largely removed. He thus describes his having been led to promote the meeting:—

"My heart has been full of praise during and since the Oxford Conference, because God so graciously led me to help in this good work. So great a blessing was enjoyed by many of those who attended the private meetings at Broadlands, that the Christians there felt that a meeting open to all should be held, and Oxford was selected. Mr. Pearsall Smith at once came to Oxford and called on me. I did then what I hope to do always, I asked the Lord to guide me, and trusted Him to do so. After prayer I felt certain that it would not please the Lord Jesus for me to refuse to help a believing effort to promote in His people, by the use of His holy Word with prayer, holiness and devotion to His service. I was on the point of leaving home for my annual rest, and Mr. P. Smith's visit was a brief one. There was no time to consult brethren, so I acted upon the conviction given me, and did what I could to promote the Conference. My mind was at once guided to two Christians to do the necessary work, and they did it admirably. Mr. Charles Badcock kindly acted as honorary secretary, and Mr. Henry Collis arranged all matters about lodgings for the visitors.

"A short time ago, I could not have believed that I should see my way to promote such a Conference, and I never had faith to expect such a manifestation of God's power as there has been."

The details of the meeting were settled during a mission week, in August, at Langley Park, the seat of the late excellent Sir Thomas Beauchamp, Bart., near Norwich, who shortly after passed from an earnest life of service to an eternity of reward. Having had a great blessing in a similar meeting the previous year, he again generously gathered about forty clergymen, and many others, for five days of consecration and prayer. With mingled sadness and joy we recall Sir Thomas's parting words:—"These have been the most blessed and the happiest days of my whole life." The corn was ripening fast, and He who alone knows when it is "fully ripe," soon thrust in the sickle and gathered him home into His own unveiled presence.

From this meeting the following call to the Oxford meeting was issued:—

"UNION MEETING FOR THE PROMOTION OF SCRIPTURAL HOLINESS.

"*To be held at Oxford, August 29th to September 7th, 1874.*

"In every part of Christendom the God of all grace has given to many of His children a feeling of deep dissatisfaction with their present spiritual state, and a strong conviction that the truths they believe might and should exercise a power over their hearts and lives, altogether beyond anything they have as yet experienced.

"They have been brought to see that personal holiness is God's *purpose* for them as well as His *command*, and that this abiding in Christ, with its results, is assuredly brought within the reach of those who will go to Him for it, with a whole-hearted surrender of their entire being, their circumstances, and their surroundings, to their Father's will.

"The Holy Spirit has given them these strong convictions, and has created a hungering and thirsting after righteousness,—practical righteousness,—a holy conformity to the will of God. They see with deep distress the grievous gap there is between what they *know* of Scriptural truth, and how they *live*. This is not a reaching out toward new forms of doctrine or of ecclesiastical system, but the felt need of more vitality in what has been already accepted. The increase of light which God has given them, has shown them the feebleness of their faith, and the proportionate scantiness of the fruits of righteousness they bear. And they feel their greatest need to be a more powerful realisation, through the Spirit, of the Gospel truth they already know and preach.

"In America this spiritual hunger has, for many years, drawn together large numbers of Christians, often five or six thousand, from a radius of fifteen hundred miles, and even some from across the Atlantic, to wait together upon God for the realisation of an entire self-surrender to the Lord Jesus Christ, and for a full trust in Him for the heart and power to serve Him. These meetings have been made memorable by the great work of the Holy Spirit in many of those who have attended them. They have been marked by freedom from excitement, and by quiet, earnest, expectant waiting upon God. Familiar truths of the Gospel, set forth from Holy Scripture in the standards of their faith, have been pressed on those assembled, with the utmost simplicity of language, and with much vocal and silent prayer. The speakers, selected have not necessarily been those of the greatest eloquence or natural power, but those who have been most walking in the power of the Holy Spirit. Removed from the bustle of their ordinary lives for several consecutive days, Christians, thus waiting on the Lord, have gained a rest of soul, in the harmony of their wills with the holy will of God, in which His searching Word and His still small voice could be heard in their listening hearts. They have realised, more than ever before, what it is to 'be filled with the Spirit.'

"It would hardly be an exaggeration to say that thousands of ministers have, through God's blessing on these Conferences, found a Divine power and unction, when they have returned to their usual work for Christ, beyond their largest expectations. We think it would not be an over-statement to say that tens of thousands of conversions have been traced to the fresh spiritual energy God has given to many of those who have attended these remarkable gatherings.

"The similar effects upon the hearts of those of different nationalities, who attended private meetings of this character last month at Broadlands Park, Hampshire, and Langley Park, Norfolk, has made those who were present feel that a similar meeting *must* be held, if God permit, open to all whose hearts may be moved to attend it.

"For this Oxford has been selected, as between one and two thousand persons can be accommodated in the hotels and lodgings now left vacant by University men.

"It is proposed to occupy as many churches, chapels, and halls as shall be offered for the purpose, every evening, for evangelistic sermons, and addresses to the unconverted. For these, special persons who offer will be appointed without interrupting the current of the meetings for Christians. So large and uniform a blessing to unbelievers also has hitherto accompanied consecration meetings of this character, that we prayerfully count on a similar blessing in Oxford.

"We earnestly advise those who attend this meeting to remain, at any practicable sacrifice, the whole Pentecostal period of ten days.

"It has been thought best by the clergy and ministers who are specially interested in this meeting, that I should myself call it.

"R. PEARSALL SMITH.

"LANGLEY PARK,
"*August* 8*th*, 1874."

A number of prominent ministers from France, Germany, and Switzerland, are to be present. Among many others, the Christians named below have also expressed their desire to co-operate in gathering this meeting. The Company of most of them, if not all, is expected at Oxford.

The Very Rev. THE DEAN OF CANTERBURY.
REV. W. HAY AITKEN, Liverpool.
,, W. ARTHUR, London.
,, W. E. BOARDMAN.
,, W. A. CHAPMAN, London.
,, A. M. W. CHRISTOPHER, Oxford.
,, THAIN DAVIDSON, London.
,, JAMES FLEMING, London.
,, C. A FOX, London.
,, W. HASLAM, London.
,, E. P. HATHAWAY.
,, E. H. HOPKINS, Richmond.
,, THEODORE MONOD, Paris.
,, E. W. MOORE, London.
,, S. C. MORGAN, Roxeth.
,, T. A. NASH, Norwich.
,, J. RICHARDSON, Camberwell.
,, W. N. RIPLEY, Norwich.
,, G. A. ROGERS, Dover.
,, G. SAVAGE, Bexley.
REV. C. B. SNEPP, Birmingham.
,, FILMER SULIVAN, Brighton.
,, G. R. THORNTON, Nottingham.
,, H. VARLEY, London.
,, A. WINDLE, Dublin.
,, J. T. WRENFORD, Newport.
The EARL OF CHICHESTER.
LORD FARNHAM.
SIR THOMAS BEAUCHAMP, BART.
RIGHT HON. W. COWPER-TEMPLE, M.P.
SAMUEL MORLEY, M.P.
HON. ARTHUR KINNAIRD, M.P.
STEVENSON A. BLACKWOOD, Esq.
HENRY KINGSCOTE, Esq.
NEVILLE SHERBROOKE, Esq.
C. LLOYD BRAITHWAITE, Esq.
G. MONOD, Paris.
PAUL KOBER GOBAT, Bale, Switzerland.
V. VON NIEBUHR Halle, Germany.

CHAPTER I.

OXFORD, SATURDAY, AUGUST 29TH, 1874.

MORNING, 11 A.M.

THE first meeting was held on Saturday morning, at 11 o'clock, in St. Aldate's Rectory large room. It was opened with prayer by Rev. A. M. W. Christopher, and the reading of Psalm ciii.

PRAISE.

R. P. SMITH remarked :—Let us set the key-note of the coming meetings with our morning Psalm, "Bless the Lord, O my soul! . . . who forgiveth, . . . who healeth, . . . who redeemeth, . . . who crowneth, . . . who satisfieth, . . . who reneweth." Let everything in our lives outwardly, or our affections inwardly, which makes a jarring note in God's harmony, be put away, so that with David we can say, "I will praise Thee, O Lord, with my *whole heart*," and let "*all* that is within me bless His Holy name." The past is under the blood. When the Lord says, "I will remember their sin no more," let us also forget the things that are behind, *and live a single moment at a time in a present Saviour*, in complete consecration and complete trust. It is only in letting go useless regrets about the past, God-dishonouring doubts about the present, and sinful anxieties about the future, that we can learn to say, "To me to live is Christ:" and no longer is it condemnation, doubt, or care. Have you escaped the position of a guilty sinner? Thank God for it. But have you also parted with that old Pharisee, your former self-righteous self? We are all born and bred Pharisees, and it is far harder to get rid of the Pharisee than of the guilty sinner. Are you willing as completely to forego self-dependence for holiness as for pardon? Did you do aught to help in the forgiveness of your sins? Can you do anything of yourself to become inwardly holy? Is it not the work of Him who justified, also Himself to sanctify? Cannot He who delivered your soul from death, also preserve your feet from falling,—and the one no less easily than the other? Freed from self-dependence for pardon, are you as free from it for holiness? Entire dependence on Christ is a life of constant praise and constant victory. You cannot praise God with your "whole heart," except in the complete trust which brings victory as well as pardon.

Our purpose in these meetings is to ask the searching light of the Spirit, that we may see the last and worst of ourselves, and that having put away all the discerned evil of our lives, which hinders free-hearted praise, we may then obey the word, "Rejoice in the Lord always:" and find that a praising position is always a victorious position. A shout is often two-thirds of the victory. It was at a shout that the walls of Jericho fell. We shall here have "the shout of a King" in our midst, instead of the wail of doubt and anxiety.

You may be disappointed in the first few meetings. We want to get quiet inwardly before the Lord. Some of us need the deep inward cuttings of the sword of the Spirit, the dividing asunder of the joints and marrow, and a depth of renunciations which we have not steadily contemplated heretofore, ere we can be a praising people. Let us be at length honest with God, and be willing to see all that is wrong in us. We need not shrink from His piercing eye, for "the blood of Jesus Christ His Son cleanseth us from all sin." The evil which the light reveals the blood cleanses.

The first days of the Oxford Conference may be painful to some partly-consecrated and half-believing ones, but the last will be praise days. I have not suffered one doubt to cross my mind as to the glorious results of this meeting. As I came up to Oxford alone in the railway carriage, I kneeled down and cast *all* care on the Lord, and found that none remained for me. I expect to have none, not a shadow, and then I can know the Spirit's guidance. God will, I know it, do glorious things for us at Oxford.

PRAISE YE THE LORD!

AFTERNOON, 3 P.M.

The meeting was opened by the exhortation:—Let us here come face to face with the Scripture. Were all those promises which are not believed by you, dear Christian, taken out of your Bible, how much smaller would it be! Do you believe God's book?—*all—every word?* Do you expect to receive when you ask? Can God save you from gross sin and not from your temper, or your trespasses as to anxiety? Look away from your past experience, your failing brethren, your rising doubts, and look at the Bible *alone*. May the Lord to-day give us trusting hearts!—or rather, shall I not say, may you *exercise* the faith which He has bestowed upon you!

Seek and Find.

Prayer was offered, and Psalm lxiii. was read. It is not a pleasant thing to be suffering from hunger and thirst. The pangs of spiritual hunger and the burnings of spiritual thirst may cause pain, but it is *the attitude of reception*. The hand of the Great High Priest is over such, saying, Blessed ones, ye shall be filled! Happy they, whatever the present pain, who are saying,—

> Early will I seek Thee.
> My soul thirsteth for Thee.
> My flesh longeth for Thee.
> My soul followeth hard after Thee.
> My soul shall be satisfied as with marrow
> and fatness.

Are you restless, unsatisfied, dear child of God? You need *Jesus*—none else can satisfy. Your child may have everything else, but it cries, "*I want mother!*" Nothing but the parent's embrace and love can satisfy its hungry heart. "My heart and my flesh crieth out for *the living God*." A doctrine about God cannot satisfy. You have come to Oxford to seek Him. They that seek *shall find*. Your soul, before you leave Oxford, "shall be *satisfied*, as with marrow and fatness," for "He satisfieth the longing soul;" and then your "mouth shall praise Him with joyful lips." Not pardon only, not victory only, not Heaven only, but the source of all these, Christ Himself, shall fill your soul, and you shall say, "My Beloved is mine, and I am His!" Trust yourself fully in His hands, your only disappointment will be that of finding Him "to do exceeding abundantly *above* all that we ask or think." Life will be filled with continual surprises of joy. Expect great things from God at Oxford, and you shall receive yet beyond your largest hopes. You are on the verge of great and glorious things, which you have always surveyed in your Bible with hungry eyes. You are now not only to survey the promised land, but to enter into it. We are saved *from* Egypt, but saved *to* a land of corn and wine and oil. The outward world is a sorrowful wilderness for us all, but let us not have *two* wildernesses—one outward and another inward—a land of spiritual barrenness!

We are saved from wrath, but saved to union with Jesus. Shame on us if, with such a Saviour and such a salvation, any have been in spiritual destitution. But we will forget the failures of the past in the wealthy place into which we are now about to enter, through Christ, at length fully trusted. Let all hungry souls then expect to be

"FILLED with all knowledge. (Rom. xv. 14.)
with the Spirit. (Eph. v. 18.)
with the knowledge of His will. (Col. i. 9.)
with the fruits of righteousness. (Phil. i. 11.)
with all the fulness of God. (Eph. iii. 19.)

Faith has strange paradoxes, and one of them is that we can be at once hungry and satisfied. Experience alone solves the contradictions.

EVENING, 7.30.

SILENT PRAYER.

The meeting commenced with silent prayer, an exercise which, as the congregations became more and more accustomed to it, proved increasingly acceptable. Persons often said that, in those times of solemn silence, God seemed Himself to deal *directly* with their souls as never before. Having escaped the bustle and tumult of our outward occupations, we seemed in those quiet seasons to get away from the tumultuous workings of our own natures, so that we could hear that still small voice which, amid the many voices outward and inward, had been scarcely distinguished by the spiritual ear. The call came to us, "*Be still and know that I am God.*" Not only believe His word, and trust in Him, but in a yet deeper meaning *know* God. An attitude and habit of quiet, restful attention to the voice of God seemed to be formed or strengthened in many hearts who learned in these Oxford days to say,—

"On Thee do I *wait* all the day;"
"My soul wait thou *only* upon God:
For my expectation is from *Him.*"

As the meetings grew in numbers and interest, we found ourselves often pausing in the midst for a season of inward recollection and consciousness of God's presence in our souls. This had a very subduing, solemnising effect on the hearts of believers, and much of the power of the meetings may be traced to the frequent recurrence of moments of silent prayer, sometimes prolonged to ten or even fifteen minutes. It was an especial help sometimes, when numerous testimonies were being given by ministers and others, to have a silent pause of a few moments after each speaker rose, and before he began to speak, for every hearer to ask for him the guidance of the Lord, and for themselves a blessing on the address. The spirit of criticism or mere curiosity seemed to die out in prayer: and constant answers were given to these petitions, in the ease and unction of those who spoke, and the grace of the heart opened to receive the message. Never have we seen such sustained harmony between speakers and hearers, and never such uniform and direct adherence by so many persons to the subject which gathered us together. We cannot recall a total of half an hour in the whole ten days in which there was digression from the special subject of the passing meeting, and very little which was not pointedly appropriate and to edification. There was throughout the constant *attitude* as well as the act of prayer.

After the silent lifting up of our hearts, the requests for prayer were brought before the Lord, a hymn was sung, and the Rev. Mr. Hankin, vicar of Christ Church, Ware, prayed; after which a running comment on 2 Chronicles xx. was given by R. PEARSALL SMITH.

THE SECRET OF VICTORY.

Israel was surrounded by real and great enemies.

Overwhelming odds were against God's people, as far as their own strength went. Defeat was almost a certainty. Jehoshaphat feared, and set himself to seek the Lord. The people did what we are now doing at Oxford, they "gathered themselves together to ask help of the Lord; even out of all the cities of Judah they came *to seek the Lord.*" They knew that if it should become a question between their enemies and the Lord,—no longer a contest against themselves only,—the victory was certain. They fully acknowledged the power of the enemy, and we do well to do this too. Satan, with his superhuman ingenuity and power, has had six thousand years of experience in dealing with silly souls. He knows our weak points far better than we know them ourselves. "*We* have no might against this great company that cometh against us: neither know we what to do: but our eyes are to *Thee*"—"none is able to withstand *Thee!*"

Then, with their wives and little ones, "all Judah *stood* before the Lord,"—the attitude of waiting, which I trust we are now taking. Then the first word from the Lord to them, and to us, to incite to *the courage of true faith,*—"Be not afraid nor dismayed, . . . for the battle is not yours but God's." Let us not forget that the One who assumed our sins, undertakes also to meet our enemies, and becomes to faith the shield to "quench *all* the fiery darts of the Evil One"; our impregnable Gibraltar; the "Rock of habitation whereunto I may *continually* resort."

Do *you* now believe this, you who assume the name of "believer"? Pause and ask yourself. Some of us in the past have been eager for more and more knowledge, and it is a blessed thirst,—but have any been going on and accumulating more and more precious things without believing the things already learned? We do not invite you to Oxford to learn anything new, we have not purposed a single thing to teach you that is new—but we urge you, *as definitely as you believe that your sins are forgiven,* also to believe that you shall "be saved from your enemies," through "the mercy promised to our fathers; and to remember His holy covenant;" confirmed by "the oath which He sware to our father Abraham, that He would grant unto us, that we, being delivered out of the hand of our enemies, might serve Him without fear, in holiness and righteousness, all the days of our life." Pause over these inspired words—and, ere you draw another breath, believe them for your own self. Expect Jesus to save you moment by moment from your greatest enemy in all the universe—Satan. As it has been failure unto you in the past according to your unbelief, in the future it shall be victory unto you "according to your faith."

First, "Be not afraid nor dismayed" at the difficulties before you. I do believe the homely Welsh proverb, "*God's a-top of the Devil!*" and in faith's contests "the battle is not yours but God's. . . . . Ye shall not need to fight in this battle; . . . . Stand ye still and see the salvation of the Lord with you; . . . . fear not, nor be dismayed; to-morrow go out against them; for the Lord will be with you." Assume the conquering position,—it is yours in Christ. It is strange how hard it is for those who do not dread to go out into an untried eternity stripped of everything of earth on which their souls have depended, or to which they have clung, simply now to trust their Lord for victory in the passing moments! They trust Him for the ages of eternity,—but not for the brief hours of their pilgrimage! Open your hearts to God's message of to-day, "Believe in the Lord *your* God, so shall ye be established." It is to bring you to a *crisis* of faith that we have come together—to a point at which you shall say, "By God's grace I *will* believe God's promises if I die in the act!" It would break my very heart, if my children distrusted my promises as many children of God distrust the promises of their Heavenly Father!

What a scene now comes before us in our chapter! A feeble army going out against overwhelming numbers with singers before them "to praise the beauty of holiness as they went out, . . . and to say, Praise the Lord!" Do you know the marvellous power involved in praise? If not, try it—no, you cannot experiment on it, for that would be doubt, and not faith—but when you meet your next temptation, just say, in holy confidence, "*Praise the Lord.*" Be sure to say it out loud — or, if others are present, in an articulate whisper. There is a marvellous reflex power in putting your thoughts into spoken words. The devil and all his angels have to flee before a note of praise.

"And when they began to sing and to praise, the Lord set ambushments against (those) which were come up against Judah, *and they were smitten.*" When God's people came to their mighty appalling enemies, "*behold they were dead!*" And *so* shall we find our liveliest temptations lose their vitality, so that, as we look again upon them, we shall wonder that we so greatly dreaded them, so dead are they to us.

"Then they returned, every man of Judah, to Jerusalem . . . . with joy; for the Lord had made them to rejoice over their enemies." And *thus* we shall leave Oxford "*more* than conquerors, through Him that loved us." Can you trust the Lord that it shall be thus?

Let praise be our attitude before our enemies, and let us begin now by all rising and singing the grand old doxology with our whole hearts :—

"Praise God from whom all blessings flow,
Praise Him all creatures here below;
Praise Him above ye heavenly host,
Praise Father, Son, and Holy Ghost."

After the Doxology had been sung, a few words were added upon the special opposition always offered by Satan to a saint, who, having been freed from the guilt of sin, was now coming to Christ to be freed from its power. We are to expect revelations of the world of darkness parallel to those of the world of light. Our Lord—who trod the path of life for us as an example—after the opened heavens and descent of the Dove, was led into the wilderness to be tempted of the devil. Having conquered in the assaults of Satan, He then healed the sick, and cast out devils. Do not be surprised by special satanic temptations in the walk of faith. "For," in the higher spheres, "we wrestle not against flesh and blood, but against . . . . wicked spirits in heavenly places." It is now that we need take to ourselves the whole armour of God. Meet these assaults with the sword of the Spirit, the Word of God, and with praise. A son of mine now in heaven used to tell me that, when he saw a temptation coming, he gave a shout of victory—*and conquered!*

DO YOU MEAN IT?

The Rev. THEODORE MONOD, of Paris, followed:—We are not come here to teach, or to hear, to make speeches, or to listen to them, but to wait before the Lord. It is not instruction in the truth of God that we so much need; not to know more, for we have knowledge enough and to spare. What we need is, to bring our knowledge to the test of faith and obedience. The kingdom of God is not in word, but in power.

With us the word and the deed are distinct, and may even be opposite things; with God it is otherwise: He means what He says, and does what He pleases. His word is power. He has but to say, "Let there be light," and there is light. He says to your soul, "Christ is thy righteousness," and, taking His word for it, you are justified. He says, "Christ is thy strength," and, taking His word for it, you are from moment to moment sanctified. There is no other way to conquer. Nor do you expect to overcome the last enemy, which is death, in any other way. Then why not *every* enemy? Why, for dying, trust Christ alone, and not trust Christ alone for living?

Probably most of us are yet too strong for Him to save them. Such is sometimes the case with a drowning man: one has to deal him a blow on the head to make him cease from the struggles which hinder the work of his deliverance. The first step towards being made strong in the Lord is a sense of utter helplessness.

The Rev. Mr. HANKIN then briefly but earnestly pressed upon believers the privilege, and therefore responsibility, of an immediate and complete surrender of self-will and of unbelief. Do it to-night. Do not wait for a week of meetings first! One Sunday evening Mr. Moody closed an impressive address in Chicago by telling the audience to go home and think about it, and to tell him next week what they would do. That night the fearful Chicago fire broke out, and before dawn some of his hearers were in eternity. From that hour he pressed instant decision for God. Now do not go home to think about a full surrender, but to *do it*.

Mr. Hankin then closed the meeting in prayer.

CHAPTER II.

The Lord's-day, August 30th.

Morning 7.30.

CARDS, with the following suggestions, were handed to those in attendance, and it was remarkable how much their spirit was acted on all through the week. We saw and heard of no controversy. All seemed more anxious to get right themselves before God than to set others right. About the need of more holiness there could be but one opinion, and those who prayed much for this found themselves averse to discussion.

OXFORD, AUGUST 31, 1874.

We have met as Christians to believe God's promises to yield ourselves wholly to the Lord Jesus Christ, and to "enter into Rest." In order for this you are entreated to act on the following suggestions:

I.

Come in a receptive spirit; submit your whole being to the teaching of the Holy Spirit. God speaks by His Word: be willing to lay aside all preconceived opinions.

II.

Heartily renounce all known evil, and even doubtful things "not of faith."

III.

Come *waiting* on the Lord. Expect confidently blessing to your own soul individually.

IV.

Lay aside, for the time, all reading except the Bible.

V.

Avoid conversation in your lodgings which shall divert your soul from the object of the Meeting. Especially avoid controversy. If any differ from you, pray with them.

VI.

Eat moderately, dress simply, retire to rest early.

VII.

Let your first waking act each morning be to remind yourself—

1. That *your* every sin is washed away by the blood of Christ.
2. That you are wholly His by purchase and by deliberate self-surrender.
3. That thus there is now no cloud nor even shadow between your soul and God.
4. That the Lord assumes the hourly keeping of the life and walk thus committed to Him.

Let this morning act be the continuing attitude of the soul all day. If interrupted by momentary failure, let instant confession restore full communion.

VIII.

It may be a help often to repeat—

Lord, I am Thine, entirely Thine,
Purchased and saved by love divine.
With full consent Thine I will be,
And own Thy sovereign right in me.

The meeting was invited to unite in silent prayer that Jesus—Jesus only—might manifest Himself in our midst, and that all our spirits might be kept free from excitement, and in a waiting attitude to hear and recognise His voice.

1 Chronicles xxix. was read: "And who then is willing to consecrate his service this day unto the Lord?" Who will say, the last thing at night as he sinks into sleep, and as he wakes to consciousness for another day, and each hour as it rolls by — *All for Jesus!* ALL FOR JESUS! This was presented as a privilege rather than a duty, though, if we fail to accept it as a privilege, it becomes a duty. Let us not turn our Bethlehem into a Sinai. "Then the people rejoiced, for that they offered willingly, because with perfect heart they offered willingly to the Lord." Let us always look at the privilege side of consecration, and make it the most glad act of our lives to give ourselves wholly to the Lord. Is it an act of painful self-denial for the bride to accept the love and support of a noble bridegroom? Shame on us if we have ever done aught else than "willingly offer."

Let us crown our Solomon "King the second time," and say, without reserve, "Thy kingdom come" in our hearts, "Thy will be done" in our lives; and then, the petition, "Deliver us from evil" will no longer be the gliding of words through our lips, but the expectant prevailing prayer of faith.

We have come to Oxford to say, "Thy kingdom come!" *and to mean it;* "Thy will be done," *and to do it.*

Rev. Mr. HANKIN then spoke on Canticles ii. 10—13: "Arise, my love, and come away,"—come away from all that has formerly kept you back—unbelief, doubts, the world, sin;—"rise up, and come away, for lo, the winter is passed, the rain is over and gone, the flowers appear on the earth." The time is come to "rejoice always" in the marvellous salvation which is, moment by moment, ours in Christ. After solemn prayer, the meeting adjourned till

MORNING 9.30.

Rev. ASA MAHAN (author of "The Baptism of the Holy Ghost," a book which has been the channel of blessing to thousands) spoke from Heb. viii. 1, and vii. 25:—"Now of the things which we have spoken *this is the sum:* We have such an high priest . . . . in an unchangeable priesthood . . . . able to save them to the *uttermost* that come unto God by Him." After Paul had dwelt on the priesthood of Christ, and the character of His work, he tells us what our High Priest is able to do for us, and what we may expect from Him. We are likely to cut ourselves off from the main blessing intended for us from defective perceptions. "Able to save to the *uttermost.*" The Greek word for uttermost is the combination of two of the strongest in the Greek language, meaning, in all respects, to the full extent. Why is that power in Christ revealed, if we are not to avail ourselves of it? Why are we told what He is able to do, if we suppose that He is not ready to do it, or that we are not authorized to expect it? Expand your hearts, expect to receive, *and receive* all that He is able to do. We *are* authorized to expect, for "He ever liveth to make intercession for us." Whilst we are *here*, Christ is *there*, interceding on our behalf; so that His Father and our Father will hear and will do, not according to what we expect, but above all that we ask or think; yea, Christ will save to the very *uttermost*. God only knows the extent of that. We must remember that *there is an exceeding abundance in reserve with God.* He knows what we want, and is "able to do exceeding abundantly *above all* that we ask or think." It is a great *sin* to "limit the Holy One of Israel." "*Save to the uttermost!*" Dare to cease to limit His power, and take Christ at His word.

Let me give you my own experience. Thirty-five years ago I became conscious of some fundamental defect in my condition. I felt I was not what the Bible teaches us to be—not a Bible Christian. Yet I laboured conscientiously; but I said to myself, "This is not Bible Christianity." At length one of the greatest revivals in our country visited our college. I went up one day to the room of one of the professors, to talk to him about what I wanted, and that was to learn the secret of the piety of Paul. I had always to gird myself up to the point by my *resolutions*, and then my feelings kept drawing me back. Paul was "*constrained.*" My friend explained it to me. I left the room, went back to my study, and thanked God that I *had found the secret.* My friend the professor came into my room, and asked me what I was going to preach about that night. I replied, "the love of Christ constraineth us." Now I began to preach; for I had not been hitherto in the fullest sense a preacher of the Gospel. I had found a Saviour from the condemnation of sin; but when under the power of my evil propensities and habits, *I resolved against* them, and relied on my own resolutions. Oh, the mistake! If you want to be sanctified, if you want power, go to Christ for sanctification and for power. Carry all your propensities to Christ! Open your heart to Him! *He is just as able to sanctify as to pardon.* I do not limit Him. I carry my temper and my appetite to Christ, and trust Him for the result. He will not disappoint me. Will He ever leave one who trusts Him under the power of sin? Never! Then put your whole trust in Him.

Now "this is the sum" of it all. "We have such an High Priest"—one that is able to sanctify, and He is before His Father to intercede for us, in order that "He may do for us exceeding abundantly above all that we ask or think." If we have faith in Christ's ability, whilst we are waiting here in these meetings, He will come to us, and we shall be filled with the Spirit; we shall be filled with all the fulness of God. We have One on our behalf in heaven who is as bountiful as ever. Christ *gave Himself* that He might sanctify the Church by the washing of water through the word. He has given Himself to *me* that He may sanctify and cleanse *me*, that I may be changed into His own image. He is here to take away our sins. Now, brethren and sisters, do you believe that if He is present to heal, He will heal? He will say, "Receive ye the Holy Ghost," and we shall rejoice in God our

Saviour, and in His plentiful redemption. We shall realise that divine promise, "Thy sun shall no more go down, neither shall thy moon withdraw itself, for the Lord shall be thine everlasting light, and the days of thy mourning shall be ended."

I have known this experience for thirty-five years. My sun does not go down, nor does my moon withdraw itself. Thus I am *waiting, enjoying, expecting.* Christ has loved you, as He has loved me. He will pour out His Spirit on you; yea, upon all—on you and on your children. Now say from the heart, "Yes, He *loved me* and gave Himself for me, in order to present me to Himself a glorious new creation."

Pastor THEODORE MONOD made a few remarks on the tendencies of modern science, and the idea so prevalent amongst men of science that we must study facts, only facts. Well, let us give them—*the great fact of a holy life.* The men of science are studying "forms of life." Let them have that form of life to study in us, a heart entirely consecrated to God, and the life of Christ in us!

At 11 o'clock the Rev. A. M. W. CHRISTOPHER preached in St. Aldate's church, from Matt. i. 21, "Thou shalt call His name JESUS, for He shall save His people *from* their sins."

The humblest believer belongs to Jesus. Though faith may be weak, though the believer may be very weak and sick, *Jesus is the same*; He never changes. He has the power of God and the sympathy of man. He is able to save, and He has the heart to save. In Him we died, in Him we live. Not that we are insensible to sin, as a corpse is to the world, but dead to the guilt and condemnation of sin. Moreover, in the 1st Epistle of Peter we are taught that Christ "bare our sin in His own body on the Tree, that we being dead to sin should live unto righteousness." Has not sin been a very bitter thing? How blessed to know that we have Jesus to cleanse not only from the guilt of sin, but to deliver us from its power.

The natural tendency of Peter was to sink. Jesus counteracted this, and Peter walked on the water until he took his eye off from Jesus and looked at the waves. Our tendency by nature is to sin, but faith in Jesus meets this tendency to evil, and God pledges His word to him who believes that sin shall not have dominion over him. Faith brings into operation the law of the Spirit of life in Christ Jesus, which sets us free from the law of sin and death. The power of "the Spirit of life," ruling those who are in union with Christ by faith, sets them free from the dominions of their natural corruption. Is, then, every Christian thus free? Yes, as to gift, but the practical privileges of the position are realised only according to the measure of his faith. Is it true that Jesus saved Saul, His persecutor, and made him able to live by faith? Will He not do this for you also? "He is able"—"who also *will do it*"—in every trusting disciple.

THE TOWN HALL.

THE CHRISTIAN LIFE.

3 O'CLOCK.

After a time of silent prayer the Rev. T. Monod guided us vocally, and the hymn was sung,—

"He wills that I should holy be;
That holiness I long to feel,
That full divine conformity
To all my Saviour's righteous will.

"On Thee, O God, my soul is stayed,
And waits to prove Thine utmost will:
The promise by Thy mercy made,
Thou canst, Thou wilt, in me fulfil."

It was remarked by R. PEARSALL SMITH, in opening this, the first meeting in the Town Hall, that we desire all to understand that the Scriptural privilege of the Christian life which we are urging upon Christians has only been named "The *Higher* Christian Life" for distinction, because so few were living it. It should be called "*The* Christian life," *the only normal Christian life.* We are not here to apologise for an unpopular doctrine, but boldly to fling out the banner of "Holiness to the Lord," and to challenge every Christian who is not living in entire consecration and full trust, with the question, "Are you living a *lower* Christian life?" Anything short of complete self-surrender, and entire faith in the promises of God, is lower than "*The* Christian life."

We preach this, not as a finality, but as the only true *commencement* of a life of progress,—the soul-attitude in which only a healthful, uniform development can be expected. It is simply soul-health. The healthy tree only developes uniformly. The youngest believer may have, and oftentimes has, in all his imperfect apprehension of the will of God, entire subjection of will and full trust. Shame on us if any of us have less of this attitude of soul than when we were babes!

I would die sooner than come to Oxford to preach anything different from "the faith once delivered to the saints," and the faith which now overcometh the world. From cover to cover the Bible is full of present salvation from sin, and of a life of unclouded communion with God. Enoch walked thus,—his life flowed on gladdened by the Spirit's "testimony that he pleased God,"—and so may you, dear Christian. It was, then, but the dim twilight of the dispensations, long before "the appearing of our Lord and Saviour Jesus Christ, who hath . . . brought life and immortality to light." Surely no less privilege is ours now in the fulness of time.

A life of full communion and victory is not a perfected condition, but simply *the* Christian life well commenced.

You expect to die thus, in the midst of weakness of mind and body—it is well. But can you not expect to *live* thus? Do not make "dying grace" your "extreme unction;"—call it "*living* grace," and live as you expect to die. Shall not Christ do more for you than death?

Some say, "I believe that there is such a state of complete trust to be arrived at, but not until death." It is well to believe in it for some time—but how long before death is it possible? An hour? A day? Peradventure a week? Possibly two or three weeks, if you are very ill? One good man granted this position until the period of six weeks was reached, but then said that more than six weeks of such living was utterly impossible! Are your views as to the limitations of dying grace only less absurd because less definite?

In San Francisco, on the Pacific, I met a Christian lady joyously engaged in a laborious work of beneficence, such as most of us would shrink from. I could not but remark on the freedom of heart, the unhindered devotedness to her life-work, and the atmosphere of *rest* in which she lived, unbroken by the pressure of her constant work. In reply to my inquiry as to the secret of a life so different from the lives of those around her, she told me that two years before, when dying, as she supposed, she found all that she had clung to passing from her grasp, and such an hitherto unconceived-of fulness in Christ opening upon her soul, as met every need of her being. Her faith, instead of being partial, was complete, unlimited, and consequently full of rest. Christ, now trusted for *all*, met every want of her soul. Fully delivered from the fear of death, she was now no less delivered from the temptations and anxieties of life. Most if not all Christians, as I judge, pass thus into eternity.

She did not die, and, as the cares and responsibility of returning life once more gathered upon her, she exercised faith that this full rest in Jesus would not be lost. Whatever were the outward agitations of life, her inward rest was kept; or if, for a moment, anything broke that sabbath, it was instantly "stoned with stones." She found that she could *live* in Christ as Christians "die in the Lord."

When she told this experience to her pastor, he said

it was precisely what he constantly met in dying Christians, but he had never known it maintained amid the pressures of active life. He added, with a sad countenance, "Your experience, my sister, is *dying grace.* We shall not have you long with us. You are being prepared for death."

"Not so!" she exclaimed. "Thank God, it is not grace for dying, but *grace for living,* and I trust Christ to keep me always living thus!"

Was it presumption in this dear Christian, by faith, thus to "obtain promises" for life as well as for death? Is this abiding in Christ in your mind a sort of extreme unction? Do you urge the unconverted sinner not to delay repentance to his death-bed? Permit me affectionately to beseech you, by the mercies of God, *not to put off a full surrender to Christ and entire trust in His promises to your death-bed!* Is there any miraculous effect in the near approach of death which cannot be wrought in you in life? Is death to be your saviour, or will you look to Christ? Let us henceforth dare to say with the Apostle, "For me to *live,*"—not merely to die,—"is Christ."

> "Jesus saves me every day,
> Jesus saves me every night;
> Jesus saves me all the way,
> Through the darkness and the light.
> Jesus saves! oh bliss sublime,
> Jesus saves me all the time!"

A True Revival.

After a hymn and prayer, part of the twenty-ninth chapter of 2 Chronicles was read. Let us notice God's own way of revival among His chosen people. It did not commence with effort, the stimulation of sick souls to work which is beyond their strength, with the resulting reaction; but with cleansing. The hidden source of weakness must be probed and healed first.

We find that Hezekiah (ver. 4) began by gathering the priests and the Levites together. In the priests we see those who walk in true communion, and in the Levites those who serve. All priests are Levites, but all Levites are not priests; for many who serve earnestly do not live in full communion. This is a meeting of priests and Levites gathered together to the King of kings.

What was the first command? "Hear me, ye Levites, sanctify now yourselves, and sanctify the house of the Lord God of your fathers, and carry forth the filthiness out of the holy place." "Having therefore these promises"—of God's indwelling and presence—"let us cleanse ourselves from all filthiness of flesh and spirit, perfecting holiness in the fear of the Lord." The only temples in this dispensation are these bodies,—"ye are the temples of the Holy Ghost,"—and we are taught to "go into the inmost recesses of our being to carry forth . . . . out of the holy place" every secret idol ambition, lust or passion which grieves the indwelling Spirit of God.

"And they gathered their brethren, and sanctified [separated] themselves, and came according to the commandment of the king by the words of the Lord, to cleanse the house of the Lord."

Did it ever strike you, dear Christian, that if the poor world could but know what we are in Christ, it would worship us. Even angels would command their homage, how much more the radiance of an unveiled child of God! When, upon the Mount, the veil of the flesh was for a brief moment withdrawn from our Lord, His glory shone through His peasant's garments, and His face was illuminated. You and I, dear believer, in the next breath, or any passing moment, may be thus transfigured, for we shall be like Him when we see Him as He is. The poor perishing world cannot conceive this, but we know it. Let the divine consciousness of such an indwelling of God and the possibilities of the immediate future impart dignity to your life, and lead you to the putting away every discerned evil of your inward, as well as outward, life.

We did not come to Oxford to set each other right, or to discuss doctrines, but each one to cry, "Search *me*, O God, and know *my* heart; try *me* and know *my* thoughts; and see if there be any wicked way in *me*." We are searching our hearts, the very inmost recesses of our existence, as with a lighted candle of the Lord; or rather, as self cannot see itself, we are imploring the light of the presence of God in these temples, that we may see the last and worst evil remaining in their recesses.

"And the priests went into the inner part of the house of the Lord to cleanse it, and brought out all uncleanness *that they found* in the temple of the Lord, into the court of the house of the Lord. And the Levites took it to carry it abroad into the brook

Kidron,"—oblivion. It was "*all that they found*," that they carried forth. We shall never know in this life the absolute purity of the Lord Jesus. We are, and ever shall be, at an immense moral distance from "the Holy One," but we cry to God for light to see the evil within us progressively as we are able to bear it; and we must accept strength from Him to "carry forth" all that in our dim vision we can see of "filthiness, out of the holy place." Painful though it may be, we need not shrink from the discoveries of evil made by the light of God, for all the needs of our moral condition are met by Christ. It is this attitude of continually bringing *all* our thoughts and acts to the light of God which we desire for ourselves. What a dreadful thing to have recognised or acknowledged evil where the Shechinah dwells!

"So," by cleansing, "they sanctified the house of the Lord in eight days," the resurrection period; "and in the sixteenth day of the first month they made an end,"—the double period of resurrection. The work will not be finished in us till complete resurrection is known. "The blood cleanseth"—is ever cleansing sin from the conscience, as it is progressively revealed.

Dear child of God, are you willing for God to show your heart to you? Are you willing here and *now* to carry forth *all* of evil that you see within? Do you in this moment put away *every* thing that you know is contrary to the mind of God? Let this be the time of decision.

Let us never preach grace as though it took away the need of personal consecration. It frees us from the yoke of the law, of selfhood, and of sin, in order that we may give ourselves to God.

Then "they brought a sin-offering for the kingdom, for the sanctuary, and for Judah." There, then, is the need of the blood. Oh, beloved, when you walk in the light, you will see your need of the cleansing blood as never before. How many of the offerings of Leviticus were for sins of ignorance! You will, now in the light of God, see so many shortcomings, which a twilight experience would obscure, that the need of the blood will be known as never before. A life of practical victory over known evil, and unclouded communion with God, is one of ever-deepening humility.

When the saintly Fletcher—than whom no more holy man, perhaps, ever preached in England, asked God to show him all the corruptions of his own heart, "his comeliness was turned into corruption," and he had to ask the Lord to withdraw His light—he could endure no more. Then he asked the Lord to show him His grace, and the vision was so much more overwhelming than the sight of the evil of his own heart, that again he cried to God to stay His hand. His great mistake was to restrain the knowledge of himself, or the vision of grace, for the one enables us to bear the other. It was after the cleansing of the Temple that the sin-offering was so fully made.

Then came the whole burnt-offering, representing completeness of consecration. There never was but One, who, from the cradle to the grave, was in every thought, affection, and action, a complete burnt-offering. Everything in us is short of the perfect holiness of

Christ. Yet we may, up to the very furthest measure of our consciousness, present ourselves living sacrifices, holy and acceptable to God. In each moment, as to the attitude of our souls we may, so far as we see and know, be wholly the Lord's, yet, with each day's increasing intelligence, being more and yet more completely the Lord's. Oh, beloved, do this, so that you may be able with Paul to say, "I know nothing against myself, yet am I not hereby justified," for Christ is my justification. Let us trust our Saviour till with the same Apostle we can say, "Ye are my witnesses, and God also, how holily, justly, and unblamably, we behaved ourselves among you that believe."

"And when the burnt-offering began, the song of the Lord began with trumpets . . . . And all the congregation worshipped, and the singers sang, and the trumpeters sounded." Why are so many Christians sad? Is it not for want of full consecration and faith? God can make our lives one long psalm of praise to Him. Shame on us if we allow ourselves to substitute for praise, sad backsliding hymns :—

"Lo! how we grovel here below."

What if some persons, long married, should get together, and delight to sing songs of how they had lost their early affections; that they loved others better now. And shall the bride of Christ sing such songs of alienated affections? Nay, my friend; if such be your experience, get you into your closet, and on your knees, or still better on your face, confess it all to your merciful Saviour; receive restoration of full communion, and then come into the congregation, and instead of wailing, *praise* God with a loud voice. Do not put such stumbling-blocks as the verse,—

"Where is the blessedness I knew
When first I saw the Lord?—"

before young Christians to cause them to fall. "If it is thus with older Christians," they say, "I must fail too,"—and down they go, all through your hymns. I would rather lose my voice than give out such hymns to congregations.

"And all this [praise] continued till the burnt-offering was finished." Our entire consecration need never be intermitted, but should be ever increasing, and Hosannas will never languish on our lips while we are giving our all to God, "They sang praises with gladness, and bowed their heads, and worshipped."

"Then Hezekiah said, Now ye have consecrated yourselves unto the Lord, come near and bring sacrifices and thank-offerings into the house of the Lord . . . . But the priests were too few," to receive all that was brought. No more urging, no more scheming, for they offered gladly. And thus we are finding it in congregations where the full privileges of the Christian life are being accepted. "Also the burnt-offerings were in abundance."

"*So*," continues this blessed narrative of a true Revival, "the service of the house of the Lord was set in order." No wonder that "soon posts passed from city to city . . . . even unto Zebulon," and "divers . . . . humbled themselves and came to Jerusalem;"

"and the hand of God was to give them one heart to do the commandment of the Lord." This is God's work, which we shall see this week at Oxford.

"And Hezekiah rejoiced, and all the people, that God had prepared the people." How will our King rejoice as He sees us thus giving all to Him, and how shall we, ere we part, praise Him that He Himself has prepared this people!

The chapter concludes with the words, "*For the thing was done suddenly.*" How long will it take you, my brother, my sister, to lay aside your last weight of unbelief or sin; to yield your last reserve as to trust or obedience; to let go the last strand of self-trusting effort, to abandon yourself wholly to Christ? Will any other moment be better than the present one? Dare you delay? The angel of God's presence is wrestling with you to-day. You cannot prevail against God:—

> "He wills that I should holy be;
> Who shall withstand His will?"

Know, not how strong, but how weak you are. No longer resist, but cling to Him. Tell Him that you have always been but Jacob—a deceiver—and your life but failure. Say, "I will not let Thee go except Thou bless me." Trust Him for all as never before, and believe His word, "Thy name shall no longer be called Jacob, but Israel: for as a prince thou hast power with God and hast prevailed,"—not by strength but by weakness, not by effort but by trust. If one night with the angel did so much for failing Jacob, shall one hour of now completed consecration and trust do less for thee? Let this be our Peniel where we have seen God face to face, a solemn epoch in the lives of many of the dear children of God!

The Rev. Robert Dawson, minister, of Nottingham, then led in prayer, and after a hymn a sermon was preached by Mr. Smith on Christ revealing Himself in the four Gospels—successively as our King, our Minister, our human Brother, and our God manifest in the flesh; and upon our accepting Him as King to rule, as our Divine Minister to bear our burdens, our Brother to sympathise and love, and our God to impart His own eternal life to us; closing with an exhortation to let *all* the glorious purposes of our Lord's incarnation be fully accomplished in our lives.

Hymn 15 was then sung, and Rev. Dr. Mahan then closed in prayer.

At 4.30 Mrs. Pearsall Smith held a Bible Reading in the same room—a meeting for ladies. Gentlemen who chose to attend were not excluded, and many were present at this and the subsequent hours devoted to her Scripture lessons.

Law and Grace.—Heb. viii.

We have here stated a great fact—that God has dealt with man in two different and entirely distinct ways—one being the covenant He made with Israel when they came out of Egypt, called the covenant of law—the other being the covenant made in Christ, called the covenant of grace. The one is called the old covenant, and is said to be decaying and waxing old and ready to vanish away. The other is called the new covenant, and is distinctly stated not to have been added on to the old, but to have come in the place of it. The old covenant, we are told, was laid aside or annulled because of the weakness and unprofitableness of it, for it made nothing perfect, while the bringing in of a better hope did.

Constantly throughout the New Testament we have the contrast between these two covenants brought out, and are emphatically told that what the law could not do in that it was weak through the flesh, Christ has accomplished.

Twice in my life did my Bible become a new book to me through discovering this contrast. The first time was when, after long years of striving to be saved by the law, I saw the truth of justification by faith, and, laying all my own doings down, trusted for salvation in what Another had done for me. From that moment on every page in the Bible, I saw written in letters of light the glorious truth, that what the law could not do in delivering me from the guilt of my sin, Christ had done.

But here I stopped; and for years, while holding clearly the doctrine of justification by faith, I still believed in sanctification by works. The law, I knew, could not give pardon, but it could, I thought, give practical righteousness. And the second time when the Bible became a new book to me, was when I discovered that the same covenant which, in verse 12 of Heb. viii., provides for our sins and our iniquities being remembered no more, provides also, in verse 10, for our loving and obeying the commandments of our

God. I saw that sanctification was by faith as well as justification. That the same Saviour who delivers from the guilt of sin, delivers also from its power. And that the very righteousness which the law demanded, but failed to procure, was made possible and easy by grace.

A second time the Bible became a new book to me, and from beginning to end I saw unveiled on its pages the blessed secret of living and walking by faith, under this new covenant of grace. Texts, which before had no meaning, now became full of light to me. I marvelled at my blindness in the past, and could not conceive with what eyes I had been all along reading it. For I had missed the grandest part of the Gospel. It had been an unspeakable blessing to me to be delivered from the guilt of my sin, but it was infinitely more glorious to be delivered from its power. For to me the consequences of sin were not so dreadful as the fact of the sin itself. And to know that Christ came to deliver from this bondage was good news indeed.

Many Christians try to live their Christian lives under the covenant of works. They trust Christ for the forgiveness of their sins, and let Him do it all, because they know they cannot help in this matter. But when it comes to their daily living, they feel as if here they could and ought to help. It seems to them that Christ has saved them from their guilt, and has started them out in their new life with certain powers of their own, which they are responsible for making the most of. And they seek, by fleshly resolutions and efforts of their own, with the *help* of the Lord, to conquer their temptations, and to keep the commandments, and to walk worthy of the high calling wherewith they have been called, instead of living and bearing fruit altogether by faith in an ever-present Saviour (Gal. ii. 20; John xv. 4-5).

No wonder the result is failure. For we are just as helpless in the matter of our daily living as we are in the matter of the forgiveness of our sins. The one must be all of grace, and not of works, just as the other was. Resolutions, and efforts, and the works of the law can no more enable us to walk in practical righteousness than they could secure to us the forgiveness of our sins. The same grace that saved us must keep us. The same Saviour who bore our guilt for us must do our daily work for us also. We cannot be Christians as to pardon, and then be Jews as to living.

The Covenant of Grace is Grace Throughout.

Now I would put the practical question to you each one. How have you lived or tried to live your Christian life? You received Christ by faith at first, how have you walked in Him—by faith or by effort? Under which covenant are you living now as to your daily walk—the covenant of law or the covenant of grace? For the two cannot be dovetailed together. They are in absolute contrast. They begin from exactly the opposite points of the compass. In the covenant of grace Christ does everything, and we simply trust it to Him to do. In the covenant of works we do it ourselves. You understand this as to conversion, and, I dare say, have, many of you, preached it very eloquently and convincingly to the poor struggling sinner, when he has been seeking to be saved by works. But have you ever thought that you yourself, on a little different plane, have been seeking to be saved by works yourself? I mean saved from your temptations and from your bondage to sin? With myself my Christian life for many years was all works. It was *do, do, do* from morning until night. I verily thought, if I did not do it, it would never be done. Grace had made me alive I knew, but I thought the law was to keep me alive. I must work, I must resolve, I must wrestle, I must strive, in my own strength!

I have no doubt many of you are just like me. You honestly think it is the right way. But, dear friends, it is the Jewish way, not the Christian. The new covenant takes hold of the matter at the other end. It is not your working in order to make yourselves right, but it is Christ making you right, in order that you may work.

He puts His laws into your minds, and writes them on your hearts. He takes away the stony heart, and gives you a heart of flesh; and He *causes* you to walk in His statutes, and promises that you *shall* keep His judgments and do them. He works in you to will and to do of His good pleasure. And your part in the whole matter is simply to yield yourself up to His working, and trust Him. *As* you have received Him, *so* are you to walk in Him. You received Him by faith, you are to walk in Him by faith also. From beginning to end of our Christian experience we are poor sinners, and nothing at all, and Jesus Christ is our all in all. He must do everything.

Now, dear Christians, will you let Him? Will you hand yourselves over utterly into His care and keeping, and yield yourselves up to His working? Will you say, "Lord, I am helpless; I can do nothing against these enemies who come out against me. My only hope is in Thee. Do Thou fight for me and deliver me?" And then will you trust Him to do it? Do you believe He is able? Do you believe He is willing? Can you leave it in His hands?

Let me entreat of every Christian present to come out from under the covenant of law, and put yourselves under the covenant of grace. You will get to a place then, where you will find God's law written on your heart so that you will love it, and where He will work in you by His own mighty power to *make* you what He wants you to be. Your Christian life will become an easy life then, and an overcoming life, and you will understand what Paul meant when he said, "What the law could not do in that it was weak through the flesh, God sending His own Son in the likeness of sinful flesh, and for sin, condemned sin in the flesh, that the righteousness of the law might be fulfilled in us who walk not after the flesh, but after the Spirit."

It is your own trying to live your life that is the greatest hindrance. Stop this, and let His life live in you. Let Christ get full possession of you, and let Him be your indwelling life, walking in you and abiding in you, and working in you all the good pleasure of His will. Then it will be easy to live right. You know that when a person is in perfect health, he need make no effort to live. Living becomes an effort only when there is disease or paralysis.

I heard once of a man who thought he could not breathe unless he made an effort to do so, and he nearly strangled himself in his struggles. His family, in great alarm, called in a physician, who, seeing at once the state of the case, called out to him peremptorily to stop. "I shall die if I do," gasped out the poor man. "Die then," said the doctor; "but STOP." The man, overborne by his authority, obeyed, and the moment he stopped trying he breathed easily and without effort.

Just so it is with some of you. You are trying to live, and your life is nearly strangled with the effort. Give up trying, and let Christ, who is your life, live in you, and you will live easily and without effort. When the soul can say with Paul, "I am crucified with Christ; nevertheless I live; yet not I, but Christ liveth in me"—then that soul has come fully into the covenant of grace, and knows experimentally what it is to have old things pass away, and all things to become new.

And now let us all bow in silent prayer, and yield ourselves up to God definitely and unreservedly for this very thing. Let it be a real transaction with each soul, so that, from this time onward, you will reckon yourself to be all the Lord's.

The whole congregation bowed in silence for several minutes, when Mrs. Smith made a prayer of full surrender on her own behalf and on behalf of each individual in the congregation, definitely handing over ALL to God. And we trust that to many it was indeed a real transaction, which will never be undone.

CHAPTER III.

Monday, August 31st.

THE previous two days had been announced as preparatory to the regular sessions for the eight days of August 31st to September 7th, inclusive; the whole, together, forming the Pentecostal period of ten days. The following order of daily meetings was arranged, with, however, the caution that none should attend so many as to cause spiritual dissipation or weariness. There proved, however, to be a simplicity, variety, and power in them that seemed to forbid fatigue. It was remarkable that persons ordinarily tired by two services a day were less tired by these meetings extending through eleven hours a day. A noticeable feature was the great *ease* of these conferences. They seemed to flow on without strain or effort on the part of the speakers, and all seemed carried together in one harmonious current.

DAILY MEETINGS.

7 to 8.30 o'clock.
BEFORE BREAKFAST.—PRAYER MEETING.

8.30 to 9.30 o'clock.
BREAKFAST AND PRIVATE PRAYER.

9.30 to 11.30 o'clock.
CONVERSATIONAL MEETINGS, in Smaller Rooms,
CONDUCTED BY

Rev. W. E. BOARDMAN,
" THEODORE MONOD,
" ASA MAHAN,
" D. B. HANKIN,
Rev. E. H. HOPKINS,
" G. R. THORNTON,
Lord RADSTOCK,
GEORGE PEARSE, of Paris,
Mrs. R. PEARSALL SMITH, FOR LADIES ONLY.

11.45 to 1.30 o'clock.
GENERAL MEETING.—Prayer and Addresses.

1.30 to 3 o'clock.
DINNER.

3 to 4 o'clock.
PRAYER MEETINGS.—In Smaller Rooms.
Mrs. PEARSALL SMITH.—BIBLE READING in the Corn Exchange.

4 to 5.30 o'clock.
GENERAL MEETING.—Prayer and Addresses.

5.30 to 6 o'clock.
TEA.

6 to 7.30 o'clock.
MINISTERIAL CONFERENCE.—Attendance free to all.

7.45 to 9.15 o'clock.
GENERAL MEETING.—Prayer and Addresses.

ON SUNDAY.—SPECIAL ARRANGEMENTS,
Leaving Free the Hours of Public Worship.

At 7 o'clock, a.m.

Isaiah li. 1-3, 11-13; liv. 5, 10, 11, 13; lvi. 6, 7; lvii. 19-21; and lviii., were read as expressing the dispensational blessings of the chosen people to be spiritually anticipated by those who realized that they were within the kingdom of "righteousness, peace, and joy in the Holy Ghost."

Pasteur Monod: You have come to Oxford seeking blessing. What are you waiting for? Is it for some great emotion? Or, till you are more able fully to come to Christ? You need no emotion, and you will never be more able. Never mind your feelings; surrender yourself to God as you are, and He will make you what you should be.

Rev. W. E. Boardman: Do not think of any preliminaries to coming to Christ; but Come, and come at once. "Just as I am" is for saints as well as sinners. Do not think that you must prepare your heart before you give it to God. He wants it in the rough. It is His work to prepare it. Christ is the Purifier, and the very first thing is to come to Him; or rather, shall I say, to let Him come in. "Behold, I stand at the door and knock." Each one has to open. *A very little latch will keep a door fast,*—a rusty lock will keep it very fast. You must undo the fastenings. It is not His way to force the door. His coming is gentle and to an open door. Does any self-will close the entrance to this Chief of ten thousands, the altogether lovely One? Renounce it here and now, and then it will be easy to believe and receive the fulfilment of the promise, "I will come to him and sup with him, and he with Me."

"Facts."

Town Hall 9.30 a.m.

In the Lecture Room, at 9.30, Pasteur Monod conducted a Conversational Meeting. "I have been announced to preside at this meeting," he said, "without being consulted about it. I do not even know what 'a conversational meeting' may be. I presume, however, it is a meeting for conversation, and I infer that each one of you, fathers and brethren, has as good a right to talk as I have. I hope you will freely make use of it. My choice would have been to attend Mr. Boardman's meeting up-stairs, for I greatly need to be taught. But we shall learn from one another, or rather, we shall all sit together at the feet of Him who says: 'Learn of me.' After all, if I have only got to the A, B, C, of a life of faith, I may be the more able to help those who are also beginners in that life.

"The Apostle John says of his gospel, and it may be applied to the whole of the Scriptures: 'These things are written that ye might believe that Jesus is the Christ, the Son of God, and that believing ye might have life through His name.' First, let us know what is written, then let us believe the testimony, and believing, we shall have *life* through the Lord Jesus. How much life? Precisely as much as we trust Him for. Christ is to each one what each one expects Him to be: if nothing be expected, He is nothing; if little, little; if much, much; if everything, everything. As to faith we can never see it; we can only see our Saviour. Faith does not even exist, much less can it be felt or considered, apart from its object. At this moment you are looking at me, and have no evidence of your doing so except that you see me; but you do not see your looking, nor does your looking at me exist, apart from me. Just so, let us look unto Jesus, and we shall be conscious, not of our faith, but of His presence, of His power, of His love. Remember, He is not only the object of faith but its author and its finisher; which must mean that He carries it on from beginning to end, not simply that He is its beginning, then that *we* continue His work, and that He again finishes it at last. If I were to tell you of an artist who is the author and finisher of a beautiful picture, you would surely not understand that he made the first sketch, and he gave the finishing touches, and someone did all the rest of the painting. And remember, this life of faith is for every one of us now, under the very circumstances in which God has placed him. Christ is, this day, made unto us, of God, 'wisdom, and righteousness, and sanctification, and redemption.' If this be not enough to satisfy us, we are hard to please. The devil will be sure to tell you: 'Oh! all this was true for Paul, and John, and this and that 'eminent Christian,' but not for *you.*' Simply answer him that it is all *yours*, and that he is a liar from the beginning."

After a most interesting conversation, and a succession of prayers, the company went up-stairs to the General Meeting. Unfortunately we have received no notes of Mr Boardman's instructive meeting held at the same hour in the large hall.

11.45 A.M.

At 11.45 o'clock, the General Meeting was con

vened. The subject of the hour was named by the leader as

THE IMPORTANCE OF DEFINITE TRUST.

We have come together to seek to have *a Scriptural experience of the grace and power of God;* such an experience as Christ came, lived, died, and rose again to give us; such an experience as Paul enjoyed when he said, "I know nothing against myself,"—washed, cleansed, justified, sanctified, and enabled to walk before God with a conscience void of offence both toward God and toward man; such an one as enabled him to say, "Follow me as I have followed Christ;"—and, "Ye are witnesses, and God also, how holily, and justly, and *unblameably* we behaved ourselves among you that believe." A child in its ignorance and imperfection is full of faults, and yet it may so love and desire to obey as to be *blameless.* A very little one once emptied an ink-pot over her dress, and in her innocence was so pleased with the sight that she finished its contents over my own light summer clothes, and then looked up with as much innocent expectation of a smile of approval as though she had brought me a flower. It was a real fault, but I could not blame her for a thing done in total ignorance. Her purpose was to do right. Zacharias and his wife Elisabeth were both righteous before God, walking in all the commandments and ordinances of the Lord *blameless.* To the Philippians, the Apostle says, "That they may be blameless." For the Thessalonians he asked the Lord to "Stablish your hearts unblameable in holiness before God, even our *Father*," in His parental relationship, not as a judge. In the same word in which he describes his own experience, he prays the God of peace to preserve the Thessalonians, spirit, soul, and body "*blameless*,"—and adds, "Faithful is He that calleth you, who also *will do it*." John, in his mature experience was able to say, "Whatsoever we ask, we receive of Him, because we keep His commandments, and do those things that are pleasing in His sight." In these passages, as I judge, all that is claimed is "a conscience void of offence." The apostles neither claim an absolute holiness, nor open the door for a defiled conscience. An unknown fault in a child will not prevent full joyous confidence in intercourse with the parent, but the smallest rebellion of will or act will destroy its freedom of heart. So an unknown, undesigned sin of ignorance, in one seeking the will of God, will not destroy communion,—while the smallest reserve of obedience, the least allowed sin, like a tiny grain of sand in the eye, will effectually mar "fellowship with the Father and His Son."

Perhaps it may help us, to recall that the word "sin" is used in common language in three separate meanings:

I. We speak of everything as sin which in its moral quality is short of the infinite holiness of God. In this sense—and it is a true one—every breath we draw is sin.

II. We speak of "living in sin," meaning thereby outbreaking moral evil.

III. We ask God to "vouchsafe to keep us this day without sin;" not meaning by this the unperceived, inevitable moral evil of our condition, but from those sins which we ought to and may, through grace, avoid—all actual, known sin.

The exceeding great and precious promises are for deliverance from sin in these two last senses. The Apostles availed themselves of them, and so may you and I, not only when dying or at some future time, but in this very day and hour.

Let us, I repeat, not forget that it is to learn to do this, to become believing "believers," we have come together at Oxford. Let us look straight at these promises of victory, and insert in each one "*for me.*" Let us begin to go through our bibles and write on the margin "T. and P.,"—for "Tried and Proved"—on each one, not sliding over a single one without thus setting our seal that God is true. It is the business of the week, and its accomplishment will change the lives of all who have not known its power. We shall with tenfold success command sinners to believe. When a pastor in Hitchin was urging upon an intelligent person to believe in Christ for his need of pardon, the inquirer looked up and asked, "Do you, Sir, trust Christ for all *your* soul's needs?" He could answer nothing, for he had hitherto failed thus to trust the Lord.

So long as we urge Christians toward an indefinite standard of holiness, we give them nothing to grasp. We desire that the marvellous blessings those here have realised from definiteness as to the pardon of their sins, may be doubled by an equal definiteness as to victory over sin, consecration to God, and unclouded communion. The entire surrender, full fellowship and overcoming faith, may be as clearly defined in experience as the knowledge of the forgiveness of transgressions. True faith not only ought to, but actually does overcome.

Do not be anxious about a life of victory and maintained communion making you self-confident. The vision of God always humbles and makes us to say, "My comeliness is turned in me to corruption"; but this is followed by the gracious assurance, "O, man, greatly beloved, *fear not;* peace be unto thee; be strong, yea be strong." Only those who are walking in faith's overcoming power, know the depths of true humiliation before God, and fully realise that in them, that is in their flesh, dwelleth no good thing; yea, nor ever will dwell there. The more we see of God, the more the ever-opening depths of the pollution of our natural heart are perceived: and the more we see, the more we find full cleansing and deliverance. I cannot explain it, but I know, and so do hundreds here, that never did they so much as now feel need of the cleansing blood.

After earnest prayer, Mr. MURRAY SHIPLEY spoke from Exodus xxxiii. 12–17. Man is never a creator, but only the discoverer of what God has created. We need to discover and realise the limitless power there is in Christ for us. The power *is yours*—use it! It would have been an act of unbelief in the disciples, if, when Christ was with them, they had kneeled and asked God to send them the Messiah. Even the Corinthians, to whom Paul said, "Ye are yet carnal," were in the same breath reminded, "Ye are the temples of God," and that "the Spirit of God dwelleth in you." Like the forces of nature, electricity and magnetism and others, which existed as really before they were discovered and used as afterwards, so Christ is dwelling in the heart of every believer, even the weakest, whether His presence is known and enjoyed or not. But unless our faith grasps Him as our indwelling Saviour, the power and realisation of His indwelling will not be ours. Have faith then to be "filled with the Spirit," and according to your faith it shall be unto you.

The indwelling Spirit—represented by all gentle things: the tender dove, the quiet dew—is easily grieved, and He waits to manifest His presence until all hindering things are put away. He must always have the entire being in subjection to Himself. Surrender yourselves to His mighty power, fully and with no reserves, and you will find your lives filled with "glory begun below."

Rev. Dr. MAHAN, of Oberlin College, Ohio, said: If the Apostle Paul stood here, he would put to us this question:—"Have ye received the Holy Ghost since ye believed?" If Christ came to us what should we most desire? That He should breathe on us and say, "Receive ye the Holy Ghost." Christ *is* here, God is here, and ready to bestow this unspeakable gift upon you and upon me; more ready than we are to give bread to a hungry child. The power of the Holy Ghost is ours when we ask the Father in the name of Christ. Do you realise this? Our Lord said to His disciples, "Hitherto ye have asked nothing in My name; ask, and ye *shall* receive, that your joy may be full." What is it to pray in the name of Jesus? A merchant in business has failed. Ruin is before him, but he has an elder brother with millions. He receives a power-of-attorney from him. Of what use is this to him? He can write cheques, draw notes, and make contracts, with the certainty of a full provision for them. His debts are paid and his means are boundless. He says to those around him, "See, here I am, the poorest of the poor; yet no one so rich, for I have my brother's name, and in that name I can claim all I want." Thus I was a bankrupt in the sight of God. When He showed me my sin, I thought that there was no such sinner out of perdition. Then Jesus said, "Ask for pardon in My name." I believed in His name, I asked in His name, and was saved. Then I wanted the Holy Spirit. I asked in His name, believed in His name, and received what I wanted. When you bow in the name of Christ, and ask believing in the efficacy of that name (I say it in deep reverence), you share the same power before the throne which Christ has. "Ask,—*and receive*—that your joy may be *full*." I have no right to be satisfied with anything less than that.

When this full life dawned on me, it was so glorious that I was tempted to ask, "Was I a Christian before;" yet I had been a sincere, conscientious child of God,—but I had missed the power of the indwelling Holy Ghost.

Christ comes to the poorest and weakest. If you get the Lamb in your heart, and the Dove in your soul, you will feel as if you were in the stable in Bethlehem, and not in the palace of pride. May this be your bliss! It will be if you believe, for "all things are possible with God," and "all things are possible to him that believeth." Rest not till your joy is "full."

After a prayer expressing the blessed realisation that we had been brought into the banqueting house, with His banner of love over us, and a hymn,

The Rev. D. B. HANKIN, of Ware, spoke from Micah vii. 14-17. When Micah prophesied, God's people were getting very little to eat. This has been the case with some of us. Many of us have been for years like a flock seeking herbage in a wood, where there has not been enough to satisfy our souls. Christ has been preached, but not fully, and we have long felt unsatisfied with the partial Gospel we have ourselves heard. We have longed for the green pastures and still waters. I had for years an overwhelming sense of the insufficiency of the Gospel as preached by me, in fully meeting the deep heart-yearnings of those who were living in the assurance of pardon. Struggles with sin and mourning over my continual inward failures and shortcomings, and a sense of lack of success at all commensurate with the power of the Gospel I preached, were my constant, reiterated experiences. I felt sure that there must be something wrong; I seemed all wrong myself, and could not believe that I enjoyed a Scriptural experience. Then came the prayer, "Lord, bring me out of this wood, where I am existing in such scanty herbage; bring me into the green pastures of the Word. My soul is starved!" Then I was led to apprehend Jesus as the Emancipator from the thraldom of sin, as the Purifier of my heart, and the One able and willing to do exceeding abundantly above all that I was able to ask or to think. I trusted the Lord as never before, and found Him faithful to His promises in keeping me from falling; when I have stumbled, as I do even now sometimes, the failure is mine not Christ's.

There is a mighty contest going on in the Church of God between two doctrines. Which will you have—sanctification by works, or sanctification by faith?—faith in the power of a risen Saviour who is able to curb your rebellious will, and bring every thought of your breast into captivity to the obedience of Christ. Exercise the faith already yours, then you will get back to your first experience; then illuminated days will come back, and, rejoicing always in Christ, we shall know the fulness of the glorious Gospel.

Then will come the effect upon the nations; "They shall see and be confounded at all their might." Ah! where has been our might in the days gone by? "They shall lay their hand upon their mouth;" they shall no more speak against this life of faith when they see us gentle, kind, meek, patient, forbearing, and loving.

The Good Shepherd.

3 P.M.

At 3 o'clock Mrs. R. Pearsall Smith gave a Bible reading on Christ our Shepherd (from Ezekiel xxxiv.) You know whether you are dwelling in the full enjoyment of the promises of the Word, or whether you are hungry and thirsty, and made a prey by your enemies (ver. 28). "I will save my flock, and they shall be no more a prey." I believe that God calls us sheep, not because of any gentleness or purity in us, but because sheep are the weakest and most helpless animals in the world.

The silliest and weakest of all, they are the best cared for, because they have a shepherd. It is not their business to choose their own way, nor to find pasture for themselves. This is the shepherd's work. They do not chafe or worry about to-morrow's food—shall we who have the Good Shepherd do so? Can we not trust Him to guide us, and see that the pastures are what we need? Do we ever think that, when darkness and trial come, He has forgotten us? He is *always* near, and if we could be more sure of His presence at one time than another, it would be when the enemy of our souls is near. When the wolf cometh the hireling fleeth—not so the Good Shepherd. "The Higher Christian Life" is just seeing that we are *sheep* who can do nothing for ourselves, and learning to leave our *all* with the Lord our Shepherd.

"He maketh me to lie down." Many Christians do not know what it is "to lie down." It means perfect rest, when every muscle of the body is relaxed, and we *let ourselves go*, as we do when we compose ourselves to sleep. Many lie down as if the couch would not support them, and are not resting for fear lest they should fall. Has the Lord caused *you* to lie down? If so, nothing can disturb you. His will is a pillow for your weary head, as you dismiss every anxiety and breathe "Thy will be done." Sheep will not lie down till they are satisfied. Can you say, "He satisfieth my soul?" He is the Good Shepherd, and He will cause the evil beasts to cease out of the land. Do *you* follow the Shepherd and leave all to Him? "The Higher Christian Life" may be summed up in two words, *Trust Jesus.* If you cannot understand everything, you can understand this, "Casting all your care upon Him, for He careth for you." If One takes the care the other may go free. Now let us say the Psalm of Rest, the twenty-third, together aloud; believing, as a present reality, that the Lord is our Shepherd, and therefore we shall not want.

The crowded congregation all bowed in response to this request, and the hearts of many were thrilled as the familiar words of this blessed Psalm were repeated by a thousand voices in childlike faith; and the Good Shepherd, who giveth His life for the sheep, was trusted in by many as never before.

The Jordan.

4 P.M.

At 4 o'clock the subject before the meeting was the passage of the Jordan by God's people. (Joshua iii.)

Canaan cannot be a type of heaven, because it was the duty of the Israelites to enter it at once on leaving Egypt, while it is not our duty to go to heaven at once upon our separating from the world in conversion. Only so much of Canaan was possessed as they conquered—we do not so gain heaven. In Canaan came failure, but in heaven is everlasting preservation. Jordan is not death, but the transition from wilderness-failure to the conquering position. At Kadesh-Barnea there was only a geographical line to be passed, but a long cherished habit of partial unbelief seems to need a marked transition line to a position of full trust.

"Sanctify yourselves, for to-morrow the Lord will do

wonders among you!" This is the message to us at Oxford to-day.—Separate yourselves from *all* known evil, and we shall see marvellous things of Divine grace and power in all our communities.

The Israelites went into Jordan in a time of very peculiar difficulty—just when the river was overflowing its banks. There will appear to you very special difficulties as to full surrender and full trust just now—but difficulties are but receding, harmless waters to faith. Step in! and "find firm footing for faith."

What was the result of faith in Israel? (Joshua xxiii. 14, and xxiv. 13–14.) "Ye know in all your hearts, and in all your souls, that not one thing hath failed of all the good things which the Lord your God spake concerning you; all are come to pass unto you, and not one thing hath failed thereof." Failure did not come till after the death of Joshua. Our great Joshua, or Jesus, never dies, but is the same yesterday, to-day, and for ever. All our victories are of grace:—"I have given you a land for which ye did not labour, and cities which ye built not, and ye dwell in them; of the vineyards and olives which ye planted not, do ye eat."

"Moses my servant is dead;"—ye are not under law—"now therefore arise, and go over this Jordan . . . . unto the land which I do give thee!" "How long are ye slack to go up and possess the land which the Lord God of your fathers *hath given you!*" Oh! that this week might see multitudes in a distinctive experience of full trust!—saying, "We which have believed do enter into Rest!"

AT 6 P.M.

The first Ministerial Conference commenced with silent prayer. After the preliminary exercises, we were reminded that, under the law, the offering for the sin of a leader of the people was the same as for the trespass of a whole tribe, showing God's view of the importance of the lives of ministers. It is a great mistake to think that ministers have fewer temptations than others—their temptations are greater than those of other Christians.

A preacher remarked:—I was once very much troubled about the limited success attending my labours compared with what I ought to expect from so glorious a Gospel. I preached in many pulpits where an Evangelist had laboured, under whose ministry a thousand or more every year found the pardon of their sins, and I everywhere heard of the permanence as well as the extent of his work. I wondered at it, for I knew that he was singularly deficient in what are commonly considered the natural elements of pulpit power. He was of cold temperament, unexpressive face, unattractive appearance and utterance, and yet had such unusual blessing on his preaching. At length he became my guest and I watched the hidings of his marvellous power and success—it was in his complete consecration at all times. *He was perfectly pliable in the Lord's hands.* With unusual natural will-power, he was as a little child in readiness to obey. He was where God could use him, and he had the power of the Holy Spirit. As I understood his life I no longer wondered at what God wrought by him. Is there the same interior life with God—the same abiding in

Christ—the same being filled with the Spirit, for every preacher of the Gospel? There is. How may it be had? By consecration and faith. When? As soon as we trust to Him for it—Now!

After a Swiss pasteur, who had preached in Egypt, had given his experience, the Rev. Mr. SNEPP, of Birmingham, said: The promise of life is in Christ Jesus, and therefore yours. Life — LIFE — spiritual life — real life, vigorous life, fulness of life! Many have testified of this life with much power. The word of God bids us all to go on unto perfection—perfection of trust with all the fruits of faith. Oh, that at length Christ might have a fully believing ministry to preach His Gospel!

The Rev. Mr. NASH, of Norwich (for many years curate to Mr. Christopher at Oxford), then described most feelingly how, after many years of earnest service, he had attended a consecration meeting at Sir Thomas Beauchamp's the previous year, and there had learned what it was to lay aside the last weight, and to trust fully for everything to Christ. Since then, in the midst of unusual difficulty and effort, life had been inwardly one long sabbath, and a blessing, manifold beyond anything before experienced, had attended his ministry.

Rev. Mr. DAWSON, of Nottingham, followed: I want to express my thankfulness to God for the Consecration Meetings held at Nottingham. I know but little of this life of full trust, but that little is so precious that I would not part with it for all the world.

Twenty-five years ago a letter from a loving faithful sister, written to me at school, opened the way of salvation. I gave myself to the Lord, and from that time tried to serve Him, though very feebly and faultily, and even sinfully, and sometimes in conscious trespass. I laboured in China till failing health compelled a return to my native country. Since then I have often been surprised that He should use one so utterly and consciously unworthy in the pastoral work. When friends said, "Everything you put your hand to seems to succeed," I cannot tell you how painfully I felt my inward deficiencies.

When I read Mr. Boardman's "Higher Christian Life," I found that there was a higher platform on to which I had not stepped, and I was led to trust Christ as never before; but even then mine was an up and down christian and ministerial life. But the Lord was teaching me in His own school. Last year was the hardest year of all. Such an awfully trying experience was mine, that I hope no one else will ever have to pass through what I did. I cannot now tell you about it. There was so much to unlearn, so much to give up. Mr. Smith said to me at Nottingham, "Well, my brother, have you passed over Jordan—clean passed over, not a hoof left behind?" I can, through grace, say that I have; and I have lived since then in friendship and fellowship with Christ such as I have never known before. "He is able" to keep me from falling. "He keepeth the feet of His saints." "He keepeth all his bones," said the Psalmist, and I am sure that He will much more keep the souls of His trusting saints. It must be a faith moment by moment. Oh take that word "*able*" into your inmost heart. I seem to have been tasting the grapes of Eshcol, but beyond are vineyards.

Dr. ZIEMANN, of Germany: It is to the glory of God that we are all here from England, France, Switzerland, Germany, America, to give the same testimony—"Ourselves nothing, Christ all!" I have worked for the Lord for some years, but it was too much in my own way, my own strength. I did not trust my Father in heaven as I ought. Through misconception I formerly greatly opposed this teaching; but now I have been taught to trust Jesus moment by moment, and He does keep me beyond my largest conceptions of the possibilities of this life.

A remarkable freedom of expression characterised this and the succeeding Ministerial Conferences. Those who took part spoke with the simplicity and ease of the family circle, so strong was the sense of Christian sympathy. The frequent intervals of silent or vocal prayer, the constant use of Scripture, and, above all, the overshadowing presence of the Spirit, made this evening hour always a time of peculiar power and blessing, both to the ministers themselves, and to those outside the centre seats, which were especially appropriated to those in the public ministry of the Gospel.

THE 8 O'CLOCK GENERAL MEETING

Commenced as usual with silent prayer. After the opening hymn and vocal prayer, Ps. cxxxix. was read by the leader of the meeting. There was a time when we shrank from the penetrating eye of God—when the thought "Thou God seest me!" was terrible to us. Now, through grace, it is no longer so with us; for we have learned that "as Christ is so are we in this world," and God sees us not as we are in ourselves, but as we stand in the Beloved. We have learned to love that Eye; but do we love it perfectly? Have we cried in the integrity of our hearts, "Teach me, O God, and know my heart; try me, and know my thoughts; and see if there be *any* wicked way in me." Is there a single thing held in reserve? Is it our purpose in all the possible honesty of our souls to come out into the piercing light of God's countenance? We need not dread the light. It may reveal many dreadful things hitherto unseen, but the light which shows the evil also shows the blood. "If we walk in the light as He is in the light . . . the blood of Jesus Christ cleanseth us from all sin." A walk in the light of God must lead to the blood—*and the blood cleanseth.*

I want the Lord's presence to go through my soul as a refiner's fire; and I think that I have felt something of this as we have waited together here in silence. I do long for as much of His holy presence with and in me as this poor body can bear. Beloved, do you cordially *hate* sin? Not merely breaking-out sin, but the refined sins just suited to your æsthetical nature? He who hates one toad hates every toad on earth, and he who hates sin, because it is contrary to God, must hate every sin, and not some only. Oh, that God may give to us here at Oxford a perfect hatred of sin, and with it an intense love of the sinner.

After silent prayer, the Rev. Mr. Hankin led us in the supplication that we might every one be brought to say, "What have I any more to do with idols?"

Rev. E. H. Hopkins: God desires us to enjoy continually His own peace, and that there should no longer be any controversy in all our being with Him.

We want God to come into the issues of life: its very springs. Has He, in moments of illumination, shown you something wrong in your life? Have you fully renounced it? Let nothing ever come between your soul and God! When I used to read passages like Hebrews xiii. 20—"The God of peace . . . make you perfect"—I felt a temptation to put them aside as presenting too high a privilege to be realised in this life. But I have learned to dare to face these promises, and to claim of God a Scriptural experience. See first what He is—"the God of peace;" and what He has done—"brought again from the dead our Lord Jesus;" and this not by virtue of His obedience, but "through the *blood* of the everlasting covenant." Begin by seeing that redemption is through the blood, not through the spotless life of Jesus. Then look at the subject of the prayer. "Make you perfect;" here, derivatively, the word means to bring into its place a dislocated joint, not to make you absolutely sinless. We are members of His body each one in particular, but we have been, even since our conversion, often out of harmony with the Head. He is now adjusting us, and we have learned to resist no longer. There is first full submission to the righteousness of God, and then full submission to His will. "Make you perfect . . . . to do His will." He has first to make us "perfect," in order that we may do His will. The law *reveals* a duty as the will of God: the Gospel *gives* a will to do it. And all this is accomplished "through Jesus Christ," not through law. Then shall shouts of victory follow close on the voice of our prayers.

Pasteur T. Monod: Do not let us be satisfied with anything short of what God has given us in Christ. If a poor man should receive as a gift a cheque for £100, he would not be content with £50, nor with £75, nor with £90, nor yet with £99, nor with anything but his full £100. Let us do the same.

A deep impression was evidently made by this day of prayer and exhortation. No devout heart could be insensible to the searching power of the Spirit in the Word, and in the personal testimonies given. Not a few came to a deep realisation that they were under solemn special responsibility, here and now, to renounce all doubtful things not of faith. In all honesty they sought to know everything in their lives, their affections, their will, contrary to the holiness of God. Such a continuous concentration upon this one thought was new to most of them. Many were brought to deep conviction for the want of full consecration and trust in their lives, very parallel to that felt when first brought to the knowledge of their guilt for committed sins, and they were ready to cry out, "O, wretched man! who shall deliver me from the body of this death?"—this remaining envy, jealousy, emulation, ambition, indolence, and the thousand results of unbelief. It was the Holy Spirit's preparation for the days of blessing which by faith we knew were to follow. We separated to our pillows in quiet prayer and praise.

CHAPTER IV.

TUESDAY, SEPTEMBER 1ST.

7 O'CLOCK A.M.

THE day commenced with the usual before breakfast prayer meeting, at 7 o'clock. The streets of Oxford formed truly a striking scene; from eight hundred up to a thousand persons passing through them at this early hour, with the quiet earnestness of their purpose depicted in their countenances. A stranger who entered the great Corn Exchange would hear no eloquent address, see no attractive ritual; his senses would be fed by no brilliant music; but far above all these was the imposing sight of about a thousand souls bowed in lengthened silent prayer. A quiet hymn is sung; they are led in words of earnest pleading for the felt presence of the Holy Ghost, for grace to make an entire surrender, and earnest breathings are expressed after a life of entire trust. Scriptures bearing upon a life of discipleship are read and briefly commented on. Again prayer is offered, for the vital realisation of what has been taught. Then the meeting is open for speaking, but prayer forms the prevailing current until we separate, at half-past eight o'clock, for breakfast. There was a subdued expression, a quiet earnestness, marked in the features of almost every one present at these simple, effortless early services. They were perhaps as effective as any we held, and they seemed to give tone to the meetings all through the day. It is impossible to put into words the quiet sweetness and sense of the presence of Christ during those early hours. The simple reading of Scripture, or the responsive repetition of a Psalm, seemed to thrill and penetrate the assembly more than an eloquent address usually does.

For an account of the ladies' daily meeting at half-past nine o'clock, put into connected form for greater interest, we refer to a later chapter. The several meetings held at the same hour in the Town Hall, though of the deepest interest, were often of too conversational a tone to be of value in a brief report.

The Conversational Meeting.

9.30 A.M.

Pasteur Monod gave a running commentary on the 30th chapter of the Second Book of Chronicles, which, he said, had lately been pointed out to him by a friend.

Verses 1, 5, 8–14, 18–22, 23, 24, 27, were more particularly dwelt upon, as suggesting obvious and important lessons in reference to the present gathering. We have been called together to keep our passover, "on such sort as it is written," "not with old leaven, neither with the leaven of malice and wickedness, but with the unleavened bread of sincerity and truth," presenting "our bodies a living sacrifice, holy, acceptable unto God, which is our reasonable service," or literally, "reasonable worship." Everything is summed up in the one command to "yield ourselves unto the Lord," casting away every idol. Never mind them that scoff, neither be hindered by anything that may yet be lacking in your full intelligence of spiritual truth; if only you have "prepared your heart to seek God," He will graciously receive you. He will give you good things that you will give Him in return. He will make us able to bless the people, and our prayer shall "come up to His holy dwelling-place, even unto heaven."

A minister said:—In prayer we have not to overcome an unwillingness of God, but our spiritual adversaries. The woman to whom Christ answered not a word overcame by quiet confidence. "The violent take the kingdom of heaven by force;" but *we* have not to overcome something put by God into the heart, nor to thrust against the door, nor to wrestle against the Lord. We are "to receive the kingdom of God as a little child"—one who has no power to wrestle, only power to take what God offers. Once in the kingdom of heaven—"righteousness, peace, and joy in the Holy Ghost"—we are to fight the good fight of faith against the devil and all his angels.

A German Christian present added: A good soldier is one who perfectly obeys his commander. I had to stand twenty-four hours before Paris almost without moving an eye. The power of a soldier is in his obedience. The power of a Christian is in complete surrender and obedience.

The General Meeting.

11.45 A.M.

This was appropriated to the thought of a definite

giving ourselves to God. Having in previous meetings sought in faith that God would show us all the remaining evil of our condition which in our present imperfection we could discern, and having, as we believed, renounced every known disobedience, with the purpose to do this in everything in which we are otherwise minded when God shall reveal anything to us, we could now, with holy sincerity of purpose, see what the Word of God taught us as to entire devotion of ourselves to Christ.

R. Pearsall Smith, after a brief synopsis of the first eleven chapters of Romans, remarked: I know that these chapters have been very diligently studied and clearly taught by many Christians. Thank God for this. The Lord would have us instructed in His ways of grace and gift before He asks anything of us. But how many have fully acted on the entreaty which follows these marvellous chapters of the grace and purposes of God?—"*I beseech you, therefore, brethren, by the mercies of God, that ye present your bodies a living sacrifice, holy, acceptable unto God.*"

You take the Apostle's words and beseech the unconverted to become reconciled in Christ to God. Listen to the same Apostle beseeching *you*, my brother, my sister, to make an actual definite transaction, as defined as any you ever made in worldly business. The motive is not command. The Apostle stoops to entreat, to beseech you, pointing as a motive to the mercies of God recounted in the past eleven chapters. If I give you a book, you take it. It is yours and not mine. I no longer think of claiming it. Having once transferred it to you, what would you think of me, if, day after day, I should say, "I am sure I do not know whether it is yours or mine?" Or if, year after year, I were to say, "I give you this book; I do give you this book," you would at length doubt whether I had ever intended to give it; or, if so, whether I had carried out my purpose and actually given it. Do not thus illusively, indefinitely, give yourself to God, but make an actual transaction, and ever afterwards recognise it as *a thing done once for all.* "Ye are not your own." Accept, in every emergency of life, something of the sense of being owned, which belongs to slavery. When, in a shipwreck, a negro was asked why, in the presence of immediate drowning, he was so unconcerned, he answered, "O it will be massa's loss!" Let in the sublime sense of being thus wholly the Lord's, first by purchase and then by voluntary gift. The heads of a family do not say the marriage covenant every day, but recognise that they have been and are married, and they adjust their lives accordingly. I gave myself, utterly and entirely, a living sacrifice to God once in a definite, voluntary gift, as the great intelligent privilege of a freeman in Christ, and I have since then only been living out the results of this clearly recognised transaction; not indeed perfectly, but with no variation as to my purpose. I hope that I have never deliberately hesitated since as to doing the known will of God. Each day shows me more and more (as I am able to bear it) the imperfection of my life, and the blood which meets my shortcoming; but each day shows me more and more that what I have done in in thus presenting myself is acceptable to God.

Here in our midst is Christ, not only our High Priest, our Sacrifice, but in another of His offices of love—our Altar. In His name I could kneel to you, and beseech you to place yourself and all that you are, or can be, all that you love or have, upon this Altar. If you have already done so without any Ananias-reserve, may a holy dread inspire you of ever withdrawing anything from that sacred place! Oh what a thrill of horror would have spread through the camp of Israel had any one dared sacrilegiously to snatch from the altar anything which had been once laid upon it! They would at once have stoned such an one with stones, burned him with fire, and covered over the remains from sight with stones—as they did Achan for a far less offence. If such be the sin of ceremonial sacrilege, what is that, in a spiritual dispensation, of those who rob from Christ any part of their thank-offerings, of which He has said, "The altar sanctifieth the gift." The Lord give us a holy horror of robbery in Divine things! Let us pause and ask ourselves before God whether our all is laid on our Altar;—or whether, having placed all there, aught has been snatched back again.

"*A living sacrifice*" is in contrast with the slain offerings of ceremonial law. We should make it a thank as well as a burnt offering, embrace it as the grandest privilege of our life, thus to give ourselves entirely to God. "What!" exclaims some one, "not leave anything for self? Utterly deny self?" Yes, utterly. Not only deny what self does, but deny the hateful self which is the doer of evil things. Well, beloved, there is such a thing as having the sentence of death in oneself, and yet living in the happy enjoyment of all we would wish to have, because self is lost in the will of God. Well might Augustine exclaim, "Love, and do what you please!" If self-will can be almost merged in that of another in the passion of human love, shall we do less for God with all the wealth of the love of God shed abroad in our hearts by the Holy Ghost?

Remember that the sacrifice once presented, and laid on the altar was *holy*: it could not be taken back again. I think we are beginning to see how utterly miserable and worthless we are in ourselves; but God makes us worthy in Christ. Having given ourselves wholly to God, faith must be exercised that the offering is acceptable, that He receives the all which we bring to Him. We are the Lord's—(1) by purchase, "bought with a price"; (2) by voluntary gift of our hearts, the "living sacrifice"; (3) by His gracious acceptance, in the words,—I will receive you; I will dwell in you; and I will never leave nor forsake you. Have you, dear Christian, a clear and *definite* experience that these three transactions are accomplished in you?

When it is thus with you, you are then ready for the words, "Be not conformed to this world." Oh, beloved, pause a moment here, for the Word of God is "quick and powerful, and sharper than any two-edged sword, ... and is a discerner of the thoughts and intents of the heart." Is there anything in your lives in which you are conformed to the Spirit of the world? . . . . "But be ye transformed"—the word here is the one rendered "transfigured" in the scene of our Lord on the Mount,—"by the renewing of your minds":—not as finality of experience, but that *now* "ye may prove what is that good, and acceptable, and perfect will of God," in the daily occurring details of life. We must come into the experience of full consecration and trust before we can prove and live the will of God.

Dr. Mahan: "But as many as received Him, to them gave He power to become the sons of God." This conveys a small idea to most minds, but it includes limitless blessings. When Christ is received by a full surrender, He endues us with power, brings us practically into a new creation, and opens the joys of the relation of sons and daughters. He puts the very spirit of adoption into our hearts, so that we live in the Father's house, abiding there as the children of God to go no more out for ever. How can we be called the "sons of God" unless we have the special characteristics of sons, so that all who see us can know us as such? He sends the Spirit into our hearts, whereby we cry. "Abba, Father!" We are entitled to "the promise of the Father," the baptism of the Holy Ghost, that we may be sons in character, in experience, in our aims and desires, in likeness to Christ. We are sons, but never in our true and proper character of sons until, by the Holy Ghost, we are made Christ-like in spirit. Oh then present yourselves definitely as living sacrifices, expecting that He will bring upon you the full power of the Spirit! Do not let in the shadow of a doubt that you will be received and transformed as sons in your Heavenly Father's house.

Mr. Shipley then gave a beautiful exposition of the Book of Ruth as teaching complete separation from the world, and full union with Boaz. After a few words by Lord Radstock, on definite anointing, the Rev. W. E.

Boardman led in prayer. It was stated that in Paris daily prayer meetings were now being held for the special object of asking a blessing on the Oxford Meeting. After silent prayer the meeting was adjourned for dinner.

At 3 o'clock

Mrs. Smith held her usual Bible Reading (John xiv.). The consummating blessing of the Christian life is God dwelling in His people. Judicially, or in gift, this is true of all believers, but comparatively few realise it. So many have lived as if Christ were shut up *in one room* of their hearts. They have not given Him the entire range of the house. Plans have been formed with little reference to Him. If some one could come and say to each one now, "The Lord Jesus is really in your house," how delightful it would be. This room would be cleared in two minutes. Some would go for joy at His presence; some, perhaps, to get something out of the way before He should see it! Well, dear friends, just so really He is living in your hearts, knowing everything better than you do yourselves. As you go about this world you carry a glorious indwelling Saviour.

The Israelites had all the responsibility of their journey in the wilderness laid on the Lord, and relief from all care. But this involved a complete giving up of their own wills. In no other way can we obtain rest from all anxiety. The Lord's sweet way of grace is first to give us something so good that we do not mind giving up what He calls for. He puts the new robe upon us before He asks us to put away the rags.

The heaviest care is the care of ourselves, and even

this He relieves us from. The words, "Be careful for nothing" include everything. But your children—your greatest care—are they included? And your health, your business, your money affairs? Yes, casting ALL your care upon Him, for He careth for you. It is enough for one to take the care. Who can manage them best, you or the Lord? You can trust Him to manage the universe, why not your life?

The submission of your will to God is the sweetest privilege that can come into your life. Heaven is full of happiness, because God's will is done there, and those who fully give up their wills receive a measure of heaven's own joy.

Recognising the Lord's indwelling presence, second causes cannot trouble us. We realise that nothing can happen to us without His will; nothing can touch us except through His presence; even cross words cannot disturb our rest. Oh, we are so safe in God!

A friend of mine was wakened one morning by a noise at her window, and on looking for the cause, she saw a butterfly inside the pane of glass, while outside on the ledge was a sparrow who followed every movement of the insect, pecking fruitlessly against the glass in its efforts to seize it, but in vain; for the bird could not touch the butterfly while the glass was there. So the protecting presence of God is between us and every enemy.

This address was followed by

THE GENERAL MEETING.

4 O'CLOCK P.M.

Ephesians i. 3-12 was read.

Rev. W. Hay Chapman, London: My beloved friends, if it is a fact in God's sight that you have presented yourselves a living sacrifice to the Lord; that all is laid on His altar—Christ; then learn from these verses what God has undertaken to do for you. God has chosen us, and it is His *purpose* "that we should be holy and without blame before Him in love." Then trust His word, and you will find Him true to His promises. By His own Spirit dwelling in you He will make your lives to be to the praise of His glory. "Thou hast wrought all our works in us."

May I here, at this time of deep feeling, utter a word of warning? Do not trust your own feelings, trust nothing but the Word. Learn God's purposes on your knees from *the Book*, and yield your heart to them. God has been teaching me the blessed *Rest* that comes from believing His promises.

Rev. E. W. Moore, London: The Christian life is a race, and there are two points out of many about a race which demand special notice. The first is *Definiteness.* A race-course is no careless haphazard track. It has a definite starting point, definite boundaries, and a definite goal. So has the Christian life. It is "a race *set* before us," and the not clearly seeing this is one cause of the unsatisfactory spiritual experience of Christians. But there is a second point not less important, and that is *Divestment.* To run a race successfully all hindrances must be laid aside; and to live the Christian life successfully all weights, the last and the least, must be cast away, and, above all, the sin of unbelief. In God's strength let us lay this sin aside to day. One word as to this point of entire surrender. Persons ask, "How am I to know that God takes me, when I yield myself up 'a living sacrifice' to Him? Our answer is from the Word, 'This is the confidence that we have in Him, that if we ask anything according to His will He heareth us, and if we know that He heareth us we know that we HAVE the petitions we desired of Him." It is His will that we should be wholly His, and thus when we honestly give ourselves to Him, and ask Him to take us, we dare to believe that He does take us. My friends, though it contradict everything—past experience and present feeling—dare to believe God.

After prayer by Rev. Mr. Mayers, especially for Lord Radstock's evangelistic service in the evening, the meeting was adjourned until

The Ministerial Conference.

6.30 P.M.

It was opened as usual with prayer, first silent and then vocal. The following incident was then told by an Evangelist: A now venerable bishop was a man of commanding abilities, and at an unusually early age was placed at the head of a college. This nourished the propensity to self-confidence and vanity, which became conspicuous even to the students. While he would have died the next hour at the stake rather than deny his Lord, he was far from having died to his self-trust, so that the Christ-life might fill his career. His stature was as much larger than that of other men as were his mental abilities. One day he visited one of his students, who was raving in a delirium of fever. As the young man caught sight of the large figure of his instructor, he turned on him, and said wildly, "Great big Mr. President! great big Mr. President! you think yourself some great one. When you preach you are so big that you hide the Cross; all that we can see is great big Mr. President!" The Lord, by these delirious ravings, brought him to see his self-conceit; that self and not Christ, had been uppermost. He at once went out "weeping bitterly" to a lonely spot in the woods, and there on his face he confessed it all to his merciful Saviour, and there learned the lesson of resurrection life. Forty years of eminently successful labour for Christ had borne the impress of that sacred hour of self-renunciation and trust. I heard him, in his old age, tell this incident, with tears in his eyes, to a company of many hundred ministerial brethren.

Behind the pulpit where I was preaching, in the chapel of the Faith Houses of Dorothea Trudel, at Mannedorf, Switzerland, I saw a large figure representing our Lord upon the cross, crowned with thorns. Much as I deplored this object, I learned a lesson from what was beneath it. "Ich," the German word for *I*, was inscribed in large letters, but through it was a deep cancelling mark, and it was substituted by "ER," or HE. May we all beneath the Cross learn the lesson of the cancelled "I," "I am crucified with Christ, nevertheless I live, *yet not I*, but Christ liveth in me, and the life that I now live in the flesh, I live by the faith of the Son of God, who loved *me*, and gave Himself for *me*."

A Minister: Madame Guyon said, "Let us have no self-reflective acts." If in our ministry, my brethren, praise is offered us, let us hand it over untouched to Him to whom it is due. If we make up our minds to leave *all* with Jesus, and put from us, as we would robbery, every thought of *our* having done well, we shall honour God, and then Christ will be also between us and blame. "Thou shalt not steal!" Oh, brethren, what thieves we have been! We have stolen that which was the Lord's! Let us do so no longer.

Sometimes our hearts have been oppressed with the care of our pressing parochial duties; our spirits have become depressed, and we think we can sustain the burden no longer,—we must leave the parish. Now, *do not leave the parish; leave the care.* My young brother, have you given up the thought of establishing a ministerial reputation? Christ made Himself of no reputation, and He was the only One ever on earth who deserved one. Will you seek what He rejected? That was my bane for a time, I sought to establish a ministerial reputation. Now, as we sing, "Leave it all with Jesus," Whose glory are you desiring? You say, "The Lord's." But, is it your Lord's exclusively? Let us hide ourselves behind the Cross.

Rev. C. B. Sawday, London: We have much to learn after we are fully consecrated. We become so hungry and thirsty that we would feed on the Word all day long. We believe in *the whole* of the Bible now. Oh, take the blessing—"the blessedness of the man that trusteth in God." I formerly wept to think that there could be cloudless communion with God, but I find it a thousand times better than I expected. The joy of the Lord is our strength. I feel it to be a burning shame upon me that all these years I kept back anything from the Lord. We ministers have often made this confession of the lack of entire consecration. I made an inventory of all I possessed, and gave it *all* to the Lord; but I found the Lord desired something yet. I said, "Lord, what more?" The answer came: "*Thy will.*" Prostrate on my face, I gave Him all; yes, my *will* itself.

What is there that you will not give up to Him? Is He not your Father? Even if it were not my duty to be wholly consecrated, I would do it for the privilege and the heaven of it! His yoke is now *so* easy, and His burden *so* light!

A leading London minister said to me, "But Mr. Sawday, you always were consecrated. I always looked on you as specially devoted to the Lord, and He has given you marvellous success." "Ah!" was my reply, "in the midst of it all my will asserted itself. I did try to submit my will, but it was not given up fully." I preached about consecration and a life of full trust to my people at King's Cross for eleven years, but never heard of a fully consecrated person in my church. As soon as I had laid aside my own last weight of self-will and unbelief, I trusted the Lord to revive my charge. Some were worldly, others carnal, others fond of money, but now near two hundred of my people have found the same blessing. Members who had long been estranged came to each other with tears to ask mutual forgiveness. One man gave up a profitable line in his business, because he could not ask a blessing on it. Another gave up a remunerative situation because he could not continue in it with a good conscience. The Sunday school teachers wept as they told the children the story of the cross. The unconverted said, "What makes these Christians so marvellously happy? we thought religion was melancholy,"—and they sought the Lord. Many were converted. Such a revival I never knew. Thank God for a testimony so distinctive as is now being given for the true Christian life.

It was here mentioned that Lord Radstock and other Christians were now waiting in the porch for reinforcements to go out into the streets to preach the Gospel. A goodly number went out for this work.

The Rev. W. J. MAYERS, of Bristol, whose deeply spiritual power in singing in the meetings can never be forgotten, was the next speaker: I was just as others, preaching, and preaching, and preaching, and all the time wanting something more myself that I would not trust Christ for. The Psalmist expressed my feelings by the words, "My soul panteth after Thee, O God." "My soul followeth hard after Thee." I longed for something in Christ I had not yet received. It came. I was satisfied with marrow and fatness.

You will say, "But you are a young man, you haven't met with trial; you don't know what sorrow is." But I do (from emotion he spoke with difficulty), and I have found this: "Thou wilt keep him in perfect peace whose mind is stayed on Thee." I had removed my sphere of labour to a larger field, where I might have more work for the Lord. I had prayed Him, if need be, to take all and prepare me for His work there. He took me at my word. He took my dearest joy; her whom He had given me, the mother of my children.

I said, "My all is on the Altar." He said, "My child, I take it." The fire consumed the best of the sacrifice, and I kissed His hand, and said, "Though He slay me, yet will I trust in Him."

Prayers followed this deeply affecting testimony, and shortly afterward commenced

The General Meeting.

8 o'clock p.m.

After prayer, the following incident was related, illustrating the personal responsibility of immediate complete obedience to God. After one of Mr. Moody's meetings some years ago, a minister of considerable prominence came to me, said the speaker, with some anxiety about the correctness of what had been taught as to consecration. After he had expressed his views, I asked him if he knew what it is to have "the peace of God which passeth all understanding," to keep his heart and mind through Christ Jesus. He replied that, while he never doubted the forgiveness of his sins, he did not live in continuous communion with God. "Is there not a cause?" I asked; "for God's purpose is to keep you—not sometimes, but always—abiding in Christ." After much hesitation, he told me of a sad entanglement in his life, which he had hesitated to keep fully in the light of God, and tried to persuade himself was not sinful. When from the Word he was shown it was contrary to the mind of God, we kneeled to ask power for him to give up the snare. When we rose from our knees, I asked "Have you given it up?" "No," said he, "I am asking for strength to do it."

Again we kneeled, and on rising I again asked if he had now really given up the sin. He replied, "I cannot do it in my own strength, I am asking God for it."

After praying a third time, when he still gave the same reply, I could not help saying, "You have asked God for power, and *you have it*. He will not make a a mere machine of you Trusting in Him you are to yield this thing up. I do not say to you, pray again; but *yield*—do it *now!*" I saw that he was depending on his prayer, and not on the Lord. "But," said he "*I cannot!* The step would be worse than death itself." I replied, "Well, my brother, there is no necessity whatever for your living, but every necessity for your obeying. Better die than disobey God. It was what the early Christians did." At length, after a sore struggle, he said, "*I do it!*" and a shadow, that might eventually have ruined his ministry, was lifted from his life. Let us not forget, though we are to depend on the strength of God, we are not to plead inability, but at once to renounce every known sin, sure that when we thus put ourselves into His will, all the resources of the Infinite One are ours to carry out the decisions of our will.

It is much like dying to give up our wills; but after the death of self-will is the Christ-life in the divine will. Oh! that this hour may be the deciding-time for many souls who have long been hesitating as to complete self-surrender. Give up even doubtful things not of faith. Give to the side of God, not to the world, the benefit of the doubt.

We know that every justified person is, in one Scripture sense, also sanctified, and that practical sanctification is the work of the Word, of the Spirit, and of Jesus; but in harmony, and not in conflict with this, the Word also says, "*Let us cleanse ourselves* from all filthiness of the flesh and spirit, perfecting holiness in the fear of God."

The hymn,—

"Nothing unclean shall enter in,"

was then sung, followed with earnest prayer by the Rev. G. R. Thornton.

Rev. E. H. Hopkins (Matt. ix. 27–31): We need a definite act of faith for a definite blessing. Some may say, "Of course I believe in Christ; but my circumstances are so trying; my temptations are so great; there is a besetting sin I cannot overcome." Well, Jesus says, "Believest thou that *I* am able to do *this?*"—this very thing. Faith answers, "Yea, Lord," and Jesus says, "According to your faith be it unto you." Believe all that you profess to believe. Christ is to you practically what He is to your faith.

In the story of the nobleman, John iv. 46–50, we have an illustration of *seeking* faith and *resting* faith. We see him first, coming to the Lord Jesus, with a faith that led him to *seek*, but not a faith that enabled him to *rest*. He has a want. He carries a burden. "Come down ere my child die!" "Go thy way, thy son liveth!" But when the word was spoken, "Go thy way, thy son liveth!" at once he loses his burden, his heart is satisfied, and his faith passes from seeking to resting. He did not rest on a sign, or an emotion, or an experience, but on the *word* of Jesus, "and the man believed the word that Jesus had spoken unto him, and he went his way." He was perfectly satisfied that the cure was effected. He acted as if he saw. So let us rest in the promises of God. Not merely ask, but believe that we have the petitions that we desire of Him.

Rev. G. R. Thornton: "The father *believed the word that Jesus had spoken and went his way.*" It was hard to believe but *he did it.* Have you not often wanted signs before you trusted? But no signs will be given to unbelief. "He did not many mighty works there because of their unbelief." Believe, and your life will be full of realisations of the presence of Christ. Signs follow not precede faith, or faith would lose its virtue of faith. Let us now, before we go any further, pause in silent prayer and each one believe for his needs, as the father did for his. (Silent prayer.)

At the time that Jesus gave the command, He had also given the blessing. The nobleman inquired at what hour he began to mend. He did not merely begin to mend, but yesterday at the seventh hour the fever left him, and he got up from his bed perfectly well. Then the father remembered that it was at the hour of healing that Jesus had said, "Thy son liveth." Now he begins to understand the reference to this in Jesus' words, "Except ye see signs and wonders *ye* will not believe." Ah! he must have thought Now indeed that I have believed I have a sign and wonder. Dear friends, Jesus does give signs and wonders, but the mistake is to want the sign and wonder *before believing.* Jesus has given them to some here, but they flowed in on us *after* we believed. He believed Christ's word, and then the Lord did yet more, beyond what he was able to ask or think; he laid hold of a little, but he did not imagine how much the promise contained.

We have been promised far more than he was, and yet it was not until lately we have proved His promises. Now we are finding out their fulness more and more day by day. Let us, who have trusted Him a little, trust Him more, so that every promise will increase in blessing. It must have been very beautiful to see all his household believers. There are your children and your servants. Remember that it was in the house of a man of faith that this took place. When you trust *fully* for your own soul's needs, you can trust as never before for the conversion of your children and servants. Oh! you who call yourselves *believers*, cannot you trust Christ for your deliverance from sin? "He that believeth not God maketh Him a liar." When, in the past, you and I have pointed the unconverted to that word, "believe," they might well have said to us, *You* are making God a liar if you do not trust Him fully yourselves.

Rev. C. B. SAWDAY, of London, rose, and said: "When the consecration meetings were held at King's Cross, the people used to wait until eleven o'clock, saying, "We cannot go home till we get this Rest of Faith." Now, if you have a besetting sin which overcomes you, and seems too big to be got out of the way, *trust Jesus at once with it;* He made the universe—it is a small thing for Him to save you from your sins. If you had a sleepless night last night in conflict of your will with God, submit your will, and have another sleepless night of "joy and *peace in believing.*" When I found Jesus in this fulness of trust, I was three days and nights praising God straight on, and ever since then, in the midst of the sharpest sorrows of life,—

> "My life flows on with endless song,
> How can I keep from singing?"

We seemed to be carried along in a holy current of consecration and faith. All the thoughts, prayers, and addresses aimed at the one point of the soul's complete surrender to Christ to give all and to take all. Dim doubts were cleared up, the will of God was becoming plain. Possibilities of a life of completed trust and devotedness, not before conceived of as for this life, were opening upon many hearts. Many this evening laid their heads upon their pillows in confident anticipation of new blessings in the Gospel.

CHAPTER V.

WEDNESDAY, SEPTEMBER 2ND.

7 O'CLOCK, A.M.

THE rain seemed to make no difference in the attendance at the early meetings, which increased day by day in numbers. The sense of the presence of God seemed to deepen. Longer periods of silent prayer than in earlier days would have been acceptable were now most grateful and in harmony with the feeling of the meeting. Persons often have said, "Those silent moments of the presence of God, when I forgot that any one else was in the room, were more to me than all the addresses. It was then that a *definite* transaction with the Lord was made in a completed surrender and entire trust. It was then that God seemed to come into my very soul, searching as with a lighted candle every secret, and it was then that I realised what it was to know the Lord's indwelling presence and power."

The LEADER: There are two of whom it is said, "*All* things are possible." "With God all things are possible," and "All things are possible to him that believeth." As the dying Adolphe Monod so well said, "Faith moves the arm that moves the universe." It is never said, All things are possible to him that feeleth, or who has an experience. Nay, but to him that *believeth.* If you are seeking a mere experience or joy as your object, you will be miserably disappointed. If you are exercising faith you will have the living Christ with you, and all the joy that is best for you. Having Him you have all; without the living Christ any "experience" will be a hollow thing, and the sooner it is pierced the better for you. I cannot have your experience, and you cannot have mine; but Christ may live the lives of us both and very differently. Even the lightning follows the grain of the wood in a tree. The Lord make us little children, for of such is His kingdom! From the cradle to the college our education was the development of *self-dependence*, but from conversion to heaven the lesson is always self-renunciation and yet more childlike dependence upon God. I get one half of my theology from the Bible, and the other half by watching my children. I learn more from them than I teach them It was Coleridge, I think, who, in one of his Table-talks, said, "Genius is simply the carrying into the maturity of our powers the simplicity and ardour of childhood." There is a divine genius in this faith-life—a sanctified, wise childhood.

If you would learn the deep mysteries of the kingdom, you must get beneath even childhood—a very babe in helplessness and docility. This is God's strange way with our proud hearts. The simplicity of the Gospel—first in pardon and then in sanctification—is its stumbling block.

A few days ago my little boy said to me, "Father, you gave Alice sixpence." He added no more. The whole argument was clear in his mind. What I had given her *of course* I would also give him. If any Christian here has a Gospel privilege which you have not, say, "Heavenly Father, Thou hast given a gift to my sister," and do not have *less* faith in Him than my child had in me.

8.30 A.M.

About a hundred and forty persons gathered, by the invitation of the Rev. A. M. W. Christopher, rector of St. Aldate's, Oxford, to breakfast at the Clarendon Hotel. All the incumbents of Oxford churches were invited, and their curates; but some were not in Oxford on that day. High Churchmen and Low Churchmen sat side by side; and Nonconformist ministers and foreign pastors, and laymen and nationalities of different portions of the one Church of Christ were mingled with them.

All united in prayer after breakfast, and then followed addresses on Scriptural Holiness, and the way in which the Lord Jesus may be fully trusted to enable and to constrain His believing people to do that which He commands,—from Mr. Christopher, Mr. R. Pearsall Smith, Revs. W. E. Boardman, T. A. Nash, of Norwich; D. B. Hankin, of Ware; Theodore Monod, G. R. Thornton, of Nottingham; F. F. Tracy, of Beccles.

It was surely a reason for praise to God that so many Christians, differing strongly on important subjects, should listen with interest for three hours to addresses on Holiness and devotion to the service of God, in Christ, and through Christ, and for the glory of Christ. All the testimonies harmonised with that of St. Paul, in Gal. ii. 20, "I am crucified with Christ: nevertheless I live; yet not I, but Christ liveth in me: and the life which I now live in the flesh, I live by the faith of the Son of God who loved me and gave Himself for me." And all the words of instruction and encouragement moved those who loved the Lord Jesus to obey His loving command in John xv. 4, "Abide in Me and I in you. As the branch cannot bear fruit of itself except it abide in the vine; no more can ye except ye abide in Me." All the glory of victory over sin and Satan, self, and the world, of the heart for Christ's work, of duty done in love, of willing service and happy labours, was given with all sincerity and singleness of mind to Christ alone.

Testimony was given that when those who are weary and heavy laden with their failures in duty, go in full trust and real surrender of their wills to Christ, He makes His burden to be light to them by dwelling in them as their strength, and His yoke easy to them by the love of it for His sake which His Holy Spirit creates in them.

CONVERSATIONAL MEETING.

9.30 A.M.

REV. W. E. BOARDMAN: In every one of us there is a whole unknown world. Sin cannot be abandoned by us till it is known. The instant we know it, we lay it on Christ, and the blood cleanseth it. We learn much of it when we are wholly given over to Christ, but now we can learn only progressively. We every moment need Christ for sins of ignorance. Nearly one-third of the offerings of Leviticus are for sins of ignorance. Be content to accept this, that there is a world within, which unfolds as we walk in the light. We see day by day what we could not see before. But every discovered need is at once met in the Lord Jesus, our mercy-seat. Condemnation for known transgression is *not* the necessity of our existence. In Him is available victory over every temptation—not partial, but complete. If you have faith in Christ, Christ acts in you, but if your faith is in self, self acts in you. Christ is the grave of self. I died with Christ. In Him I have resurrection. My body has not gone into the grave, as His did, nor have I risen again as He did, but Christ is my spiritual burial-place and resurrection-place. I died and am risen in Christ.

General Meeting.

11.45 A.M.

Psalm xlvi. was read, and after prayer, R. Pearsall Smith suggested the current of thought for the meeting: In the midst of fearful tumult raging all around His people hear His voice, "Be still and *know* that I am God." Oh, that we may this morning get away from every tumult of this nature, and "enter into Rest." There is such a thing as keeping the soul's inward sabbath unbroken in the midst of trial and conflict.

Now let us turn to Matthew xi. 28-30. Do you know the Rest *given*, and also the Rest *found?* You remember your first coming to Christ, and rolling off your burden of guilt—not part only—and how Rest came into your soul. Is it so now? Have you less communion with God now than you had then? Oh, dear child of God, is there not a cause? "As ye have received Christ Jesus the Lord, *so walk ye in Him.*" How did you at first receive Him? Was it not in pure grace for pardon? Has there been anything of Pharisaism in your method of sanctification? You can no more save yourself from fresh sinning, than from the guilt of past sin. Part trust and part effort is to be "fallen from grace" into legality. Oh, I feel so thankful to-night that, whatever it may cost us before we learn it, the Lord will have His salvation from the first step of justification to the last step in sanctification all of grace, pure grace, free grace! Did you in your conversion expiate one sin? No. God could not give you peace until you received it in His own sweet way of grace. So now many dear Christians fail of victory because they will not let Christ do *all* for them. Having begun in the spirit, they seek to be made perfect partly by fleshly effort. We may fall from grace in the matter of sanctification as well as justification.

What is it to fall from grace as to sanctification and come under law? It is to lose the sense of responsive, grateful obedience, and to act from law or constraint. So long as the bride trusts her husband's love, she does all from love. Her house becomes a prison when she begins to act from mere duty. She may redouble her efforts, but the sense of pleasing and the joyous impulse of love-service is gone. Directly there come temptations to disobey the law of her husband, where, when his will had been taken as her delight, she had rejoiced in everything done for him. She must resume her confidence in her husband's love. The moment she does so, her "soul dwelleth at ease," and she resumes the joyous, responsive, grateful service of love.

There are two sets of three which always go together in experience :—

Under the law,	Under grace ;
In the flesh,	In the Spirit ;
Sinning,	Holiness.

If you are under law you are in the flesh and sinning ; and if you are sinning you are under the law and in the flesh ; and if in the flesh you are under law and sinning. Conversely—free grace, the Holy Spirit, and holiness belong together. Give me one and I have all. If in grace, you are in the Spirit and under a life of holiness. Before I had learned the "rest of faith" I used to be very much troubled with a painful sense of legal compulsion. If I got into a railway carriage, I had an uneasy sense that I ought to be all the time giving away tracts and speaking to the people, but it was not in the joyous sense of constraining love of Christ ; but when I trusted the Lord the same thing was a real joy to me, and I learned that it was not the Lord's mind that I should be always pressing these things upon strangers, but that He would open the way and make it a privilege instead of a burden. We must get away from legality, for in it the sweetness of serving the Lord is gone. My prayer in the railway carriage became, "Lord, give me what Thou wilt to do ; but let me only do it in the joy and sweetness of communion with Thee." Since then I have seen a number of distinct conversions in the railway carriages. I guard my life of obedience by maintaining an inward surrender and responsiveness to the will of

God, doing nothing under the constraint of law but of love.

It is not a life to be lived on a strain, away, far off from ordinary duties, but a free, lovely life, to be lived amidst all our hourly, homely duties, in an undisturbed, inward sabbath, whatever may be the outward pressures; not one day of a week, but seven days every week, and three hundred and sixty-five days every year. It is a contest, but the fight of *faith* is always a victory—unbelief is defeat. We had, most of us, much of the overcoming faith in our conversion; but we had not intelligence enough to see where the old Pharisee-principle came in, and when we came to our Kadesh Barnea, where entrance to the land was across a mere geographical line, alas! we "limited" God in His power to save, and "turned back into the wilderness," or as it is repeatedly called in Scripture, "the *provocation.*" We always "provoke God in the wilderness" if we stay there by unbelief and consequent failure. I speak of an inward wilderness, for outwardly the world must always be to the saint a wilderness; but within should be corn and wine and oil, the peace of God keeping our hearts and minds through Christ Jesus. Is not the Jordan-entrance into this immediately before you in our text? Let us read it as if we had never seen it before, and, as we read it, act on its injunctions and grasp its privileges.

You came with your burden of guilt to *Jesus*—not to a moral life, or an ecclesiastical connection merely—and He gave you rest. Now hear Him say, "Take my yoke upon you and learn of *Me*, for I am meek and lowly of heart, and ye shall find rest to your souls."

The one rest is given to the repentant sinner, the other found by the fully consecrated saint. A yoke may be put upon an unwilling disciple by the law, or sense of obligation to obedience. Or it may be gladly taken upon him as the sweetest privilege in life in every moment to accept the will of God, and say, as to the soul attitude, every moment, "Thy will be done!"—even when it seems to cost us what is dearer than life itself. Then the now unresisted yoke becomes easy; it is lined with contentment. Truly many Christians have less sense than the dumb animals. When they find that they must wear it they are content, and chafe and worry under it no longer—their "yoke is easy." How quietly they come to be yoked.

Have you thus taken the yoke of the sweet will of God in everything? Are you at any point of your lives resisting it in your will or your affections? Say, with full consent, "*Yes, Lord*," to each expression of His will in His providential dealings with you. I love to say it out loud when any one is aggravating me, and I do testify that it is easy. In the severest agonies and bereavements of life the "Yes, Lord," takes the smart and sting out. Few have had more suffering than I have, but with all my soul I testify that His yoke is just what He declares it to be—an easy yoke.

Now pause, and go over your family life, your life in the world, and especially your inward life, and see if there is anything, however small, in which you are resisting this easy yoke. Christ says, "*Take*." I like the word. Do not wait for the yoke to be forced on you. Put out your hand and take it as your greatest privilege.

"And learn of Me." When our resisting will is surrendered, how He does teach us! "I have learned more in one day now that I am fully surrendered to the Lord, than I formerly did in months," said a clergyman to me.

"For I am meek." Ah, there are souls here who long to be meek like Christ! who are more eager to get down into the lowest place than they ever were to rise in the world. And if you want this meekness He will give it to you. Not an exterior humility expressed in ostentatious ways, but the ornament of a meek and quiet spirit. Do not be discouraged, dear soul, if you seem slow in obtaining this. The architect lays the foundations, builds the walls, and last of all puts on the ornaments. I think that this adorning of meekness is one of the latest received gifts. When you receive it, you will no longer covet the praise of men; you will shrink from it as from a file on your teeth. If it comes it will be passed over untouched to the Lord. Then blame will affect you as little as praise.

"And lowly of heart." The only One ever on this earth who merited admiration, "made Himself of no reputation." Men will give up everything before they will resign reputation—even religious reputation and ministerial reputation are hard to part with. Christ had none in His day. Have you any not fully handed over to Christ? Do not be discouraged. People who live constantly with one another gain a resemblance even in their countenances. Live in and with Christ, and His likeness will come into your soul, and out into your life and appearance.

"And ye shall find rest." Christ carries us and our burdens too. Give Him your life-long burden to-day. It has not helped you on your journey heretofore. With a yielded will, renounced unbelief, entire consecration, you may claim the Saviour's promise—"Rest"—not at some other time, but *now!*

After a hymn, the Rev. Mr. BOARDMAN spoke: If our Lord were here this morning, I think He would take a little child and set him before us, and teach us, by His character of complete obedience and trust, to take His yoke upon us.

You have had from my brother two trios as to our position; he told us that we are either

Under law,	In the flesh,	Sinning;
	or,	
Under grace,	In the Spirit,	Obeying God.

Let me give you two other trios. You are either:—

In Christ,	Under grace,	On God's promises;
	or,	
In self,	Under law,	On your own responsibility.

These trios are never separated.

Some of us fail—I know it by bitter experience in the past—because of looking to ourselves, and not leaving *all* to Christ. We cannot put into words what a rest comes through a yoke gladly taken; but we know in our own souls that we have rest, soul-sabbath. He will not let you be an idle rester, nor an unrestful disciple. No. He will fill your heart with His love and your hand with effective service for Himself.

Our attitude toward difficulties and spiritual foes is

ever resistance, but toward God it is rest. "The kingdom of Heaven suffereth violence" is rendered in the margin "They who thrust men take it by force,"—the idea being that whatever stood in the way must be thrust aside. But towards God we are in rest—that of a receptive "little child." If we do not receive the kingdom thus we may not enter in. Jacob's own strength must fail before he could receive the blessing. The only offensive weapon given to the Christian is "the sword of the Spirit," but in order to use it we must have such confidence in it as implies perfect rest in God, and then it is resistless.

The Rev. D. B. HANKIN then remarked, as one of the characteristics of the meeting, on the surprising uniformity of thought in leading us, previous to the speaking, to the same texts and the same current of meditation.

If we had been asked to assign a reason why the Israelites did not enter into the promised land for forty years, we should have specified some grosser outbreaking sins in their history; but the Apostle tells us that they could not enter in *because of unbelief.* Canaan typified full rest in Christ, and the overcoming life, no longer, as in the wilderness, on the defensive and in defeat. It is the present heaven to go to the future heaven. We might have gone in at Kadesh Barnea, but we magnified our enemies, and ignored the mighty power of God. Let us not again fail by the same example of unbelief. The highest attainment of the Apostle Paul was that, through faith, he did not now any longer "frustrate the grace of God," or erect barriers of unbelief to His purposes toward his soul.

Oh! do not let unbelief rob you of the promise left you of entering into rest. Let not distrust shut the door of plenty in your face.

Christ is able to do "exceeding abundantly above all that we are able to ask or to think;" He can now keep us from falling. Whoever heard of a Christian being able to keep order in his own heart? Is not Christ ready to do this for you now in answer to faith? There is a crisis of faith in the experience of Christians. The great Napoleon used to say that there was always one ten minutes which decided the fate of every battle. Is such a crisis of faith before you now? Have you been crying, "*What* shall deliver me from this life of sinning?" and trying every expedient in your reach, only to fail again and again? Look away from everything else. Look up and say, not "what" but "*Who* shall deliver me from this body of death?" Salvation from sin is in a Person, the blessed person of our Lord Jesus. Look unto Him, and in faith say with Paul, "I thank God, through our Lord Jesus Christ."

As in the other meetings, a deep solemnity was spread over the great assembly. The victorious position of faith, before dimly seen, now was a reality to many souls who felt themselves being drawn by the Holy Spirit to such an act of full trust in Jesus as they had not before known. Many spoke of it as only paralleled by their first experience when they trusted the Lord Jesus for pardon. To some the realisation of how much more they could now trust Christ for, came with overwhelming emotions of joy. To others, no less filled with faith, there was no change in their emotions, but only the quiet divinely-inspired resolution, that, without emotion or with it, they would now trust Jesus every moment. We were taught that faith was above and separate from emotion, and that a higher faith was exercised when there was no conscious joy. We must walk *by faith*—and that does not mean feeling—though sooner or later the path of faith is filled with conscious "joy and peace in believing." Happy they who have not seen or felt and yet believe.

After the Address, by Mrs. R. P. SMITH, on "Joseph a type of the risen life," at 3 o'clock, and the regular 4 o'clock General Meeting, we adjourned for tea.

THE MINISTERIAL MEETING.

6 O'CLOCK, P.M.

After a time of silence, Rev. W. E. BOARDMAN led us in prayer. Pasteur STOCKMEYER, of Switzerland, said, under deep emotion, in broken English: May the Lord help me to speak from my heart to the heart of each one before me! I had faith when I received the invitation to come to Oxford that I should here receive the baptism of the Holy Ghost. I am of myself a poor sinner. If the Saviour cannot save me from myself, He is no Saviour. But He does save me, and I have my Heavenly Father's face shining on me. I feel now that, through the Spirit, I have been enabled to separate myself from the world and the flesh as never before. I have carried about with me the body of death long enough, a corpse like that of Lazarus when it had been buried four days: you remember what is written of it. I could not go on living in such an atmosphere. I have found deliverance. These moments are so sweet and the Lord is so near to me, I feel like a bird escaped from a cage. I have found something new; I no longer look into my own heart, but into my Saviour's face.

Pasteur T. MONOD: "If He cannot save me from myself, He is no Saviour." These are bold words that our brother has just spoken. And yet they are true. What would it avail us to be delivered from every foe except from self, the most powerful, the most deceitful, the most distressing of them all? The very purpose of Christ's life, death, and resurrection is to save us out of the life of self-reliance, self-will, self-seeking, self-glorifying, into a life of which He is the inspiration, the object, the rule, and the glory. He is able to do it; He is willing to do it; He gave Himself to do it; He is doing it for many; will you let Him do it for you? Oh! let us lose sight even of these meetings, lose sight of self altogether, and see "Jesus only."

Rev. W. J. MAYERS (2 Kings vii.): "Then"—Elisha spoke in a day of darkness and sorrow, not feasting but famine—"to-morrow, about this time"—he knew even the hour—"shall a measure of flour be sold for a shekel, and two measures of barley for a shekel in the gate of Samaria." The king on his throne was shaking with terror, and the poor people devouring their own children. But he had a "Thus saith the Lord." We need not fear too high a superstructure if we have the Lord for our foundation. But, to unbelief, what is a world full of promises? *If—if—"if* the Lord would make windows in heaven, might this thing be?" And he said, "Behold thou shalt see it with thine eyes, *but shalt not eat thereof.*" And He did open windows in heaven, and the lord on whose arm the king leaned saw the plenty and never ate of it. There was the plenty, the joy, the feasting—oh! what gladness in many a heart!—and yet that great one never tasted of it; and why? Because he did not believe.

Many here have suffered famine, and now you can testify of the plenty that has come down into your hearts. But are there any yet hungering and thirsting? I entreat you not to say, "If—*if*—*if* there can come such a baptism;" or, "It will not come to *me.*" Oh! beware of closing the hand of Jehovah by your unbelief. You are in the place of the unbelieving lord. God save you from this. It is a solemn thing to be in the midst of such blessings and to refuse to trust for them.

When lately standing by the open grave, and sitting in the house before the emptied place, I felt so glad that in prosperity I had given all to the Lord. Oh! I felt Him so near. He must have come very near to have taken one so dear to me; and how could He come so near and not leave a blessing behind Him?

Oh! that God would look into your hearts and find them empty; and if not now empty, then empty them, so that He may fill them with Himself. "Be filled with the Spirit," as with wine. That means that the Spirit should have the mastery over us. After such a blessed meeting, what manner of men and women ought we to be in all holy conversation and godliness! Grace is not given for a parlour ornament, but a thing to be taken, so to speak, into the kitchen to use.

Do not say, "*If* the Lord do it in some extraordinary way: if He would use some remarkable means . . . then!" Nay, brethren. It is in an *ordinary* way, in the Scriptural way, that you must have this life of abiding in Christ. Simply renounce all else, all self-dependence, and trust for it to the Lord Jesus Christ.

Rev. C. B. Sawday: When the great revival in our Church commenced, we had to urge Christians to do just what they had often taught others to do—Give up their *all* to Jesus, and trust Him perfectly. "As ye have received Christ Jesus the Lord so walk ye in Him," is the life-long lesson; but, alas, how few do it! How many have to be taught to once more walk in Him just as they received Him at first!

After I had left the meeting last evening, a dear pasteur came to my lodgings, and, sending for me, said, "My wife and I have come all the way from Switzerland to get this blessing. It has cost us a large sum, and we cannot afford to go away without it." He asked if he could have a little conversation with me, and if I would pray with him. After silently asking counsel of the Lord, I saw that he was in danger of depending too much on me, and so said to him, "Now the Conference card tells us to go to bed early, and I mean to do as the card directs. Go home, and just give your whole heart to Jesus, and the thing will be done. We will pray for you, and to-morrow you will have the blessing"—the blessedness of the man that really and fully trusteth in God. This morning I was told that he had found it, and you have just heard him tell what he has now found in Christ. Oh! brethren, feeling or no feeling, joy or no joy, rest or no rest, peace or no peace, I will trust in Jesus. I purpose, through grace, to walk in divine fellowship seven days every week, and fifty-two weeks every year. When a minister and people are together rejoicing in the Lord, sinners see it and believe in the Christ who saves them fully. This is my ministerial experience of late.

A sweetly persuasive appeal followed, closing with the words: "If ever there was one who could not be kept from falling, I was that one. If Christ can keep me, He can keep you, every one."

R. Pearsall Smith: President Edwards' teaching of the affections governing the will I believe to be untrue. The will governs the affections. I believe in the yet older saying, that "True religion resides in the will alone." Many are feeling deeply, but I desire to take you away from your emotions. When I make a large, important transaction, I wish to be calm, deliberate, free from excitement, and in full possession of my judgment; if emotions come into it, let them come afterward. Our emotions are treacherous things, likely to obscure our ideas of the nature of the transaction. Now put your will over on to the side of God thus without emotion. If you will do this without emotion, God will, in His own good time, give you all the emotion you need or can bear. I made the transaction of a full surrender of my whole being, and it was not till months afterward that those holy tides of feeling—the overwhelming sense of the presence of God—came in, which have made life almost a psalm of praise. Then came a fall upon my head causing a congestion of the brain, and a degree of nervous depression and suffering my physicians said never exceeded in their experience. I was physically incapable of religious emotion. In the interior of South America, alone, and weeks away from any Christian communion, instead of health I found yet deeper depths; and in their midst the powerful assaults of Satan suggesting even infidelity. I was thankful then that religion was in my will and not in my emotions. To all his attacks I said, "I *will* believe: live or die, in agony or in joy, *I will believe!*" I seemed as one with his back to a rock and beset by devils. "When neither sun nor stars in many days appeared, and no small tempest lay on me," no sensible religious emotion for almost months, I *did* trust God, not only for final salvation, but for a conscience void of offence. I know whereof I affirm; I speak what I know, when I say God's salvation is beyond the region of our emotions, though at times they may be deeply affected by it. Some here go on for months without so much as thinking whether we are happy or not—they are occupied with Christ. Ask a joyous child if he is happy; set him to analysing his feelings, and he becomes worried and sad.

Try to analyse your emotions of love for your dearest friend for five minutes, and you will not be able to realise that you love the dear one at all. Think of the virtues and kindness of the dear one, and your heart will glow with affection. Present your entire being a living sacrifice to God. Do it as an actual mental transaction, recognise that *it is done,* just as really done in conflict as in rest. God does accept that which He beseeches you to give, and it is for Him to give you the emotions best for you.

Do not be misled when we speak about having

learned to "rejoice always." We do not want you to get joy instead of Christ. You do not need an experience like that of Mr. Boardman, or Mr. Monod. You cannot copy their experiences. You need Christ in your heart. Forget the experiences you have heard; say in your very soul and with your lips, "Thy will be done in me; keep me from evil,"—*and then trust the Lord to do it.*

Now cross this Jordan in an emotionless condition, and may God hold you thus till you learn to live in His will, and not confound the act of faith with the joy. I am of course with increasing intelligence always more completely given to God, yet as regards the deliberate, full surrender, I did it but once. Thenceforward I looked on it as a thing irrevocably done, just as we look on our marriage for life. We do not say, the "I will;" "I give thee my troth," of the marriage ceremony year after year, however more holy and complete may become the union of heart. Give yourself to Christ with a devotion beyond your highest ideal of the bride's heart-surrender in marriage, and more than in any earthly union keep your heart with all diligence true to Him. The Scripture is full of this aspect of consecration, and warning against the loathsomeness of divided affections. It is not pardon in believing. It is the heart irrevocably yielded to the heavenly Bridegroom.

We have had mostly heretofore to dwell on the negative side of consecration. I have come, meeting after meeting, longing to open the positive side of this life; but I felt the Lord leading us to lay deep foundations in a through searching of His Spirit, and a complete consecration to the Lord. We will come to the other side of gift and privilege when the obstacles to their reception are removed. We must first lay all our own burdens down before we can take His easy yoke and light burden. Lord, give us this blessing when we are able to receive it!

I naturally shrink from speaking of myself, but this I give to the Lord, and say, to His praise, that what I preach I have, through grace, learned to practise—to cast all my care on Him. In coming up to Oxford I felt a shade gathering over my spirit, and I kneeled alone in the railway carriage, and laid not part, but *all* the burden of this meeting on the Lord. Deeply as I felt the responsibility of calling it, I have not felt a burden about it since. My whole family were on the ocean last winter, after the many terrible losses of the last autumn, and I said, By the grace of God, I will practise what I preach. I kept saying in my heart, "He shall not be afraid of evil tidings," and He saved me from having a single anxious minute; and, at length, at the Mildmay consecration meeting, the telegram of the vessel's reaching Queenstown came. The Lord takes the care, we have none; and as to the work, He works in those who speak, as we reverently trust, to will and to do of His good pleasure. He taught me the lesson of having no care, not in a place of contemplative retirement, but in the busy pressure of the administration of the factories of two whole villages, where I heard His voice, "Be still and know that *I* am God." Since then my soul has kept her sabbaths almost unbroken.

"I have no cares, oh! blessed Lord,
For all my cares are Thine;
I live in triumph, Lord, for Thou
Hast made Thy triumphs mine."

A Swiss pasteur engaged in prayer. Those who could truthfully do so then sang—some still upon their knees:—

"'Tis done, the great transaction's done,
I am my Lord's and He is mine,
He drew me and I followed on,
Charmed to confess His love divine.

"Take my poor heart, and let it be
For ever closed to all but Thee,
Seal Thou my breast and let me wear
The pledge of love for ever there"

After the Doxology the meeting closed under a deep sense of the presence and power of God in our souls.

The foreign pasteurs then convened at the hotel, where a meeting for Saturday was arranged.

CHAPTER VI.

Thursday, September 3rd.

7 o'clock Early Meeting.

AGAIN a great company came together before breakfast to seek the Lord—*and to find Him* in the fulness of the Gospel, in the sweetness of His love, in the glory of His person, in the power of His Spirit, in the blessedness of His in-dwelling presence. In the earlier meetings of the Conference we were like a frequently-defeated army, lacking the confidence to expect a victory. A few "armed men" were there, who had passed over Jordan to an aggressive life of victory, but too many were in the wilderness attitude of defence, and demoralised by frequent failure. We had heard the call, "Sanctify yourselves; for to-morrow the Lord will do wonders among you . . . Ye shall know that the living God is among you, and that He will without fail drive out from before you the Canaanites." Now many were no longer looking upon the crossing of Jordan as an impossible thing for them; nay, very many could say that they were on the Canaan side. The obstacles to believing were put away,—the partial submission of will, the seeking the honour that cometh from men, and the indulgence of known evil, and all things not of faith. Few had ever known such a time of solemn searching and humbling before the Lord. The night had witnessed many sleepless pillows. and many "waited for the Lord more than they that watch for the morning." The many Scripture scenes of gathering the people together before the Lord, for cleansing from their sins, and for the restoration of the presence and blessing of Jehovah, seemed reproduced. A deepening tone of reverential awe pervaded the meetings. We now began to feel that the Lord was indeed lifting up the light of His countenance upon His people.

The sense of discouragement was at last being replaced by the courage of faith;—we were learning to dare to trust God, moment by moment, to "preserve our feet from falling." We suppose it safe to say that hundreds had found a crisis in their soul's history, an epochal experience of the Lord's power, never to be forgotten in time or eternity. As had been said in the Evening Meeting, there was "a great sweep on to the believing side." The work of years of experience seemed wrought as in an hour. Longer periods were now spent in silent waiting prayer. We can no more define the baptising presence of the Spirit than we can picture the shining of the mid-day sun, but we are conscious of its warmth when the clouds are gone; our words fail in describing the "morning dew" of these early meetings, and the profound and lasting impression made upon many hearts in them. Our hearts almost feared, much as we rejoiced, as we entered the cloud of the Lord's presence. How precious, as never before in those days, the Word of God became! How thankful we felt that we were not drifting at the mercy of our own imaginations, or bewildered by Satan transformed into an angel of light, but that we could rest upon and be guided by the revealed and written mind of God. How its difficulties disappeared, and its paradoxes were solved in the light of the known presence of the Lord!

The deep realisation of the evil of self accompanied the deeper knowledge of Christ. We saw and abhorred ourselves, not in despair, but in trust in the cleansing blood. As we were able to cry, "Woe is me! for I am undone; because I am a man of unclean lips; . . . for mine eyes have seen the King, the Lord of hosts," —we felt that the live coal from off the altar had touched our lips, and we could say, "Here am I; send *me*" on Thy message of mercy. It was when our "comeliness was turned into corruption," that we could hear the words, "Fear not: . . . for from the day that thou didst set thy heart to understand, and to chasten thyself before thy God, thy words were heard. . . . O man, greatly beloved, fear not; peace be unto thee; be strong, *yea, be strong.*" We could now as never before bear the deep things of Scripture, and say without shrinking, "Let my Lord speak; for Thou hast strengthened me."

9.30 O'CLOCK.

The several Conversational Meetings re-assembled, including the one exclusively for ladies. None were of more interest than that in the Town Hall, in which the baptism of the Holy Spirit was the special subject.

Dr. MAHAN: "Truly our fellowship is with the Father and with His Son Jesus Christ." It is else where termed, "the fellowship of the Spirit," because the Spirit brings it. He manifests Christ, takes His things and shows them unto us. Before I met you at Oxford you may have heard of me, but you could not have communion with me. It is the voluntary union of two minds brought into contact one with another. You may believe in Christ, and be assured that your sins are forgiven through His name, but how can you have fellowship until He is *manifested* to you? When you call Him is He far off? When He is with the Father, can He come and dwell with me? Can I have communion with Him? Christ promised that it should be so. How particularly He said that this should be done by the Spirit. It is one thing to read the Bible, and another to read it in communion through the Spirit.

What a thing it is to have all that is meant by the promise to the obedient disciple, "We will come unto him, and make our abode with him." "He that believeth on Me, out of his belly shall flow rivers of living water." This surely follows the presence of the living Christ.

Can any one speak as if justification were the finality of the Christian life, with the words before him, "Ye shall be baptised with the Holy Ghost not many days hence?" To "be filled with the Spirit" is your immediate privilege. Love to God and man is not an effort then, but the outflow of a full heart. When Christ comes thus to abide in you, you will not want to abide anywhere else. Do not attempt to have fellowship with the Father, or to abide in the Son, but through the Spirit.

This morning a Conversational Meeting, led by Lord Radstock, was crowded by ministers who were earnestly longing to be filled with the Spirit. Towards its close, in a lengthened time of prayer and silent waiting, there was deep feeling, many being in tears. The hearts of all seemed filled with earnest longings for the presence of God. One of the French pasteurs present remarked, that he nowhere in Scripture read of promises of *consciousness* of power;—that even Paul said, "When I am weak, *then* am I strong." The secret of power is realised union with Christ, and this may come with or without deep emotion.

Day after day Dr. Mahan pressed upon us the privilege of being here and now "filled with the Spirit," as a Scriptural experience which we should not and must not be without; and many, it is believed, realised in his conversational meetings the baptism of the Holy Ghost in all its essential characteristics of a subdued will, an obedient heart, and deep love to God and man.

Pasteur TH. MONOD led another Conversation Meeting: Our subject for this morning is

GUIDANCE.

Will you turn to the 32nd Psalm, from the seventh verse to the end? "Thou art my hiding-place, Thou shalt preserve me from trouble." That is very precious, but it is not enough; it is not enough for Him, though sometimes we think it is enough for us. We see next, "I will instruct thee," &c. Who is this spoken to? Look at the last verse again: it is to the upright in heart. And now, How will He guide them? First of all they believe He will guide them—the beginning of it is expectation of guidance. This does not mean thinking "I will try and see whether He will guide me:" that is not the way. Simply *trust* Him; or rather, as has been well said during these meetings, simply trust *Him*. How will the guidance come? "I will guide thee with mine eye." That means that we are to be looking out for it, looking up at Him. If we do not do this, how can we get the guidance? Yesterday morning I came into the meeting rather late, and I knew Mr. Smith would be looking at me to catch my eye to get me to come up on the platform. I did not want to go, so what did I do? I simply did not look at him. He may have been looking at me to guide me with his eye, but I do not know, for I did not look at him. If we treat God's guidance like that, of course we do not get it.

Now turn, if you please, to Proverbs iii. 5, 6, which throws fresh light on the subject. "Trust in the Lord with all thine heart" comes in again here; and then come three other things to be done, or rather one thing not to do, and one thing to do, and one thing for God to do.

First, the thing *not* to do: "Lean not to thine own understanding;" don't think you are wise in little things. Some man of the world will say, "That is really silly; it is good for babies." Yes, it is very good for babies; we want to be little babes before Him. He would take all "the pride of life" out of us. Now the thing *to* do is, "in all thy ways acknowledge Him"—all thy ways. Is it hard to trust Him for that? Don't you think that, when He died to lead you to glory, He will lead you every step? Then the thing is done as far as you are concerned. God will do all the rest. He will take different ways for different people; different ways, perhaps, for the same man on different days. If you begin thinking how it is to come about, you will make mistakes; you must get quite away from your own wisdom. This is not so easy; it is easier to distrust our own strength than our own wisdom, just as it is easier to distrust our own righteousness than our own strength. But He is "made unto us wisdom:" there could be nothing stronger than that. Now will you turn to John x. 1-6. "They understood not." So it is still; people say it is all very mystical, very impracticable. It happens to be the most practical thing in the world. We see the matter put very beautifully here. "A stranger will they not follow." Even if the stranger wants to lead you to-day, when Christ led you yesterday, you won't follow; you have only got to follow *Him*, to hear His voice. This simplifies the whole of life. You may get up in the morning with the feeling, "How am I to get through the day? I have so many things to do, so many people to speak to, I hardly know what to do first, or how I shall get through them all." You will never have more than one thing to do at a time, and that one thing will be to follow the voice of Jesus. How are you to hear that voice? You will hear it in many ways, in the voice of circumstances—in the voice of friends. Of course in His Word, and by the Holy Spirit in your heart, or by your minister, in these things you will hear His voice, and if you don't hear His voice—His "It is I!"—don't follow; don't do anything that in the least obscures communion with Him.

Perhaps there will sometimes be something hard which you want to do for Him, but which He does not want you to do. Sometimes there will be something hard which He *does* want you to do. An instance of guidance occurred at this morning meeting. God laid it on the heart of one present to repeat a promise from His Word; it was done in trembling, just done because it seemed His will, and the note was pitched in which many, perhaps 200, joined.

There is one other thing to be noticed about this guidance, if you want guidance for something far off in in the future. He won't show it you to-day; it will just come step by step as it is needed. We have noticed that so clearly with regard to this Oxford meeting. It was first just a suggestion from some brother at Broadlands, that we must have some meeting like the one there, to which all might come; then the idea was taken up; then Oxford was thought of; then all the arrangements were made, so quickly, so easily. It was just God guiding it all, and I think every one here would say it could not have been ordered better. If some brother had taken it into his head that he would get up such a meeting, and had advertised it largely and taken a great deal of trouble to get people to attend, would the result have been the same? Brethren, where the future is concerned just trust for it, leave it with Him. When the day comes the guidance will come, and it will be quite quietly.

In the last place, we will just turn to St. Paul's story. In his conversion his first question is "Who art Thou, Lord?" His second question is "Lord, what wilt Thou have me to do?" That last question was the motto of his life. We see it again in Acts xxii. 22, 23. He went about "not knowing the things that shall befall me there," but still in perfect peace. When we go away from this quiet time with Jesus we know not the things that will befall us, but we know He will guide us much more than even here. As somebody said when we were leaving Broadlands, if a child in this beautiful place is led and kept and guided, much more it will be led and kept and guided in the bustle and confusion of the streets. Brethren, if Jesus has been guiding us in these meetings, much more will He guide us in the din and whirl of outer life.

There was one question raised at the end of our meeting yesterday, which there was not time then to answer fully, and I should like to say a few words about it, before going on to-day's subjects. The question in many minds is "To what extent am I to be kept from sinning? *when* am I to expect to be kept?" The only answer we can give is, "You are to expect to be kept from sinning *now*." God does not give a reserve stock of grace which you can look at and say "that is mine." He just gives you, minute by minute, and moment by moment, what is needed. It is like this: suppose a man says to his friend—"I will give you an empty purse, and in it you shall find any money you want the very minute you want it. I shall never give you any to keep in your pocket, but you may go to your purse for *anything*." Would that man be a very rich man, or a very poor man? I think he would be both. If he wanted a penny to buy a newspaper, he must call on his friend, and go to his purse for it, if he wanted a shilling, he could go for that; if he wanted a hundred pounds, he could go for that; he could get anything he wanted, but there would be something he could not do—he could not put money on the table, and look at it, and say, "What a rich man I am!" He would get up with an empty purse, and go to bed with an empty purse, and yet he would have all he needed. That is the way God gives us His grace, never more than we need for that very minute—always quite enough.

Rev. SHOLTO DOUGLAS (1 Samuel x.): This chapter gives a beautiful picture of guidance. Saul was born to rule. He was anointed and consecrated, and now God's guidance was to be his. How minute were the directions. First he was to meet two men at a certain place, who shall say certain words; then three men carrying certain things; then past the hill of God a company of prophets, and then the Spirit should come upon him, and he should be turned in another man. "And let it be when these signs are come upon thee, that thou shalt do as occasion serve thee, for God is with thee."

Here is a picture of the Christian life—first chosen, then consecrated, then God's great broad principles given, then left to do as occasion serves, to use an illuminated, sanctified common-sense. In this matter of guidance, see what you have got. Have you senses—education—influence? "Bring them hither to Me," says Christ, and as He multiplied the bread they already had, He will also multiply your gifts for the blessing of the multitude.

"But how am I to know God's will?" If there is

nothing special to lead you, ask guidance, believe that your prayer is answered according to that word, "The meek will He guide *in judgment*," and act in a sanctified judgment. Balaam had a will of his own, and so he had to have a hedge of thorns, and an angel with a drawn sword for guidance. Special sensible guidance is mostly to restrain, or to the obedient for special occasions. Let *us*, in the current of our lives, know the sweetness of that word, "I will guide thee by mine eye."

THE GENERAL MEETING.

11.45 A.M.

This was opened first by silent and then vocal prayer. "The Cleansing Wave" was sung, and we were then reminded, before the requests for prayer were opened, that God's plan is that what we ask for, believing, we receive, and that we should pray in the restfulness of faith, bringing all our burdens to the Lord, and not taking them back again. If we should pray about anything, and then be anxious, it would not be faith. Let us pray thus for those who in so many circumstances affecting their lives have asked us to pray for the objects of their love. It was mentioned that to-day, five thousand persons in a similar meeting, on the other side of the Atlantic, are probably in prayer for us in Oxford.

After many requests had been presented before the Lord, R. PEARSALL SMITH continued: Do not, dear friends, be thinking to-day about the speakers, but their message. As each one rises to speak, pause and pray for him. This will obtain help for him, and open your own hearts to receive his message.

We do not need again to remind you that our teaching is the exact antithesis of perfection in the flesh. Nay, we may say not only that in the flesh dwelleth no good thing, but that there never will be any good thing in it, or coming out of it. It was judged and condemned in the Cross of Christ. As the Articles of the Church of England so truly say, "This infection of nature doth remain, yea, in them that are regenerate." We should tremble to lead any one beyond saying daily, "Forgive us our debts;" for, even where we are not immediately conscious of displeasing God, there is so much in the debilitated condition of our moral nature, and in our lives, at an immense moral distance from the perfect holiness of God. Trespass against the known will of God is one, but not the only, definition of sin. What we know, or can see, is not any true standard of holiness. Christ is our only standard. When we "have done all," or our nearest approach to it, we feel the most deeply that we are unprofitable servants. I have never so felt my need of the blood of Christ, as after times of special blessing in preaching, when the very windows of heaven seemed opened upon my soul; for then I was most in the light, and saw most of my coming short of the holiness of Christ.

Yet when we have freely stated all this, and much more of the same import, it does not mean that we are to "continue in sin," in the sense of known evil. Christ came to save us from this, and to meet, in the atonement, not only all conscious guilt, but also all unperceived evil in our moral condition or ways. In the midst of all, He can give us continual and satisfying communion with Himself—soul-health amid all the infirmity, cares and sorrows of this life. How sad it would be if our children were as frequently out of health as God's children are. Christ came to heal us, not to leave His Church one general hospital of sick souls. There will always be a distance between what we know ourselves to be in the imputed work of Christ, and in our own practical condition, but there need not be the fearful gap that we have known in the past. Let us open our Bibles and read the promises—pause before each one, and say, "I trust Thee, O Christ, for this one also," and you will find that, as persons are continually telling us, "The Bible is now really a new book to me. I must read it all over afresh, for it is filled with light—and now *true*, not only in itself, but to me also!"

A young man once said to his pastor, "I wish you preachers would just lay the Gospel down so that a poor fellow could pick it up!" Let us again try to show you the fulness of the Gospel privilege in such a way that by faith you can, here and now, "pick it up."

The first thing — invite the all-searching light of God in your consciences, that you may see in what you are displeasing God, and trust Him, progressively, as you can bear it, to show the evil of your hearts. Many dear, honest Christians, were made unhappy at first by these meetings, but they have learned that all Christ shows of evil in us He will deliver us from, if we only trust Him—He will give not pardon only, but deliverance from the power and act of sin.

The next thing—accept fully consecration, not as a duty merely, but as a most glorious privilege; for you must always look at the privilege, rather than the duty side of full surrender. Then, the offering you bring is accepted by Him who calls for it, and you must dare to believe that now the Altar, Christ, sanctifies the living sacrifice, the thank-offering of our hearts laid upon it. As you definitely turned your back to the world, and accepted pardon through Christ, so now, with equal definiteness, give yourself to be the Lord's, wholly the Lord's, and for ever the Lord's ; to accept His will, to let Him live your lives for you. With or without emotion, joyous or sad, give yourself to a life of trust. Many of us here are confident that we have thus had a work of God wrought in our souls, which, while it has given us victory over sin (Romans vi. 14 ; 1 John v. 4, 5), has humbled us in an ever-deepening sense of our sinfulness in ourselves apart from Christ. We lean on Him as never before.

Then having learned the secret of full rest and communion, we are asking Him that we may walk with Him, and, weak as we know ourselves to be, we dare to believe that He will go on to "perfect that which concerneth us." We no longer faithlessly say, "I shall some day fall by the hand of the enemy"; but, rather, "I will yet praise Him more and more." We are beginning to feel the power of that word, "elect unto obedience;" and have given ourselves to a life of instantaneous, implicit, uniform obedience to God. We do not expect to be doing and doing this again and again, but always to recognise that we *have done it*. Liable in each moment to fail, we expect, in the hourly miracle of grace, to be "kept by the power of God."

For several meetings I had purposed to seek to turn

the course from the negative side of giving up, to the positive side of the development of a Scriptural experience of full trust, but I think we have all together been held by the Spirit to the one thought of self-surrender until now. The Word of God has ploughed deep in many souls, who are finding that God must have *realities* of completed consecration and trust. Now that so many have found blessing, may we have the guidance of the Lord while we together meditate on other aspects of privilege in Christ.

Henceforth let us "walk in the Spirit," and accept the glorious emancipation promised to those who do this. "Sin *shall not* have dominion over you, for ye are not under the law, but under grace." The Spirit is stronger than the flesh, and shall so control it that we cannot obey its lusts. We read of the *works* of the flesh, but of the *fruits* of the Spirit brought forth by abiding in Christ our true Vine. Do not try to make fruit, but place yourself in the beams of the Sun of Righteousness, and let it ripen all heavenly fruits in you. "I have chosen you that ye should go and bring forth *fruit.*"

Let us notice the comely order in which the *fruits* of the Spirit are produced. Love comes first—through "the love of God shed abroad in our hearts by the Holy Ghost." It is blessed to notice that this is not our mere natural love, but the divine love to us which God Himself, who "is love," possesses in Himself unchanged and unchangeable through all our failures—a love irrespective of the unloveliness of its object. It is blessed to know that we have this divine attribute of God put into our souls. No wonder that with it there is no limit to our bearing unmoved the daily worry and irritations of life. Knowledge too often puffeth up, but love "beareth all things." Then comes joy, then peace. The one, like the head-waters of the Mississippi—boiling and tumbling, but not deep; the other, like the same river, twenty-five hundred miles below—a quiet current three hundred feet deep. Long-suffering comes after the peace, and is all but impossible without it. Gentleness—"the ornament of a meek and quiet spirit,"—like the ornaments of a house, is put in after the saint is rooted, grounded, and built up in faith. It is, perhaps, one of the last things in Christian development to be gentle and meek under provocation and care. Do not be discouraged in your eager restless zeal, if this grace be not matured in you. You are in the good Husbandman's hands, and, as you trust Him, He will bring you out a tree of His own planting, bearing your fruits in their season.

May the Holy Spirit give us to-day the gift of Divine love in every heart! How many graces and how few defects we shall then see in our brethren. Barnabas, when he had come to Antioch, "saw the grace of God and was glad. . . . For he was a good man full of faith and the Holy Ghost." Some of us know how little grace it takes to see defects in our fellow-Christians; but to see grace in ignorant and immature brethren we must have the grace of God in our own souls.

Rev. F. Sulivan, of Brighton: I came here to seek a blessing, and it has not been withheld from me. At first I received this message with prejudiced ears. I did not and I do not believe in "perfectionism," nor could I sympathise with those who, I wrongly imagined, had got beyond the Cross. But I find none so far from the thought of perfectionism, and none who more faithfully preach the blood of Christ. This is just the very teaching I have proclaimed for years past, but with what a want of trust myself! But it has become so definite and in such power of the Spirit that we have been compelled to open our hearts to the faith-life. I trust that henceforth our lives will run safely on the lines of trust and holy expectation.

After a pause of silent prayer for realisation of this:—

Pasteur Monod, in prayer: "O God, our Guide, our Comforter, our All and in All, let us come to Thee again, but let none say that they are waiting for Thee, for indeed Thou art waiting for us, waiting by the well, waiting to give the water of life freely. Thou knowest what has brought us here—our desires, our expectations. Oh! let us have a solemn sense of Thy presence this morning. We have asked Thy guidance; now let us test Thy guidance. Let us go on day by day, seeing the way more clearly, that we may walk in it more simply, more truthfully, more watchfully."

He then said: Our Lord made use of very homely illustrations; even such as that of a woman sweeping a floor. Let me take a very homely one. Suppose we take a sponge, and dip it in a pail of water. Do we say that the water is in the sponge, or the sponge in the water? It is both. So Christ is in me, and I in Him; not talking about it, but *being*. Oh! that is the best verb, the verb *to be*. Not wishing to be, but *being*. But some one may ask whether there is not so much evil in me to get rid of before I can be in Christ? It is because we are in ourselves so full of evil that we must take Christ. Let us look at the sponge again. Is there nothing in the sponge before it is put in the water? Oh yes, there is air. Well, shall I try to squeeze out the air before putting the sponge in the water? No; to get rid of the air you must put it in the water, and then the water will force out the air, which will come to the surface in bubbles. The two cannot co-exist, the water and the air; for the water drives out the air.

When Mr. Smith came to see me in Paris, I had no difficulty as to the doctrine he preached; but it looked very difficult to give up *everything* to Christ. In my inmost heart I did wish a little margin for self-indulgence. I did not conceive how perfectly Christ could in this life satisfy every need of my being, and I half-consciously reserved a corner for the world. It was unconsecrated indulgence in literature that partially took the place of Christ's love. Now, abiding in Him, I can prayerfully use the same things, but with no longing for what is not done for and in Him. Put yourself practically into Christ by consecration, and He will drive out the sin. I do believe we have been very foolish in the past to allow a divided heart. My Bible, now fully believed, does not seem the same Bible. Faith has given me an illuminated edition.

"Without Me ye can do nothing"? What, *nothing*, Lord? Surely a little! No; nothing! The trouble is that we did not believe the *nothing*. Is this meant to discourage? A thousand times No! for "I can do *all things* through Christ which strengtheneth me." We must realise experimentally the "nothing," to grasp the "all things."

There may be some one here feeling like a withered branch. I know what the feeling is. All our works dry—oh, so dry! But to think that out of that dry branch faith, once more uniting it to the vine, shall make it bring forth beautiful fruit! "These things have I spoken unto you." Why? That we may know our duty? More than this: "that My joy might remain in you." Remain in *me?* Yes! "rejoice always." "And that your joy may be full?" It should not be less, and it cannot be more than full, can it? It seems to me that this is enough about growth in grace, and it is but one diamond out of a mine full.

Prayer: O Father, we have Thy promise to give to those who ask, and Thou hast something to give, and the power to give. We desire to receive. We would not depend on our feelings, our experiences—but on Thy Holy Spirit. Thy breath, O Father! in us, O fill us with this afresh to-day!

Rev. Mr. Barne: There are many buildings in this ancient city of which you might say the architecture is Gothic, or it is ancient English, and both may be true. The truth our beloved brother has given us we may call the divine aspect. The human is St. Peter's word, "Add to your faith virtue." The word *add* refers to the Greek officer who supplied the funds for an Athenian chorus. So we are to *supply* to our faith virtue—moral courage—manly energy. (Mr. Barne developed this in thoughts of practical life, but we find no sufficient report.)

In going back to my parish I take with me a fresh sense of the presence and power of the Holy Ghost among Christ's people. I may have had misgivings about this line of teaching before I came here, but I shall be most glad to welcome it to my parish of Faringdon.

HENRY VARLEY: To follow on this teaching of union with Christ—Are we clear as to what spiritual life is? We have not merely moral change, but *life*. "Jesus Christ is in you, except ye be reprobates." Out of His fulness flows His life to millions of the sons and daughters of men. This is spiritual life, for Christ "is *our life*." Some speak of circumstances hindering, but Paul only made them the occasion for showing through the earthly vessels the excellency of the power of God. If the Christ-life be developed in us, what dignity, what grace, what gentleness, must express themselves in all our existence; not the poor, weak, starved, melancholy thing too often seen around us, but "life more abundantly" exuberant, divine, glorious, overcoming life, manifested—shown and recognised by men—in these mortal bodies. Remove the obstacles, and then let the thrill of Christ's own eternal life surge and thrill through all your being. Let the Sons of God, the Kings and Priests of this age, show that they believe that God has made them such.

At 3 o'clock, in the Corn Exchange, Mrs. SMITH gave her daily Bible reading (Eph. iv. 1): "I therefore, the prisoner of the Lord, beseech you that ye walk worthy of the vocation wherewith ye are called." In order to walk worthy of any vocation, we must first know what that vocation is. If a prince is to act like a prince, he must know that he is one, or it will be impossible for him to display a princely character. And if a Christian is to walk worthy of his calling, he must know first of all that he *is* called, and then must also know what the calling is.

To begin with then, dear friends, do you all know that you *are* called with this high calling? Do you know that you are God's children, and that you have been translated out of the kingdom of Satan into the kingdom of God's dear Son? For unless you know this it is useless to talk to you about walking worthy of it. Any doubt as to our relations with our fellow-men effectually hinders the development of the proper feelings and actions which belong to such relations. And any doubt as to our relations with God, is equally a complete barrier to the development of the right feelings and actions towards Him. In considering therefore this subject of a walk that shall please God, the first point to be settled is—what are your relations to Him? Have you any doubts as to the forgiveness of your sins? Do you *know* you are His child, or do you only *hope* so? Let me beg of you to ask, and answer this question to yourself now and here, in order that you may be able to go on to the further consideration of our subject. And if you have a single doubt, let me tell you how to settle it. Find out what God says about it, for He knows, and what He says must of course be the truth. Do not look inside yourself to see how you feel; but look inside the Bible to see what God says.

And He says that "whosoever believeth that Jesus is the Christ *is born* of God;" "He that believeth on the Son *hath* everlasting life;" "He that believeth on Him is not condemned." It is always the tense of present possession that is used in these declarations. If you believe on the Lord Jesus Christ, God does not say you may perhaps be His child, or you will be some day, but He says you *are* His child now. And this settles the question.

Being His child then, the next question is, what position this gives you, and what are your possessions, that you may know how to walk worthy of them.

As to your position—let me read you a few of the names by which you are called. A man's titles show his rank and position in the kingdoms of this world, and the names and titles given to the Christian show his rank and position in the kingdom of God. Beloved friends, we are said to be children of God, children of the light, heirs of God, heirs of the kingdom, the bride of Christ, partakers of the Divine nature, holy brethren, a chosen generation, a royal priesthood, a holy nation, a peculiar people, the household of God, the temple of God, the habitation of God, God's workmanship, God's building, the flock of God, members of Christ, beloved of God, friends of God, the body of Christ, strangers and pilgrims, kings and priests, the light of the world, followers of God, servants of Christ, fellow-citizens with the saints, blessed of the Father, sons and daughters of the Lord Almighty.

God seems to have exhausted our language of its titles of grace, and blessing, and privilege, in order to show us who and what we are.

Then as to our possessions—what are they? Eternal life, the spirit of adoption, redemption through the blood of Christ, the forgiveness of sins, peace with God, access to God, grace for all our needs, completeness in Christ, comfort in all our tribulations, joy unspeakable and full of glory, rest, liberty, deliverance from all our enemies, fellowship with the Father and with His Son Jesus Christ, a kingdom which cannot be moved, a peace which passes understanding, the same love wherewith God has loved His Son, all spiritual blessings in heavenly places in Christ.

Such are we, and such are our possessions—a grand people with a glorious inheritance; and now God calls upon us to walk worthy of it.

Have you ever thought how astonished the angels—who know who and what we are far better than we ourselves ever can do in this world—must be at our ignorance and indifference concerning our amazing privileges; and how they must pity us with the profoundest compassion, for the poor grovelling pursuits and interests that occupy our time and our thoughts? Our feelings at seeing the heir to a mighty throne, and the possessor of unbounded wealth, raking up an ash-heap, may give us a faint glimpse of their wondering gaze. They see us beggars, where we ought to be millionaires. They see us serving, where we ought to reign. They see us starving, where we ought to be satisfied with marrow and fatness. They see us walking in darkness when we ought to be filled with light. And do not some of you see yourselves thus, too?

In Nehemiah ix. the Children of Israel, upon their return from a long captivity in Babylon, confess before the Lord their sad condition, and say, "Behold we are servants this day; and for the land that Thou gavest unto our fathers to eat the fruit thereof, and the good thereof, behold we are servants in it: and it yieldeth much increase unto the kings whom Thou hast set over us because of our sins: also they have dominion over our bodies, and over our cattle at their pleasure, and we are in great distress."

Is not this a typical picture of many Christians present? Instead of being kings, reigning triumphantly over the land, and eating of the fat things thereof, you are in bondage to your enemies, and in great distress. But I hardly think you need to be convinced of this, you are only too sadly conscious of your unhappy case; and what you need now is to be told how to get deliverance from it.

The way of deliverance has been pointed out to you over and over during these days of our meeting here. The very purpose of this Conference is to bring all who are attending it, out of their bondage and distress, into the liberty, and joy, and peace, promised us in the Gospel. The way is by the steps of entire consecration and simple trust.

Come, as the children of Israel came in the Book of Nehemiah—confessing your wanderings and your sore need, and yield yourselves definitely and wholly unto the Lord to be His. "And because of all this," they said, "we make a sure covenant and write it; and our princes, Levites, and priests seal unto it." "And all they that had separated themselves from the people of the lands unto the law of God, their wives, their sons, and their daughters, every one having knowledge and having understanding; they clave to their brethren, their nobles, and entered into a curse and into an oath to walk in God's law, which was given by Moses, the servant of God, and to observe and do all the commandments of the Lord, our Lord, and His judgments, and His statutes." This answers to the command to us in Romans xii. 1: "I beseech you, therefore, brethren, by the mercies of God, that ye present your bodies a living sacrifice, holy, acceptable unto God, which is your reasonable service." And we are here to-day to do it. You have always known that you ought to do it, you have even wished to do it, but now you must do it. I believe Satan often makes that word "ought" into a real hindrance in our way. We stop short at it, and satisfy our consciences with it. Do not say "I ought" to-day, but say "I do."

But you may say, You keep telling us here, that we are utterly helpless, how then can we ever hope to obey Him, even if we should give ourselves up to Him? Ah, dear friends, this is the way of it. When you give yourselves up to Him, He takes possession of you, and your strength lies just here. You tell the Lord that you will keep His law, and He immediately takes possession of you, and says you shall. You put yourselves into His hands, and He takes you, and begins "to make you perfect in every good work to do His will, working in you that which is well-pleasing in His sight, through Jesus Christ." He does it all. Your part is to surrender, His part is to take that which you surrender. You avouch Him to be you God, and to walk in His ways, and to keep His statutes, and His commandments, and His judgments, and to hearken unto His voice;" and He then avouches you to be His peculiar people, and that you *shall* keep all His commandments. He undertakes to accomplish it, and He is able. You have but to surrender your will into His hands—and by your will I mean your liberty of choice—and He will take possession of it, and work in you by His own mighty power "to will and to do of His good pleasure. He will actually make you want to do the very things that have seemed heretofore impossible to you. He works miracles in a man's will when it is put in his hands. Can you not see that it is possible for you to walk worthy of your high calling, if the mighty power of God is to accomplish it?

If you could but know what an unspeakable privilege this surrender of yourselves to God is! Have you realised what an untold blessing it is to have your eyes opened to see the length and breadth of God's law? Sometimes Christians are frightened when they first begin to understand what the law of God is. They are afraid of it, and begin to mourn. This was the case with the uninstructed Israelites, when the long-lost and forgotten law was found again, and read in their hearing; "For all the people wept when they heard the words of the law." But those who were better instructed—the priests and the Levites—said: "This day is holy unto the Lord your God; mourn not nor weep." "Go your way, eat the fat, and drink the sweet, and send portions unto them for whom nothing is prepared: for this day is holy unto our Lord: neither be ye sorry: for the joy of the Lord is your strength. So the Levites stilled all the people, saying, Hold your peace, for the day is holy; neither be ye grieved." And all the people went their way to eat, and to drink, and to send portions, and to make great mirth, because they had understood the words that were declared unto them."

Are you rejoicing at the hearing and understanding of God's most lovely and lovable law? He commands, "Be ye holy." Are you *glad* that you may be holy? Ah, do we not catch at this moment a glimpse of the unutterable sweetness of the sweet will of God? Is it not blessed that He has commanded us to walk worthy of the vocation wherewith we are called? In the very command there is hidden the power to obey it, for He Himself has undertaken to work in us all the good pleasure of His will, and He is able to do it. He only asks your consent that it shall be done. He only wants you to say, "Yes," to Him.

Most intensely do I long that there should be something *done* here to-day, as well as something *talked about*. I entreat of you to make a definite transaction between your souls and God. Begin to say "Yes" to Him now, throughout the whole length and breadth of your being. Say, "Thy will be done," to everything. Then you will find that God takes possession of you, and that He will, by His own power working in you mightily, enable you to walk worthy of the glorious vocation wherewith you are called.

Mrs. Smith then said that she supposed all present had repeated the Lord's Prayer many hundreds if not thousands of times during their lives, but, she asked, had they ever really meant it? And she suggested that it should now be repeated aloud, together, by every one who did indeed take the will of God as their portion, resting in the fact that His was the power to do all for them and in them.

The crowded congregation then bowed for a few moments in silent prayer, and then the Lord's Prayer was believingly and solemnly repeated by the larger proportion of all present, under a deep feeling of the glorious privilege opened out before them in its divine depths of holiness and rest.

After the Bible-reading,

AT 4 O'CLOCK THE GENERAL MEETING

commenced. It seemed as though almost the ease and freedom of a family circle pervaded the addresses, or rather conversations, which flowed on from day to day; and as we are seeking to give a faithful picture of the meetings, we will transfer with freedom these social talks, hoping that the spiritual sympathy and the absence of the spirit of criticism which made it so easy there to break through the ice of a lifetime of reserve, and to speak freely of personal experiences before more than a thousand hearers, may also be in the heart of dear Christians who read the records of these sacred hours. These words are not to be judged by the standard of pulpit or platform addresses, or of doctrinal expositions, but by that of the confidential intercourse of Christians, whose hearts are "knit together in love." Surely in "the one family" our hearts may sometimes thus speak one to another.

A great help to this ease was found in a new selection of "Faith Hymns," largely composed of words of triumph in a present redemption, such as:—

"O'er sin and uncleanness exulting I stand,
And point to the print of the nails in His hand,
O sing of His mighty love, mighty to save!"

No one who was there can forget the spiritual power

of these moments of heartfelt praise. We understood and lived in the meaning of these words, "Filled with the Spirit, speaking to yourselves in psalms and hymns, and spiritual songs, singing and making melody in your heart to the Lord."

After prayer and a hymn, the General Meeting was opened with Isa. xxvi. 12, "Lord, Thou wilt ordain peace for us, for Thou hast wrought all our works in us." R. PEARSALL SMITH said: We cannot know full peace until we cease from our own works, that the Lord may work in us. Every privilege involves a corresponding responsibility. Every command has a yet larger promise attached to it; the commands are smaller than the promises. The yoke fully adopted is easier than resistance. The burden of our own self-will is like a mountain, while that of Christ "is light." We do want to save you from the agonies of a divided heart, an unsubdued will, and a half-believing life. "Thou wilt keep him in perfect peace whose mind is stayed on Thee, because he trusteth in Thee." Is this your experience? If not, why, with the indwelling Holy Ghost and the exceeding great promises your own, is it not so with you? Was it so once—and yet not now? Once more take God's promises as the realities of your present life. Are you in comparative rest here in these meetings, but anxious for the future? The present is yours, the future is God's, and of it He says to those who trust Him, "I the Lord do keep it; I will water it every moment; lest any hurt it, I will keep it night and day." When we have realised union with Christ, we have no less real fellowship in the crowded 'Change or social gathering than in the Church,—as one of your Oxford poets so well said:

> "There are in this loud and stunning tide
> Of human care and crime,
> With whom the melodies abide,
> Of the everlasting chime;
> Who carry music in their heart
> Through crowded streets and wrangling mart,
> Plying their tasks with busier feet,
> Because their hearts the sacred melodies repeat."

I am myself not aware of any more full communion with the Lord here at Oxford than I have often had amid the busy whirl of a large business: not that my mind could be then occupied with spiritual things, but as we may be conscious of a friend's presence and sympathy when quite absorbed in any pursuit, so the quiet realisation of a Divine companionship has been with me amid the most absorbing engagements of life. I have often in the busy streets raised my heart, and my voice, so far as I might without attracting notice, to praise God. I do not expect this Christ-life to fade out or become dim. My principal joy in looking forward to the remainder of my pilgrimage is the confident expectation that it will increase. "I will yet praise Thee *more and more.*"

It was not always thus with me. I had been a "religious man" for ten long and toilsome years, when one day, in the railway carriage, I for the first time saw in the Scripture what the blood of Christ had done for me. Reaching my journey's end I found that my wife, in the same way from the Scriptures had, a few hours before, also found eternal life in believing. The next night found me preaching to the sailors at our seaside summer home, and I have been at it ever since. It seemed to me after my long years of legality that free grace, pure grace, could not be so dear and clear to any other human being as myself. But in the midst of all my earnestness I found a life of frequent inward trespasses and interrupted or clouded communion. I never for an hour doubted my pardon and adoption—but this only made it more painful to grieve my Saviour so often. Nor did the immediateness and completeness of forgiveness on confession prevent sad and painful experiences of spiritual failure. Then came the completed consecration and faith—the laying all upon the altar—religious reputation and all—and being willing and glad to be a fool in the eyes of others for Christ's sake. It seemed then as if the very heavens opened upon me, and again I learned, in a deeper lesson, that *all* was of grace—sanctification as well as pardon. I cannot say that I have never failed since, but I have always known that I was to live and walk and work by faith alone; and I have found a heaven of communion to go to heaven in. Each year is like a new life, so greatly does this life in Christ expand. I could not have conceived a year ago what Christ now is to me, and next year I expect to find immensely beyond this. "It is better further on," ever better to faith.

Do not be discouraged if, as yet, you are walking by faith alone, an emotionless life—even having a dry time; God knows what is best for *you*. To some of us weak ones God perhaps gives more signs and emotions—but faith-life glorifies Him more, and has many blessings specially its own. The most successful preachers I have ever known had but little emotion.

The Spirit moved more in the range of their intellect and judgment. It was so, I think, with John Wesley.

You long for this life of heart-union with the Lord. It comes by self-surrender, and faith. We do not by consecration mean a covenant of works—God forbid! —but it simply removes the obstacles to grace. Then faith is not a mysterious sacrament, but just an honest determination that I will believe God if I die in doing it, and no longer make Him a liar in His promises to me. For this we are made temples of the Holy Ghost, and, in a deep sense, we already thus *have* faith. We are now to *act* faith as we act it in trusting ourselves to a vessel in the ocean. I had not a moment's anxiety in crossing the Atlantic: I trusted the captain of the vessel. Faith and anxiety cannot be simultaneous. Faith knows no anxious care.

If you are not in rest in Christ as to your daily life, there is a cause. If there is anything in all your life not consecrated to God, are you willing to give it up? You perhaps are unconscious of anything not yielded to Him. If I tell you of something, will you, in the strength of grace, yield it up? Pause and make up your mind and say, mentally, "*I will.*" Now let me tell you what it is. *Your unbelief.* "My unbelief?" you say. Yes, *your* unbelief of a thousand promises of being "kept from falling," in "perfect peace," of sabbath rest of soul. The Lord cannot do many mighty works in and for you because of your remaining unbelief. You "cannot enter in because of unbelief." You "receive the witness of men" all day long, but the "greater" witness of God you doubt all day long. It would break my heart if my children treated the promises of their earthly father as you treat those of your Heavenly Father. We have many of us obeyed the twelfth of Romans in the presenting ourselves living sacrifices. Now let us obey the twelfth of Hebrews by "laying aside every weight and the sin which doth so easily beset us," *unbelief* evidently being meant, as we see from the "*wherefore*" of the passage and the faith examples of the previous chapter.

Do not look on unbelief with any allowance. Never say, "I do not trust God," as if it were a small sin. It is a dreadful sin. You do not apologetically say, "Well, I do steal a little, I do lie a little;" and is making God a liar in His promises a less serious sin? In its effect possibly it is worse, for if you committed an outbreaking sin you would confess it and be fully restored, to live more humbly and watchfully; while you indulge unbelief, which is the foundation of all other sins, and forget what a sin it is.

I pray you then, here and now, with all the definiteness with which you ever laid aside any other sin, *lay aside unbelief;* and in the power of the indwelling Spirit commit yourself to a life of full trust. Never again slur over the promises of God, but sit down before each one as it comes before you till it is believed, received, and the reality it involves is your own in possession.

Pastor Monod: "Open to me the gates of righteousness; I will go into them, and I will praise the Lord: this gate of the Lord, into which the righteous shall enter." Our Lord says, "I am the Door." Whenever you are willing, you can enter in, but too many keep standing at the threshold. Oh! why do you not come in? I know that once I was like a boy who rang violently at a door and then ran away. I formerly asked, but never expected to enter.

"He is *able* to save to the uttermost." If any ask how long this life will last, I say for ever; what does everlasting life mean, but *ever-lasting*—lasting for ever. But this is not the best. It gets better and better. It is always possible to leave off believing, but the habit of faith will make it difficult to disbelieve. We do not say that it is impossible to sin, but that it is possible to "sin not." Do you ask when?—why *now*.

(Prayer): We feel, O Almighty God, what a Saviour we have in Jesus, and we bring our souls to Thee to rest them there, to find in Thee our protection from the power of sin. From this hour we take a more abiding place in Thy love and tenderness than ever we have done in the past. We think that we now know what it is to abandon our whole being to a life of trust in the Son of God. "Hold Thou us up"—stay us against our very selves. O save us from ever leaving this our Rock, our Hiding-place, and losing all those blessed things which belong to abiding in Thee—the sinning not, the asking whatsoever we will, the bringing forth much fruit. We give up our wills, our ambitions, our affections, our whole hearts to Thee, believing that Thou dost and wilt keep what we now commit to Thee.

At 6 o'clock a social meeting of the Continental Pastors took place at the residence of a lady in Bradmore-road.

Those who spoke were not the only ones who received a definite lift heavenward. When it was suggested that a special song of praise be sung by those who had received the blessing at Oxford, between one and two hundred arose. If it be asked, What was "the blessing" they received? It is the blessedness of the man who "maketh the Lord his trust," "whose strength is in Thee"—of them who have not seen and yet have believed—who stand by night in the house of the Lord, believing where they cannot see Him—who present their bodies a living sacrifice to God as a reasonable service; and, doing this, are henceforward "not conformed to this world, but transformed by the renewing of their minds," proving in actual life in doing it, "what is the acceptable and perfect will of God."

6 O'CLOCK, P.M.

The usual Ministerial Conference assembled. The centre seats were reserved for those in the ministry, the rest of the great Corn Exchange being occupied by others. These meetings were of deep and sometimes thrilling interest, from the ease and simplicity with which those occupied in the public preaching of the Gospel told of their past and present spiritual history. Those who, in their parishes or churches, had lived out the life of full consecration, gave, one after another, the strongest testimony to the power they had found resulting from the epochal experience, in which even things doubtful and not of faith were laid aside, and the promises of Scripture fully trusted. Though still encompassed by infirmity, and under even specially increased assaults of Satan, they had found victory where before had been defeat, and soul-sabbath where before had been unrest. And even though there had been moments when they had not availed themselves of their blessed shield of faith, and had consequently been overcome, it had been but a momentary experience, all being in the very instant of confession cleansed by the blood. Their testimony was not that they had not sinned for so many months or years, but that they had found the secret of victory and acted on it, and that even remaining failure was fading out of their lives as they more uniformly practised the lesson of faith. It was freely stated that there had been greatly increased results from their ministry now that, in telling the sinner to trust Christ for his needs of pardon and life, they felt that they had indeed themselves trusted Him for their own needs of victory and communion.

Canon BATTERSBY: "See that ye refuse not Him that speaketh!" I feel most thankful to have shared in this Pentecostal season. I have read the recent books on the subject now before our minds and hearts, pondered over them, and tried to say a word in defence of them, when I thought myself required; but I felt that I wanted myself the very blessing I had advocated. I think that we clergy are apt to look at doctrines as if they were for others, and not see them for ourselves. But now I have seen the simplicity of this way of faith, and accepted it for myself. It was when I heard a dear brother-clergyman speak of the faith of the nobleman whose son was healed, that the truth flashed on my mind, and afterward God enabled me to trust and make a full surrender. It is a difficult thing to speak of my own experience, and very distasteful, yet perhaps for this reason it may be right for one to do so, and to acknowledge the blessing I have received.

Mr. Bryan: I have found at Oxford what I sought for. The first address that opened my eyes was one from Mrs. Pearsall Smith; and when I tell you that it was my greatest antipathy to hear a woman speak, you will see how God has humbled my pride and self-will. I now trust that if it be His will to spare me to work for Him, I shall do it more as an ambassador for Christ —Christ speaking in me.

R. Pearsall Smith (in prayer): O! Thou who hearest and answerest prayer, we pray for another blessing, for the blessing of the last meeting will not do for this. We cast ourselves upon Thee. We feel Thy hand upon us. Oh, our Father, this is a very solemn season to Thy servants, and we pray that nothing may hinder the work of the Holy Ghost among us. We feel that our inmost being is yielded to Thee, —all that we have, all that we are. Some of us are so weary of ourselves, of our own wills and characters, and we are finding that Thy holy will is no longer a load, but a pillow to lay our tired heads upon. And now we place the government upon Thy shoulders for ever more. Amen.

Pastor Goulden: I have preached the Gospel for five-and-twenty years, but I shall now go back from Oxford, I hope, to begin afresh, and with larger blessings.

A Gentleman: Fourteen years ago I was led to look into this subject. I believed that I then made a full surrender, and that I realised this Gospel blessing; but I made a great mistake—I trusted too much to my *experience*, instead of to Christ, and so lost the joy I had. It is now regained.

ANOTHER GENTLEMAN: I had been living with Christ, but yet felt to need something more. I went to the Conversational Meeting on the Baptism of the Holy Ghost, and wrote down these words:—"I believe it is coming." I felt the power of God coming down upon me, humbling me, and causing me to sob like a child. I felt that I was, indeed, blessed with the very presence of God. One of the weakest of His creatures, I do thank Jesus in the presence of you all, that I have received the Baptism of the Holy Ghost.

"The more Thy glory strikes the eye,
The humbler shall my spirit lie."

Mr. T.,—a very young man,—asked leave to speak, and, stepping up upon the platform, he said: "I feel called on to tell you, that while Brother Sawday was speaking, I gave myself up to the Lord. So many venerable men said they had not entered this pathway of trust, that I thought it must be too difficult for me, and then I found that I *had* peace, and I remembered that, 'These things are hid from the wise and prudent, and revealed unto babes.'"

Rev. E. H. HOPKINS: About eighteen months since I met a Christian at a meeting appointed for him in London. Many irritating things were said, and I watched his countenance to see their effect. When I saw that they did not disturb him at all, I felt that, in spite of the objections of good earnest Christians, which were my greatest difficulty, a faith which gave such inward rest could scarcely be wrong; and soon I myself found a fulness of rest and trust which I had never known before. I want to tell those who have just entered into this Rest,—it gets better and better every day:—no worry now about preaching, about texts, about subjects—IT'S ALL JESUS. I roll over my cares to Him, *and leave them there.* I do not fear God's will, for it and my happiness are now one. I can say, as never before, "Thy will be done!" God has infinite things beyond to teach us, and as time rolls along, "It is better further on!"

A BAPTIST MINISTER: The idol which prevented supreme love to God in my heart was scientific pursuits. Harmless and instructive in themselves, they were so absorbing as to become my snare, and damped the enthusiasm demanded by my work. There was only tumult in the effort to repulse them, till my restless affections were withdrawn from them to be centred in Christ. Still I did not realise full rest until Mr. Sawday's address last evening, when, "feeling or no feeling, joy or no joy," I determined to yield myself wholly to Jesus, and henceforth to trust Him to keep me. Feelings are either good things or bad things. If they be bad, we do not want them; if good, we cannot make them.

I beseech you, my brethren, to abandon at once whatever you feel to be *to you* of an entangling or questionable character. If you disobey God, you know not how low you may fall.

The effect of these meetings has been to kindle an intense love to my brethren. I have had few opportunities of becoming acquainted with my brethren in the Establishment, but never have I felt so warm a glow of Christian love as toward those with whom I have been associated in the Oxford meetings. The several divisions of the Church of Christ are too much like a flotilla of fishing-boats high and dry at low tide, with their keels lying exposed and showing their different colours. But when the tides set in they float, and the many-coloured keels, instead of being seen are seen no more, but they are now steadying the vessels. All names at Oxford have been lost sight of in the holy tides of Christian faith and communion.

Rev. F. F. TRACEY: I had strong misgivings as to this line of teaching, and dreaded contact with it. I shall never forget my first interview with the leader of this meeting at Langley Park Mission. He asked us whether we were willing for God to search us through and through. There was a need that my heart should be searched. Our friend entreated God to lay His hand on any point in which He had a controversy with each of us, and to give deliverance, pressing upon the necessity of complete self-surrender. I said, "If this fulness of the Gospel be possible, it shall be mine!" That night I placed myself before God, and made an offering of myself, body, soul and spirit,—parish troubles and all,—to live or to die—only to be in the will of God. The Lord accepted me in this full sense. His by purchase I was now His in my own consciousness, by a complete self-surrender also. Since then my relations to my parish and to the world are marvellously changed.

The Rev. Mr. D——: The Lord has not had my *whole* heart heretofore, and my life was full of ups and downs, till I got very much discouraged. The Lord save you from so bitter an experience! It is very hard to expound the Bible, the soul meantime being itself not at liberty. The heavens seemed to me as brass. Then a holier light dawned on my soul. I saw the newly-received power in my wife's life, and yet I would not surrender. Then I came to Oxford without hope in my heart, till, in one of the meetings, the words came into my very soul in a new light, "the blood cleanseth." I knelt down, and, when I rose, I realised for the first time that I was wholly the Lord's.

R. PEARSALL SMITH: When holding meetings among the young men at Cambridge, I had to close them exactly at ten o'clock, that they might obey the commands of the boat captain to be on their pillows at half-past ten. They must sleep just so many hours, eat just so much of such and such food, and drink just so much every day. It was not taken as a hardship, but gladly submitted to—and for what? That they might win a boy's trifling prize—the cup! *Shame on us if we do less for the heavenly prize of our high calling in Christ Jesus!* Shame on us, too, if we do as a task, feeling as if we were doing bitter things, what they joyously did as a privilege. Through the grace given you, "whether ye eat or *drink*, or whatsoever ye do, do all to the glory of God." Permit me to emphasise the word *drink* in the presence of *the* great national sin, and *the* great source of failure in the church in England, and entreat you, upon your knees, to ask God's mind for yourself in reference to this. Never again lift the cup to your lips unless you are sure that it is "to the glory of God." I do not remember to have ever seen a wine-glass in my own household, nor do I expect to till I have faith for a blessing in it. I do not dictate to any one else in the details of life, save to take all to God, and only do what is of faith. Visiting a house near London lately, some ladies said (what I had not noticed) that some conspicuous jewellery had disappeared from their persons. I said, "You did not hear me speak about this?" "Not a word," was the reply; "but when you got us in that meeting to kneeling and asking the Lord if there was anything in our eyes He would have different, we, for the first time, saw these things. The Lord, not you, did it." What the Lord does He does better than I can. I might have tried for a year in vain to get off these things, which were in their way in visiting among poor young women, to whom such things are a very special snare. The Christian may lose full communion by the most minute thing in which the will opposes that of God. Yield, I entreat you, your *whole* hearts to God, and NOW!

The great "company of them that believed" read together Psalm cxlv. under deep feeling. "I will extol Thee, my God, O *King!* and I will bless Thy name for ever and ever. The Lord is nigh unto all them that call on Him, to all that call on Him *in truth.*"

In the 8 o'clock meeting the deep tone of prayerful expectation continued. It was not so much what was said, in the purely extempore remarks or addresses, as the prayerful readiness to accept—the receptiveness of hungering hearts—which gave interest to the meeting. These notes are simply to recall to those there the holy influences of the days of Oxford.

R. PEARSALL SMITH: If you have any doubt whether you are fully consecrated, ask those in your household;

they know if they would tell you. Are you sweet at home—tender and Christ-like? Does the sudden pull of the bell ever give notice in the kitchen that a good temper has been lost by the head of the household? Trust Christ at home first. The Gospel is preached all the way along the street by the face of one who has not failed in the trials of His home-life. Have faith for the continual presence of your Lord in your home regulating all the life there. His personal nearness is as real as it was in the sacred home in Bethany. You, dear friends, who are in danger of freezing, do not guard yourself against excitement. A good shout of praise, such as David gave, would do you good for all your life. It is more Scriptural to shout than to freeze. I never scarcely myself got beyond a deep Amen! but I am not fully Scriptural in the quietness of my own experience. *Average* with our excellent expressive Methodist friend and it will do you both good. Do not let him get more and more afraid of deadness and you of excitement.

Keep some word of God hid in your heart to meditate on. I get most of my blessings this way, by some word pondered and prayed over for days, and even weeks, till, like the seed in Genesis, it "brings forth fruit after its kind." For instance, lately the word, "*Thy soul shall dwell at ease*," was in my heart and prayers, until a hitherto unconceived-of ease in walking with God came into my life. The Spirit will suggest the word your soul needs.

I do not cling tenaciously to the idea of having "dark seasons," for I would "walk in the light." I have asked for the Scriptural experience of "everlasting joy upon my head," and I expect to have it "though He slay me." "The joy of the Lord shall be your strength." If you would but take Him in His own sweet ways of grace He would *make you happy in order to make you holy*, rather than holy in order to be happy. Let us trust Him, and continue to learn the lesson of our conversion when the joy He gave us carried us sweetly through the confession of our subjection to the despised Nazarene and our break with the world.

Give up the expectation of failure; it is a foregone conclusion to those who expect it. Pray in faith, "Deliver us from evil," and expect nothing different. Have you strong peculiarities, specially besetting sins? He can make you the strongest on the weakest side of your character, as He did Moses, who in his haste slew the Egyptian and yet was made "the meekest man on earth." Have you a strong will? I find such in consecrated lives generally made the most pliable in the hand of God. Are you fond of admiration—you will hate it, and lose your sensitiveness to both praise and blame. Are you ambitious—you will be as eager to take the lowest as you ever were to take the highest place.

Preservation from sinning is the smallest part of the Gospel we preach. The Christian life is a large, generous Christ-life that lives itself. Continue to save you? Oh, more than that! Why He is giving you His own eternal life—*life!*—an overcoming life, a joyous life, a graceful life, a tender life—a divine *life.*

Have faith in God for these things. It was well

said by a great preacher two centuries ago, one who himself "subdued kingdoms," "One man of faith will always shake the country for ten miles around him!"

Henry Varley: You who have received Christ have entered on a course of endless development. Your conversion is not a climax, but only a commencement of a path "shining more and more unto the perfect day." And now, "leaving the first principles of the doctrine of Christ," let us go on to perfection. (Ezekiel xlvii.) He longs for us to go on to deeper life. "The Spirit that dwelleth in us lusteth to envy"—that is, the Holy Spirit is enviously jealous to hold us wholly for Christ—He cannot bear that any part of us should be held by the Devil. The stream under the temple reaches "to the loins"—grace is in the place of strength. "Waters to swim in," not to drown in. Some Christians, I verily believe, think that if they were to trust themselves fully to the will of God they would be drowned. Wherever the stream came was life—fishes to swim in it—trees by its side—marshes healed. Wherever we go we carry *life* with us. Living waters speak of Christ. Oh! cast yourself to-night fully into the current of God's grace which will carry you on to glory. Do you know anything of the might of His power?

I went to Liverpool lately in five hours. Had I done any great thing to congratulate myself on? Nay, I simply trusted the engine. My carriage was linked to the mighty locomotive—the coupling was firm and we went a mile a minute. If faith will but grasp it, there is something in spiritual dynamics to be had parallel to the forces of nature, and in the present awful combinations of human ingenuity and power in rebellion against God we need in spiritual things a corresponding and yet greater power; this we have in Christ. Let us see to it that we avail ourselves of our divine resources.

After solemn prayer by Rev. Mr. SAWDAY, this day of blessing closed with the grand old doxology,—

"Praise God from whom all blessings flow,"

the use of which really seemed a necessity to express our feelings.

CHAPTER VII.

MORNING PRAYER MEETING.

7 O'CLOCK A.M.

THE punctuality of the gatherings of the early meetings was remarkable. The intensity of interest of the spiritual exercises seemed to keep every one fully roused to embrace each opportunity of communion and prayer. No word of urging to early rising was needed.

After prayer by H. Varley,

R. PEARSALL SMITH (on Heb. xii. 13) said: Many restless souls are seeking rest in some change of pastor or of ecclesiastical connection, thinking that with more congenial surroundings they will have more blessing. Such have often found in changed relationships that, while some burdens are lessened, other and different ones are far greater. If you find the soul-sabbath of communion with Jesus, the temptation to change will be gone—Christ will satisfy; and you will be surprised to find how much more that is of Christ there is in your pastor, or your church, or your form of worship than you ever saw before. While I know of none who have, in consequence of this line of teaching, changed their ecclesiastical connections, I have reason to believe that hundreds have been saved by it from temptation to change.

The great thing is, to get souls into vital conscious union with Christ. Then the effects of any errors of judgment are neutralised, while the truth embraced is vitalised. When you are near to Christ, the paradoxes of Scripture are solved; you are no longer worried about Election, and the thousand things which once perplexed you in doctrine. It is only dark when the world is between us and the sun; when it no longer separates us from the source of light, the confusions of darkness have passed away. Even a tiny grain of sand will obstruct your vision until removed, and the smallest act of known disobedience will cloud the truth of Scripture.

Christ will be to your consciousness—in a life of complete, implicit, instantaneous obedience and trust—nearer than the nearest and dearer than the dearest friend on earth. With habits of restful obedience once formed, the strain is all gone. It becomes easier to obey than to disobey. Shall the larger part of my being be held by Satan? Nay, henceforth it shall gravitate, not toward sin, but towards God, for we have now given all to Him. No longer "prone to wander," though *liable* to it every moment, the current of our being sets toward God and not toward sin. Let us keep our soul-sabbaths in the will of God, and instantly put to death whatever rebellious thought or act breaks them.

Do not be discouraged if at first you stumble, as you did on first learning to walk. Learn by your failures to trust yet more implicitly, and, if not gone all at once, they will fade out of your life by the maturing of your faith. But *give up the expectation of sinning.*

Unless you are doing this, you are not trusting. Yielding up this expectation is to many the key to the life of faith.

HENRY VARLEY (Matt. iv. 4): "Man shall not live by bread alone, but by every word that proceedeth out of the mouth of God." When a man is hungry in the service of the Lord, it is not for him to be fed at the table of the Devil. I want to press upon you the importance of feeding on the words of God. "How precious are Thy thoughts unto me." "I hate vain thoughts," or properly, "I hate thoughts, but Thy law do I love"—God's mind. "Every imagination of the thoughts of his [man's] heart is only evil continually," —is it strange that David hated his own natural thoughts, and loved those of God. Jesus places evil thoughts as the first issue of the heart of man, before even murders. Oh! the importance of having our hearts furnished with God's thoughts. If a man makes his mind a sink for the receptacle of all kinds of rubbish, he must pay the penalty.

After prayer, by Lord Radstock and Rev. G. R. Thornton, the meeting adjourned for breakfast.

BREAKFAST MEETING OF PASTORS FROM THE CONTINENT.

MR. T. B. SMITHIES invited the foreign Pastors to breakfast at the Randolph on Friday morning, after which two hours were spent in hearing from them.

A German brother, son of a pietist family, spoke of his early conversion, his going out as a missionary to India, great domestic and other sorrows; of always carefully avoiding sin, but latterly he had become melancholy and despondent, which in Germany it is considered that Christians ought to be. If asked what I have found here? I have every night given myself to my Saviour—surrendered myself unconditionally to Him. I have not had so full an experience as some of you, but I am *at peace.*

A brother from Crischona: The Lord had given me power and health to work for Him, but I was not quite happy. I was ready to give my strength, but I had not given *myself.* Some besetting sins which I was not quite willing to leave troubled me. When I came here I soon understood the first thing was to get rid of self. Mr. Smith said the surrender of self must be done deliberately, and with the will. During the night, I gave not my strength only, and my work, but myself. He the Vine, I the branch; He the Sun of Righteousness, His beams are mine. I don't wish to be a great man, but to do all He would have me do. In Crischona a hundred people are praying every day that I may come home with a great blessing. *Oxford is the highest University to me, where the deepest knowledge of Christ has been received.* I go home rejoicing; it will not be the Jesus of Oxford, but the Jesus that will be everywhere.

A brother spoke of Dr. Wichern, who has been preaching the kingdom of Christ these twenty-six years. This I have found here. I came expecting, with tears of hope, of repentance, of wishing to have this blessing. Now they are tears of joy and thanks to God. My brethren, I am poor and weak, and this is all my strength, that He shall be *all.* Now I have

Him, and He has me. Pray for Germany; there is orthodox preaching, but too little power—too little of the Holy Ghost.

A French Pastor, whose name is well known, admitted that he had not come without strong prejudice to these meetings, and although he hoped for a blessing, it was in a general way. He could not say he had got the full blessing, but he had got something new. There are people who are converted, but not well converted. I thank God I came to Oxford. I hope that many who are not well converted will be thoroughly converted here. Now I understand why God could not fully bless me; because I was not *fully* yielded to Him.

Pastor O. PANK, from Berlin, translated by Miss von Niebuhr, of Halle: By the special guidance of God I came here. I came not with great expectation—I had a secret fear they were not orthodox. Now I am at Oxford, I praise God; it is a sea-bath tonic for my soul—a journey to the mountains where spiritual health comes. I am quite convinced that what I hear here is according to the Scripture, and what I have experienced is of the Holy Ghost. Not that I had never known the power of the Lord. I never knew justification, without a growing sanctification, and being justified by Christ seemed always a delightful thing. Therefore, I preached, "Not I, but Christ liveth in me;" "Whatsoever things ye shall ask the Father in my name, He will give you." I have known this for others, but *have not believed it for myself;* and this is the blessing I have received in these days. I now know why the power of God was weak in me and did not grow, but I also know how this want can be supplied—alone in God. I go home with this faith strengthened, willing to sacrifice my all to the Lord; to say, "Lord, I believe; help Thou my unbelief." I purpose surely to preach this full salvation to my fellow-Christians, and to trust in the Lord Jesus for everything. *Not as if it were a new Gospel, but a new treasury of the Gospel opened.* Paul says, if one member suffer, all suffer; if one rejoice, all rejoice. There is a member here in Oxford rejoicing; I praise God, and rejoice with you; will you, dear brethren, see a member in Germany suffer, and not help us? My own, evangelical Lutheran Church is a member of the body; it was once glorified by the Lord, but now it suffers grievously. It is a double strife—Romanism and Infidelity. Luther wrote with chalk on the table, in a time of difficulty, "*Jesus lives;*" I go home with a new experience, "Jesus lives *in me.*"

A Swiss Pastor: I had gone into depths of sin; was converted, and used of God in His service, but I became dissatisfied with His experience and with the result of my labours. Seeking a deeper work of grace I went to Mannedorf, and left it with a deep sense of sin in my soul. I wrote to Pastor Zeller, "I can come no more; I am broken." Zeller replied, "Come." I went, out of health and was healed of my sickness, after full confession of my sinfulness, with the imposition of hands, and experienced the cleansing of the blood of Christ From this time I passed through different phases—new experiences of deliverance and judgment. And now I am here at Oxford, by the grace of the Lord. Since I spoke yesterday, I see things that want to be rectified. I can't tell you what the Lord has done for me this night, but He has been and is working. I will tell in my country what the Lord has revealed in Oxford. As I get nearer to the Lord, I feel all barriers of denomination fall down.

A Pastor from Italy: This is not new. Luther was just preaching that Gospel—the reason why the Reformation succeeded. He took sinners, and put them at once in the arms of Jesus. I was converted through the instrumentality of a monk. I was dwelling upon myself and my sins. He said at last, "Now have you put your hands in your own mud long enough? You are trying to make yourself better before you come to Jesus. You are putting the cart before the horse. and it won't go." Luther said, "God has spoken to me: as a lion He hath broken my bones: so hath God spoken to me." In this easy century men have an easier way. Why don't the French accept Christianity? Because they don't find earnestness. They do find monks and nuns seem to be in earnest. How can we overcome but by showing that we are in earnest. If we are earnest in our joy, they will come. Pray for us.

At a later meeting this Pastor said he was going to Paris to preach, on Sunday, from the text, "The joy of the Lord is your strength."

We have dwelt at length on this meeting of foreign Pastors because we believe it will appear that one of the most important and beneficent results of this Conference will be the blessing of a clearer, fuller trust in the Lord Jesus for life and godliness among them. These Pastors, many of them prominent and representative men, have carried with them an influence which not only powerfully affects their own congregations, but, gathering similar Conferences, they are spreading the flame over the Continent of Europe.

At the 11.45 Meeting

numerous requests for prayer were read under deep feeling of sympathy for those who had requested our intercessions. A deep and quiet, but intense feeling seemed to pervade the meeting.

Dr. Mahan (2 Pet. i. 1–4): I had been struggling for holiness, but was at length taught that I was to receive it by faith in "the exceeding great and precious promises" of which we have just read. I had long believed and preached the promises of pardon and eternal life, but when I came to the words, "And the very God of peace sanctify you wholly," I stumbled at it, although it was added, "Faithful is He that calleth you, *who also will do it.*" "Spirit, soul, and body be preserved blameless"—How long? "Unto the coming of our Lord Jesus Christ"—in every moment that we will trust Him for this marvellous grace. *I dared to believe the promises of God.*

In like manner I saw that I was to believe in Acts i. 4, "*The* promise of the Father." I did believe for it, the promised blessing of the Baptism of the Holy Ghost came, and in that power I intend to walk until He calls me home.

Isaiah tells us, "The Lord shall be an everlasting light. Thy sun shall no more go down; neither shall thy moon withdraw itself, for the Lord shall be unto thee an everlasting light, and the days of thy mourning shall be ended." I trusted God for this promise, and did He not do it? As a witness for God, I tell you that "*All* the promises are Yea and Amen in Christ Jesus." I have stood beside the death-bed of my dearest and best, have been left alone in the world, but through all the light was unchanged. When in sorrow the shade is but the creation of light, and light but the shadow of the infiniteness of God. We sang,—

"All things are possible to him
That can on Jesus' name believe."

R. Pearsall Smith: Let us read some promises of Scripture, first pausing that each one present may feel responsibility for trusting them HERE and NOW. We preach to sinners, "How shall we escape if we neglect so great salvation?" But how shall you and I suffer present, and, in some respects, eternal loss, if we fail to appreciate and appropriate such promises as these! Isaiah xxvii. 3, "I, the Lord, do keep it: *I will water it every moment:* lest any hurt it, *I will keep it night and day.*" Beloved, some of us here believe this; we believe that He now keeps us, and that we shall be kept more and more. In looking back and seeing how this rest of faith has increased year by year, I feel that I would rather lose my life than to doubt this promise. I could not last year have conceived that Christ could be, in this life, so much as He is to me now, and thus it has been year by year since I learned the life of full trust; and I believe that next year's blessings will be to you as much beyond those of 1874 as they are beyond 1873. "The path of the just is as the shining light, which shineth more and more unto the perfect day." "I will yet praise Thee more and more," year by year, and not less. It is the great joy of continued life to know more and more of Christ. When a Christian believes with his whole heart, it is marvellous how his whole theology expands on the Godward side. I formerly was afraid to face the promises of God, and I have the most respectful appreciation of the feelings of those dear Christians who honestly fear lest we give too large a present interpretation to them; but they seem instead of being exhausted to grow more limitless as we go further on the line of perfect trust. I may say that in the urgent pressing cares and bustle of commercial life, I find quite as free a communion as here in Oxford. I am just as truly in the will of God then as now. The secret is to hand *everything*, each thing as it comes up, over to the Lord—and *to leave it there*. Anxiety then can only come when He gives it back to us, and that He will never do.

When the Lord showed me the secret of victory over sin, and of maintained communion with Himself, I found what seemed a new life—a very heaven to go to heaven in. Then He revealed to my soul the marvels of His love, satisfying every craving of my heart, and it seemed as though a yet higher heaven of privilege opened to me.

It seems to me that God keeps the best of His saints in reserve, as is done in a battle. I am sure that He puts some of the weakest forward to preach, while the strongest and best are behind to pray. Let us in our weakness read and commit our souls to one more promise,—"Thou wilt keep him in perfect peace whose mind is stayed on Thee, because he trusteth in Thee." This is "*the peace of God* that passeth all understanding"—His Divine unchangeable peace put into our hearts. Now I am sure that there are hearts here upon whom is laid the solemn responsibility of a total surrender of unbelief. Having given up much to the Lord, they are now called to give up the last reserve of distrust in the grace of God.

I once brought to a suffering Southern soldier, who had been captured in the invasion of Pennsylvania, some fine ripe peaches. Instead of receiving them, he turned to the other side of the cot, weeping freely. When on my return to his tent I found him composed, I asked him why he had not accepted my gift—did it bring overwhelming associations of home? "No, not that," he replied, "but I came into your State an enemy, to pillage it, and when you treated me so, it seemed too good to be true! Your kindness broke my heart. But I believe it now, and I can take your gift." Can you not let grace break your heart to-night, and accept its wealth of privilege? After having helped a man in poor health along for years, he turned on me and acted very unkindly and even maliciously. Soon the man was again in distress, and came to me to help him. I can never forget the deep joy of realising what grace is, when I said to him "My poor fellow, you know all that I have done for you, I know all that you have done against me"—and I then gave him what he asked for. Shame on us if that man could trust more in the measure of grace in me, than any of us trust in Him who is "*full* of grace!"

I fear that some are going on asking, and yet refusing to *take* what God has already given them in Christ—never grasping what is put into their very hands. You are the temples of the Holy Ghost. You therefore can believe God fully. He cannot be satisfied with a part only of your heart. I thank God that He will not allow any to be fully at rest till they fully trust Him. I would not put salt into any one's wounds, but there are those who need awakening about this matter of their responsibility for trusting fully. When pure grace fails to draw us to Himself, He has sometimes to try sorrow to drive us to His heart; but one is as much love as the other. I have a father's heart, and I know a father's yearnings over his child, and yet I knew what it was to say to a beloved son, "I would rather that your every earthly hope should be dashed to pieces; that you should lose all the results of your college course, all your bright prospects in life, than that you should be a half-hearted Christian." If a failing earthly parent could feel thus, is it strange that God in His vaster love and knowledge should deal with us "as with sons" by chastisements? And now that my boy has gone to be with the Lord, I feel so thankful that in the midst of unusual earthly prosperity he did give his *whole* heart to His Saviour. If your Heavenly Father shall dash every earthly hope here, it is that He may lead you to the higher joys of communion with Himself. If the sweet presence which illuminated all life for you has passed away, and the voice which vibrated in music through your heart is still, it is love's call to a higher love.

There is no joy in all my work so great as to plead

with young hearts that, while the strong pulses of youth and health beat through their veins, and everything is prosperous around them, they should give their *all* to the Lord. How infinitely more acceptable an offering, than to bring a broken life to Him because of sorrow. I praise God that so many bright young lives are now consecrated to Christ. He will Himself give you "all things richly *to enjoy*," and keep you from every pleasure which is not doubled by His approving smile. He will take all the sting out of sorrow, and multiply all true joys.

After a time of thanksgiving for the glorious things true, not only in the Bible, but in our experience, and prayer that we might henceforth dwell in love and in God;

HENRY VARLEY said: "In whom ye are builded for an habitation of God." He is teaching us to say, "Not my wife, not my family, not my money, not my friends, but *God* is my possession." We get the other side of this truth opened to us when Jesus says, "If any man love Me, he will keep my words; and my Father will love him, and we will come to him and make our abode with him." It is indeed true that "the tabernacle of God is with men."

There are four thoughts expressed in John xv.:—

1. Verse 9, "Abide in My love." Not your love to Christ, but His love to you. I have lived long enough to be ashamed of my love to Him a thousand times; but I have also lived long enough to look on His love to me as my chief possession.

2. In verse 11, He speaks of His joy. Not our joy in Him, but His in us. Rejoicing in His love to

us, our hearts overflow in returning it to Him. This joy is what the fruit is to the blossom. In Zeph. iii. 17 we read, "He will rejoice over thee with joy; He will *rest in His love;* He will joy over thee with singing." I pray God that our faith may be exercised in these things! They are expressed in our hymns; they are on our lips; would that they were in all hearts! Never forget the joy that God has in you. The house does not support the foundation, but the foundation the house.

3. In verse 15, He calls us His friends. It is not here that we call Him our Friend, but He calls us *His* friends; and he does it with the perfect knowledge of what we are. I should not like to bring an unworthy young man to my father as my friend; but Jesus has renounced every disqualification that stood in the way of our introduction into His Father's house.

4. Again, in verse 16, we have His *choice* of us. "Ye have not chosen Me, but I have chosen you." I bless God from my heart for the love that reached from the past eternity to us in time, and which will shine on in all the blissful eternity to come.

These, beloved, are as four walls to your house. Live *inside* this house whose walls are salvation and its gates praise.

1. Side by side with each is the other side, that of personal responsibility. We have to go hence to fight the good fight of faith in the world. In verse 10 we read, "If ye keep my commandments, ye shall abide in my love." I charge you not to talk about abiding in the love of Christ unless you are keeping His commandments. There is nothing more demoralising than *to hold the truth* of God in disobedience. A dishonest

conscience belongs to a man twice dead. "If ye love me, keep my commandments."

2. With the obedience and joy come unfeigned humility and unfeigned love of the brethren—the loving with a pure heart fervently. Love one another; not only this, but with a pure heart; and yet more—*fervently*. Now grasp this in its fulness.

3. Now comes verse 15, "For *all* things that I have heard of my Father I have made known unto you." "All things!" Unless you have an increasing knowledge of His will you cannot walk in fellowship. To know the will of God we must know the book of God. I do not know any human being as I know that book. It talks to me morning, noon, and night.

4. In verse 16 is God's choice of us for fruit-bearing. I do say that if there is a terrible thing to hear, it is when people talk of God's choice of them, while yet no corresponding fruit is to be seen in their lives. If you have been chosen by God, it is through sanctification unto obedience, in order that you may bear fruit. The fruit of the Spirit is love, joy, peace, long-suffering, gentleness, goodness, faith, meekness, temperance. Abiding in Christ will make you sweet, mild, and gentle; kind and loving in your homes; not selfish or proud, or hasty.

We thus have as correlatives:—

GRACE.	RESPONSIBILITY.
1. Abiding in His love.	1. Keeping His commandments.
2. His joy in us.	2. Loving one another.
3. Called His friends.	3. Learning His will.
4. His choice of us.	4. Our fruit-bearing.

Let us see to it that we never dissociate these things which God has put together. God enables all who trust Him to live within the four walls of His love, His joy, His friendship, His choice; and then, when we go out into the sin-stricken world, it shall be to carry to fevered souls the water of life—the *life* that is permeating our own being.

3 O'CLOCK P.M.

The Corn Exchange was densely filled at Mrs. SMITH's Bible Reading, the subject being "The Victory of Faith."

4 O'CLOCK P.M.

The General Meeting again commenced. The interest of these gatherings was not so much in what was said in the unpremeditated extempore addresses, as in the preparedness of heart to listen. Probably the speakers never in their lives found it so easy to speak even to a dozen persons as it now was to address a thousand or fifteen hundred. Naturalness and ease are the charm of Christian exhortations, and this charm we had. Brilliant essays, or even eloquent efforts, would have fallen like a pall upon the meeting, just as they would in the fireside circle. The company "had been with Jesus," and something of childlike simplicity seemed to have been restored to our lives—a feeling which cannot be put into words, but which those at the Oxford meeting can never forget.

R. PEARSALL SMITH: Let us meditate a little on the practical living-out of this faith-life. I think that we can bear to speak one to another now in a way that we could not have done at the earlier meetings. Drawing near to Jesus has brought us near to *each other.*

Permit me to entreat those who have to leave to-morrow not to argue at home about this life of trust. We do not argue about facts—we know them, and that is enough. Christ has become, in a deeper sense than ever before, *your life*, and living out His life in us is your best argument. I do not press food on persons not hungry. They will either find fault with it or be injured by strong meat. Give your time to those hungering for righteousness. Few opposed these things more than I once did, and it would ill become me to be other than respectful and humble to those who have honest objections to our teaching. Do not press these things on others till you are conscious that your wife, your children, your family, your servants, have seen the fruits of the Spirit in your home-life.

I would that I could ring out in the ears of every child of God the word, OBEY! Oh! that all knew the joy, the ease, the freedom, the cloudless communion of a life of implicit, unquestioning, instantaneous, free-hearted obedience, and how seemingly almost inevitable it in time becomes! Partial obedience is a very thorny path; full obedience is the easy yoke promised us. I always look on the privilege side of consecration. I have gained infinitely more than I have given. I forget anything that I have given up for Him in the joy of what He is giving me.

The more you receive of Him, the less you will judge those who to-day are where you were yesterday. I used to judge very severely those who came short of my ideal; but I have been pushed out of the chair of infallibility by a deep sense of how little I know as I ought to know. Pray don't expect others to walk by your standard. The child cannot act as a man. The Lord teaches consecrated people as they can bear the knowledge of His will. The great thing is to get *the will* right. Then all gradually comes into harmony.

In America, where the use of wine is but little known among Christians, smoking tobacco is as universal as is the use of intoxicating drinks here. A brother present had never perhaps so much as had a wine-glass in his house, but, with an entirely easy conscience, smoked cigars in his exhausting work as an evangelist; asking a blessing on the rest afforded by them with the same ease of conscience as on his refreshing cup of tea before preaching. But, a year after having learned the faith-life, one day, as he was preaching holiness, it came to him, "Is this consistent with the purity that becomes a temple of the Holy Ghost?" He saw, for the first time, that smoking could not now be of faith, and, without a questioning thought, he renounced it. There was not a divided will, and therefore no struggle with himself. At once all taste or inclination for it was lost. It was far better for God Himself thus to deal effectually with him. I believe that our great work is to lead souls to God in entire self-surrender, and then we may well trust the details to the guiding Spirit. I believe that those who are thus guided will find themselves, sooner or later, ceasing from the use of the special national snare which, in England, causes their brethren to offend.

So also in regard to ecclesiastical position, I might not think that of another so Scriptural as my own; but were I, upon my light and guidance, to lead ut of a position of usefulness to walk in the path laid out for me, I might only cause him to stumble.

In every question go to God. You will find a marvellous guidance in the Bible on subjects on which you expect nothing. For instance, about servants, study all that the Word teaches and apply it—not so much looking what servants should do as what *you* should do. We are apt to look for one another's duties in the Bible instead of our own.

Dress to please Jesus. For twenty years there has been running through my heart these words :—

"I've none to please but Jesus."

When you go into a shop ask the Lord Jesus what you shall buy; as a woman would seek to please her lover or husband, so consult His wishes. He has a very perfect taste, and if you dress for Him you will be dressed with refinement and simple inexpensive elegance. Avoid scrupulosity and worry in dress. He who counts the hairs of your head will guide you what to wear. I have met a few good women to whom I might wisely emphasise the word "*adorn*" in the apostolic injunctions on dress; I mean those who were too careless about dress—but to most we must pass by the word adorn to emphasise the admonition as to modest apparel and the avoidance of gold, pearls, and costly array. Some dear souls seem to think that when the Apostle said "gold, costly array," &c., he meant something else —*but he did not.*

How the Lord must love us to care for these little details of our lives! I care little how strangers dress, but every item of my own children's attire is interesting to me. You may not at once see all the Lord's mind in details, but as you obey He will tone it down till it pleases Him. He dwells in you, and He will set His house in order, outside and in, if you will permit Him to rule.

But all these things seem almost unconsciously to regulate themselves in the lives of trusting, obedient saints. There comes by living with the Lord, as there does in the earthly marriage relation, an instinctive consciousness of what will please *the* Beloved. We do not worry ourselves about it, but just easily, naturally, joyously, walk in His companionship, and find that "we do those things which are pleasing in His sight." Love has a profound and true sense of the taste and choice of another. You will not gain this simplicity and ease all at once, but as you live in intimate, holy union with the Lord, there will, like the gentle dew, distil over your spirit the promised rest of the cheerful yoke-bearer. While you adore and worship Christ as your Lord and your God, you will, like John, so know His infinite depths of love, as to lie upon His bosom in holy, restful acceptance of the place He Himself calls you to. Let our hearts be simple with Him, as children are, and not make our Bethlehem of joy into a Sinai of fear.

HENRY VARLEY: The Holy Ghost is not an influence, but a Person. The work that the Lord Jesus laid down He takes up:—"He shall take of Mine, and shall show it unto you." God could not let our Lord's work pass into any hands but the hands of the Spirit of God. No power but the power of the Spirit can raise the dead. Christ Himself was anointed by the

Holy Spirit for His ministry. In this respect we must follow the example of the Master. "Come from the four winds O breath, and breathe upon these dry bones that they may live!"

In those ten days at Jerusalem, while the disciples waited, how much they must have got the restlessness out of them. Peter had to learn that his zeal and energy were not enough, and John to find that he must not depend for strength for service even upon the fervency of his love. The lesson they learned during these ten days of quiet waiting was this:—"Not by might nor by power, but by My Spirit." Are we not learning something of this at Oxford?

The acceptance of Christ in His Father's presence was the acceptance of the whole Church, and now, "accepted in the Beloved," they were being inwardly emptied and prepared to receive the Baptism of the Holy Ghost.

At length came the "rushing mighty wind." This may show, if we may so speak, the impetuosity of the love of Christ. He came to them early in the morning to be the strength of His Church, and abide with them for ever.

My friends, we may have a very humble opinion of ourselves, but even a cracked vessel, kept under the fountain, will be always full. We do not receive the Spirit because we deserve it, but because Jesus is glorified. It is the Father's reward to Christ, a gift on the day of His coronation.

The Spirit of God has been given us to enable us to fill every department of daily duty, however humble. If you cast yourself into His current, He will bear you along safely and gloriously. Our cold natures need the warmth of the Spirit.

The Spirit is likened to the wind. I have often stood at sunset upon the deck of a vessel when the ocean was like glass, with not a breath of wind to stir the sails. Far away in the distance the rippled water showed the coming breeze, and presently the becalmed and waiting ship, with filled sails, would spring like a thing of life upon our course. Thus may the Spirit now energise many waiting saints here to preach the Gospel in the Holy Ghost!

My sister, your body is the temple of the Spirit. Be careful where you take Him. The ball-room and opera are not His choice. He is as a gentle dove. Have a care that there are no thorns in the nest. Your heart is His dwelling-place. Let Him have the whole range of the house. Do not keep the drawing-room of the soul for worldly company. He may indeed not leave you altogether, but He will, as it were, retire grieved to some of the upper rooms, and leave that drawing-room to worldly company.

We can hardly know what the full meaning of "the power of the Spirit" is, but we can always come to ask "the promise of the Father," and say, "Father, Thou knowest what it is—teach it to me!" We want the fire to descend on us, in mighty rushing power. We are called enthusiasts. We accept the name, for it means *God in us.* It is a name worth bearing.

"When human cisterns all are drained,
Thy fulness is the same."

Wait for the quieting, energising power of the Spirit and take no denial, till you hear the Word, "Great is thy faith, be it unto thee even as thou wilt."

We want to see the sweetness of the Master brought out in our lives. To Paul to live was Christ, who wrought all his works in him. Shall life be less to you and to me? *"Lord! permeate me with Thy Spirit in my house, in the church, in the world!"*

The Six o'clock Ministerial Conference

Opened with the ministers each giving their *present* experience of grace in a verse of Scripture.

"Christ, who is *our Life*."

"*No more I*, but Christ."

"*My* cup runneth over."

"Jesus said, I am the Way."

"God worketh in you, *to will and to do* of His good-pleasure."

"The Lord is a Sun and *Shield*."

"Blessed be the man unto whom the Lord imputeth not iniquity, and *in whose spirit there is no guile*."

"Thanks be unto God, for *His unspeakable gift*."

"*One thing* have I desired of the Lord, that will I seek after, that I may dwell in the house of the Lord all the days of my life, to behold the beauty of the Lord, and to inquire in His temple."

"All power is given unto Me in heaven and earth."

"Barnabas, ... when he came, and had seen the grace of God, was glad, and exhorted them all, that *with purpose of heart they would cleave unto the Lord*."

"*The Lord is risen indeed*."

"God is faithful, who also *will do it.*"

"The Lord shall deliver me from *every* evil work, and will preserve me unto His heavenly kingdom."

"There remaineth therefore a rest to the people of God . . . . We which have believed *do enter into rest.*"

"Thou hast delivered my soul from death: *wilt Thou not* keep mine eyes from tears, and my feet from falling?"

"*I know* in whom I have believed."

"The Master is come, and calleth for *thee.*"

"Behold, how good and pleasant it is for brethren to dwell together in unity."

"Now, unto Him who is *able to keep you from falling,* and to present you faultless before the presence of His glory with exceeding joy, to the only wise God our Saviour, be glory and majesty, dominion and power, both now and for ever. Amen."

"Then were the disciples glad when they saw the Lord."

In a brief space a multitude of such testimonies of *present experience* were poured rapidly into our ears. We had heard witnesses for Jesus, but here was "*a cloud* of witnesses." The effect was marvellous. Never had the Scriptures seemed so full of present privilege. Could anyone for a moment longer doubt the truths pressed upon our attention, or delay to grasp what seemed placed before us as in letters of fire?

M. STOCKMEYER, a Swiss Pastor: Shall I give you the story of my past? No; it is buried. Yesterday I wrote to my wife that in this moment, by the almighty grace of the Lord, I am in fellowship with Him, and it is peace. It is joyful; it is gladness. Oh, it is no mistake,

I shall feel more and more a great and poor sinner; but I am impatient to finish with myself, and wish to have done with self for ever. There are some in Switzerland who said, "You will very much rejoice in Oxford." But I am not come to Oxford to rejoice; not to find something better, but something new; it is the baptism of the Holy Ghost.

Another said:—I have had great reluctance to speak here to-day. I have had great privileges in attending Mr. Moody's meetings, and in conversations with Mr. Varley. *Theoretically I have known this blessing, but have never fully realised it until now.* There has been one thing in my heart not given up; I have preached to others, but this has always remained. By the grace of God I have cut this cable this afternoon. I do feel thankful that the one distinct thing that came between me and Jesus has been removed, and I am looking for the blessing to flow in, now the hindrance is taken away.

Rev. E. W. MOORE: On May 1, 1873, I was pressed to go and hear an address on this subject. I had disliked some papers in the *Christian*, and laid it aside and refused to take it in. However, I went, expecting to hear some new doctrine. The speaker said great blessing had come into his life through deep searchings of heart, and unreserved surrender and trust in Jesus. I said, "Search *me*, O God." He showed me things I had never seen before; and I yielded them, and myself, to Him. I ventured a fortnight after, with bated breath, to say that it did seem as if the Lord Jesus had come and taken the throne of my heart. I can say to-day it is better than ever, and the last Lord's-day was the best of my life, and still "It's better on before."

Rev. Mr. GRANE (Shanklin, I. W.): I rise, on behalf of a friend and myself, to thank God for the benefit we have received here. I came here because I felt a great want in my ministry. Crowds came and went, and yet with small result. I could not believe that all was right, and I came to see what was the secret of the spiritual power which some of my brethren possess. What have I got here? Just nothing—but the strongest conviction that my dear Saviour will help me. Nothing but this to go back with—I go back to trust Him. My dear brother has received great blessing, joy and peace are now resting on him.

Rev. Mr. F.: The other day I did do one thing; what was it? Just ceasing to do. I came to Oxford for a purpose, at great inconvenience; yet I felt that it was of God. I had the feeling of self-despair; the cold, intellectual light showed the want of power in my ministry; but though I had this sense of weakness, it did not bring the sense of shame it should have done. I did hope for a blessing here. Should I test whether this trusting would do or not? A voice said in my heart, "Thou shalt not tempt the Lord thy God." I could not say, "I'll see if Thou canst and wilt." No; I must just give myself up to God. I had no ecstatic expectation, but I felt that self must be done with. It seemed as if all my friends whom I knew most intimately were receiving the blessing, and I left high and dry. When I was an undergraduate, ten years ago, I had a friend of whom I was thought far ahead in spirituality. I met him at Mildmay, and found that he had left me behind, and I was terribly vexed. Another I used to look up to had had great objection to this doctrine of sanctification by faith, but he told me that now he can sing—

> "My life flows on in endless song,
> Beyond earth's lamentation;
> I hear the sweet, the far-off song
> That hails a new creation."

When all my friends were thus coming in I felt I must not be left behind. Don't we feel that a great wave of blessing is passing over us? But individual souls must take it at the flood, and how sad to be left in the shallows of a Christ-dishonouring Christianity!

Rev. Mr. TOKE: I rise as one of the weakest here, to testify for the comfort of other weak ones. Months ago I had learnt the secret of dominion over sin. I had been overcome by a besetting sin—irritability of temper. I learnt that there was victory, by handing it over to the Lord Jesus Christ and letting Him conquer, and He has done it. I used to lift up the shield of faith little by little instead of instantly and all together; but when I raised my shield, He always gained the victory for me. But I had not entered the full rest. I have now yielded my will. It is only by His strength I am able to stand up and say this before you.

Rev. E. H. HOPKINS: This life makes Jesus so precious, and the Bible seems like a new book. Preaching is quite another thing—no more worry—not only the sins gone, but the cares. *God's will and my happiness are synonymous terms now.* I fear it no longer. The Lord has yet infinite things to teach us, as we sing—

> "It is better farther on."

Rev. HENRY SHARPE (vicar of Trinity Church, Hampstead, London): Before I came to Oxford, I read a paper at our local clerical meeting, *against* these views of "Holiness through Faith." I preached against them only a Sunday before I left home, and I also opposed these views at our monthly Bible-reading. I longed for a holier walk, and OFTEN *failed*. I was led here, and arrived on the Wednesday morning. Again, in conversation with a Christian friend, I said, "It is dangerous to state truth so fully." But on that remarkable Thursday morning prayer-meeting, the whole matter was revealed to me. A dear friend was enabled on that morning to make the surrender, and to receive the peace; and when those friends who had received *the* blessing were asked to stand up and praise God, my friend was enabled to do so. I could not stand up. My poor, unhappy soul was in deep distress. I felt the power of the Divine Spirit in the meeting: so silent, and so gentle, yet like a mighty river flowing through the meeting, and my poor little vessel left behind on the shore. We left the meeting, weeping all the way back to our abode; my friend looking up, and the young men, from the shop windows, seeing his tears flowing with deep emotion. I kept my head down, and my dear brother said to me, "I so missed YOU, when I found you were not by my side. Dear brother, we must have the blessing TOGETHER." On reaching our rooms, he kneeled down, and poured out his soul to God for me, so that my heart was nearly broken. On rising, he said, "How is it *now?*" I said, "The surrender is made;" and he said, "Praise the Lord!"

I had no joy that day; and so, in the evening, I said, "My dear friend has been enabled to make the surrender, and has received the peace too; but I have only made the surrender." I was asked, "Has God accepted it?" I could not tell. However, the next morning I mentioned my difficulty to an experienced clergyman, and he said, "Thank God for what you have already, and *feeling* will certainly be the result." And so it was. Never since I heard those words, years ago, "Thy sins *are* forgiven thee; go in peace," have I been so happy. When I was chaplain to the railway men at Hampstead, a lady came to us, and I longed for her power to speak to others; but until now I knew not the secret of such joy. One difficulty in not receiving these views was a dread of losing sight of the judicial aspect of the Atonement, and the work of our divine Substitute on the cross; but there is the experimental side, as well as the divine side of the subject. There is the *repose* of faith, and the *life* of faith. You will pray for me, that I may now make known unto my people a complete and a FULL salvation.

Pastor THEODORE MONOD, after speaking of Christ being to us what we take Him for, that according to our faith He would be unto us, said: Faith is very difficult to define, but is something like this: if you look at me, you *know* that you see me, but you cannot *see* that you see me. So, with our faith. We cannot see our faith, but we can see Christ, and then we know that we have faith; but though we live by faith, we must not live upon our faith, only upon Christ, as Paul says in the Hebrews, "Looking unto Jesus, the author and finisher of our faith." What more can we desire than this declaration, "Author and Finisher?" If one were given a blank piece of paper, and asked, "What more can you think of to write on it that you need than the promises of God?" What could one write? Nothing, nothing at all. We can conceive of nothing more; they are exceeding abundant, above all we can ask or think. The more we live by them, the more we shall find in them; and we have not so much to *ask* again and again for them, as to *take* them. We must come to the marriage-supper of the Lamb, He has made all things ready for us, He wants nothing of ours at this feast. We must not bring our own bit of bread, but we must trust Him for all, and we must abandon all. But here lies a difficulty. We cling to something, and this something keeps us from Christ's supper. In the siege of Paris, when we went to dine at a restaurant, we had to take our own bit of bread, bad as it was; but at this feast we must leave our all, or give all to Christ, and He will either throw it entirely away—in which case we may well thank Him for getting rid of it for us—or He will give it back to us in his own time and way, and we shall then enjoy it *in* and from Him. Some little thing it may be, some foolish thing, something we cannot tell a fellow-creature, some little game, or some occupation—we must bring it to Christ, and then, instead, we shall have His food to enjoy, His presence, His love.

I gave myself to Christ without any feeling of faith, joy, or love, but still I *did* it, and after a time all these came to me. I did well that I did not wait for them to come first, and obeyed the command of God to come at once; just as I was, cold, half-unbelieving, sinful.

I am very unfit to speak to you this morning. I have been only a few weeks in this pathway of entire trust and consecration; but perhaps it is well that we should hear from beginners as well as from those who are more experienced in this life of faith, and so I have endeavoured to *speak* of it to *you*.

8 O'CLOCK P.M.

Mr. VARLEY and others spoke in the Town Hall, while another large meeting was going on in the Corn Exchange. It became necessary as the Conference went on to open several places of worship in addition, and the preaching in the streets was continued. A quiet awe seemed to pervade the town. The blessing extended much among the residents of Oxford. No opportunity was had of definitely gathering up the results, but many conversions were reported. One cabman, who had long been a drunkard, the bane of his family, as he waited on the stand, overheard the preaching and was converted. It was "a still small voice," free from pressure or excitement; but the quiet whisper of the love of Jesus, and the power of the Spirit seemed to reach many in the city. Visitors seem to have acted faithfully on the exhortation to preach the Gospel at their lodgings.

There had been an address announced for the eight o'clock meeting on "the Baptism of the Holy Ghost," but when the hour came there was so much of the practical reality of that which was to be the subject of the address, that the Ministerial Conference was continued in the crowded Corn Exchange, while other meetings were held elsewhere. There was much silent prayer, and the quiet pause as each speaker arose, that all might join in intercession for him. The confessions from ministers of past failure and present trust were very touching. The pressure for time was such among the many ministers, who desired to speak, that many had to express by a single passage of Scripture their present heart experience.

Rev. C. B. Sawday (London): The Bible is a new book to me every day. I have to put aside my old sermons. Prayer is a different and more real thing. Yet let none of us look to feelings and emotions. No one is happier than I am, though in circumstances of sore trial, but I am persuaded that we cannot look at our own emotions and at Jesus at the same time. Do not try to look out of the windows of your soul with eyes shut and looking inward. The Sun of Righteousness will not thus reach you. When any one asks us what we have learned here—we answer, Just to *do* what we always should have done—*trust Jesus fully.*

Rev. G. A. Rogers (Christ Church, Dover): My experience for thirty-five years has been of intermittent communion—joy was a tide that ebbed as well as flowed. Fifteen months since I had been much blessed in mission services and was rejoicing in the Lord, but damped by the expectation of losing my joy. I told a friend present that this took away half of my Christian joyfulness. He replied, "Cannot you trust as much for this as for His keeping you for eternity?" "Is that all?" I exclaimed, and I saw that true faith gives up all expectation of loss of communion. And my joy and confidence have never been shaken since.

I trust the Lord as never before, giving up all anxiety about the future to live—as the children do—an instant at a time, and to find Christ the Saviour of this passing moment.

ANOTHER: This life of trust is a great change after a dull sad experience. I have now no care, no fear. As He keeps and saves me now, He will all through. I have had intellectual perceptions of this Scriptural life of trust for a long time, but now there is not one step where I do not find soul-rest in the will of God. Do not look for something afar off which is nigh you, even in your heart, the word of faith which we preach. When you have asked, then *take* from God the answer to your prayer.

Pastor OTTO MULLER, of Berlin: It is not without trembling that I testify that I have received here a *great* blessing.

Gal. vi. 14: "God forbid that I should glory save in the cross of our Lord Jesus Christ"—I had stopped here at the half text through my whole life hitherto; now I can finish it—"by whom the world is crucified to me and I unto the world." Now I realise that the *whole* Gospel is true, and I will trust without feelings. I know that I shall have joy in trusting the Lord Jesus Christ; a joy strong as the truth. That is my hope. The whole verse is now mine. Pray for Germany, above all for an inner mission in our own hearts throughout my country, that we may show people what the love of Christ is. Prayer meetings have here been turned into praise meetings, and I will close with praise.

The meeting ended in a solemn sense of the presence

and power of God. We were reminded that in proportion as we have here learned real consecration and trust, the future of our lives would be not less, but even more illuminated. The best days of similar Conferences have been, not its services, but those which followed them, when it was found that Christ went with us through all the plain homely details of ordinary life, imparting to the lowliest duties the glow and illumination of His own divine presence. Let us guard against mere excitement of the emotions, and go with yet deeper trust to the Word of God. Great dangers attend great spiritual as well as temporal wealth. The Devil may come, not now to offer the kingdoms of this world, for the fascination of its glare is gone, but as an angel of light, seeking to guide us away from the Cross, away from the blood, away from the Bible, away from prayer, to a specious spirituality, an emotional, impulsive guidance. He who was tempted in all points, like as we are, was solicited to a presumptuous disregard to God's laws, by casting Himself down from the pinnacle of the temple, and all under the guise of faith. The Devil's first solicitation is to transgression, the second to fanaticism. I dread the latter as thoroughly as the former, because it wrecks such devoted souls. "The meek will He guide *in judgment*," which might be not irreverently paraphrased by "the gift of sanctified common-sense," or an illuminated intellect. A *wise* heart have they who fear the Lord.

CHAPTER VIII.—Saturday.

Before-Breakfast Meeting.

7 o'clock a.m.

THE meeting was opened with prayer by the Rev. A. M. W. Christopher. There was much deep, though quiet, feeling, and we were exhorted—Eph. iv. 12—as the tide of your feeling rises high, turn to the Word of God. Seek no experiences not set before us there. Do not get away from the Cross. A true progress and victory only deepens your sense of the continual need of the blood of Christ. Thus you will walk humbly and softly before God, and be able not only to speak the truth, but to speak it always "*in love*,"—not contentiousness. Love is the bond or girdle that binds up all other graces into harmony in the character. Let us guard the reputations of others more carefully even than we do our own. You would shrink with horror from stealing, then shrink with horror from speaking evil of your brother. Both are alike forbidden. May the Lord preserve us from being jostled from a quiet, restful abiding in Christ. May the very tones of our voice convey the gentleness of Christ!

After prayer for the numerous cases brought before the meeting, R. Pearsall Smith said: Those who are learning that they may and ought to dare to say,

"The life which I now live, I live by the faith of the Son of God," are discovering it to be a marvellously simple life. When the Lord finds us perfectly pliable, He gives us His own will to be lived in us, our work being simply to hand everything over to Him. If you can conceive of my pen having some will of its own, and sometimes asserting its own choice of words, you will see that I should lay it aside for another pen; and so, many a time in the past have we been laid aside while He has used others more wholly pliable. When He finds us perfectly yielded, He will do more by us than we can conceive of. Suffer Christ to live out His own glorious life in you hour by hour, and while it grows more simple, and free from effort each day, it will grow more effective and full of results. In one of the paradoxes of faith, the inward sabbath and intensity of outward action belong together. Quietness and strength unite in the Christ-life. There is conflict, often severe, but it need not break the inward sabbath when victory is certain.

One whose life had been crowded with sharp sorrows, such as fall to the lot of few, said at Oxford, "I am afraid that there is something wrong with me. I do not find the road rough as some Christians seem to do. It is so easy!" In the midst of conflict she had found Rest! Another had said that the wear of the daily care of a restless insane father had been such that she had usually found herself quite exhausted in her nerves before breakfast was over; but that since she had learned to *rest* in the will of God, the evening found her less weary than formerly she had been in early morning. There comes into the soul a sublime sense of the sweetness of oneness with Christ, when the heart responds every moment, "Yes, Lord," to each expression of the will of God. Say with each cross that comes, "Thy will be done!" *and be sure to say it aloud*—there is marvellous power reflected by thoughts put into spoken words. Keep on saying it, even when the heart rebels, until it becomes easy and joyful, as it surely will do.

We have dwelt much on great principles and doctrines in these meetings. It may be well now to say a few words of plain, practical experience. This life of faith is not, firstly, for the pulpit and prayer-meeting. *It must begin at home.* If you are questioning yourself whether you are wholly consecrated to the Lord, permit me to say that your wife, or husband, your children, your clerks, or your servants know—those who see you hour by hour could inform you, if they would. Your own consciousness in their presence would tell you whether Christ is first in your purposes.

Many long years ago I had asked the Lord not to send me out till the Divine seal had been set on my work at home—and when all my children, my servants, and many of my work-people had been converted, and brought to live the faith-life, it was easy to go "to the parts beyond." The Lord would train us in small things before He can safely trust us with larger. If you have found "the blessing"—the blessedness of the man who trusteth in God—it will make you *sweet at home*—at the breakfast table, and all day long. Those who live with you, saints and sinners, must feel that you have Christ in your life. If they do not, go at once to God about it, for you have not yet the love which "endureth all things." There is a humility, sweetness, and tenderness in the home-lives of those who have Christ dwelling in their hearts, which *must* be felt, even where it causes the opposition of the natural mind. Do not press this fulness of the Gospel, in its doctrinal, dogmatic side. It is not so much a doctrine to be argued as a *life* to be lived. *Confess* Christ—do not *profess* to be anything. Acknowledge His grace courageously, for nothing so reaches the hearts of others, but remember that *you* are now no better in and of yourself—only you have learned that you may dare to trust Christ for more than you ever conceived of before. Your life must be your argument to those who see you constantly. Do not worry them by doctrinal statements, but love them into the fulness of salvation. It is usual to hear persons say, "I was wrong. I could meet the arguments, but *the life* of my friend has convinced me that she was right."

Avoid *scrupulosity*. The word, derivatively, means pebbles under the feet. It is not nice to walk on pebbles in our shoes—but it is less painful than a restless worrying conscience. The Lord intends us to lead a free, graceful, generous, royal, overcoming life. I meet Christians who step the streets erect amid all the homely, chafing, details of life, like kings and princes, walking in royal palaces. Others, with the same surroundings, are more like beggars. Some among us have misrepresented our Heavenly Father, as a ragged starved child, who would not wear good clothes or eat the liberal fare of his father's house, would do dishonour to his wealthy parents. A fully consecrated heart trusts God to deliver it from evil, and, conscious that in each moment it is yielded to God, rests all in Him. If you have "rest" you have not worry; if you have worry you have not rest. The trusting soul hears the word, "Thy soul shall dwell *at ease*," and it accepts the Spirit's testimony that, even in all its imperfectness of service, it pleases God by its faith and consecration. Do not permit the Devil to suggest difficulties, as that a life of full consecration to God will make you miserable. Banish instantly a thought so unworthy of God! *He is your Father*—your *Heavenly* Father. Does an earthly parent make the thoroughly obedient child miserable? Shame on the thought! Let it never be allowed entrance to any heart here!

Be very careful not to judge others when they do not see as you do. "My views" are what I am able to see—nothing more. I am not Pope—nor you either, my dogmatic friend. Low down I can see but little. Seated with Christ in heavenly places I see more, and when there I am sure to be humbled by my ignorance. Your humility and forbearance toward others is the measure of your true elevation in Christ.

Especially do not find fault with your minister, even if he does not yet see what has become very precious to you, and has not found faith's full victory himself. You could not so effectually close his eyes to this life of faith as by the sin of lessening his influence by needless criticism. Perhaps he has been on his face before the Lord this very day in the sense of his infirmities and short-comings. Pray earnestly for him, and you will then not like speaking of his failures. He stands for God before the people, and in lessening his personal influence you may be hindering the blessed Gospel. As a Christian woman left a church with an unconverted husband, she made some critical remark on the peculiarities of the minister, and then as she looked into her husband's eyes she saw them filled with tears. The minister's message had reached her husband's heart, and she, who would have laid down her life to win him to Christ, had broken the power of God's message to his soul.

Ministers are men of like passions with yourselves, and they have peculiar temptations. I know personally the inward life of hundreds, who pray, and even weep before the Lord for the souls committed to their charge. They *need* your prayers. Do not give them your sneers! Do not suppose that God has one standard of life for them and another for you, because you don't preach! They are liable to be deadened by constant familiarity with sacred things—you come to them fresh with a rebound from the world. They have many temptations which you have not. By the measure of your love to the blessed Gospel, strengthen the hands of those who preach the "Good News."

Rev. M. Witney: I have preached this grace, but I did not know that it could be obtained at once through consecration and faith. I followed the closing exhortation last night by going to my room quietly and prayerfully. I was enabled to give myself entirely to God. I have had songs in the night season. I go home rejoicing and hoping to preach the Gospel more lovingly, more livingly, more trustfully.

Another: Like so many others, I did not come here at my own wish, for I had doubts about these meetings, but the matter was ordered for me. Now I am, indeed, thankful to have been here, for I have received great blessing on my soul. I shall henceforth preach, I trust, with a much deeper sense of the meaning of what I preach. I have told people to merge their will in the will of God, without myself doing it; but, by the grace of God, *I did it last night.*

AT 9.30 O'CLOCK.

There was a special meeting in the Town Hall for prayer for the ministers and others from the Continent. The following were present:—

FROM FRANCE.—Rev. Theodore Monod, and wife, 114, Place Lafayette; Rev. Mr. Fisch, son, and wife, 38, Rue de Turin, Paris; Rev. J. G. Cook, Nancy (Methodiste); Rev. Mr. Combe, au Pialoux par Chabeuil, Drôme; Rev. Mr. Good, Rochelle; Rev. George Appia, Rue du Vieux Colombier, Paris.

FROM SWITZERLAND.—Professor Felix Bovet, and family, Grandechamp, Neufchatel; Rev. Arnold Bovet, and wife, Souvillier, Berne; Rev. Rau Vaucher, Bienne, Berne; Rev. Stockmayer Auberson, near St. Croix, Vaud; Rev. Vautier de Begnin, Vaud; Rev. Heinrich Rappard, Inspector of the Missionary College, Crischona, Bale; M. Kober Gobat, Editor, 4, Stappelberg, Bâle.

FROM GERMANY.—Baron Julius de Gemmingen and wife, Gernabach, Baden; M. Vernier, Professor, Kornthal; Rev. Mr. Muller, Professor, of the Evangelical Johannesst, Moabit, Berlin; Rev. O. Pank, St. Philip's, Berlin; Rev. T. Jellinghaus, of Raednitz, near Crossen.

From Holland.—Hon. P. J. Elout de Loeterwonde, ancient member of the State Council in Holland, at the Hague; Hon. J. W. Van Loome, Heerengracht, Amsterdam.

Pastor T. Monod (in prayer):

"O God, our Father, from whom cometh every good and perfect gift, we ask Thee for a special gift this morning, that of Thy Holy Spirit. We give thanks that we have found here in the love of Christ the love of the brethren; and that we know also that we are in the love of Christ, because we love the brethren. We are here to be prayed for. O, give to our brethren and sisters the prayer of faith that always prevaileth. Thou hast put it into the hearts of many to expect a great blessing here, *and we have got it*, and now we ask for it for the Continent. Has the time not come, O our Father? Put great expectations into our hearts, and if they are from Thee, they must be fulfilled."

A hymn was then sung in French, followed by one in German.

R. Pearsall Smith: The work of the Spirit is not so much in breaking down outward lines of separation, as in an inward fusion of soul which must make us overpass all barriers of sect or of nation to realise "the fellowship of the Spirit," the effortless communion of saints. In the tender out-reaching love of Jesus, we greet you, our brethren in Christ. We know and feel no lines of separation—one with Christ, we are one with each other.

We will venture to ask you to tell us, so far as you feel free to do so what blessing you have found at

Oxford? This will cheer and help us, and as you speak, our hearts will ascend in prayer for you, and not only now, but in days to come.

After prayer, in French and German,

Pastor MONOD said: I should like to say that from the glowing fellowship we have received at Oxford, we have felt *at home here.* This meeting is of the deepest interest to us. Is there any brother who has not taken the final step,—letting *everything* go? *Here, now, upon this platform,* is the time, the place to do it.

We are going back to an atmosphere of which you in England can have but little conception. It is an atmosphere that is *deadly;* like carbonic acid gas, ready to put out the light. It seems that the infidelity of ten years ago was nothing to what, alas! it is to-day. *Now,* even the heart is called but a piece of chemistry, and they say, Jesus can have nothing to do with their souls.

Such is the atmosphere. But we can by faith live above it—hidden with God in Christ—even in France. But I believe there is yet to be a special grace for France from God. The Huguenots were people who might be set beside any here. Yet, though the material has degenerated, God can "make the weak things of the world to confound the wise, and things that are *not* to bring to nought things that are." Nothing can be less than things *that are not.* I begin to see what the Gospel means, and we are beginning to feel that we are men that do not belong to ourselves any longer. Brethren, pray for us, and if I dared say it,—*pray for me.* I feel that God has brought me up out of the dust in order that I may know nothing but His sweet and mighty will and do *all* in Him.

After Mr. Monod, and each speaker after him, took their seats, a space was given for united silent prayer for him.

Pastor APPIA, of Paris: We have practically no Lord's day, no family life, no Bible, in France. A gentleman to whom we offered a Bible, said, "*Did you write it?* Very nice!" We have Roman Catholics. Be very careful, brethren; they make a show of *consecration.* We hope to have a little band of joyful loving Christians, and that the Roman Catholics will see it. I go back to preach to-morrow in Paris—"The joy of the Lord is your strength."

Pastor O. PANK, St. Philippus, Berlin (taking the hand of Pastor Appia, who translated for him): That a French brother is translating for me shows that war does not divide Christian hearts.

I was seeking refreshment from my work, when my brother Otto Müller invited me to go to Oxford. I knew nothing of it, and decided to go without any expectations. Now I know that another Hand has led me to Oxford, and led me to see what, as a blind man, I did not see in my own land. We were both miserable at home. I had the Lord, but I did not know what I had in having Him. Long ago I had found the treasure in the field, but these meetings have taken away the dust and rubbish which covered the treasure; I praise the Lord for what I have found here. I shall go home with another Jesus than I had when I came here; thus you see the child of the German Reformation of Luther has got great riches in England,

Saussen at Halle is preaching both Christ for us and Christ in us. His life is his preaching, and his preaching his life.

Like Paul I was blind, not three days, but three years; but now, like him, I trust God may make me a chosen vessel. The Gospel in Germany is surrounded by flames. If I am right, the night will be darker, till the old rotten things are quite cast down, and there will be no hope in the things that were. But we see there is hope in the things that *are*, in Christ Jesus. If Germany is the heart of Protestantism on the Continent, Berlin is the heart of Germany. Through her flows the poison and the truth.

I pray for a blessing on you all! And now I ask God to cover with His grace the past, to guide with His grace the future.

Pastor HEINRICH RAPPARD, of Chrischona: Four things have come to me here. (1.) I have found strength to give up self by the grace of God. (2.) I have found the exceeding preciousness of the Lord Jesus. (3.) I have found my own exceeding vileness. (4.) I have found what flowers and fruit are in the Bible. I could scarcely leave off reading it last night.

Hon. Mr. ELOUT, of Holland: I crossed the Channel a few years ago to share in the union of Christians, and I crossed it now to get a fresh blessing, and I have found it. You had from us William the Third, to whom you are indebted for much of your liberty. Impart now to our land the liberty that is in Christ!

Admiral FISHBOURNE solicited our sympathies and prayers for Italy, whose reformers were noble men and very early in the field.

Lord RADSTOCK: There are eighty million souls in Russia. I believe that they have some feeling of the power of God. They are not infidels. Many of the priests are believers, and are circulating the Word of God. I can look in faith for a mighty work of God in Russia.

Hon. J. W. VAN LOOME, of Amsterdam: I went to Spain to procure the liberation of Matamoros. Carasco, who might have been the head of the reformation in Spain, God has taken. So now the work has to be carried on in much trouble and under many difficulties. Spain has a special claim on the prayers of God's people. There is very little strength and very great ignorance. Spain has had many martyrs, and their blood will be the seed of the Church. Pray that the light of the small flock there may be kindled in such a way that it will be impossible for the Government and people not to know that there is a work of God in Spain.

The meeting closed with earnest prayer.

11.45 A.M.

The General Meeting commenced, as usual, with silent prayer, singing, and the offering of the special petitions.

Rev. W. HASLAM (Psalm ciii.): It is when our faith is fixed on God that our thanksgivings flow freely. People put faith first, feeling next, and praise last. They say, "When I *feel* all the promises to be true, I will never cease thanking God." But if you really believe God, you will praise Him, whether you feel it or not. Put believing first, praise next, and the feeling you crave will follow. The unsaved say, "If I only *felt* saved, it would be all right." You teach them to believe and praise God irrespective of their feelings. Are you doing this on another level as to sanctification?

One day a gentleman called on me, saying that he could not find peace because he did not *feel* that he was saved. I took three books and said, "We will call the first 'Faith,' the second 'Feeling,' the third 'Thanks.' Now," said I, "Do you believe that Jesus died for you?" "I do not know that He did," the man replied "Do you believe that He left you out?" "Oh, no," he replied. "Then you believe Him, that He did not?" I said. "Change the order of the books and say, First faith, then thanks, then feeling. You believe that He did not leave you out of the covenant of His blood. Then thank Him for it, and the feelings will come all right."

Always, in all circumstances, put faith first, thanks second, and *last of all* feelings.

Now look at what God has given you,—not only pardon, but *Christ*,—Christ as a friend, a brother, a companion; to heal your diseases, to crown you with loving-kindness every hour, yea, to dwell in you. Do you say, "I never saw all this before." You must now look for it, believe for it, praise for it. Then will your cup overflow in blessing to all about you.

Rev. Filmer Sulivan: In these meetings Christ has kept the best wine to the last. How sweet this hundred-and-third Psalm of praise! It begins with, "Who forgiveth all thine iniquities." Dear fellow-sinner, are all your sins forgiven? If one is, then all are. There is no channel for the blessing we are here seeking till this point is settled. My question is not, Do you feel your sins forgiven—for feeling is not the basis—but Do you accept the word, that whosoever believeth in Christ shall not perish, but have everlasting life? I used to read it thus,—"whosoever, except Filmer Sulivan," but God makes no exceptions. Take, then, the sinner's place, and accept eternal life,—and NOW.

Having received pardon, the young believer thinks his whole life will be one of victory. But in too many cases temptation overcomes him again and again, till he begins to think that anything else than this frequent sinning is impossible, because he is so weak. He gets this doctrine from experience, and then tries to find it in Scripture. But I have learned that I am not *weak* merely, but *dead,* and that as to any overcoming in future, it is "not I, but Christ." Is He able to overcome these temptations? Do we not hear His gentle voice, almost of reproach, "Believest thou that I am able to do this?" I praise God that so many here can answer, "Yea, Lord." This is what Christ is waiting for; not "I think so;" or, "I hope so;" or, "I wish so," but "Yea, Lord!" Then we can read the hundred-and-third Psalm aright, for it is true to our own experience. "Forgiveth—healeth—redeemeth—crowneth—satisfieth." The thing that has hindered our being fully blessed in the heart, has been saying, or thinking, "partly of Christ and partly of myself." But, from first to last, we now find it is, "*Jesus* only."

This truth was brought particularly before me by Rev.

E. H. Hopkins, who came down to labour at Brighton, some months ago. I had heard rumours of "perfectionism" and so forth, and was prejudiced against this teaching, but I saw that it gave him continuous communion and joy, while mine was intermittent. Then at the six days' Conference at Langley Park I received a great blessing. I am now, so far as I know, wholly in the arms of Jesus. He saves me *now;* the future I leave with Him. I have learned in the strength of Christ to say, "I *will* trust," and to keep on saying it whatever my feelings may be. When we *thus* trust Jesus, and then by faith praise Him, joy and peace fill the heart.

Pastor Monod: I confess that only a few months ago my heart was sore with telling the people of a religion which had such imperfect results. I do hope that those who have come to us with this message, have opened our way for a very different life—one of victory and joy.

"But," some may say, "how long will this happiness *last?*" Why, it is *everlasting* life. What does that mean if not that it is to *last* for ever?

The motto of Oxford is, "*Fortis est veritas*"—Truth is strong. Do not think that you are going to bear up this truth. The living truth will bear you up. If you have to go to London carrying a dead horse, it will be a hard journey; but if the horse is living, and carries you, you will get there easily.

Where is *watchfulness* in this life of faith? It is everywhere. Where is "fear and trembling"? I never knew what fear and trembling were before. Do not let us come with abstract truths to the people, but with the *living* Truth. Suppose I had discovered a new light, more beautiful than gas, or any other light; I might tire other people and myself too with trying to make them understand it by descriptions. But if I lighted up my own room with the soft and lovely light, and they came to see it for themselves, the light would need no explanation from me. It would speak for itself.

After the 3 o'clock Bible Reading by Mrs. Pearsall Smith, on Rest, as taught by the reign of King Solomon—

The 4 o'clock Regular Meeting

commenced. About two hundred requests for prayer were collectively presented before the Lord.

R. Pearsall Smith: An act, whether of sin or of obedience, repeated again and again, becomes a second nature, and life flows on in the grooves of habit naturally and easily. It is cheering to know that the faith in Christ to "deliver us from evil," and the yielding up of the expectation of sin, which at the first has been to some here such an effort, will become by continued repetition easy. Breathing after drowning or swooning is an effort, but each breath makes the next less difficult; and every act of implicit, instantaneous obedience makes the next easier; while every failure opens the door for another.

Form, I pray you, the holy habit of reading your Bible in faith that the promises your eye meets are now your own; or if they be not yours in possession, do not go on to the next one till you can say, "Mine."

This faith is now making the Bible, by their own statement, a new book to many Christians. Pardon me for a homely illustration of the way God's gifts are too often treated. A Scotch friend told me that after feeding his dog with a scrap now and then, which he ate eagerly, he set the whole joint on the floor before the animal. The dog could not believe that *all* was for him, and turning round he walked away. It was "too good to be true"—he would not be so presumptuous. I would not provoke a smile—but have you treated the exceeding great and precious promises of God thus? Do you accept a small one now and then, but turn from a great one?

Now let us, in this *habit of full trust* which we are forming, read Ezekiel xxxvi. 25, &c., and dare to accept what is so plainly taught here. It is true in God's grace and purpose—shall it not also be true in your own experience? "Then will I sprinkle clean water upon you, *and ye shall be clean;* from all your filthiness and from all your idols, will I cleanse you." If you cannot in your system of doctrine conceive how this can be true to you, just kneel down at once and say, "Lord I do not know what this promise means. Whatever Thy meaning is in it, give *that* to me. 'Create in me a clean heart.' 'Out of a pure heart,' permit me to call upon Thee. Cleanse me 'from all unrighteousness.' Make me to hear Thy word 'Now ye are clean.'" On your knees, in childlike trust, is the place to understand the promises of God. They are *all* for you. Do not let your unbelief answer, "They are too good to be true." The Devil, who has had six thousand years of experience in deluding silly souls, would conceal your wretched unbelief in the grace of God under the name of humility.

It is for His "holy name's sake" (verse 22) that He does these great things for us. Now, if you have never before had faith to "call upon God out of a pure heart," just let your heart go now, and trust God to enable you to do it in His own Scriptural sense. The "love of God shed abroad in your hearts by the Holy Ghost," effects marvels in personal experience. "A new heart also will I give you, and a new spirit will I put within you; and I will take away the stony heart out of you, and I will give you a heart of flesh. And I will put my Spirit within you, and cause you to walk in my statutes, and ye shall keep my judgments and do them."

We have here in our text the being cleansed from our idols, and the word, "Ye shall be clean." Next we have a new heart, a new spirit, and keeping His commandments. "God is love," and His two great commandments are included in *love*—to be like Himself in character. Is this just added to the rest of the law to make it more difficult? Nay, not so; for love is the fulfilling of the law. How can it be love? *Not by trying to love, but by a fully submitted heart yielding to love.*

You know that in human relationships there is a certain point at which a true woman breaks through all the reserve of her nature, and lets her heart go in an abandonment of trust and love to one who has sought her affections. Just so there is a point in our spiritual life, in which all self-imposed barriers break down, and the heart is poured out in a torrent of confidence and *love to* Jesus. It is the time of the soul's espousals, when it realises its union to the heavenly Lover. You have borne a true allegiance to Him as King; you call Him Master and Lord, and so He is, but now the time has come to give Him your heart. Do not be afraid of unlimited trust; you cannot go too far on that side.

Are you capable of earthly love? Have you loved a fellow-creature, a mother, a wife, a husband, children, with all the enthusiasm of your being? Will you love the Lord Jesus less? No! a thousand times, No! By His grace we will love "the chief of ten thousands, the altogether lovely" One, more than we do any of His creatures. Love and consecration to Him shall be the passion of the soul. We say to our dear ones that we love them with all our heart, and yet when God removes them from our sight, we say from the heart, "Thy will be done;" and shall we not admit to our own consciousness that we love Christ with all our heart?

Now, beloved, if you are withholding nothing from your Lord, the best thing you can do is to go to your closet and say, "Lord, I love Thee with all my heart." In the intimacies of near relationships we may express our feelings in such language as we may not use toward others, and when we learn what it is to dwell in love and in God (1 John iv. 16), the Bible becomes a psalm of love and praise, its marvellous wealth of language being all needed to express the heart's language. Now do not go and tell the Lord Jesus that you love Him a little, but that you give Him your whole heart. Saints of old were not afraid to say, "I love the Lord;" "Thou knowest that I love Thee." You are in different relations to a person when you have said out your heart in words, "I love you!" The barriers are gone; your soul flows freely now.

Shall we tell out our earthly love and not our love to Christ? All the wealth of England would not tempt me to refrain from telling the Lord Jesus that I love Him. Go to Him and tell Him all your heart, and there will spring up a sweet soul-intercourse between your soul and Him such as you have never conceived the thought of. Often has my whole being thrilled as I have just said, "I love Thee, Jesus." It is in such experiences of unbinding our too formal hearts, that He re-creates and moulds our characters to His own blessed will.

We are controlled by those we love. If they have our affections they can do anything with us. Our faith works by love. Many had for years noticed the peculiar gentle attractiveness of a Christian, when a friend asked her the secret of her life. She looked up and said, "It is the sweetness of love." It is this sweetness of Christ's love in our hearts which we need to mould all our characters to the image of Jesus. I could not understand this when I was contentious about doctrine; and always ready to make a man an offender for a word. I have had but one drop of His love—the ocean is beyond. Love's yoke is now "easy" and all His burdens light.

As we sit here do not our hearts vibrate with the words, "My beloved spake, and said unto *me*, Rise up my love, my fair one, and come away. For lo, the winter is past, the rain is over and gone. The flowers appear on the earth; the time of singing of birds is come, and the voice of the turtle is heard in our land.

. . . . My beloved is mine, and I am His. . . . . I am my beloved's and my beloved is mine." Will you yield yourself to Him in this the day of your espousals? I think that earthly types were not selected only, but created to teach us heavenly things. If we find so great a delight in those we love, if earthly love be so sweet, shall not Divine love satisfy our whole being, redoubling our joys, and taking all the sting and restlessness out of sorrow?

Beloved, listen to-day to the pleadings of Divine love, "*Give me thy heart!*"—break down every barrier in your nature to the love of God, and let your heart go out in unhindered fulness of devotion to Christ, trusting Him to set all right in His dwelling-place of your soul.

Pastor THEODORE MONOD: If we think that every thought will be given to Christ, oh! that will be a wonderful thought! He will speak to us more and more frequently and sweetly when we see that the greatest thing is not merely knowing doctrine more perfectly, but knowing Himself. We shall give a new meaning to the words, "I will manifest Myself unto him."

AT THE SIX O'CLOCK MEETING

for Ministerial Conference a large body of clergy and ministers occupied the reserved central seats. After prayer, the meeting was opened with reading Deuteronomy xxvi. "And it shall be when thou *art come* in unto the land which the Lord thy God giveth thee . . . . and possessest it, and dwellest therein, that thou shall take the first of all the fruit, ... and shalt go unto the priest that shall be in those days, and say unto him, I profess this day unto the Lord thy God, that I *am* come unto the country which the Lord sware unto our fathers to give us." The Lord is calling us to acknowledge every good thing which is in us by Christ Jesus. The saints of all ages have set us the holy example. The Bible is a book of personal experience. The Israelite was in the land, but he was to say so. He had to acknowledge not only his deliverance from Egypt, but his entrance on the land flowing with milk and honey. Then he could "rejoice in every good thing" from God.

"Thou hast avouched the Lord this day to be thy God, and to walk in His ways, ... and to hearken to His voice. And the Lord hath avouched thee this day to be His peculiar people, as He hath promised thee, and that thou shouldst keep all His commandments."

It is important to dwell on what we are *saved to*, as well as what we are saved *from*. Now let us rejoice in this good land which the Lord hath given us, and bring Him the first-fruits of our lips. I think myself to be as responsible for acknowledging my spiritual as my temporal blessings. I love to be commanded to "rejoice always." It is more pleasing to God than continued mourning. May we, in the simplicity of this holy fellowship, now say, "Come and hear, and I will tell what the Lord hath done for my soul.

Rev. H. Sharpe (Hampstead): Gal. v. 16. We have three expressions, "Walk in the Spirit," "Led by the Spirit," and "the fruit of the Spirit." I have *tried* not to fulfil the lust of the flesh, in order that I might walk in the Spirit: but this was reversing the order of Scripture, which says, "Walk in the Spirit, and ye shall not fulfil the lust of the flesh."

Most of the emblems of the Spirit express tranquillity and rest, as the dew, the breath. They walk gently who are "led by the Spirit of God," hearing a "still small voice," which was inaudible while the inward restlessness of the soul lasted.

Fruit is an effortless thing, it comes by abiding in the vine. The fruit of the Spirit is the antithesis of the *works* of the flesh.

How may we obtain more of the Spirit of Christ? Not by imitating others, not by struggles; but by faith. "Received ye the Spirit by the works of the law or by the hearing of faith?"

R. C. MORGAN (London): I should like to say that I have got a great blessing here at Oxford. The Lord is my Shepherd; He feeds His flock, and seeks the scattered sheep. When I got Jesus, I got Him to care for me; and when I keep in Him, and know and trust Him, I am satisfied. "The blessing" we have received is "the blessedness of the man who trusts the Lord, and whose hope the Lord is."

I regard these meetings as a wonderful manifestation of the Lord's grace, love, and power. "The Lord hath visited His people."

Rev. Mr. HODGSON: I came to Oxford with a definite desire for the baptism of the Holy Ghost, and I can say that the Lord who kept me, has suddenly come to this His temple. How can I again grieve One so gentle. I have endeavoured earnestly to preach the truth; but now I have found in a new sense how the Lord can fill His saints with joy to live in, as well as to die in.

Admiral FISHBOURNE: We have enjoyed great privileges here. Great responsibilities are joined to great privileges. We have been drinking out of the wells of salvation, and God's purpose is that we shall continue to do so. Let us take counsel together, that we may be filled with all the fulness of God, so that the Devil shall not occupy an empty place with some idol. See that none overlook the foxes that spoil our tender vines.

Not till I came to Oxford had I learned the indispensable importance of seeking for, and finding, a life of continual trust. The blessing I have received is the entire confidence that God, for His own glory, will support those who put entire trust in Him.

Rev. W. HAY CHAPMAN (London): Why have I ever lost this blessed rest? Only because of self. We must have done with self in order for Christ's power to be manifested. The will must be surrendered. I am determined not to doubt my Father's purpose that I should always enjoy the light of His countenance. Let us go home realising not only that we have been with Christ, but that we are rooted and grounded in Him.

The vessel must be emptied in order to be filled, and then will come such power as you have not thought of before. Never rest till you can say experimentally, "Christ liveth in me."

Pastor BOUVET: I learned this truth from Dorothea Trudel, but all that I had received has been greatly expanded at Oxford.

Rev. E. Boys (All Saints, Derby): A few nights ago it would have been a bondage to stand up before you all, but it is a joy now. I was discouraged from seeking this rest of faith by three persons. Now all these three have taken an active part in these meetings during the week. One of them sent me books against the teaching, and said, "I hope you are not falling into error." Now he is here in full sympathy.

Rev. R. D. Monro: With me it has been a gradual thing. For months I have been learning to turn to Jesus whenever temptation arose, and He has kept me in great rest of soul. I speak sometimes thirty times a week in missions, but it is friction that wears me out, not the work. I long for those here to prove what Jesus is able to do for them. Life is one constant song of praise now.

Mr. Clifford (Bristol): It was at the time of the Hanover Square Rooms Consecration meeting that I received this great blessing. I learnt there that God had said He would overcome for us what our own efforts could not overcome. The next morning I consecrated everything to the Lord—health, money, friends, success, and everything that I could think of as mine. But I have since received from Him much more in every way than I could have conceived possible. Persons said at the Broadlands meeting that we should never again witness such a scene in this life, but that has been even exceeded at Oxford. What Christ is desiring from His people is the heart. Their service is acceptable, but He longs for the responsive love of the heart. He says, "Thou hast ravished my heart with one of thine eyes. . . . . How much better is thy love than wine?" He does not say thou hast ravished my heart with thy earnest devotedness, thy painful sacrifices, thy successful service; but "with one of thine eyes," that is, with loving to contemplate Him.

The meeting closed after a rapid succession of earnest testimonies to the present saving power of Christ, of the power and joy of which it is impossible to convey an impression.

CHAPTER IX.

THE LORD'S DAY, SEPTEMBER 6TH, 1874.

THE address of Saturday night was connected so closely with the meetings of the Lord's Day that we include it in the present chapter. We had felt that we were drawing near to a crisis of the meeting. The overshadowing presence of the Lord had more and more filled all hearts. An increased simplicity and ease pervaded the meetings, with yet a tone of earnest expectancy. We felt that victory over sin, and the avoidance of evil, was at best only the negative side of holiness, but the preparations for the positive, that of the Divine energies of the Spirit, were permeating our being. True holiness is active, outreaching, aggressive on the kingdom of Satan. In the wilderness Israel was on the defensive, and often failed. In the Land of Promise they were aggressive and victorious. It is needful first to find Christ a Saviour from sin in our daily walk, in order that the energies of the now ungrieved Spirit may be developed. We felt that the time, which we had from the first been led to expect, had now come, for receiving "the promise of the Father," "the baptism of the Holy Ghost," in a definite experience.

SATURDAY EVENING 7.45 O'CLOCK.

R. PEARSALL SMITH: There never was but One in this world who lived the Truth and He was "*The Truth.*" We find individuals and Churches ever swinging from the great centre. We have preached one part of truth and neglect the other. I speak not of "truths;" the Truth of God, the Truth of the Bible is but one. I praise God that justification by faith was never more fully received than now; but has the Baptism of the Spirit been duly pressed upon the believer? Now, beloved, it may be that we have pressed—never, oh, never, too much—but too *exclusively*, justification by faith. When John the Baptist first spoke of Jesus, his chief thought concerning Him, was that it was He who should baptise with the Holy Ghost and with fire. Dear Christian, have you been accustomed to dwell upon Jesus as the baptiser with the Holy Ghost and with fire? He told His disciples that it was expedient for them that He should go away: there was something better than His personal presence. Do you feel that to have shared His personal presence, that to have sat at His feet and gazed upon His spotless perfect humanity would have been to you the greatest of blessings, a heaven upon earth? Do you not remember that His own brethren believed not in Him? Do you not remember that His disciples did not understand, and were ever swerving from His ways? We are far more favoured than those who had His personal presence. Oh that all would value the Holy Ghost as Jesus estimated His value.

We find that when Jesus came to His disciples after His resurrection He breathed upon them and said,

"Receive ye the Holy Ghost." They had been with Him during the three years of His public ministry, they had walked with Him, had learnt out of the prophets and of Him in private; were they not fitted for the work that was before them? Not until they had been endued with power from on high in the reception of the promise of the Father. Now I know that every one here who believes in Jesus is the temple of the Holy Ghost. You may not be conscious of His presence, but He is there. The very way which the Apostle took to bring the Corinthians out of their carnality was to remind them that they were the temple of God, and that His Spirit dwelt in them (1 Cor. iii. 16); and when rousing them to the Lord's standard of personal holiness he says, "Know ye not that your body is the temple of the Holy Ghost? . . . therefore glorify God in your body and in your spirit, which are God's."

Now, it is one thing to have been breathed upon and to have received the Holy Ghost, but quite another to be *filled* with the Spirit. We most of us remember the last words of the dear ones who are gone; oh, how we cherish them in our memory! What were the last words of Christ to His disciples? "Tarry at Jerusalem until ye be endued with power from on high." What! were they not ready to be witnesses to Him? Since they had been with Him from the beginning, were not their minds furnished with all necesary power? No. "Tarry at Jerusalem—wait for the promise of the Father." And they waited there, "continuing with one accord in prayer and supplication with the women," &c.—not merely the Apostles, but "the *women* and Mary the mother of Jesus and His brethren." I am so glad that they were all together. Beloved, we need not wait for ten days. All believers in Jesus may have it this evening if the temple is prepared. You know that when the temple was cleansed the priests brought out "all the uncleanness that they found and sanctified the house of the Lord." (2 Chron. xxix. 16–18,) He cannot manifest Himself in all the fulness of His grace while there is one secret thing lurking within the temple.

"Ye shall receive power after that the Holy Ghost is come unto you." They waited upon the Lord for this in obedience to His command. I think a large part of the blessing received by us has come in *waiting* before the Lord; and now I think we have come where we shall see and receive in the Word and promises of God such blessings as we have never conceived possible before.

Dear Christian, have you ever waited ten days before the Lord? In this waiting, evil things and wrong things are burned out of our souls by the spirit of judgment. We have been waiting thus, and perhaps our hearts are being prepared more than we are conscious of. Have you ever waited ten hours for God's answer? *Have you ever waited ten minutes?* I can imagine that company as they waited during the long expectant period of the ten days. I think there must have been a great deal of solemn heart-searching before the Lord, and of telling what the Lord had done and would do for them. They were getting the house ready that the Heavenly Guest might come in. Are we setting our house in order? Oh, it is to me such a delightful thought that *I* may be "filled with the Spirit;" that the King may rule in His Kingdom. Oh, believer, is there anything between Him and thee? This matter is of far more moment than the things of this world. Beloved, I say it thoughtfully, that the setting up of Christ's kingdom in your heart is of more importance in reference to eternity than the fate of battles, yea, of the whole kingdom. The angels look on these things. *We* are privileged to look into things into which they desired to look and could not. We cannot put into words the vast importance of these minutes, hours, and days, as it will appear in eternity.

The believing ones waited—five, six, seven days passed yet it came not—eight, nine. How their hearts must have beat with expectation! I wonder if their faith began to fail. The promise is always sure; *it* cannot fail. At length it came. It took no visible form—it came as a mighty rushing wind, and filled all the house where they were sitting. Then the cloven tongues appeared.

And they were all filled with the Holy Ghost, and "began to speak as the Spirit gave them utterance." Think of that little company going up into that room like a flock of poor frightened sheep ready to be torn to pieces by the wolves without, hiding themselves away in an upper chamber. What a change has come over them! The poor trembling sheep with that very man at their head who, when taunted by a servant girl had in cowardice denied his Lord—these burst forth among the wolves and boldly preached Him of whom the cruel mob had cried, "Crucify Him; Crucify Him." Many wondered, others charged them with being drunk; but the Apostle Peter, at their head, declared that it was a fulfilment of the prophecy of Joel: "I will pour my Spirit upon all flesh," &c.; then, having charged them with the crucifixion and death of the Son of God, and having affirmed His resurrection by the power of God, and His ascension to the right hand of the Father, he testifies that "He hath shed forth—this which ye now see and hear." Three thousand on that day were converted and baptised.

"Upon all"—yes *all;* for as their ruin was common so "grace came upon all men unto justification of life." As when John the Baptist came, so when Christ came they preached that there should be "repentance;" then follows "baptism in the name of Jesus for the remission of sins"; then, "the reception of the promise of the Father." In speaking of this the Apostle says: "Therefore, having received of the Father the promise of the Holy Ghost, He hath shed forth this which ye see and hear."

Beloved Christian, let me ask you, have you had this baptism, the promise of the Father, as your expectation so prominently as the Scriptures place it?

In chapter iv. 31, we read that "when they had prayed, the place was shaken where they were assembled together; and they were *all* filled with the Holy Ghost." In the eighth chapter we see that the believers in Samaria who had been previously baptised in the name of Jesus, received the gift of the Holy Ghost at the hands of Peter and John. And again, in chapters x. 44 and xi. 15, we read that the Holy Ghost fell on others *as on these at the beginning.* I pray you to note these words, for many Christians seem to forget that this happened again and again. It was not the characteristic of the beginning only, but of the continuance of the dispensation in which we live.

Barnabas, "when he saw the grace of God, was glad, for he was a good man and full of the Holy Ghost." Some Christians very readily discover the faults of others; but Barnabas saw the grace of God in fellow-believers "*because* he was a good man and full of the Holy Ghost." Again, we find Paul—who was not with the Apostles at the beginning, but was rather persecuting the Church and wasting it—we find him spoken of as being "filled with the Holy Ghost." We only quote a few passages out of a large number, for the sake of brevity, but search for them, and you will find there are a great many. No doubt the early Christians walked in the Spirit, and as occasion arose, they became filled with the Spirit for special service. Ought we not to seek this with our whole heart?

But let me caution believing brethren and sisters not to look for any particular emotions in connection with it. The Lord is a Sovereign in the dispensing of His gifts: no two receive them in the same way. I know many who are not conscious of the baptism they have received, just as some do not know the hour of their conversion, but the fruits are there. I do not wish to point so much to the phenomena of the coming of the Spirit upon individuals, as to the reality of it. It may be received in the will and not into the emotional part of our nature.

Now, one word as to its effects. I think it will lead to a most quiet life. It will make us meek, even in the very tones of our voices. Remember what a tender thing it is—it is likened to the gentle dew which can easily be brushed away; to the gentle dove which is so easily frightened away. We must walk so softly and so tenderly that we grieve not the Spirit. Being filled with the Spirit will take all the friction out of our lives; everything will go like the flowing of a river. This baptism effects just that in our characters which makes our lives restful and quiet. It may not make much outward difference to many dear earnest Christians here, but it will give inward quiet.

This baptism comes by faith. The Apostle asked the Galatians: "Received ye the Spirit by the works of the law, or by the hearing of faith?" I have met with few Christians who have studied the Scriptures so carefully as to expect this baptism. It is not strange, therefore, that it should have been so long lost to the Church. I am ashamed to say that though devoting myself for years to the work of the Lord, I did not conceive of such a thing as being "filled with the Spirit" until a ten-days' meeting was gathered like this. It was with fear and trembling and anxiety that they came together. In my self-conceit, I went to criticise. I sat down among them to set them right; for I felt sure they were all wrong, and I thought it such a pity; but I gradually became conscious that they had something that I had not; something that made their faces shine—that made them gentle and sweet in all their lives. I wondered at it, and felt that though they were all wrong, they had something good which I could not understand. At length, one day, a little company of us, two or three hundred, went out into the woods to pray. We kneeled down before God, and just waited half an hour or more asking for the baptism of the Spirit (some people get very restless in five minutes); there was no preaching, no exhortation, but as we waited there was a growing sense of the distance, the vanity and the nothingness of this world, and of the consciousness that ourselves and all around us were just being covered with the mantle of His presence. Then we praised God. At length the baptism came. It filled all the capacities of our being and showed us the glorious reality of the Father, Son, and Holy Ghost. Nothing that we could see with our bodily eyes was half so real as the glorious reality of the presence of the Father, Son, and Spirit. All was perfect quiet beside us; no leaf moved, but our hearts were stirred to their very centre; it was strange that we did not shrink from it. We had asked God to search us, and—oh, I wish I could put it into words. . . . all in life seemed like a dream—God only a reality. There has been no period since when God has not been more or less in my consciousness as the living Being unto Whom I looked. These things are not to be argued about—we *live* them. As I have since preached to the unconverted about their souls, I seem to have seen my blessed Saviour on the cross in all the measureless love of His divine nature and His tender humanity, looking upon the assembly. I have seen His sad, pitying, tender, scarcely reproachful look, but oh, I have seen Him too drawing them to Himself, and again and again it has seemed to be as it was at the beginning—the Holy Ghost has fallen on the assembly.

I hesitate about telling how it was with me lest I

should put my experience between any soul and Christ. There is the greatest variety possible in the experience of different individuals. Yet we must be witnesses, and a witness must tell what he has himself seen.

Now do you desire to be filled with the Spirit? Do not answer hastily. When He shall take possession of your hearts, the lives of some here may be very different from what they have been. Are you willing to surrender *all* to God? Oh, it is only mocking Him to ask to be filled with the Spirit while one thing is kept back. He may fill the heart in which there is still much imperfection, but not where there is one cherished or allowed sin. Before we ask God for this on our knees, see to it—be honest within your own souls—oh, see to it, that there is nothing unyielded—no sin, no idols, no carnal desire, no love of the world!

Are you ready to go home to-night believing that the Holy Ghost is ready to take possession of His temple? Is the temple in readiness for Him? Is all adjusted? Is every thought, every feeling, every wish or desire in harmony with the mind of the Spirit? If so, God is ready to do great things for us. Let us wait on Him in silence. . . . .

A person present writes: "At the conclusion of Mr. Smith's address he called on us to place ourselves in an attitude of waiting, and expectant believing prayer. The large meeting remained on their knees for some time in most impressive silence. A feeling of inexpressible sweetness and awe filled many hearts. There were no visible signs—no emotion of any kind to be seen. A hymn was then sung, and a few words addressed to us to the effect that we were to wait and let the blessing descend just in God's own way; to expect no sign or any unusual manifestation. The Rev. Mr. Christopher closed in prayer, the blessing was pronounced, and the meeting quietly separated. Almost every one went home in silence, and there is reason to believe that great numbers received 'in quietness and assurance' 'the promise of the Father' that night. Many Christians testify that they awoke that memorable Sabbath morning with not merely a full sense, but an overflowing consciousness of the blessed Saviour's presence. As these went to their settled homes in various parts of the globe, they carry, we trust, with them the blessing of 'the living water' to many thirsty souls. To these indeed had the experience been realised more than they had ever conceived it possible —'To appoint unto them that mourn in Zion, to give them beauty for ashes, the oil of joy for mourning, the garment of praise for the spirit of heaviness.'

"At the early morning prayer meeting of that true Sabbath day, or rather it should be called '*Praise* meeting,' the new-born spirit of full trust seemed to burst forth spontaneously from lips now anointed with true fire from God's altar. Mr. Smith observed that he had no doubt that there were many present who would wish to express their feelings of thankfulness and praise, but who would not venture to speak before so large an audience, and suggested the happy thought that any such should just express themselves in Scripture language as they sat, any sisters as well. Surely none of those fifteen hundred present will ever forget the scene which followed. For fifteen or twenty minutes there was a running utterance of praise all over the great Corn Exchange, and in exact Scripture language. Some, whose timidity was so great that they dared not venture to speak before so many, opened their Bibles, and, with trembling lips but with full hearts, *read* their own happy portion. Once I noticed when the praise seemed to have subsided a little and there seemed a little hesitancy, that a clear voice was heard, 'Let *everything that hath breath* praise the Lord!' This seemed to bring out scores of voices which had not been heard before.

"Return unto thy Sabbath, O my soul, for the Lord hath dealt bountifully with thee.'"

At 9.30 o'clock we again assembled to spend a quiet hour before the time of public worship. After prayer by Rev. Canon Battersby, Psalm cxlix. was read: "Sing unto the Lord a *new* song," every day; an old one will not do, for "His mercies are new every morning." It may be old words, but it must have a new meaning in the heart. "Let the children of Zion be joyful in their King." This is impossible till they have fully submitted to Him. "Let them praise His name in the dance!" I do not advocate a literal rendering of this now; but it would be less unscriptural to do it than to "go mourning all the day." I have seen those whose religion seemed like an ache to them; but I never saw so many restful countenances together as are now in this meeting. "The Lord taketh pleasure in His people." We cannot comprehend how He can do so, but we believe it. "The meek will He beautify with salvation." Who are the meek? Those who submit themselves to Him every hour. "He will beautify the meek with salvation, and they shall sing aloud on their beds." We ask every Christian present to have a Scriptural experience by doing this to-night,—singing aloud on your bed. It is not enough to think sweet thoughts of the Lord. "I will praise Thee with joyful *mouth*." You know not what you miss when you keep the praise in. Say out your love to a friend, and your relations to him will be changed by the act. Your soul will go out freely to Him now. Praise God out loud, and see how it will help you to live with Him. Go to sleep praising Him, and in the morning it will not be a getting back to a distant God, but "*when I awake* I am still with Thee." "Let the high praises of God be *in your mouth*," on your lips. Try the effect of saying frequently (in an undertone or whisper, where a louder voice is unsuitable), "*Praise the Lord!*"—not mechanically, but with your heart in it, and see how it will turn life to one long psalm. Then the two-edged sword will be yours; one edge to divide between joint and marrow, separating the vile from us in our inmost souls, and the other edge against the King's enemies. "To bind their kings with fetters." He now binds the sins that once ruled over us as kings. "What all? Even my peculiar temper?" says one. Cannot God, who made the universe, control your tempers! Let us "execute upon them the judgment written: This honour have all His saints. PRAISE YE THE LORD!" Thus endeth the 149th Psalm. Thus may your life and mine be lived and ended on earth.

R. PEARSALL SMITH: The time will come for the proving of your faith. You may have special temptations of Satan after this time of baptism at Oxford.

You may fancy that your faith will change the order of the Word and Providence of God. You may be tempted to do, under the name of faith, presumptuous things, or even to turn back to the world. Be careful to answer the devil in the words given you by God. Dread a cold life of mere duty, but *flee* fanaticism; it is the devil's special lure to saintly souls, and it has prevailed where all else has failed. "Be sober, be vigilant;" the devil walks about seeking to destroy you. Having resisted the devil for yourself, you can then have faith to deal with his work in other souls.

Learn to keep your soul's sabbath in God. I would rather have God use me to settle ten persons in abiding communion with Himself, than to see a hundred conversions of those who would live on the average level of professing Christians; for the ten who learned to walk with God would do more in the conversion of souls than the hundred, many of whom would be but stumbling-blocks in the way of sinners.

As you walk in quietness of soul with Christ, and gain more of the mind that was in Him, you will not only rejoice with your Lord, but find it your highest joy to "fill up that which is behind of the sufferings of Christ for His body's sake"—yet not in any approach to the thought of atonement. "If we suffer we shall also reign with Him." If you weep with a friend you come far nearer than when you rejoice with him. Nothing so binds hearts together. This is fellowship. We are not always sitting in clouds tuning spiritual harps, for life is a plain homely thing to be lived out, not in doing great things, but in doing plain things well. Christ sanctified labour, sorrow, and weariness for us. Yet there comes a thrill, an intense emotion, into the most ordinary life and occupation which is illuminated by the presence of Jesus.

Never forget that the highest elevations of experience involve the most fearful dangers. Yet do not look too much at man. The sailor's safety at the mast-head is in looking *up*. Be it ours to be ever "looking unto Jesus."

Rev. F. SULIVAN (Brighton): We have heard great things, and received great things. We have seen Jesus! As we have gone on and on there has been more and more unveiling of self, and then the Sun of Righteousness has risen with healing in His wings. May others take knowledge of us that we have been with Jesus—not with saints only at Oxford! —Jesus has been "in the midst," and we have received "grace for grace,"—"wave upon wave" is the meaning,—an ever-flowing tide of grace, pardon, life, strength, love, joy, peace. "All my springs are in *Thee*";—not in the Oxford Conference, but in Jesus.

Pastor THEODORE MONOD, at the Wesleyan Chapel: (John xiv. 6).—"Let not your heart," &c. Thomas asks the way, and Jesus said, "I am the Way," &c. Man has completely lost his way, and many are saying, like the fool of old, "there is no God." They don't know how to approach God, and would not wish it if they could. The world is not holy. Take up the first newspaper that comes in your way, and you will see the proof of this—you need no more. Left to Nature, what do we know about heaven? I wonder *where* and *how* it is to be found in nature? And if we look at death, it does not seem that *that* is the way to a better world; and if we are sure there is a better world, how do we find the way to get there? Happiness is living in your own element, and being at liberty there. We were made *by* and *for* God, and because we have lost God, the voice of sighing goes up from this little world day and night. But if man could not set up a ladder from earth to heaven, could God let down a ladder from heaven to earth? Indeed He could, and He has done it through Jesus Christ. He brings God to man, and therefore brings men to God. He took upon Him our nature, that we might take His. He has reconciled us unto God. He came to tell us that God loves us and is *love*. "He that hath seen me, hath seen the Father." "God so loved the world," &c. In Him, we are one with God. Then we are on the way not only to God, but holiness. You might as well look at the sun, and say you did not see the light, as be in God, and not be holy. So with happiness—Jesus Christ is our happiness. Do you think your children are the losers when they give themselves up to your will? Do they have a hard time of it when they trust themselves to you? Jesus is the way to Heaven and to happiness; and if it were not so, He says, He would have told us.

A little child on her dying-bed said—"It's so dark, I want my father to come with me." Her father had to tell her he could not go with her. Then she said, "I want my mother"; but her mother had to say the same. But they said, "Jesus will go with you." Then she said, "I am so happy now, I have found Jesus." Having found Jesus, we have found the *Way*. Many people think Christ is a good way; but there are other ways. If I were speaking to other than believers, I might speak of these other ways, but *you* know that He is the *way*. But how? You might ask the way to Paris, and you may teach others, but that won't take you there. You remain here just the same. You have to take the steps. The first step you must take yourself if you will go there. The most remarkable phrase in the text is, "*I am the way.*" Do you think any one who was not the way would have said this? They might say, I'll show you, or teach you, the way. He, Jesus, says, "I am the way." What does it mean? It means that it is a living way: a living person. When you have found Him; you have found the way. "I am the way, the truth, and *the life*." Now there are souls in this very town, at this very time, inquiring of this brother and that, for the *way*. A simple illustration may help us to understand it. A child wanders a few steps out of his father's house. Then he gets further away, running after some flower, some butterfly, till he finds himself in the midst of a forest, and he is tired and hungry, and he wants his home, and cannot find the way. It gets dark, and he cries bitterly, "Father, Father!" Presently he hears footsteps, a voice; it is his brother's voice. His brother is seeking him. He finds him. carries him away to his father. Well, if that child is asked what way he took to get there, he would say, pointing to his brother, "He was my way. I trusted myself to him. I never even thought about trusting him, for I knew he would take me home." Now every soul in heaven will have nothing else to say than this,—"When I heard my Saviour's voice, I opened my heart, and said I wanted to go home!" Now do you think, brothers and sisters, He could have made the way more accessible than He has made it? The way begins on the very seat where you are sitting. He is nearer than the one who touches your elbow as you sit. Will you let Him take you home? Now is it necessary that I should tell you that if He is *the way* He is *all* the way? He carries the wandering sheep all the way rejoicing. I havē preached on that text, and yet did not trust Him *altogether*. I trusted Him sometimes, when I had a great thing to do (as if anything was great in His eyes!) But for the little things, I trusted Him not (as if anything was little in His eyes!) If He is the way *at all*, He is *all* the way. What would you think of a piece of a bridge, and not a whole bridge; built at each end, and not in the middle? All Christians have seen these things, but all have not practically believed them. Oh! that this might be to some the last moment of a partial faith, the first of complete trust!

3 O'CLOCK P.M.

The Corn Exchange was again filled to hear Mrs. R. P. SMITH'S daily "Bible Lesson," and after it the

FOUR O'CLOCK MEETING

was convened. Many had made great sacrifices, and come long distances, from the Continent and elsewhere, and there was an eager desire to embrace every opportunity of being in the atmosphere of the prayer, hymns, and teaching. It was remarked that the meetings were solemn enough for Episcopalians, orderly enough for Presbyterians, warm enough for Methodists, and quiet enough for the Society of Friends. We do not remember to have heard a single discussion or controversy. The hearts of those present were too much absorbed in seeking a realisation of full surrender, full trust, and full union with the Lord to stop to argue. Those who had come up to Oxford with deep prejudices heard, as they freely and often said, nothing which had not been in substance taught by themselves. The point that was kept before the meeting was, that *holiness by faith is practicable.* If we want others to believe that this is true, our best way is not to argue, but to *practise* it.

This had been grasped by many, and the remainder of the meeting was now largely occupied in seeking to be "rooted and grounded in love," established in the marvellous grace which had opened upon our souls.

Pastor THEODORE MONOD (Luke viii.): It was Jesus' work to preach *glad* tidings. If our preaching does not make people glad, we have not got the right message. Until they see that it makes *us* happy, people will not believe that it is glad tidings. The seed is the Word of God. That is what we have to sow; not flowers, but seed; not our experience, though our witnessing is helpful, as it corroborates the Word of God—but we are to sow *the* Word which, being God's, has life and power in itself. And if we want proof that this Oxford meeting has been of Him, it is this, that it has led us to more searching of God's Word, more love for it, and more complete trust in it.

Verse 12. The seed having been sown, "*then* cometh the Devil." Remember that. When you leave the meeting Satan will come to you to take it away, "lest they should believe." God's Word is clear enough for any thirsty soul, but He will not *force* us into obedience. Verse 13: "They receive the word with joy." So it has been received here. We see it not only on the platform and meeting, but even in the street, because the presence of the Lord is here. "In time of temptation they fall away." You say, "Don't say that. It alarms us." No, no! Just pray in faith, "Deliver us from evil—*for Thine is the power.*" "Choked with cares." It takes many cares to choke a man. You need never have another anxious care if you will yield obedience to the Word, "Casting all your care upon Him, for He careth for you." It is not needful for two to take care; if God cares for you, you need to take none. Nay, but we believe the seed has here been sown in good ground, and in honest and true hearts, who will "bring forth fruit" in abundance.

Rev. F. Sulivan: "Believest thou that I am able to do this?" I am sure that the response of many hearts is, as never before, "Yea, Lord." This is what He has been so long waiting for. Jesus is all and in all now. Failure came before because it was partly Christ and partly self. We sought to make the great God an instrument in our hands, now we abandon ourselves to be an instrument in His hands. It is just a question of simple full trust; the full surrender of self, and then trusting Him to keep us. Some say, "What will you do to-morrow?" I have nothing to do with to-morrow. It is living a moment at a time, my soul hanging on Him, and saying, "I will" to every indication of His will. May our chariot wheels run henceforth in the two lines of trust and expectation.

R. Pearsall Smith: Do you not hear the gentle voice of Jesus saying to your soul, "Lovest thou Me?" After a meeting, a young man came to me and said, "When a boy you asked me, 'Do you love Jesus?' It brought me under conviction of sin, and I was converted. I gave myself to the ministry, and at the college one day, as we were kneeling in the young men's meeting, another voice than yours seemed to say to me, 'Lovest thou Me?' I answered, quickly, 'Yes, Lord, thou knowest that I love Thee.' Again, and in more searching tones, the question came to my soul, '*Lovest thou Me?*' Again I answered, but less confidently. When a third time the question sounded in my heart, I felt how dearly I loved my own reputation, and ease, and many other things. My heart seemed all at once like a cage of unclean birds, as I saw my remaining sins. There and then I renounced all that I could see, and gave myself to the Lord for a life of obedience and trust as never before. When we rose from our knees, I told my fellow-students what I had done, and since then I have lived in and for Christ as never before."

Can you answer to the Lord's question, dear Christian, "Lovest thou Me?" Does any idol of position, wealth, reputation, remain in the temple of your soul? Do you, so far as you know, give your all to Christ? If an earthly lover cannot be satisfied with less than the whole heart, will you put off Christ with less than the supreme devotion of your soul?

Do not, however, try to analyse your love. You cannot ascertain the fact of your vision by closing your eyes and seeking a consciousness of sight. You can n realise faith thus, but by looking at its object—Christ. If you try for five minutes to analyse your love to your dearest earthly friend, you will not know if you love that one at all. But in proportion as you give yourself to another will you love that one. Never *try* to love another, it will paralyse your affections. When your *all* is given to God, love will spring up unsought.

"He that keepeth My commandments, he it is that loveth Me." Let us see to it that love to Christ is not a mere sentiment, but the power of our life reaching out to sinners and saints. I have seen some deplorable cases of a religion of sentiment apart from practical obedience. It is my greatest dread in watching for souls. God must have *realities.* "*Lovest thou Me?*" Do you know the voice that to-day whispers this in your heart. "I died for thee, wilt thou live for Me?" May we not say, "Lord, Thou knowest all things; Thou knowest that I love Thee!" Let each evermore carry with him the solemn consciousness of having given himself, without a single reserve, to the Lord Jesus. We are thus learning that "He that dwelleth in love dwelleth in God, and God in Him."

The meeting gathered at 8.15 in the evening, after the close of the public services.

R. PEARSALL SMITH (Joshua vii.): A great triumph had been gained at Jericho. By faith even its untouched walls had fallen. How strong Israel felt after it when they came to little Ai. They did not feel the need of all their force, were defeated, and under a loss of only thirty-five men were completely demoralised, their hearts like water. A small failure paralyses our tongue for the Gospel message; continued failure breaks our spirit, destroys the courage of faith which brings the victory. On their faces on the ground they now lie, confessing and confessing again, and bewailing the failure. This looks humble, but it is not what God wants. "Wherefore liest thou thus upon thy face? Get thee up!" Israel could not stand before their enemies till they put away the accursed thing. There was good intention in Joshua, but he had not watched God's way. He now, in three lots among 1,200,000 people, found the cause. "Be sure your sin will find you out." If you are not in full communion and victory let God show you your hidden sin—it may be in your household, and almost forgotten.

A Babylonish garment had been hidden by Achan. Babylon is false religion. Have you any rags of your own righteousness left? Any wedge of gold, the heart's precious idol, in your household state? Or is the love of money, "the root of all evil," festering in the secret places of your soul? Bring them to the valley of Achor and stone them with stones, burn them with fire, and raise over them a great heap of stones so that you shall never see them again. Do this with your easily-besetting sin, whether it be external act or inward evil, or that root of all other sin, unbelief. Do it now as you sit in your seat. At Waterloo the possession of a little cottage decided the fate of nations. Satan intrenches himself in some small thing in the will. A child who yields 999 things to his parent, must be unhappy if the thousandth thing is withheld; nor can the parent express his love till the last point is yielded. Now hundreds in this room have said that it was in yielding their last reserve that they have found full communion; then harmony was realised, and they could utter a perpetual "Yes, Lord," to each expression of His will.

There is another mention of the Valley of Achor (Hosea ii. 14-21) which, in this quiet peaceful gathering, we shall do well to turn to in order to open the glorious possibilities of the Christian's life. "I will allure her, and bring her into the wilderness, and speak comfortably to her." The wilderness here is not the wilderness of disobedience, but of trial. God never meant us to have two wildernesses, an inward and an outward. "In Me ye shall have peace," a life of unbroken communion, though in the world ye have tribulation. Happy they who have only an outward wilderness, while within is corn and wine.

Beloved, the Lord may be drawing your soul to Himself by sorrow. Has the light of your household, the sunshine of your life been withdrawn? Our Father knows that eternity outweighs time, and He is preparing you for it. The polishing is sharp, but it prepares the rough diamond for honour. Ah! dear young friends, are you finding earth's joys but apples of Sodom, bitter ashes on your lips? Do you know that sorrow, worse than that from circumstances, the interior sense of desolation and despair at times to overshadow your heart? Your Beloved is leading you into the wilderness of separation, but it is that He may speak comfortably to you. He will give you vineyards—joy —from thence; a joy that will remain. You shall know the Valley of Achor, the place of entire absolute renunciation of all discovered evil, for a door of heavenly blessing. To some Oxford has been like death itself in the yielding of unlawful things dearer than life, but let us die to the world, not groaning, but singing. Let us have sudden deaths to self, and then see to it that there is no revival of the old sins.

"And she shall sing as in the days of her youth, even as in the day when I brought her up out of the land of Egypt." Did you ever before share such notes of praise as have ascended within the past few days? They are higher, clearer notes than even the joy of conversion. The coming up out of the wilderness leaning on the arm of your Beloved, is a deeper joy than coming up out of the world. Jordan opens a better land than the Red Sea. A new song has been put into many mouths here, and their sorrow turned to laughter; for they have found their Achor, the place of entire renunciation.

But this is not all, the best is to come. "And it shall be in that day, saith the Lord, that thou shalt call me Husband, and shalt call me no more Master." Our Lord can never be satisfied until He teaches us to "dwell at ease" in the sweet restful communion of His Divine love. Conceive of a prince calling the poorest scullery-maid to his throne. He could never be satisfied till she knew and believed in his love so as to be "at ease" in his companionship. Beloved, have you not in your earlier experiences of grace known something of this? Why was it? You were in grace and in full obedience. Are you so now? Have you fallen from grace into a legal life, one of mere duty, with its anxious face and restless effort, instead of the joyous ease of a responsive love? Yield up your distrust, put away every conflicting affection. Let your doubting heart abandon itself to the loving call of Jesus.

The point at which I have learned to guard my obedience is in serving Him from love, and not duty, which is but a cold word. When the mother does her "*duty*" to her child, the joy, the tender sweetness of maternal relationship is gone. When the hitherto responsive happy wife has begun a *duty*-life, her home becomes a prison. There is no obedience, yea slavery, like that of a mother's or a wife's love, but it is a delicious bondage. It knows nothing of "sacrifice," whatever may be given up; its very life is lost in that of another. Happy they who understand the self-forgetfulness of love!

"I will betroth thee unto Me for ever." This is more than pardon. Scripture opens with an earthly marriage, and closes with a heavenly, and throughout its pages are types and songs for those who, themselves in a risen life, are "married to Him that is risen from the dead." Earthly relationships are created but to reveal heavenly realities of union with our Lord. "This is a great mystery, but I speak concerning Christ and the Church." "My Beloved is mine and I am His." This is glorious; but further on a deeper apprehension of Christ's love says, "I am my Beloved's, and my Beloved is mine." Faith contradicts even our moral sense of our unworthiness of such communion, and accepts the wonderful thought that Christ delights in us; that we are even necessary to His happiness. Let us be careful as we speak of these things. I believe that the most loathsome thing in the sight of God is the truth held in unrighteousness; talking of being "whiter than snow," while indulging in unforsaken sin; of being "seated in heavenly places" while walking in the mire. Would to God that we may never again let our hearts go out to any conflicting love. May the Lord save us from preaching "high doctrines" and living in low practice!

(Canticles ii. 10-12). The birds have been singing though we heard them not, but now the winter of our soul is gone; the ice-bound heart is melted, and the summer time has come. We are to have henceforth the warmth and life of Christ in all our being. We are in the new creation; all things are become new. With Christ in the heart all the day there is now no need to wrestle for a blessing; we will but whisper our wants in the ear of the Bridegroom of our souls. Look up in the face of our Beloved to-night. Oh, that some rays of His love may illumine our faces; that we may with Him love and serve even the unlovely! There are traces of true beauty, an imparted radiance, in the faces of the "pure in heart," who, even in this life, "see God."

The heavenly Lord is offering His love and communion to many hearts this evening as really as ever did any earthly suitor to the object of His love. *Will you take Him* NOW?

(Prayer.) Oh, Thou, the Chief among ten thousand, the altogether lovely One, Thou hast come to us to-night, not in the terror of the law; but in love to claim our hearts for Thyself. We worship Thee, O Son of God. We adore Thee in thine infinite holiness. We are utterly unworthy, but we know and believe Thy love. We yield to Thee to-night every reserve of our being. We renounce every idol of our affections. Utterly and entirely, in every department of our being, we rejoice to give ourselves to Thee. Thou dost accept what Thou hast in love called for. We are Thine; Thine alone; Thine for time and for eternity. With the intelligent apprehension of faith, we give Thee our hearts, and accept Thine own word put upon our lips, "Thy Maker is Thy Husband."

Hymn—"Safe in the arms of Jesus."

CHAPTER X.

Monday Morning.

7 o'clock a.m.

A LETTER of praise was read, and, after prayer by Lord Radstock, Psalm xci. was repeated in response. A morning doxology was then sung.

R. Pearsall Smith: It was needful for a time to turn our attention inward to find the causes of the soul-sickness of which so many complained. A good physician first finds the cause and then heals. The Lord has given us the secret of soul-health, and we have put ourselves into His hands without reserve. I am so anxious, now that we have learned these lessons of faith, that we should not be dwelling on our own experience, but on Christ. Let us walk in the light of God, not in the dimness of our own emotions. We will let the rays of the Sun of Righteousness fill our souls.

We have got much from the Lord—let us honour His grace by asking for more. My own rule is, when He gives me a blessing at once to ask for twice as much. I would not be outdone in coveting by any merchant prince. "Covet earnestly the best gifts." Let us not be afraid to ask great things, glorious things. Let us get our souls into harmony with the Lord Jesus and we may ask what we will. Napoleon "subdued kingdoms" with the sword. We are to do it "by faith." We cannot pray this prayer of faith while a single known sin, however small, is allowed. Let us begin each day, realising by simple trust that not a cloud, nay, nor a shadow, is between our souls and the great throne. Abide thus. Should failure come, let us never delay for one instant a full confession and restoration. Sometimes in this life of full faith, there may come a momentary parenthesis of failure. We must expect these, but if we stumble we will not lie there an instant. The way back is open. "If we confess our sins, He is faithful and just to forgive us our sins, and to cleanse us from all unrighteousness." He who thus claims instantaneous restoration, finds failure to fade out of the life and communion to become more and more unbroken.

Let not our conscience be clouded because we find it impossible to *like* every Christian. There is many a Christian whom I do *love* "with a pure heart fervently" whom I do not *like*. When two sisters in the higher experience of grace, living alone with each other, were congratulated on their happiness in having such companionship, the reply was, "It takes all the grace we have received to bear each other's peculiarities." I love my brother, but the black dog that goes with him I dislike. I love the Christian, but dislike his infirmities. It was a great relief when I understood this.

Such a dread comes over my soul lest I should take any of the glory that belongs to God. "If ye will not hear, and if ye will not lay it to heart to give glory unto My name, saith the Lord of Hosts, I will even send a curse upon you, and I will curse your blessings."

The Lord save you and me from robbery of God, and from ever snatching our thank-offerings of service from off His altar. Beloved minister, forget your "good" sermons, and trust the Lord about the "poor" ones preached in faith. Let us have no retrospective acts—make our lives a succession of "henceforths." It is marvellous how indifferent the soul becomes to praise or blame while it is "looking unto Jesus." Praise then makes us feel our unworthiness and littleness, and persecution makes us rejoice.

In regard to money, we read, "Having food and raiment let us be therewith content." Can you, dear Christian, say that in this thing you are obeying the Lord? Has He all your cares, if you are poor; and if you are rich you may be a faithful steward. Give what costs you something in self-denial, and not your surplus only. I know a Christian who began life by giving away one-half his income to the Lord; when his income was £50 a-year he gave away £25; when £100 he gave £50, and so on as he increased. Notwithstanding all this he became very wealthy. Another, rich in faith, whose princely gifts have for nearly half a century been poured in the Lord's treasury, and who was for some days here with us at Oxford, began with giving one-tenth, and, as he was prospered, he increased to two, then three-tenths of his income, and so on till he bestowed nine-tenths; and still his estate grew larger. This may not be for all to do, but the Lord can trust consecrated stewards with wealth. The rust does not reach money that is in use, nor the moth fret garments that are worn.

Permit me here to say that those who preach the

Gospel should be, in many cases, better cared for than they are. Not having myself to accept aught from anyone for my own use or expenses, I can speak the more freely of this. I have been distressed to see Evangelists making long journeys, preaching ten and twelve times a-week, pouring out their very lives for the Gospel, and receiving but a pittance from Christians. I pray you to care for such, and to see that the advancing cost of living is met by corresponding supplies to ministers of the Gospel. I know the inner life of many ministers, godly, spiritual, men who would die for their people, and yet, who are allowed to suffer painfully from the advanced price of necessaries. It is a part of your love and consecration to Christ to care for your minister. After you have prayed for him nd supplied his needs generously, you will be surprised how many more virtues you find in him than when you prayed little, gave little, and criticised much. If consecration is of the Lord it is immensely practical and reaches into the minutest details of Christian life. Let us receive Jesus into our souls, and all these details will, without effort or strain, adjust themselves in harmony with His mind. Restless scrupulosity will be lost in love and communion. We well know the truth of Augustine's celebrated saying, "Love and do what you please!"—because our desires will be in harmony with God."

The Rev. J. Turner (vicar of Deddington, Oxfordshire) observed: This is not the time to act the part of a timid Nicodemus, and therefore I dare not resist the dictates of the Spirit by keeping any longer silent. I learned much of the truth spoken of at these meetings about sanctification, from the teaching and example of a departed sainted mother. But I have to say with regret that I learned these truths only in *theory.* During these meetings the Spirit has taught me the doctrine as to "the higher Christian life," and enabled me to enter upon it as a *reality.* One effect of this rest of faith I will state. I was called by God to occupy a peculiarly trying post in His Church; I have no hesitation in saying, from much knowledge of parishes in various parts of the country, that I have unusual trials and difficulties. These were so great that I had prayed to be removed to some other place of work, though I felt assured God had placed me where I now am. I might liken myself to a lion confined in a cage, ever knocking his head against the iron bars. Thank God, I have learned during these happy days (the happiest of my life) "To be content in that state wherein God has placed me," and I shal return to my parish, and regard it as the ante-chamber of heaven, so long as it may please God to keep me labouring there.

Another blessed result I would mention. I experienced unusual blessing in my church yesterday (Sunday). I gave notice at the morning service that in the evening an account would be given of the outpouring of the Spirit at these Oxford meetings; but even that short description of what God had done, seemed to bring a blessing with it to the congregation. To enable the Nonconformists to attend, they closed one of their chapels, and preacher and people all came to church, and at the two other chapels the services were shortened. I am glad to say that my Dissenting parishioners are willing thus to act with me on all occasions of special services in my church or schoolroom. The church was crowded in the evening; and as it was in the morning, so in the evening, when the gracious times of refreshing at Oxford were made known, "the Holy Ghost fell on them that heard the word." There was an after-meeting at the close of the service, in which assistance was given by a dear friend, Mr. Richardson, of St. Benet's, London. Such a scene Deddington Church never presented before within the memory of living men, though there have been many seasons of great blessing within the last ten years. All, it is believed, felt the presence of the Spirit. Some gave themselves to Christ for the first time, and others experienced a fresh baptism of the Spirit.

Mr. Turner concluded by asking prayer for his parish, that God may mightily carry on the work He has begun, so that many souls may be added to Christ, and all believing led into the full experience of entire sanctification.

So many were anxious to bear testimony to the blessing received at Oxford, who could not be heard for want of time, that those who had found a definite step of faith were invited to rise and sing a doxology, which was done with much feeling by a large number.

11.45 O'CLOCK A.M.

The meeting was opened with prayer by the Rev. G. R. Thornton, followed by R. Pearsall Smith (Rom. xii.): Before we part I desire again to impress upon you that the privilege of the Rest of Faith we are *setting* before you here is not a finality but the true and only commencement of a life of progressive sanctification. After beseeching us to present our bodies a living sacrifice to the Lord, the Apostle, from this point of entire consecration, teaches us to be not conformed to this world but transformed; proving in each daily, hourly duty what is the good and acceptable will of God. There is no finality short of the Throne of God. We find that we have but just commenced on a life of uniform progress—the healthful growth of the soul—and we will be very tender of those who are to-day where we were yesterday. Let us not expect any one else to walk by *our* present light. My ignorance of God's will may permit me to do some things that you cannot, and *vice versa*. Bear with me till I receive your light, and I will bear with you; for as we walk in entire consecration God will teach us both that "true religion resides *in the will*." Let us place *our will*, not merely under, but *in* the will of God, and the details of life will soon be adjusted by the indwelling Spirit opening the Word to our hearts and understanding. For this let us read our Bible sometimes on our knees. As young Hallam said, after a wearying search for rest in the philosophies of the day, "It is God's truth because it is man's book. It fits into every fold of the human heart"—and so it does, meeting every need and satisfying it.

Henry Varley: Since Christ is my strength I shall with ease mount up with wings as eagles. It is no strain to the eagle to mount. Faith receives a graceful glorious overcoming life, for it is Christ's own eternal life. It gravitates to its own centre in God and not toward the world. If we receive the "life more abundantly," it is not hard to obey—obedience is joyous. It comes by faith. What overcomes the world? "Even our faith." How is the devil to be resisted? "Steadfast in the faith." What is our defence? "The shield of faith." Paul began with, "What wilt Thou have me to *do?*" but ended with, "I've kept the faith." Oh, sirs, it was faith that subdued kingdoms, obtained promises! Put your foot on each promise and say, "*It is mine.*" Believe against your own consciousness. I would a thousand times sooner believe God than my own feelings. The one we love most is the one we would trust in the darkest place of our history. If, with the best of earth's saints, you now and then pass through a tunnel where God is not seen, trust Him in the dark.

Faith stopped the mouth of lions. When in their midst Daniel's nerves were unshaken, as shown by his preserving the polite form of speech used to Eastern monarchs, "O King live for ever!" As you gaze upon Jesus in His book, the Spirit will take of the glory and make it over to you, "changed into the same image" by beholding. What makes yonder moon, shining in her fulness, so bright? She is looking at the sun; and if you and I are looking unto Jesus we shall reflect His light, though in ourselves opaque bodies.

This address was followed by the reading of Mark xiv. 3-9. by the leader of the meeting: It was not the "*duty*" of the woman to break the alabaster box. She would not have been under any condemnation had she not done it. No injunction urged her to the act. A command would have deprived it of the joyful spontaneousness of love. Nothing in the life of Christ seems to have met the wants of his human heart so much as this. Forget for the time the very thought of duty and let your hearts act to the response of love. Some here know the joy of giving their best and dearest to the Lord. We will now kneel. Shut out the thought that you "must" give anything, and if your heart prompts you to any rich gift to the Lord pour it out as an alabaster box of ointment upon His blessed person. I am not asking you for money. We "have all and abound;" even if poor in the eyes of men faith has "the cattle on a thousand hills." We desire to carry on God's work on the Continent, but we do not ask even for this. Does the way open for you to leave a profitable business to preach? Have you a son, a daughter, to offer for the missionary field. Upon your knees let your inmost heart respond to the love of Jesus.

We knelt in vocal and then silent prayer. We have reason to believe that many then and there joyously devoted their best to the Lord. Many special gifts of jewellery and money were sent in, and some days after came a cheque, from one who would not communicate his name, for a thousand pounds, marked "*An Alabaster Box.*" This and the surplus of expenses at Oxford, over the cost of rooms, &c., was appropriated to the spread of the Gospel in its fulness on the Continent. Many will long remember those minutes of silent prayer and the joy of thankofferings there poured out to the Lord.

THE GENERAL MEETING AT 4 O'CLOCK*

was devoted mostly to some practical suggestions as to

* A report of Mrs. Smith's address, at 3 o'clock, will be found in the numbers of *The Christian* for September.

living out the life of faith. "Why," asked one, "do you not urge Christians to work?" "There is no need, if they but accept the privileges we press upon them," was the reply. "The great trouble we have with those who have found the joy and communion of a life of full trust is to keep them from ruining their health by overwork, and from giving away more than their circumstances will rightly admit of. Guided by experience in the past, we look for more conversions at the Oxford Meetings than if we had held purely evangelistic services, and in their after-results an hundred-fold. "Restore unto me the joy of Thy salvation, and uphold me with Thy free Spirit"—this first—"*then will I teach transgressors Thy ways; and sinners shall be converted unto Thee.*"

R. PEARSALL SMITH: We have sought here a Scriptural experience of faith, of victory, of communion, of love, of worship. "They that seek *shall* find"—it is no uncertain search. If we have got up higher, it is but to see how much more of the land is yet to be possessed. If we have got down lower, it is at the foot of the Cross. If we have learned any "new views," they are visions of the evil of self and of the exceeding power of Christ to us-ward. I believe that you will always greet with joy any with whom you have here worshipped. We "believe in the communion of saints" as never before. It does seem as if something almost more than an earthly illumination were on faces around me. We Anglo-Saxon people are so cold! In danger of freezing, we would defend ourselves against warmth. I wish we had more of the glow and *fire in which* the Bible was written. We have done too much toward interpreting it as a book of doctrines, instead of a *life*. Thank God for the well-worn Bibles of England. Nowhere is *the* Book so much studied. Is the law written in your minds? Now let the Lord put it in your heart's affections. Jesus would win *enthusiasm*. Love is a passion in the human soul, and when we devote ourselves in the entireness of our being to God, His love becomes the absorbing life of our life. The victory over sin is an immense blessing, but only a negative. Love is positive. It is the outflowing exertive life of God in our souls.

Never was the Bible so sweet as now. The simple reading of a passage seems to affect the hearts of the hearers more than the most eloquent sermon ordinarily. We have learned to trust the promise in the present moment. It is now five minutes to five o'clock, and He is saving us from our sins. Will He not do this at five o'clock, and in each succeeding five minutes of our life, yea, until His coming to receive us to Himself?

Out upon the Sierra Nevada Mountains, near to the busy whirl of the Pacific metropolis, San Francisco, lies Lake Tahoe. It is twenty-three miles long, ten miles wide, and so deep that the line at nineteen hundred feet does not touch bottom; and all this five thousand feet above the neighbouring ocean. Storms come and go below its level. Its surface the while is so still and the water so clear that the eye can penetrate, it is said, a hundred feet into its depths. A bell can be heard for ten or twenty miles. Around its mild verdant sides are the mountains, ever crowned with snow. The sky above is as calm as the motionless water. Nature loses scarcely anything of its clear outline as it is reflected there. Here I learned something of what *rest* is. Day after day I opened my heart to let the sweet influences of Nature's sabbath pervade my soul. It was a faint type of what I have found in Christ.

In the pressure of the greatest responsibilities, in the worry of small cares, in the pressure of the crises of your life, you may have the Lake Tahoe rest in the will of God. Learn to walk in that calm. The power and effectiveness of your life will be doubled; your cares will be gone. From this inward rest you will be able to look into the souls of men before you in your ministry. Then, with the gentle dew of the Spirit upon you, the effectual "communication of the Spirit" shall be felt by thousands.

(Prayer.) Lord! fill us with Thy Spirit this afternoon. In this calm, quiet Sabbath hour penetrate our very souls with Thine own restful presence. Thou art so great, Thou canst not be agitated; and Thou art so great in us that we will not be agitated. Now, Lord, teach us to keep Thy sabbath in every remaining moment of our lives, that, like a river, they may flow on, without return tides or cross-currents, till we reach the great ocean of eternity. Our prayer to Thee this afternoon is for Thy promised rest for the weary souls of Thy children—for yet deeper *rest*. We have asked for rest—THOU ART GIVING IT TO US.

MINISTERIAL CONFERENCE.

6 O'CLOCK P.M.

We were reminded that we were not to be ashamed *before* men of Christ's words or Christ's truth. None retain the blessing of full faith, and its consequent victory, who refuse to acknowledge, on suitable occasions, what God has done for them. The saintly John Fletcher four times fell back into the old level of life by fearing to witness for this grace of God. The Lord will not have secret disciples. In common life we should esteem him mean who allowed others to stand forward and receive persecution for a truth enjoyed secretly by himself.

Would that there were written inside of every pulpit, in full view of the preacher, "HE *made Himself of no reputation.*" He, the only One in all the universe who ever deserved a reputation, put it away from Him. Shame on us if any are seeking reputation for ourselves! Let the Lord of life and glory, once the servant of men, be your only reputation. Be as eager to escape it as ever you were to win it. It is often the last weight laid aside in entire consecration.

If you would speak to a brother about a fault, get down *beneath him.* It fell to my lot once to admonish a servant of God in a conspicuous position, and I went to the Lord to prepare me for it. The means He took were to give me such a vivid remembrance of my own failures, since I was a Christian, as I had never had before. I felt that I could weep for myself. This gave me place in the Christian's heart.

Probably the greatest sin of the ministry is speaking evil needlessly of brethren. We obey God when He says, "Thou shalt not steal." Obey Him no less when He says, "Speak evil of no man." I entreat you let this sink in your hearts. If we see failure, let us speak to God; then to the unhappy one who has stumbled, "restoring such an one in the spirit of meekness, considering whether thou also be tempted."

Prayer by Rev. F. Sulivan.

Rev. BARON HART (Paris): This meeting has been a great blessing to me—not in any great joy or rapture, but in finding full rest in the Lord. It is, indeed, a wonderful change since those dark times when I had to teach to others what I did not fully receive myself. I have been reminded of the Saviour's loving reproach, "Have I been so long time with you, and yet hast Thou not known ME, Philip?" Do not look for something afar off when the blessing is at hand. Like Hagar in the wilderness, there has been ever beside us a well of water, and we "knew it not."

Pastor F. MONOD (John i.): "The Life was the light of men." We get this light and life in coming to Christ. More light has been shed on the evil of our hearts, more on God's promises, than ever before. Some things seem of so much greater importance, and some of so much less, when seen by the light of the sanctuary.

And now how shall we spread this but by living it? We may have admirable ways of teaching a faith-life, but if our conduct contradicts it, people will not believe us. "Take heed to *thyself* and the doctrine" —"*thyself*," the practice first.

The Lord will guide us each in his own way; not you in mine and I in yours. We shall each moment have all we need, not a little after, nor a little before, but when we *need* it. We are as unable now to do what we did yesterday, as now to do what is for to-morrow. Walk each day in its own light, keeping your obedience at its extreme verge at each moment. "It is more blessed to give than to receive. Freely ye have received, freely give."

Lord RADSTOCK (who had come in while Mr. Monod was speaking) rose and said: I thank the Lord that He has put it into my brother's heart to say those last words. I have just come from the Oxford fair, and there those for whom nothing is prepared are hungering and thirsting for the word of Life. It is impossible in the hubbub of the fair to have full opportunity for open-air preaching, but I have found great openness to receive tracts and a few words of loving counsel. I have come back to see if any here feel called to go out with me for this work. "It is more blessed to give than to receive."

Many left the room at this intimation. The great fair was quite overshadowed by the Christian conference. The common talk of the market-place was the "joyful message." "How happy these people look," seemed to be a common remark. Here was a crowd of listeners drawn from the fair, addressed by Admiral Fishbourne, and there, near the Martyrs' Memorial, from the midst of a similar circle could be heard Lord Radstock's clear voice. Walking around the edge of the crowd numbers of people in twos and threes could be heard in earnest conversation. A young lady, in company with her brother, was preaching the Gospel to a labouring man. A young man in his teens said he had found the rest of faith, had been to speak to his companions, and that one had been converted. The water of life seemed to be flowing everywhere. All reserve seemed to be done away with. The new wine warmed the hearts and opened the lips of all who had been to the feast. Those who let lodgings were spoken to about their souls, and told of the blessing received. One man before leaving his hotel called the porter and other servants into his room, and so spoke to them from the fulness of his heart that every one left the room, it was said, in tears.

Walking down the streets of Oxford you could not help noticing the people engaged in earnest conversation, and then the words would catch the ear, such as "Over Jordan now," or, "What must I do to be saved?"

While the meeting in the Corn Exchange was continued another meeting was held in the Town Hall, for children and young people, by R. Pearsall Smith, followed by a solemn inquiry meeting, in which a number professed to have found the Lord in the pardon of their sins.

CHAPTER XI.

Ladies' Meetings.

AT 9.30 each morning of the Conference, meetings were held exclusively for ladies, conducted by Mrs. R. Pearsall Smith and Mrs. Boardman. They were generally opened by prayer and singing, and short addresses from the leaders of the meeting, and were then thrown open to the guidance of the Spirit, liberty being left for any to speak, or pray, or sing, as they might feel led. These meetings were seasons of deep spiritual interest, and of much definite blessing to many souls. As in the more general meetings, the presence and power of the Holy Ghost was wonderfully realised in the progressive character of the meetings. Each one seemed to be, as to power, in advance of the one before, and the line of truth taught and realised developed daily more and more from the starting point of entire consecration, on to the blessed consciousness of union with Christ.

The subject of the first day (Monday) was the reality nd Scripturalness of the experience of the life of full trust and victory, to consider which the Conference had been gathered. It was felt that in order to make people hungry for anything, they must first be convinced that it is possible for them to get it, and therefore attention was called to the Scripture teaching on the subject, and to the experience of the Apostles and early Christians, who, it is very manifest, knew a rest and triumph in their Christian lives far beyond what is the usual portion of Christians in the present day.

The frequent use of the personal pronoun "I" in Paul's writings was especially noticed, and also the fact of our being all called to be God's witnesses, and that a witness must necessarily say *I*. In a court of law a witness is not allowed to talk about what other people have done or seen, and is obliged to tell what *he himself* knows personally of the case; and any witness who cannot say "I saw," or "I heard," or "I felt," is not permitted to testify. Those present, therefore who could tell anything from their own personal experience of this wonderful life of full trust were urged to do so, that all might be made to hunger and thirst after it.

The meeting was thrown open, and several deeply-interesting testimonies followed from some who had for many years known and rejoiced in an experimental knowledge of the power of Christ to deliver them from the dominion of sin, and to give them a daily victory over their enemies. These testimonies all agreed in this, that the speakers had not for a greater or less period after their conversion experimentally known the secret of victory, and that consequently for a longer or shorter time their Christian lives had been full of failure and defeat; but that *at last* they had been taught—either directly by the

Spirit through the Scriptures, or through the testimony of others—that the Lord Jesus Christ was able and willing to deliver them, not only from the guilt of their sins, but also from their power; and that, having trusted Him, He had proved Himself faithful to save and to deliver.

The convincing nature of these testimonies, and the Scripture teaching that was brought forward, seemed to carry the truth home to many hearts, and the Lord was felt to be in the midst of His people.

The subject of the meeting on Tuesday morning was God working in us both to will and to do of His good pleasure, and our surrender to Him in order for this. The attention of the congregation was especially directed to the fact that when a soul is really given up to God, He never fails to take possession of it; and that He then begins to work in that soul all the good pleasure of His will. It is like making the junction between the machinery and the steam-engine: the machinery is yielded up to the power of the engine, and the engine works it, and it goes easily and without effort because of the mighty power that is behind it. Thus the Christian life becomes an easy and natural life, when it is the outward development of the Divine life working within. When we give ourselves to Him He claims us, and this is where our safety lies—not in our giving, but in His taking. What we have to do is to put our will right over on His side, and then He will take possession of it, and work for us, making us really willing to do His will. And if God thus gets possession of us, and causes us to walk in His statutes and to keep His commandments and do them, we shall find it an easy and happy thing to live in conformity with His will. The great point is to be made right inside, for the right inward life produces, easily and without painful effort, the right outward living. All present were urged, therefore, to surrender their wills to God—to say to Him at once, "Lord, we will be Thine; we yield ourselves to Thee"; and then to trust Him to take possession of them, and Himself to work in them all the good pleasure of His will. Several after this rose to testify to the joy and power they had found in thus surrendering their wills to the Lord. One lady spoke of having given up a great many separate things but of not finding the deliverance she expected, and of discovering at last that it was because all the while the stronghold of her *will* was not surrendered; that at length she had taken her will to the Lord and abandoned it to Him, surrendering for ever the liberty of choice, and consenting to His will throughout the whole range of her being; and that immediately her soul had entered into a path of wonderful rest and liberty.

Another lady said she had been for over thirty years working for her Master, but that during that time, while teaching others to cast their cares upon the Lord, she had often lived under burdens herself. She said when she left home for Oxford an invalid daughter had said to her, "Mother, I do not think you need to be made more useful: but I should like to see you happier, and less burdened with care." And, she continued, "I am going back to her far happier, for in this meeting yesterday morning I learned how to trust the Lord with *everything*, as I never knew before, and the burden has rolled off and I feel like a child in its mother's arms."

Several others spoke, giving similar testimony, and some very earnest prayers followed. At the close, all those who felt that they had given up their wills into the hands of the Lord, or that they heartily desired to do so, were asked to rise and sing the last two verses of

"Jesus saves me all the time."

A great many, under deep feeling, responded to the invitation.

On Wednesday morning the subject was in reference to obedience, and the blessed promises made to those who have and who keep the blessed commandments of the Lord. John xiv. 21, 23, was read and commented on; and every soul that was hungry for this promised manifestation was urged to start out on a path of simple obedience. Reference was made to the difference between a believer of doctrines and a disciple: that among the Greeks there were certain great teachers who had, what were called, disciples—that is, those who left everything else to follow them, who went with them from place to place, who sat at their feet, and hung on their words; eating where the master ate, sleeping where he slept, walking in his footsteps, and imbibing his very spirit. Others might listen to their teachings, and believe their doctrines, but still might have their own separate interests and pursuits, and, while called believers, could not be counted among their disciples. Christians are called to be Christ's *disciples*, to leave all to follow Him, and to sit at His feet and hang on His words continually. We shall then *have* His commandments in a very different sense from those who follow Him afar off, and the blessings promised to those who both have and keep them, will assuredly be ours. All who desired this manifestation of Christ to their souls were urged then and there to put themselves deliberately and definitely under the guidance of their Lord, and to let Him lead them in their daily and hourly walk, with the assurance that He never fails to guide by His blessed Spirit every soul that thus surrenders itself to Him. (Luke xiv. 26-33). The forsaking all was commented on as being the necessary attitude of every soul that would indeed become a *disciple* of the Lord Jesus Christ; and it was shown that this and similar passages were to be understood as setting forth the way to become disciples.

All who longed after this blessed place of nearness to the Lord were asked to rise, as an expression of their desire, and that they might be prayed for. Very many at once responded to this invitation; some, as they rose, expressing in a few broken words the great hunger of their souls. One poor woman said she had never dreamed, until the day before, when she had chanced to stray into one of the meetings, that there was any such soul-satisfying religion in the world anywhere; but she saw that it was just what she needed, and felt now that she *must* have it.

Very earnest prayer was offered for these seeking, hungry souls; and, as the meeting closed, many testimonies to blessing received then and there were to be heard on every hand.

The subject on Thursday morning was the necessity

and the privilege of entire and immediate consecration. Reference was made to the numerous difficulties which arise in the way of the believer, who seeks to enter into the life hid with Christ in God; and it was urged that these difficulties would surely be made to disappear before a maintained *attitude* of entire consecration and perfect trust.

The illustration was given of a lump of clay in the hands of the skilful potter, who purposed to make it into a vessel unto his own honour. The part of the clay is simply to be put into the potter's hands, and to abide there passively. The potter must do all the work. The clay cannot make itself into a beautiful vessel, neither can it help to do it—it must lie passive in the potter's hands, and know no will but his, and he will then mould and fashion it by his own skill into just such a vessel as he sees fit. And just so are we God's workmanship, not our own; and He, and He only, is able to make us into a vessel unto His honour, sanctified and meet for the Master's use, and fitted to every good work. Our part is simply in faith to abandon ourselves to His working—which is what consecration implies—and then to trust Him to do it all. We may know ourselves to be very poor lumps, full of stones, and sand, and hard places, and may despair of ever being made into anything to the glory of the Potter; but He is able to make out of the vilest lump a beautiful vessel; and since the work is His, and not our own, none need despair, let them be as poor a lump as they may. He will work in us "both to will and to do."

"Put yourselves then into God's hands, as clay in

the hands of the potter, and trust Him. But do not take yourselves back. Having given yourselves to Him you must abide in Him—you must *stay* there. You must let Him mould and fashion you; you must let Him arrange your days and your hours for you; you must yield up the control and management of everything that concerns you into His hands; you must say to yourself continually, "The Lord Jesus has undertaken my case, and He will take care of it; I will leave it all to Him. He shall have His own way with me, and I will say, '*Yes,*' to Him continually."

"But some of you are afraid of the will of God. How can you be? for He loves you! If you could only see into His heart, and could get the least faint idea of how He loves you, you would only be too glad to be in His hands, and to give up your wills to Him. You would be afraid to be for a single moment in your own hands, and would feel safe only when He had taken possession of you. To surrender yourselves wholly to God is to enter into the sweetest privilege of your whole life."

A solemn appeal was then made to all present to surrender themselves at once in entire consecration to the Lord, for Him to fashion them into just such a vessel as pleases Him, and all who could unite in doing this were asked to bow in silent prayer. Nearly the whole congregation responded to this; and after a season of very solemn silence, followed by an earnest prayer of surrender, we all sang, while still bowed before the Lord, the following verse of solemn consecration—

"Lord, I am Thine—entirely Thine—
Purchased and saved by love divine;
With full consent Thine would I be,
And own Thy sovereign right in me."

It is believed that most of the large company present did, in a very definite manner at this solemn hour, abandon themselves wholly to the Lord. It was a season never to be forgotten.

At the next meeting, on Friday morning, it was felt that the point to be urged now was that of trusting. We had presented ourselves to the Lord, and had abandoned ourselves to His working, and now we were called upon to *trust* Him. The passage read and commented on was Ruth iii. 18: "Sit still, my daughter, until thou know how the matter will fall: for the man will not be in rest, until he have finished the thing this day." And all those who had the day before consecrated themselves altogether to the Lord, were now urged to "sit still," and trust Him to finish the matter; for He who had undertaken their case would not rest until He had accomplished in them all the good pleasure of His will. It was shown that we could not do anything but yield ourselves up to His working and trust Him; that He who had begun the work must also finish it; and that having put ourselves into His hands we must now trust Him day by day, and hour by hour, to carry it on in His own way, and by His own means. His own way may not be our way, nor His means our means; but He is the Heavenly Potter, and knows the best way and means, and we must simply trust. We must trust Him with ourselves and all our affairs, both inward and outward, we must trust Him with our money, with our health, with our reputation, with our children, with our husbands, with our work, with our experiences—with *everything.* We must trust as children trust. We must obey that command literally, "Be careful for nothing,"—absolutely *nothing*—" but in everything by prayer and supplication, with thanksgiving, make our requests known unto God," and leave it all with Him.

But it was shown that we cannot trust Him unless we are satisfied with His will, and know it to be the sweetest and best thing that can come to us. And, therefore, until we had consecrated ourselves unto Him, and had begun to say, "Thy will be done," throughout all the range of our being, we could not go on to trusting. For He does not always do things the way we would have them done. We ask Him to fit us for His service, and perhaps He shuts us up to some plain domestic duties, and then we are tempted to think He is not answering our prayers. But if we trust Him we shall be satisfied with all His dealings, whether we understand them or not.

The illustration was given of a little girl, of six years, who wanted a string put to a bag she had for marbles, and who asked her mother to do it. The child expected the mother to sew a string on at each side, but the mother knew that a far better way was to run it through the hem with a bodkin. The child looked on eagerly to see the work accomplished, but when she saw the bodkin and the string both disappear inside the hem, her heart began to fail, and she said, anxiously, "But, mother, I want a string." "Yes, my darling," said her mother, "I am putting in a string." For another moment the little girl watched with a troubled brow, and then said again, "Oh, but, mother, I *do* want a string so badly!" "Well, darling," replied her mother, "I *am* putting in a string; just trust me, I know how, and you do not." So the child smiled and trusted, and in a few minutes the string came out all right, and was tied in a knot, and the little girl hung it on her arm with great delight. She stood for a moment thinking, and then said, "Oh, mother, that's just like Jesus: We give Him things to do and we think He is not doing them right, and we are going to get worried, and then we remember that He knows, and we just trust Him, and He brings it out all right." When we have put our case in the Lord's hands our part is simply to "sit still," for He will not rest until He has finished the matter. How can a child of God worry when God has undertaken his case? What is there to worry about? And we must remember this—that *if we carry a burden ourselves the Lord does not carry it.*

An earnest appeal was then made to all who had definitely consecrated themselves to the Lord, to *trust* Him now as definitely; and it was proposed that all who could unite in this should bow in a season of silent trusting. Each one was urged to take their own especial burden and lay it on the Lord, and leave it with Him. Again, as on the day before, nearly the whole congregation of several hundred ladies responded to this invitation, and it is believed that to most of them it *was* a period of definite trust. A prayer was then offered by one of the leaders of the meeting, in which she said: "Now, Lord, we trust Thee with everything; do Thou take the management of all for us. We trust Thee with ourselves, we trust Thee with our experiences, we trust Thee with our husbands, with our children, our servants, our money, our time. We trust Thee with the management of our households, with our work for Thee, with our reputation, with our names, with our emotions, with our intellects. With all we are and all we have WE TRUST THEE!"

Then, while still bowed before the Lord we sang twice, with deep feeling, this verse—

> "I am trusting, Lord, in Thee,
> Dear Lamb of Calvary;
> Humbly at Thy cross I bow,
> Jesus saves me—saves me now."

This was followed by many short expressions of trust from one and another, as burden after burden was rolled off weary shoulders, and laid upon Jesus. One lady said, "Lord, I trust Thee with my dissipated son." Another said, "Lord I trust Thee with my Bible-women." Another—"Lord, I trust Thee with my business." Another—"Lord, I trust Thee with my health." It was a deeply impressive time.

After rising from our knees a lady rose and said that she had attended many a *prayer* meeting before, but never a *trust* meeting.

She was followed by a lady who is engaged in extensive mission work in Paris, who said she felt she had a message to deliver to her sisters from the Lord. She wanted to tell them how every need of a woman's heart could be met and satisfied with the love of Christ. She said, "I had worked for the Lord for *many years*, and loved and trusted Him, but my *heart* was not satisfied. The void grew greater and greater; it felt as if my heart was as large as the world, and there was nothing to fill it. I hungered, but I knew not for what. But about two years ago the Lord revealed Himself to me as the heavenly Bridegroom, who would henceforth carry me in His arms of love, and would make my life bright with His presence; and from that moment my soul has been satisfied with His fulness, and has found in Him more than it had ever entered into my heart to conceive of blessedness and joy. I feel that to me is fulfilled that promise, "The beloved of the Lord shall dwell in safety by Him; and the Lord shall cover him all the day long, and he shall dwell between His shoulders."

"Now," she said, "my heart is too small to contain the joy that is mine."

She then urged all hungering and thirsting souls present to claim the Lord as their heavenly Bridegroom, assuring them that He could and would satisfy the need of every heart.

It was a thrilling message, and stirred the meeting so deeply that it seemed almost a necessity to give some expression to our feelings by singing—

> "Safe in the arms of Jesus,
> Safe on His gentle breast,
> There by His love o'ershadowed,
> Sweetly my soul shall rest."

Several others then followed, testifying to the same blessed experience as our sister had described, and the meeting separated under a very solemn feeling that the Lord Whom we had trusted, had been revealing to us wondrous secrets of His love. Many hearts had been roused to a great hunger after Himself.

On Saturday morning it was suggested that we should open the meeting by doing, as had been done at the Ministers' Meeting the evening before—by each one giving in their present experience in a text of Scripture. One after another rose with texts of richest blessing and rest; some with gray hairs, some young, some with trembling voices, often five or six rising at once; so full was the tide of blessing that all seemed to want to speak to the glory of their Lord. It was like being in the very land of Promise itself, listening to the words of the great Promiser.

Some very striking testimonies followed, as to the reality and power of a life of faith and victory. And then the subject of trust was again resumed from the day before, as it was felt that the only thing left for a consecrated soul was to trust in the Lord at all times. Attention was called to Psalm cxviii. 8. "It is better to trust in the Lord than to put confidence in man," and it was stated that this was the central verse in the whole Bible, and the keystone of God's wonderful arch of truth. We were told that "man" here must mean our own selves as well as others, and that trust in self was as utterly unreliable as trust in any one else. We must trust in the Lord for everything, and never expect to find anything in self to which we can trust. Reference was made to the natural desire to find something in self to trust to—some goodness, or wisdom, or earnestness, or something; but we were urged to settle *it once for* all that we shall never find anything good in ourselves of any kind whatever. Christians are apt to think they can have stocks of virtues laid up in themselves—a stock of wisdom or patience, or of love. We have all these things laid up in Christ, and, at the moment we need any one of them, we must go to Him for the supply. Some one said once, "Most Christians are too thrifty to live by the moment; they are not contented unless they have a stock of piety laid up for a year ahead. But God's way is to give grace to help in the time of need, *and not before*."

A Christian who knew that circumstances were about to arise in his life when he would need a great deal of wisdom, not understanding God's plan of a supply, moment by moment, felt that it would be necessary for him to pray a long while in order to lay up a sufficient stock to carry him through the difficult time. He therefore began to pray, and prayed on day after day for wisdom, but, to his surprise, he did not feel himself growing any wiser; but, on the contrary, his own foolishness and ignorance only became more and more apparent. He was very much puzzled, and tried to pray more earnestly. But one day it was suddenly flashed into his soul; Christ is made unto us "wisdom, and righteousness, and sanctification, and redemption," and he saw that he already had wisdom in Christ, and that what he must do was, at the moment of need to go to Him for it. He could never be wise in himself, nor have any stock of wisdom laid up there; but in Christ he had all he needed or could ever need. It is just like drawing on a bank. Our money is in the bank, not in our pockets. God never gives us anything apart from Christ. We get up each morning with nothing, and we go to bed with nothing, and yet we are rich all day. For we have Christ, and, having Him, we have everything. We sing:—

> "Thou, O Christ, art all I want,
> More than all in Thee I find."

Do we believe it when we sing it?

We were then very solemnly urged to be satisfied with Christ, and to take Him for the supply for each moment's need. It was pressed upon us that He is a present Saviour, able and willing to save and deliver in each present moment, and we were exhorted to put into His hands the management of all our affairs, both inward and outward. He says: Commit thy way unto Me, and cast thy cares upon Me. Take everything to Him then, and keep back no reserves. If you should put a case into the hands of a lawyer, you surely would not keep back from him some of the points, and say, "I can manage these myself." No lawyer would undertake any case unless he was put in possession of every particular. *All* must be handed over to Christ, therefore,—everything. And be definite about it. Take with you words and go to the Lord. Put your case and your need into words. Do not be satisfied with vague floating desires. If you want to get a door opened, you do not stand before it, and just wish it was opened, but you ring or knock. Prayer is a real transaction. It is as really laying your burdens off on the Lord as you would put a load on a cart; and you must leave them just as much in the one case as you would in the other. Whatever else you do you must trust. Our Lord commands us about this, saying,

"Let not your heart be troubled, neither let it be afraid." "Be careful for nothing." And we are disobeying His commands when we are anxious or worried for a single moment. WE MUST TRUST!

At this point in the meeting a lady rose and said she would like to repeat what she had often heard said that if we trusted we did not worry, and if we worried we were not trusting. She then went on to say that it had taken her a long while to learn this lesson. And that since she had come to Oxford it had been made more clear to her than ever. That she had been detained from some of the meetings by a bad nervous headache, and felt very much worried. But that the Lord had showed her that He was able to come between even the joints and marrow, and therefore also between herself and her nerves, and she had put herself into His hands and trusted Him, and had found a complete deliverance.

Another lady followed, saying that she also had experienced a similar deliverance from nervousness, and she knew from blessed experience that the Lord Jesus can quiet the most restless nerves when they are trusted to Him. She then went on to urge our trusting Him to regulate our lives for us, even when they seem to be going wrong. She said, when she had fully surrendered herself to the Lord, she expected to be immediately put into some great work. But that, instead, she had been shut up for the first time in her life to domestic duties. She was tempted to rebel, but the Lord showed her that He knew what was best for her; and she accepted His will, and took the training He had provided for her thankfully, satisfied to leave the management of her life to Him. And the result had proved that it was the very best training possible.

A letter was read from Miss Havergal, from Switzerland, illustrating the blessedness of a life of implicit following of the Lord, by a circumstance that had happened to her in climbing the mountains there. She and her friends were following a guide who cut steps for them in the snow as they went up. They followed him, but were rather negligent of watching his exact footsteps, and, as a consequence, found themselves continually stumbling, and thought the pathway very difficult. At last one of the party called out to the rest, "If you will put your feet *exactly* in the footsteps of the guide you will find it quite easy to walk, but you must be particular to be very exact." They all tried it, and found it true. And so it was shown that implicit following of the Lord, with perfect confidence in His wisdom and power to guide, would make an easy path for the Christian through the most difficult places.

On Sunday it was felt that as in the previous meetings we had learned deeply the lessons of entire consecration and simple trust, we needed now to go on to consider more fully the blessed secret of the love of Christ and our union with Him.

The meeting was opened with reading Eph. v. 22-32; Isaiah lxii. 4, 5, liv. 5; Hosea ii. 16, 19, 20; Song of Sol. iv. 7-12, and it was said that only the soul that had entered into rest could understand these *passages*. The Song of Songs could not be written *until* Solomon's reign—the reign of peace. This blessed secret is one that the soul is slow to understand.

We sing many beautiful songs before we are ready to sing this one concerning the love of Christ and His Church. There is the Song of Moses when we are first delivered out of Egypt; the Song of Deborah and Barak after their triumph over Sisera; the Song of Hannah for the gift she had received from God. But none of these was like the Song of Songs, and none held out such heights and depths of blessedness and love. When the soul reaches that point in which it cries out—

> "Thy gifts, alas! cannot suffice
> Except Thyself be given,"

then it is ready for this glorious revelation.

The story of love is a very short story, and yet its depths are unfathomable. And this little book is one of the shortest, but one of the deepest, in the whole Bible. The most enthusiastic love is expressed and described here. It is not the ways of filial affection, nor of the affection due to a benefactor, but rather the actings of the love of espousals in both Christ's heart and ours. The joy of hearing the Bridegroom's voice is here fulfilled in the heart of the believer.

The believer does not fully know what Christ is until he comes to this. Every need is supplied here. Every empty place is filled. Every longing satisfied.

But to come to this place the soul must surrender all. Christ is wooing us to say "Yes," to Him, and when we are able to do so throughout the whole range of our being, we are then ready to have revealed to us this blessed life of union with Himself.

The heart is made deeply susceptible of an overmastering affection, and Christ is the offered object of it. He proposes Himself to it. He claims the supreme place in our hearts. "He that loveth father and mother more than Me is not worthy of Me." This may sound very solemn, but is it not also glorious? Is it not blessed to know that our Lord wants our love; that it is worth something to Him?

We often sing, "Jesus, lover of my soul," but have we ever recognized Him as such? Have we listened to the wooings of His love, and have we consented to leave all else to be His and His only? There comes a moment in the life of a woman when she says "Yes" to the proposals of her beloved. Has this moment come to you in your relationship with your Lord? Have you said "Yes" to Him? Our sister from Paris the other day brought us a very solemn message as to this, and the Lord would have us open our hearts wide to receive it. For the consecration we have been pressing in these meetings, and the full and childlike trust, are only stepping-stones to this glorious consummation of soul-union with the Beloved. He has bought us for this, and our souls have not reached their highest destiny until it is known and rejoiced in. Let your hearts go then in an absolute abandonment to His love, and you will find that in His presence there is fulness of joy, and at His right hand there are pleasures for evermore.

Another lady followed this opening address, by calling attention to the different sorts of love in life, which are types of the love between Christ and ourselves; all sweet and precious, but only one an overmastering love.

There is the love of a servant and master, of a parent and child, of a subject and sovereign, of the love of brethren and the love of friends. These are all high and blessed to know, but they are not the highest. The love of a bridegroom and his bride is the dearest and best of all, and it is our privilege to know this love between our souls and Christ. But in entering into this relationship with Him, the other loves are not lost. It is only that a love is gained which includes and overtops all the rest. But we must not be discouraged if as yet we do not know this highest love. If we keep close to Christ and wait on Him, though we now have only the child's love, the deeper affection will be sure to come.

Several ladies followed, testifying briefly to the joy and rest their souls had found in thus knowing Christ as the Heavenly Bridegroom. One told how, through many years of widowhood and heavy cares, she had been sustained and comforted, and known the Lord to be to her far more than earthly friend or husband could ever have been.

It was a deeply solemn meeting. Many hearts were melted, and many souls were bowed before the Lord in view of such glorious privileges as were opened up before us. The feeling was so great, that at the close of the meeting several met more privately for a season of earnest prayer, that to each one of them this wondrous soul-union with Jesus might become an experimental reality.

On Monday morning the meeting met under a feeling of the deepest solemnity. In all that large congregation of several hundred ladies there was hardly one who had not in a most definite way surrendered herself and all that she had to the Lord, and had started on a life of simple momentary trust. And it seemed as though, having brought all the tithes into the storehouse, we were now only waiting until the Lord should open the windows of Heaven and pour out such a blessing as there should not be room to contain.

The meeting was opened with some remarks on the Book of Ruth, based upon what had already been said concerning it in one of the General Meetings. Ruth was a type of the Church. She was a Gentile bride united to a Jewish husband, and advanced to a place of especial honour. She took the first step out of her own country, and into the land of Israel; not because she expected to get a bridegroom there, but because her heart was desolate and lonely in her own land, and she was attracted by the religion of Naomi. She began to receive blessings as soon as she reached the land where the God of Israel reigned, and her "hap was" almost at once "to light on a part of the field belonging unto Boaz, her near kinsman." So we, who turn our backs on the world to seek the God of Israel, even although very ignorant of all the blessings in store for us, find ourselves soon gleaning in the field of Christ, our near Kinsman, and He shows kindness to us in causing many blessings to be scattered for our gleaning.

Then Naomi urged her to press a nearer claim. Boaz was her kinsman, and as such had a right to redeem her and give her rest in his house. In submission to the advice of Naomi, Ruth made her claim. And often the more advanced Christian is able similarly to help the younger ones on to their higher privileges, where there is the true spirit of Christian submission of one to another.

Boaz was touched with the thought that Ruth cared for him more than for any one else, and he called the claim she had made "showing kindness." It looked like presuming, but he felt it to be kindness. Wonderful thought—that our Lord delights in every claim we make upon Him for union with Himself, and calls it kindness—"the kindness of thine espousals."

Having made her claim, Ruth then was simply to sit still until she should see how the matter would fall, for Naomi told her that "the man would not be in rest until he had finished the thing that day."

And to those of us who have been stirred up by the solemn and searching teaching of God's Spirit among us during these last few days, to make our claim for this realised union with our Lord, the message comes to-day, "Sit still, my daughter, until thou know how the matter will fall, for the man will not be in rest until he have finished the thing this day."

Before Boaz could make Ruth his bride, he had to redeem her from a kinsman who was nearer than himself. And before Christ can unite us to Himself in a realised soul-union, He must fully redeem us from under the law, as we read, "Wherefore, my brethren, ye also are become dead to the law by the body of Christ, that ye should be married to another, even to Him who is raised from the dead, that we should bring forth fruit unto God." (Romans vii. 4.)

At last Boaz did indeed "finish the thing," and *called the elders* and the people to witness that he had purchased Ruth to be his wife. And so also we read that "Christ loved the Church, and gave Himself for it."

Nothing will satisfy the heart but this realised union with our Beloved. Many of us have our *intellects* satisfied with our knowledge of Jesus, but our *hearts* are aching and hungry. But there are some who can say that the deepest cravings of their hearts are most blessedly satisfied, and Jesus is to them more than any earthly friend or lover ever could be. And if this is the privilege of some, it surely may be the privilege of every one of us, for the prayer of our Lord was that "they ALL may be one."

This is the consummation of all Christian experience—to "know the love of Christ that passeth knowledge." Pray that it may speedily be yours!

After these opening remarks, the meeting was thrown open for the Spirit to lead, and many testimonies and prayers followed one another in quick succession. Every heart seemed full, and longing to tell what God had done for their souls.

One lady said: "I feel my soul has entered the home for which it was created, in the bosom of my loving Saviour. Here I am at rest. Nothing but a living Jesus, fully received into my heart and affections, ever satisfied me. Until I received Him there, I was sad and hungry. The soul was created for union with Him, and until this union is realised nothing can fully satisfy it. But I am satisfied now. 'I am my Beloved's, and His desire is toward me.' All my life *is bound* up in Him. I never see myself apart from *Him.*"

Another said: "I only wish I could tell you what it is to be consciously the beloved of the Lord; to dwell in safety by Him, and to have Him cover you with His wings as He does me all the day long. But no words can tell out this wondrous secret. It can only be learned by each one experimentally for herself on her knees before the Lord. None can know it saving he that receiveth it. 'My Beloved is mine, and I am His,' and my soul is satisfied as with marrow and fatness."

Another said: "Dear friends, this revelation of the wonderful treasures we have in Christ must not discourage any of you, and make you think you do not know Him at all, because your experience is not so full and deep. What you already have is very blessed, and this is only going on to know the fulness of that which you have as yet but tasted. You have wants in your hearts. They are made capacious for happiness, and nothing earthly ever satisfies. But this realised love of Christ will more than satisfy. My heart is too small now to hold the blessing He gives me, but once it was like a wilderness. I have to cry now continually 'Oh, enlarge my heart!' Dear friends, Christ is wooing you to-day, He wants you to come and share this blessing. Come, for all things are ready. Surrender yourselves to the Lord, to be His only and His altogether, and obey His wondrous command in Hosea ii. 16, 'And it shall be at that day, saith the Lord, thou shalt call me Ishi, (that is, Husband,) and shalt call me no more Baali, (that is, Lord.') For He will betroth you unto Him for ever."

The deep solemnity over the meeting during all this

time is indescribable. The Lord was felt to be in our midst, and all hearts were thrilled with the sweetness of His love.

A lady well known in the Christian world as an eminent worker for Christ, rose to testify to what Christ had done for her. She said: "I have been a Christian for thirty years, and a rejoicing one too, as many of you here well know. But during all that time I was conscious of a lack in my experience. I had not perfect inward victory, nor perfect rest. I felt that I did not live as the Bible seemed to expect and command Christians to live. When I first heard of this life of full trust I felt that it was what I wanted, and I sought earnestly to lay hold of it for myself, but could not. My daughter, who was a young Christian, received it joyfully, and for more than a year now has lived in the power of it. I could not understand why she could do what I could not. I prayed, and struggled, read all the books I could find on the subject, and attended every meeting. But in vain; I seemed to get no nearer, but only further and further away. I resolved to come to this Oxford meeting, hoping to receive the blessing here. The day before I came I went into my room to pray, and asked the Lord to show me what was the matter. Suddenly, as though scales had fallen from my eyes, I saw it. All these years I saw that I had been holding on to Christ, and my weak grasp had often seemed almost to fail, and my soul had struggled and strained to hold on. But now I saw that Christ was holding me, and, *instead of* straining, I might fall back and rest in His *strong* and loving embrace. The words came home to me with power, 'Hold thou me up and I shall be safe,' and I saw that I was safe only there. Since then my soul has rested in perfect peace, Jesus has taken me into His arms, and is carrying me on His bosom, and I have not a care or a fear. It is so simple that I wonder I never saw it before. And since I have known this rest, I find that things which were hard before have become wonderfully easy. Two weeks ago I could not have opened my mouth in this assembly; but now I rejoice to tell of the wonderful goodness of my Lord."

Another earnest Christian worker next arose, and said: I want to give you a word that has come home to my heart with great power this morning, "That the life also of Jesus may be made manifest in our mortal body." This is the summing up of the whole matter. If the life that is made manifest in our mortal body is Christ's life, then all must be in harmony with His will, and we shall have the mind that was in Him, and shall walk in His steps. I am longing to know this blessed experience fully for myself, and I know there are many other longing hearts present. I know something of the life of faith, but I want to know the life of union also. It seems to me that the whole secret must be to let no obstacle in ourselves prevent Him from taking possession of us, and working in us to will and to do of His good pleasure. We must put our wills—the mainspring of our beings—into His hands, and then simply trust Him. And I feel assured He will then work in us mightily, and then manifest His own glorious life in our mortal bodies. Then we shall *thirst for souls,* we shall have power to overcome, we shall be gentle, and meek, and easy to be entreated. We shall, in short, be Christ-like. Dear friends, it is the only way; let us get His life within, and it will be manifested outwardly.

Many others were longing to speak, but it was necessary at this point to close the meeting; and under a very manifest and solemn influence of the Holy Spirit we bowed in silent prayer. After a few moments thus spent, the following prayer, by a lady well known for her life-long faithfulness to the Lord, was offered with the power of simplicity and reality :—

"Oh, Lord! Thou hast been walking through Oxford with royal progress. Those who have come here longing for the life hid in God, have entered upon it. Those who knew something of it before, but whose communion had become dimmed, have had it restored brighter than ever before. Now, O Father, do not suffer Satan to bring one single doubt that it is better further on. We claim it of Thy love and Thy faithfulness, that Thou wilt sustain this soul-union with Jesus in its power. Increase our enjoyment of it continually. We are waiting on Thee for further revelations of Thine unutterable beauty and strength. We give Thee thanks for Thy great glory. We glory in Thy spotless holiness. O, lift us up in Thy arms, that we may look straight into Thine eyes of love. Hold Thou us and we shall be safe. We delight in the thought that a life of obedience is a life of love. We realize that love is above all law, fulfilling all law. Thy law is written on our hearts now, and we love it. We beseech Thee let no shadow of doubt come in. Let us for ever delight to do Thy will. Give us such tender consciences that at the first approach of the tempter we may flee to Thee to shelter us.

"Let the unutterable sweetness of Thy love be a perpetually constraining power over every thought, look, and action from the greatest down to the most insignificant. We have left ourselves in Thy hands, and we trust Thee continually to take us out of self, and self out of us. O turn out everything that is not of Jesus, and possess us wholly! Give us power to dwell in Thee continually, and to leave all to Thee. Make us astonished at the way in which Thou wilt do all things for us. Let us each one go home from here with such a presence of Thee around us, that others shall see, not only that we have been with Jesus, but that Jesus has come back with us. In all the little details of life make us study more and more Thy mind and will, that our families and our servants may see the effect of the blessing we have found. We do not want this for our own glory, but for Thine.

"Manifest Thyself, we pray Thee, to any one who has not yet received full rest and joy. Our Saviour, our Lord, we want Thee to the last moment of life, and throughout all eternity, to fill up our whole being. Some of us know, from tenderest experience, that Thou hast never forsaken us; our very sorrows and trials have been Thy blessed opportunity for sweetest words of love. Faithful and True, we adore Thee! We love to call Thee Master! We would so live in Thee that Thy mind may come out in all the minutest details of our daily life. We want to reflect Thine infinite tenderness, Thy truth, Thy holiness, Thy purity, Thy fulness. All Thy glories that are not for Thyself alone dispense, we pray Thee, to us also, that we may manifest Thee among others.

"Bring a mighty army for Christ from amongst the young men of Oxford, especially those preparing for the ministry. Teach us every possible way whereby we can glorify Thee. Win every soul present to whole-hearted consecration to Thee. Make those who have hitherto held the Lord with only one hand, now surrender up to Him the whole being. We would especially bring before Thee our tongues. Let every tongue among us be laid upon Thine altar, that Thine own healing power may come upon our lips. When we are any of us about to say an unnecessary or harmful word, keep us from it; let us speak always as if Thou wert standing personally beside us. Lord, we consecrate our lips and tongues to Thee; and we do ask Thee to show us all that is ungenerous or unlovely in our conversation, and keep us from it.

"Thou knowest what a volume of prayer we would pour out to Thee—for our dearly beloved Queen—for that beloved son of hers who was called back to life through the prayers of Thy people—for that sweet young wife the princess. Thou knowest all we would ask. Oh Lord, bless them with Thy richest blessings! Take every unuttered prayer of every heart now before Thee, and undertake every cause. We leave it all with Thee!"

There were a few more Ladies' Meetings after the close of the Conference, but as no notes appear to have been taken of these no report can be made.

In summing up the wonderful manifestations of God's power and guidance during these meetings, the soul can but marvel and adore. The striking characteristic of the whole work was that Jesus was lifted up continually, and His mighty power to save was made plain to the people. No new truths were taught, but the old ones were made real and experimental. Things Christians have always known they *ought* to do, were here *done*.

Consecration advanced from being a *prospective duty*, to being an *accomplished fact*. Perfect trust, which had been always acknowledged to be the true theory of the Christian life, became here a reality of soul-experience. The promises of the Bible, heretofore only longed for, were now actually laid hold of and believed. Life-long aspirations after rest, and liberty, and peace, were here turned into present possessions. And the Lord Jesus was revealed to hundreds of souls as a present living Saviour, able to keep and able to deliver even now and here in this daily earthly life.

The creeds and doctrines of Christians were not changed, but their experience was. They laid hold of the things which, hitherto, they had too much only talked about. They dropped the future tense out of God's blessings, which had heretofore put them off indefinitely, and adopted the tense of present realisation. It was no longer, "I trust He *will* do," but, "I know He *has* done." And it is safe to say that to many of the hundreds present at these meetings there began, during their course, a new life of entire consecration and perfect trust, whose possibilities of progress and development are infinite and glorious and which if steadfastly continued in, will make the whole future of their pilgrimage-journey all sunshine in the gladness of their Lord's presence and love. Letters pour in continually telling of rich harvests of blessings to many hungry, weary souls as the results of these meetings. And although some may not sympathise fully with the means used, surely every follower of the Lord Jesus Christ must rejoice at whatever exalts Him, and brings rest and power to the souls of His disciples.

If mistakes in interpretation of texts of Scripture have been made, these are easily exposed and can be corrected.

The truth itself which brought about this wondrous emancipation was simply the old story of our utter nothingness and Christ's all-sufficiency, made a living and experimental reality to the soul of each individual believer. And the text, more than any other, that would express what was here taught and experienced, is simply this: "As ye have therefore received Christ Jesus the Lord, so walk ye in Him: rooted and built up in Him, and stablished in the faith, as ye have been taught, abounding therein with thanksgiving." (Col. ii. 6, 7.)

CHAPTER XII.

ON Tuesday morning, at 7 o'clock, a brief Praise Meeting was held.

MR. R. PEARSALL SMITH: We are but just entering the cloud now. We know not what glorious things are coming on the land. The Lord seems to be marvellously hastening His purposes in these last times, accomplishing in the history of kingdoms the work of centuries in days. It may be so in His heavenly kingdom.

If it please God that we shall have another meeting in 1875, let us ask and expect twice as great a blessing as we have here had. Learn to honour the grace of God by asking with each gift for its double, and even this does not exhaust what He gives. The Oxford meeting is more than the double of the Broadlands meeting.

Let us part with a few words about practical life. You will find that every hour of implicit, holy obedience makes the next easier, until obedience seems to be almost inevitable. The interior forces of the will, the bent of the affections, the action of the intellect, the very appetites of the body, by a life in "the obedience of faith," become harmonised to God. The old nature is liable in each moment once more to assume its sway, and yet it may in each moment be kept in the place of death and beneath our feet. Faith's power over it becomes more uniform every day. There will be conflict all along, but victory, not defeat.

Live out this life in little things. Most of us are called to glorify our Lord by a faith-life in small details, but small things are illuminated by His presence. The current of existence is made up of small rills. Our peace shall now flow as a river, ever more deep, and therefore more calm. Salvation does not confound our individuality. Let us not chafe if others have very different experiences. Some spend whole nights in prayer, others but brief periods, but with no less answers. Scripture prayers are mostly very brief. Prayer by habit becomes the *attitude* as well as the special act of the soul. "Pray without ceasing." Let us not make speeches to God, but talk to Him easily and naturally, though reverently.

Let us walk by our own measure of faith and light, and expect others to act by theirs. The more we judge ourselves, the more forbearing we shall be to others. If those around us, after hearing us tell of what we have found in Christ, reject what we bring them, let us not burden them, but take the food to hungering souls. The Church is full of these. But let us never be silent as if ashamed of Christ or of His words. This will suspend our communion. Let us not speak of anyone's "views," but of Christ and of His salvation. We shall find all that we need as to the doctrine, in every evangelical creed, prayer-book and hymn-book in use, as well as in the Bible. Let us avoid using the names of men. We cannot do them a greater unkindness and injustice than to speak of this life of faith as "the views" of such and such an one. A man's "*views*" are limited by what he can see, which is but little. They will be larger next year.

Since we have given up ourselves to a life of full consecration and faith, we need not now be analysing our experience. With some even months pass without their thinking of their own experience, unless they can use it to help others. Sick souls cannot forget their inward pains. Well, people forget that they have any inward bodily organs. I often recall the words of an eloquent preacher, "Thank God that One came into the world able to do our work for us! We'll speak of Him. 'Twould make us mad to think about ourselves: *we'll speak of* HIM!"

Remember that soul-health is very different from maturity. The sour apples in April are perfect. In October they are mature, or "perfected." At the best we are but ripening, and yet I do not shrink from Scripture terms. The Bible speaks of many perfect men—"as many as be *perfect*"—but adds, "Not as though I were already *perfected*." Little children are "perfect" in all their immaturity. Do not confound an unattainable, absolute, or divine holiness with an attainable victory over known sin. When Paul asserted, "I know nothing against myself"—not as the ground of his justification, but of his conscience void of offence; and when John said, "We keep His commandments, and do those things that are pleasing in His sight;" they neither claimed absolute holiness, nor opened a door for a defiled conscience. In Leviticus we read, "*The priest shall* make an atonement for him concerning his ignorance wherein he erred and wist it not, and it shall be forgiven him. It is a trespass offering; *he hath certainly trespassed against the Lord.*" We shall never in this life get beyond the need of saying, "Forgive us our trespasses."

After all the deductions from what we would be here and what we shall be hereafter, and all the limitations of our enfeebled moral condition, it is still a glorious salvation; "I know not the numbers thereof." To many souls now here "to live is Christ," no longer sin and failure and shame. "In God have we righteousness and strength."

As we cannot all speak here, those who have received at Oxford the fresh blessing of a full trust in our Lord for this life as well as for that to come—the soul-sabbath in Christ—will be glad to rise and praise God in the Doxology.

A large number then rose and sang:—

"Praise God from whom all blessings flow."

Then *all* who were in a definite experience of full trust were invited to sing:—

"Glory, honour, praise and power,
Be unto the Lamb for ever,
Jesus Christ is our Redeemer;
Praise ye the Lord."

At this suggestion, out of about a thousand persons nearly all, it is believed, rose to their feet and sang, with deep feeling, these grand old lines.

Mr. Smith continued: "We are specially commanded to pray for kings, and for all that are in authority;"

and ended with the prayers for the Queen and the royal family.

The Rev. Canon BATTERSBY requested those present to rise and join him in repeating together 2 Thess. i. 3, and iii. 16, "We are bound to thank God always for you, beloved, because that your faith groweth exceedingly, and the charity of every one of you all toward each other aboundeth." "Now the Lord of peace Himself give you peace always by all means. The Lord be with you all." With these words the Oxford Conference ended.

CHAPTER XIII.

"GOD hath visited His people."* If any one had said a year ago that we should see, in the city of Oxford, an assembly of Christians, very largely composed of ministers of the Establishment and various Nonconformist bodies, and including twenty or thirty Continental Pastors, gathered for the alone purpose of seeking, by mutual counsel and united prayer and consecration, to reach a higher condition of Christian life, it would have been considered far more devoutly to be wished than likely to occur. And if it had been added that we should see early morning meetings of nearly a thousand of these men and women, of all ranks in society, and of all denominations, gathered for prayer, and for the communication of their experiences in the divine life, clergymen and laymen standing up and declaring what God had done for their souls, there would have been not a few to say, with the lord on whose hand the king of Israel leaned, "If the Lord would open windows in heaven might such a thing be!" But God *has* opened the windows of heaven, and is pouring out a blessing that there shall not be room to receive it. And not *only* so, but God hath chosen the foolish things of the

* See *The Christian* of September 10 and 17.

world to confound the wise; and God hath chosen the weak things of the world to confound the things which are mighty; that no flesh should glory in His presence. Could anything have been more unlikely than that Scotland should have been stirred from end to end by two strangers like our brethren Moody and Sankey? or that at Oxford, another layman should have been able to convene such a congress as that which has for the past ten days been gathered there? Looking either at the evangelical work in the North, or at these assemblies of Christians "for the Promotion of Scriptural Holiness," no one unblinded by prejudice could fail to see that the blessed Spirit of God is moving upon the waters, and that a work of grace and power, not less divine and omnipotent than that of the six days' creation, is already begun. God forbid that any of His people, like the lord above alluded to, should see it with their eyes, and yet not partake thereof.

The truth is, the risen Lord has breathed upon His disciples, and said, "Receive ye the Holy Ghost;" and the Eternal Spirit has breathed upon the slain, no matter through what human lips, so that the prophesying is as He hath commanded, and there is a noise, and behold a shaking, and the bones come together, bone to his bone. Thus far at least have we seen, and we shall see greater things than these; we shall see the breath come into them, and they shall live, and stand upon their feet, an exceeding great army.

In connection with the union of England with America in this movement, let us also notice the fact *that the* Continent of Europe was well represented at this Conference. It would have touched any heart to see a score of pastors—French, German, Dutch, Swiss—gathered on the platform of the Town Hall at Oxford, an American Christian presiding, while hymns were sung and prayers offered in German and French, and a Frenchman translated the address of his German brother. These men, members of the two nations so recently at deadly war, are going back to their French and German homes, to tell the people of the same Jesus, the Author and Finisher of their common faith, the Centre of their one hope, the Object of their united love. They are going home to bear witness that Jesus lives; that He lives in them; and that their life is hid with Christ in God. Is not this full of hope and encouragement? Will not all His people rejoice in hope of the glory of God? Does it not at least remind us of the prophecy and promise, "Neither shall they learn war any more"?

We have attended many Conferences, including a ten days' Convention in America, the prototype of that at Oxford, but in many respects this excelleth them all. It is the fruit and flower of those which have gone before—of those at Barnet, and Mildmay, and Perth, and other places at home, as well as of Mannheim, and Vineland, and Round Lake, in the United States. Conferences must be of another type henceforth; the stiffness and reserve have been broken through, and such a brotherly confidence has possessed a thousand gathered saints of God, that they could hear with deepest sympathy while others told the secrets of their *hearts*—their past failures—their pantings after God, *the living* God—their surrender now, not only of their character, influence, reputations, but of themselves, and the full joy of some, and the expectant hope of others, who had thus come to the seat of learning to learn their own nothingness and yield that up to God ; to learn also the glory of the Word made flesh, the only begotten of the Father, full of grace and truth, and to receive of His fulness grace for grace.

The most characteristic features of the Conference were the union of nationalities ; the spirit of love and unity which, so far as we are aware, was undisturbed throughout by one unkind or bitter word (though, as might be expected, things were spoken in which all were not agreed) ; the reception of individual blessing ; and the restrained expression of heart-experience, which was listened to with respectful attention and love toward the speakers, and with devout thanksgiving to God, not unaccompanied by deep searchings of heart, and silent cries and tears for a like blessing.

If it be asked what is the "blessing?" it is the blessedness of the man "who maketh the Lord his trust," "whose strength is in Thee," of them who have not seen and yet have believed—who stand by night in the house of the Lord, trusting where they cannot see Him—who present their bodies a living sacrifice, holy, acceptable to God, their reasonable service ; and who, doing this, are not conformed to this world, but are being daily transformed by the renewing of their minds, that they may know what that good and acceptable and perfect will of the Lord is.

Let this also be remarked—those who had waited on God before they came, and who came expecting to *receive*, were those whose praises were the clearest, and those whom the Saviour had most evidently met. Those who came with prejudice, but in a candid spirit, had their doubts removed. If any came with a foregone conclusion, determined not to see the grace of God, doubtless they have left more hardened in their own opinion; but we really do not think there can have been any such cases. Of this we are assured, each has had this promise fulfilled: "According to your faith be it unto you."

The Conference was not a disjointed collection of meetings, but a symmetrical whole, advancing day by day in a continuous development of Christian experience.

Commencing with the prayers for the searching light of God's presence in our hearts, and a deep desire to know the remaining evil of our lives, we were led on to such new discoveries of inward and outward failure as brought a deep sense of conviction into many hearts. The light had been let into the cavern, and we were alarmed to find what forms of loathsome life had been sheltered within by the twilight. But the light which shows the evil reveals also the cleansing blood, and we felt that we were not to shrink from this solemn searching, but rather to invite it more and more fully.

Then came solemn renunciation of the revealed evil in the presence and power of the Great Searcher of all hearts. Lurking ambitions, half-recognized self-indulgences, social rivalries, pride of opinion, the things written on the walls of the secret chambers of imagery, idolatrous affections, and especially *the great* SIN of unbelief in the promises of God, which lay at the root of all other sins,—all, *all* that we could discern, were yielded. The principal purpose of the earlier days was to get us away not only from the outward bustle of our lives, but from the inward restlessness of our being, to get quiet before God, so that we might indeed hear and know all that He had a controversy with. Many could not understand it, but leaders and congregations were carried along together by the same divine guidance.

Next we found ourselves occupied with the yielding of our whole hearts to God, because of "the mercies of God" already received; presenting our whole being a living sacrifice to the Lord, jealously guarding against any secret reserves; and having brought all, watching lest anything should be sacrilegiously snatched from the altar which sanctifieth the gift. "Every devoted thing is most holy to the Lord"; we felt that nothing should ever again be taken back for the purposes of the old selfhood. We are not to be always giving ourselves afresh to God, as though we had not already done so once for all; but to realize that *we have already done it*, as persons are married once for all; not day by day saying the ceremony of marriage as though they had not already been bound together. Once done, the Christian should in every moment realize that he is the Lord's—wholly and for ever the Lord's.

Then faith grasped the fact that the offering made with the whole heart, with or without emotion, was acceptable to God. The interior consciousness and emotions will, sooner or later, be conformed to the divinely-directed acts of the will and of faith. It was a saying of Fenelon that true religion resides in the will alone; so that, irrespective of the uncertain, varying emotions of our lives, we may give ourselves fully and utterly to God in our will alone, disregarding our feelings, and live henceforth as those wholly given to God, however our emotions and inclinations might rebel. It is for this that we had in Christ been made free from the law, from the dominion of sin, from the control of the old life, free men; free, not to sin, but to give ourselves thus to God. His by purchase and right, we felt that we became, in the most full sense, His also by choice, and by an act of surrender and trust.

It was constantly pointed out that, so far from this being the finality of Christian experience, it was *but the commencement of a course of "progressive sanctification,"* which, through grace, by faith, should never again be retrogressive, but ever developing.

From this point of entire self-surrender and trust we were shown that we were no longer to be conformed to this world, but transformed, "transfigured," by the renewing of our minds, proving, with an upright purpose, in each detail of life day by day, what is that good and acceptable and perfect will of God. In this attitude of full consecration and trust, "if in anything we be otherwise minded, God shall reveal even this unto us," our habitual position being instantaneous, implicit, and unreserved obedience.

We were, day by day, reminded, that while this is what Scripture calls "a perfect heart," — an entire loyalty—it was human imperfection all through, and at an infinite distance from our only standard,—Christ. It is the antithesis of "perfectionism." As we thus walked *in the light* of God, we should daily by that light see so *much* more of the evil of our own condition by nature, that we should, as never before, be saved from the thought of "perfection in the flesh."

No words can describe the solemnity imparted to the meetings by the general exercise of soul, so profound, so engrossing. Hundreds were brought before God as never before, and led to yield both known and half-suspected sins, things "not of faith;" the peace of "a conscience void of offence," a "heart that condemns us not," was found by hundreds. With this came a greatly deeper apprehension of the value and meaning of the cross of Christ, as separating not only from the guilt of sin, but, through death, from the old life of sin.

After several days of exercises of this character, and after hundreds of clergymen, ministers, and others had publicly and privately acknowledged their realization of a new position as to practical full self-surrender and faith before the Lord, the character of the meetings was changed to teaching how this life of full trust was to be maintained, not by struggle, but by faith in our Lord. Fierce contests would come, but they would be "the fight of faith," the fight behind our shield, no longer a doubtful contest, but a continuous march to victory.

Next the being "filled with the Spirit" was pressed upon us as a command, and therefore a promise. Many hearts were deeply exercised as to the power from on high for their ministry. On Saturday night, under a sermon, "Be *filled* with the Spirit," the hearts of the congregation were deeply bowed under the sense of the presence and power of a baptism of the Holy Spirit.

A noticeable feature of the meetings was their great

ease. They seemed to flow on without strain or effort on the part of the speakers, all being carried on in one harmonious current.

The friend who attended to the details of procuring lodgings, and arranging the details, stated that he had not heard a hasty word, or seen a disturbed countenance, amid all the perplexing detail and crowding of so large an assembly. People along the street were heard to remark, "What happy people these people are!" Except in a single instance, we heard of no hasty word, nor any contention as to doctrine.

A dear friend said: "When I entered heaven, I expected to feel such joy, but never till then. 'My life flows on in endless song;' that began to be true at Oxford, and is still."

Another friend said: "I do not know how to describe the time, except by saying it was a ten days' heaven upon earth."

A dear child of seventeen, who had known the Lord only two years, said to me: "I can't tell you anything about the grand buildings at Oxford, but I know a good deal about the small lanes and homes of the poor. We went there with some ministers singing for Jesus, and the people following us in troops. Dear J. W—— preached the Gospel to them, and now I am longing to go back to school to tell them all about the blessing."

But it is said by some that these Conferences are not practical; that they are mere manifestations of sentimentality and mysticism; that no plans are devised, no schemes elaborated, no committees formed; that the *people just* come and go with no result, beyond the *useless pleasure* of having met. And indeed it is quite true that no plans or schemes are proposed and discussed; and the whole charge is true, unless it be a practical thing to entreat the face of the living God. There were no plans or schemes laid down at Pentecost; nothing could have been less practical, in the eyes of those who believe in the wisdom and power of man, than for a hundred and twenty men and women to meet together day after day, for ten days, waiting for the promised Spirit; but when that Spirit was poured out, and they went forth without having formed a committee or decided upon any method of operation, to preach this mighty Gospel, that Jesus is the Christ, and three thousand were converted before the night closed in, that surely was neither empty sentiment nor vague mysticism, but practical work, effected, not indeed by human might or power, but by the Spirit of the Lord of Hosts. And when the preaching had been found so practical that the captain of the Temple and the Sadducees laid hands on them and put them in hold until the next day; and rulers, and elders, and scribes, and the high priest and all his kindred, were gathered together to put this thing down; and the apostles and their company again entreated the face of Jehovah, and the house was shaken where they were assembled, and they were all filled with the Holy Ghost, and spake the Word of God with boldness—surely this was practical. And the life of Paul was practical, though he had no scheme of his own, no committee—only the risen Jesus in heaven and the Holy Spirit on earth.

And in that prophetic word is it not practical when *ten men* of all languages take hold of the skirts of one that is a Jew inwardly, whose heart is circumcised, and say, "We will go with you;" not because your plan of Christian work is so well devised, so free from extravagance and undue excitement—no, but because "we have heard that God is with you?"

Oh, brethren, the great necessity of the age is GOD. Vain man, in the name of science, falsely so called, is deifying matter and denying God; will human plans and methods, will men's ingenuity and administration, meet the exigencies of the case? No, never! The Church and the world want GOD; therefore the one most practical thing is for God's assembled people to entreat the face of the Lord of Hosts. "Wherefore should they say among the heathen, Where is their God?" "Sanctify ye a fast, call a solemn assembly; gather the elders, and all the inhabitants of the land, into the house of the Lord your God, and cry unto the Lord. . . . Then will the Lord be jealous for His land, and pity His people; . . . and my people shall never be ashamed."—(*The Christian.*)

CHAPTER XIV.

Results.

ONE of the gratifying effects of the Oxford Meeting was the deep impression made upon the unconverted. No means have been taken to gather up results; but a Congregational minister speaks of many conversions in his congregation. A clergyman was told in the train by a young woman that her two sisters and herself were all then converted to God, and that she had gladly given a sum of money, carefully reserved for worldly indulgence, to the Lord's treasury. The servants of the principal hotels were gathered together by several ladies, and were deeply moved by the power of the Gospel.

Meetings were continued, under the care of Lord Radstock, through the week, in the Corn Exchange, at 7 and 3 o'clock for believers, and in the evenings for the unconverted. We do not like to "number the people of Israel," but large blessings are reported as following the meetings in different quarters of Oxford and its neighbourhood. In the pages of the *Christian*, and the *Christian's Pathway of Power*, will be found some accounts of the tide of blessing which followed the return of those at the Oxford Meeting to their homes in various parts of Great Britain and the Continent.

Similar meetings were convened in all directions, and special blessing has been reported in the organization of those in France. The hymns used at Oxford were translated into German and French, and also the books on the Life of Faith. In Paris the monthly periodical, *La Liberateur*, and another in Basle, *Des Christen Glaubensweg*, were at once commenced, and devoted specially, like the *Christian's Pathway of Power*, to teaching the privileges of consecration and the life of trust.

Our limits forbid more than specimens of the reports coming in from various quarters.

From Rev. D. Martin, Congregational Minister, Oxford :—

September 9th, 1874.

My dear Brother in the Lord,—I feel it to be an honour to bear my humble testimony to this glorious work of God. I wish it to be considered as coming from my people. I am their representative ; I intended to be their spokesman at the meetings, but my heart was too full for utterance. They will now be heard praising the Lord for the blessings they have received—blessings without number, as they will be without end.

1. We are profoundly thankful that the banner of "holiness to the Lord," through faith in Jesus, has been unfurled in our much-loved city, and for two special reasons—the Church generally needs it, because holiness is sadly neglected. It is written, "and let every *one that* nameth the name of Christ depart from iniquity;" but, alas! we have not departed from all

iniquity, and we have been too much accustomed to believe it to be an impossibility to "perfect holiness in the fear of the Lord," and *so have failed.* But it is not enough to have "holiness to the Lord" on our banner; we must have it also "through faith in Jesus," because there are multitudes looking for holiness by other means. According to Popish teaching people are to be made holy by rites, ceremonies, penance, purgatory, &c., &c. So that we feel profoundly thankful that, in the midst of so much darkness, this light has come, and the people have been taught that sanctification—as justification—comes by constantly looking unto Jesus *only.* Our prayer is that this banner may be unfurled everywhere, till all see, believe, and rejoice.

2. We are thankful that one effect of the presentation of this truth has been "*conviction for holiness.*" This is greatly needed, that, as sinners must be convinced in order to be justified, so believers may be more deeply convinced in order to be sanctified. The teaching has been very tender and loving, but very searching; and, as the result, many have been led to discover what enemy within has hindered their heavenward progress. I confess that, to my view, *unbelief* is that terrible foe. I have always regarded it as the chief devil and tormentor; it has been now made to appear *a blacker devil than ever.* Most solemnly were the words of God pressed on our attention, "He that believeth not God hath made Him a liar, because he believeth not the record that God gave of His Son." The conviction flashed upon me, Why, what have I been doing? I have been listening to the *chief liar in creation.* Who is the chief liar? Surely he that makes

the God of truth a liar must himself be the greatest; and this is what God says we do by listening to this terrible lying spirit within us, *unbelief*. Let this suffice as an example. Doubtless to multitudes of believers sins innumerable have been brought to light. This I regard as a priceless blessing, as leading to holiness.

3. We have received glorious encouragement in the way of holiness. I know instances of persons reading of the "higher life," and having been sadly depressed thereby, because they have not seen *how* it may be realized; and it has been a source of exquisite mental torture, unfolding before them a glorious life, but entirely above their reach. But the testimony of so many witnesses—their profound peace and joy, and abounding hope—has removed all doubts, has caused them to see that there is no longer any need of being constantly beaten and buffeted by the enemy, but theirs may be the privilege of daily, hourly victory; that "the old man" may be so subdued, so manacled, so crippled, as to be unable to reign—for "sin shall not have dominion over you, for ye are not under law, but under grace." No words can express the delight of some of my people on account of *this grand spiritual fact*. It has lifted off a mighty burden from their spirits, and opened up visions of brightness and blessedness attainable even in this present life by holiness through faith; whilst in other instances that have come under my observation, it has awakened earnest longings which I trust will lead to invincible determination to wait upon the Lord until this blessing is *theirs*—for "blessed are they that *hunger and thirst after* righteousness, for they shall be filled."

4. I have reason to believe that a great number have been led to *decide for Jesus* and a life of holiness through faith in Him. There were many not far from the kingdom, some of my own congregation amongst them, and they have given their hearts to Jesus. Others, who have not been entire strangers to the rest of faith, have been led, in the marvellous spiritual atmosphere in which we had been living during this pentecostal season, into a deeper, more confident, more joyous and triumphant rest.

5. *Last Lord's Day.*—Probably there never was such a Sabbath in this city, never such a collection of God's people, never such prayers for the baptism of the Holy Ghost, and never such manifest answers. I will briefly describe what happened in my own chapel. I had preached from 1 Pet. i. 8, 9, and had endeavoured to bring out this fact—that the whole secret of this life of faith is here—that the vivid realization of Jesus "moment by moment" with believing prayer, prevents sin being *an inevitable fact;* that evil thoughts brought thus into this light, instead of remaining to reign, fade away, as the beasts of prey retire to their dens when the sun rises; that as it is impossible for sin to live in the full view of Jesus in heaven, so the nearer we attain to this by His manifestation of Himself to us, the more complete will be our victory over sin and sorrow in this world. Peter says, *I have* seen the Lord, but *you* have not, but you believe and that is enough, since it causes you to love and to rejoice. Whilst thus believing, loving, and rejoicing, you are actually receiving—what?—the end of your faith, the *salvation* of your souls; including, without a doubt,

sanctification. At the Lord's table, immediately after, a beloved brother from Bristol, who is associated with Mr. Müller, rose and asked permission to confirm what I had been saying, and stated that it was his privilege to be able to say that he had lived in unbroken unclouded communion with Jesus for very many years, and after explaining how it may be, and urging us to seek it, prayed most fervently that all might be led into this most blessed life. Afterwards several visitors rose up spontaneously, to declare with great gratitude that they had found this blessed peace in the meetings which had been held. The place seemed full of the presence of God, so melting, so soul-subduing, and so gladsome, that the like had never before been realized by us.

In the evening our beloved brother Monod, from Paris, preached to a remarkable congregation. Such was the desire to hear, that people were round the doors long before the time of service. The building was perfectly packed, with a rapt audience. The brotherhood of the Gospel was here realized, there being representatives of all sections of the Church, and almost every condition in society—Clergymen, Baptist, Wesleyan, Congregationalists, &c., the rich and the poor, all met together to praise the Lord and to hear His word.

Our brother preached from 2 Cor. xiii. 9, with all the simplicity, fervour, and unction for which he is so remarkable, to the comfort and rejoicing of the multitude of believers who were gathered together to hear *him*.

Many went away from this service to the larger

gatherings in the Town Hall, or the Corn Exchange, and so concluded the most remarkable Sabbath we ever spent in Oxford.

I cannot describe the joy I have felt all through this season of spiritual refreshing, in witnessing the earnestness of my people. Young disciples, whom I have been the means of converting and training for usefulness, so interested, overflowing with happiness; men of business, giving up all thought of business for the time; careful Marthas, ceasing to be troubled about domestic difficulties—all absorbed in the desire and the determination to receive as much as possible of the blessing which was being poured out on Oxford.

Am I not bound to hope that this is the commencement of the time of refreshing that has been sought for in believing prayer during the closing years of my ministry here? But even this is but a small matter compared with what is in every Christian's thought throughout Christendom, that as Oxford has been and still is, in a measure, a fountain whence flows the deadliest spiritual poison, it may in the future become a fountain of all that is true, and holy, and good; and my impression is that of all means hitherto employed, none are more likely to succeed than this movement. I write most deliberately, after much prayerful thought and observation, that I have never witnessed so much of God—of God's presence, God's power, God's grace, as I have in this; so little of the flesh, so much of the Spirit; so little of man, so much of Jesus—never! never!

Our prayer here is that this Conference may become annual *in this city*; that in every town in this land,

and in every land under the sun, such holy gatherings may be held, until the blood-stained banner of holiness to the Lord, by faith in Jesus, may be waving in triumph over the whole world, fulfilling the immutable word of our faithful God: "When the enemy cometh in like a flood, the Spirit of the Lord shall lift up a standard against him."—Beseeching an interest in your constant prayers for this city, yours affectionately in the love of Jesus,

DAVID MARTIN, Congregational Minister.

To the Editor of *The Christian*.

A letter from Birmingham says: "You cannot think what a bond 'Oxford' still is among those who were there. The brightness shed over so many souls is constantly coming to our notice, shining out here and there, in unlooked-for quarters. We had a very blessed miniature repetition here a fortnight ago. Just when people got warmed up, and many were flocking in, we had to separate; but it will be an encouragement to be bolder next time; and, as a first effort, we were very thankful for this."

At Brighton, on Monday evening, September 21st, a crowded meeting was held at the Dome, with reference to the recent Evangelical Conference at Oxford. Several gentlemen had been announced to give an account of the proceedings at the Conference, and about 2,000 persons assembled, the Dome being well filled. The Rev. E. L. Roxby, Incumbent of All Souls', presided. The chairman stated that the object of the meeting was to hear an account of the wonderful blessing that had attended the Conference that had recently been held at Oxford. This Conference had been so helpful, so useful, that many of those who were present, when they came home, determined to give an account of the great work God had done there. The tendency of the teaching that was brought forward there seemed to be this — fuller trust in the Lord Jesus Christ, moment by moment. And the result of this meeting was that many persons went back to their parishes or their dwelling-places, possessing a joy and a peace which they had been strangers to before. And this work, which had humbled them so much on account of their sins and shortcomings, which had taught them to love more and think more of their blessed Saviour, must have been of God; and, therefore, he asked them to give themselves *wholly* up to Him, and ask Him to make them wholly His own.

The subsequent speakers all testified to the blessing so generally experienced at the Oxford meetings.—(*The Christian.*)

With the view of hearing more of the truths enunciated at the Oxford Conference, another meeting of a similar kind was held in the Music Room of the Royal Pavilion, on the evening of the 28th ult. The room was literally crowded by ladies and gentlemen, every available space, not excluding that upon the platform, being occupied, while many endeavoured in vain to gain admission.

The presiding clergyman, the Rev. E. H. Hopkins, read and spoke upon Eph. iii. 14. Rev. J. B. Figgis, whose heart was full, and who felt that the hearts of many were full, and that words could give but poor expression to the feelings which were passing through their hearts under that wave of blessing with which God had touched their town, directed attention to the Pentecostal presence of the Holy Ghost, as recorded in the Acts of the Apostles. One after another had, he said, characterised the blessed time at Oxford as another Pentecost, and he prayerfully desired that whatever blessing was poured out at Oxford might be poured out at Brighton; whatever grace was received at the former place might be received at the latter, that the same Holy Spirit that was given at the one town might be given at the other.

An impressive prayer was offered by Rev. Dr. O. Winslow, who supplicated that Christ might preside over all their hearts; that in anticipation of the great and important gathering which was to take place during the succeeding week at Brighton, the holy atmosphere of these assemblies might spread around, and that the Spirit of the Lord might brood over the Congress.

Similar meetings are being held in St. Margaret's schoolroom on Wednesday evenings, and in Union Street Chapel on Thursday evenings, and will be held in the Countess of Huntingdon's Church on Monday evenings.—(*Sussex Daily News.*)

The following meetings have just been commenced: Daily prayer-meeting, at Young Men's Christian Association, Prince Albert Street, noon. Consecration meeting at the same place on Wednesday, at 7.30 a.m., and Saturday, at 8 p.m. Also at the "British Workman," Sunday, 7.30 a.m.

The following accounts are from a parish near *Oxford*:—

"*The* revival in the parish of Deddington, Oxfordshire, has been the first known fruit of the Oxford meetings. On Sunday last the evening service in the parish church was largely attended. The services in the chapels were held earlier, and that in the parish church an hour later, to enable all to attend. One chapel in a hamlet of the parish was closed, and the preacher at a chapel five miles off gave up his evening service, and brought his congregation to Deddington, that they might hear of the outpouring of the Spirit on the Oxford meetings.

"This was the subject of the vicar's sermon; and as he told of the many manifestations of the Holy Spirit's power, again, as on the previous Sunday evening, the Spirit fell on them that heard the word.

"The people came miles, and such a scene has never before been witnessed in this town. The large church was crowded, and the Holy Spirit descended in such power that sinners were convinced of sin, and some realised pardon and peace before they left the church. The vicar said he would not leave the church while there was one anxious soul who would remain. A large prayer-meeting was held in the vestry, which continued up to ten o'clock. The chancel was nearly full of anxious inquirers, and many that night were plucked as brands from the burning. Yesterday five men went to the vicarage to know what they must do to be saved.

"I have known this parish for more than thirty years, and I can truly say that I never saw the like before. The vicar, who has for many years been a devoted servant of Christ, seems to have received new life since the Conference at Oxford. He has the *sympathy* of every Dissenter, and all are one in this great movement. Everywhere there are 'signs of abundance of rain,' and I believe God is about to work mightily in the hearts and consciences of the people here. We only add that every Christian to whom the writer has spoken—and he has had a liberty never before given him to speak to sinner and to saint, —every Christian, save one, has declared the last few weeks have been the happiest and most blessed time of their Christian experience.

"The good work is spreading to the neighbouring villages. We conclude with words which a dear aged believer says he uses every day for what has been done amongst us by the power of the Holy Spirit, "We praise Thee, O God, we acknowledge Thee to be the Lord.'"

APPENDIX.

A SELECTION FROM THE LETTERS RECEIVED.

I.

October 1st, 1874.

"CONTINUOUS victory by the power of the Holy Ghost" expresses, in few words, the inestimable blessing imparted to me by the Lord Jesus at the Oxford ten-day meeting.

For many years I had enjoyed the peace of Christ, the joy of the Holy Ghost, the love of God and sweet rest of soul in Jesus but fitfully, and while I longed for more conformity to the Lord, and more spirituality of mind, and for unbroken communion, I had insensibly fallen into a sort of misty conclusion that it was not intended we should attain to holiness in this life, but that our halting ways were meant to keep us humble and to exalt the Lord. Gradually, from day to day, direct manifestation of the Holy Ghost was made to my wondering soul, and I learned the possibilities of faith, and that Jesus is as able as He is willing to keep the trusting soul in abiding peace, continuous joy, perfect love, and heavenly rest.

"Eye hath not seen, nor ear heard, neither have entered into the heart of man, the things which God hath prepared for them that love Him, but God HATH revealed them unto us by His Spirit."

Now in a measure I can pray believingly (Eph. iii. 14-21) that "I may be able to comprehend with all saints what is the breadth and length and depth and height, and to know the love of Christ which passeth knowledge, that we may be filled with all the fulness of God;" and I can shout the praises of Him that is "able to do *exceeding* ABUNDANTLY ABOVE ALL that we ask or think, according to the power that worketh in us."

CHEYNE BRADY.

II.

9, Montague Place, Russell Square,
London, September, 1874.

I am a barrister, 71 years old, and have been converted about thirty-five years, having first realised a sense of pardoned sin on the 16th April, 1838. I have since then, and specially in later years, been a good deal engaged in the Lord's work—Bible classes, &c., and not, I believe, without some tokens of the Lord's blessing; but all the while with an inner experience which is very much a counterpart of that recorded by Mr. T. Monod in his letter, printed in the *Pathway of Power*.

My mind had been a good deal exercised about these precious truths during the last half year; as I had seen the wonderful result upon the lives of others who had embraced them; and I went to Oxford in a state of mental uncertainty, and not by any means predisposed to enter fully into them.

But on Tuesday evening—for I reached Oxford in time for the last meeting that day—I was led to see the prerequisite of a definite absolute surrender of all to God; and in my chamber that night, to a certain extent, I believe, I *did* surrender my all to Him, and each meeting afterwards, I obtained more light; but it was not until I was alone for two hours in a carriage by myself on the railway, on Friday night, that the surrender of *all* was complete, and I felt that my will was truly on the Lord's side. And, that being done, I was enabled to realise that He would keep that which I had committed to Him; and, thank God, He has done so hitherto, and *I believe He will*, even to the end. The Bible is a new book to me, though I knew the letter of it, and rested on many of its precious promises before. Prayer is also a new thing to me. It used often to be a burden, and wandering was irresistible. *Now* it is a delight, and I rarely find myself even tempted to wander, and if I do, it is instantaneously checked.

If you publish any names, I give you full liberty to

publish mine. I delight to proclaim far and near the blessing which has been brought to my soul through definite consecration and definite trust. I found it a hard matter for the first ten days to trust the Lord entirely; but now, the Lord be praised, it seems to be the normal state of my soul, without an effort.

MARCUS MARTIN.

III.

Park Hill, Moseley, Birmingham,
September 28th, 1874.

I am a Baptist minister in this town, have been converted about eighteen years, and had much intercourse with the "brethren," so that for years I have known the truths of union with Christ.

At first I was prejudiced against teachings known as "sanctification by faith." I thought they were unsound, tending to perfection in the flesh. Gradually, upon examination, I became convinced that they were according to Scripture, but could not say they were my experience.

In June last I attended the meeting at Mildmay, and although much enjoying it, did not receive what I desired—the perfect rest of faith.

Months went on, and I at last persuaded myself that what these good people had was what I for years had seen—union with Christ.

I came to Oxford on the Thursday morning, being unable to come before, and when I heard the experience of one minister after another, I was convinced that I was ignorant of any such real experience as they testified of.

Friday evening I had to return again here; oh! I did desire to remain longer, yet I thought, The Lord can give me this experience even while going home. Before leaving the Hall, Canon Battersby gave his experience most clearly, and after him a minister arose and stated what blessings he had received at the meetings, but he could not yet say he had entire rest. Just my case, I thought. Leaving the Hall I met Canon Battersby, and asked him why he thought it was the last speaker failed to know the blessing; for, I said, his case is just mine.

"In all probability," was the reply, "because of his want of faith." And then he referred me to the nobleman at Cana of Galilee, who desired Jesus to come down and heal his son, and when Christ told him his son lived, he waited not for signs, but just believed the word that Jesus had spoken, and went his way.

In the train, in one corner of the carriage, in the light of truth, I examined my heart to see if there was any one thing I was unwilling to give up. "No, Lord," I felt, "all, all is thine." Then what more was needed? *Faith*, and that word came sweetly to my soul; "Faithful is He that calleth you, Who also will do it." "Yes, Lord," I said, "and Thou shalt do it now and for ever."

At once a sweet consciousness of rest and peace stole over my heart, the troubled waters subsided, and there was a great calm.

There was one gentleman in the carriage with me. "Now, Lord," I said, "I am wholly Thine; hast Thou a word for me to speak, if so put it into my mouth." In a few minutes I was enabled to commence a conversation with him, and soon was dealing personally with his soul. When I came home, I told my wife and my people on the next Sunday that they might rejoice with me. Since this time I have proved the reality of the rest of faith and the victory over sin and the power for service in my everyday life; yet I find the constant need of watching against getting into my old way, of planning for myself, instead of at once, when the need comes, looking to the Lord; or of engaging in my own strength in His service, instead of yielding up my heart continually for Him to work in me both to *will* and to *do* of His good pleasure.

The life of faith, instead of being distinct acts, is becoming more a constant habit, and I am confident that He who has begun the good work will perform it unto the end. Desiring an interest in your prayers, that I may not only be myself blessed, but prove a blessing to others.

Yours in the love of Christ,

G. E. THOMAS.

IV.

Tunbridge Wells, October 19th, 1874.

I am asked, as a thanksgiving to God, to say in a few words what I received at the Oxford Conference. The great treasure of rest in Jesus; for everything was made a more tangible reality. Through God's goodness I had known something of it experimentally before, but it was there reduced to Scripture form, and it became more than experience, an actual fact, which one would no more doubt than one would doubt one's justification. I think I have now grasped it intellectually, as I had before received it into my heart, so that I find myself better able to teach it, and have already been blessed to the leading of others into this happy rest.

R. D. Monro.

V.

October 6th, 1874.

I feel so glad to tell you what a great help and joy the Oxford Meetings have been to me. For years since my conversion, I have been seeking for a full salvation, and hungering and thirsting to know what was meant by resurrection-life in Jesus, and constant abiding in Him. Some papers in the *Christian*, which appeared last year, on the subject of "holiness," gave me the hope of more light, and then the *Pathway of Power* was such a help to me, especially the papers by H. W. S.

Still it remained for the blessed work in Oxford to confirm and deepen my consecration, and lead me as never before to abandon myself to Jesus.

The past struggling faithless prayers are exchanged for an attitude of *trust* for all, hour by hour. I do not know much of rejoicing in the Lord, for the privileges upon which I have thus entered seem so glorious, so overwhelming in their unmerited grace, they make me tremble, and my faith is very weak, but I think I would rather die than give them up. There is no more goodness in me than before. I think I never felt so mean and utterly sinful, but "He is able," and I cling to Him. I hope I have not done wrong in responding to your request for the testimony of those who received a blessing at Oxford, I was so happy to do so. I will thank you so very much not to mention my name. . . .

VI.

I had heard of the "Higher Christian Life," by Mr. Boardman, and had also heard of the correspondence concerning Mr. P. Smith's views on "Perfection," but I took very little interest in the subject; and not caring to study the opinions of either, I had an idea that they were visionary and unpractical.

Having learnt, however, that meetings of a semi-private character were held at Broadlands for the promotion of Scriptural and practical holiness, and that much blessing had attended the gatherings, I longed to have a share of such blessing. I had for some time desired and prayed that God would awaken and save souls in my parish; and when the announcement was made that a public Conference would be held at Oxford, the question arose,—"Shall I go to this, or travel to Scotland and see the work of God in that land?" for I felt I wanted the blessing more for my parish, through me, than for myself.

Never can I be too thankful that I was led by God to meet Him at Oxford. I came in a *receptive* spirit, expecting to be much refreshed; but instead of there being simply "times of refreshing," I was enabled to lay hold of a new power, of which I had no previous knowledge. I seemed to have gathered strength each day of the meetings, as God revealed Himself to our waiting souls, to drop off one by one the "garments spotted by the flesh," then to "*crucify* the flesh," and lastly to follow self to its burial. The final step of *self-surrender* was made as I cut the cable that held me to the shore by publicly testifying before the Conference that I had found the blessing, and longed to return to my parish in Ireland to bear witness of the *reality* of the new life I had found.

I had never thought that I ought to expect to have an uniform daily victory over known sin, but I now see that God not only commanded, but *intends* that His people should have the conquest. Moreover He is, I find, *true to His word,* and being able, *does* keep me from falling whenever, and as long as, I trust Him.

Oh, the rest and the power that I now have is an unspeakable surprise to myself and others!

The energy of faith is evinced in overcoming inward and outward temptation, or impelling to joyful service. Often for years have I resolved and struggled and prayed against a certain besetting sin, threatening even to dash my watch to the ground if I again yielded, hoping by this threat of costly sacrifice I might succeed. Alas, my time-piece had soon to suffer, and my strength and my prayers availed but little. *Now* (to God be ascribed everlasting praise) I find the conquest easy, through "Him who has redeemed us to God by His blood."

Formerly my Bible was read, my parish was worked, and my sermons were preached in a very perfunctory manner, now they are the joy of my life.

W. J. McCormick,
Incumbent of Kilbride, Arklow.

September 25th, 1874.

VII.

It was my blessed privilege to attend a large portion of the meetings at Oxford, and I humbly confess to have received an abundant blessing in my own soul. It was indeed a rich Pentecostal season, a time of refreshing from the presence of the Lord!

There was no apparent excitement, but a holy calmness pervaded the dense mass of hearers as they listened to the scriptural teaching of the holy men of God who addressed them.

I have been permitted to preach the blessed truths of the Gospel for forty years, and God has in mercy made me the instrument of good to numbers of souls; but still I never felt the power of those truths so forcibly in my own heart as I did while listening to the various speakers.

New life seems to have been imparted to me, and I feel now, as I have never done before, how blessed it is to surrender ourselves entirely to the Lord Jesus, to trust in Him momentarily each passing day, and, abiding in Christ, to enter into the joys of a present salvation, the glorious and happy liberty of God's dear children. I doubt not numbers of others can testify in like manner to the spiritual blessing received at these meetings, and I am sure can record with gratitude, that, during the remaining years of their earthly pilgrimage, they can never forget the Oxford Conference. To me it seemed to be really a previous foretaste of that blessed time when the whole company of the Lord's redeemed shall stand before His throne, clad in white robes, with palms in their hands. May the Lord soon accomplish the number of His elect, and hasten that day when Jesus shall present them to His Father, and say, "Behold I, and the children thou hast given me!"

JOHN W. WATTS,
Vicar of Bicester.

September 10th, 1874.

VIII.

Montague Square, London,
September 26th, 1874.

After forty years of a very depressing wilderness experience I found rest in Jesus in the spring of last year from the long, and for the most part, fruitless struggle with sin; but it was not till my visit to Oxford that I was taught how to obtain victory over earthly cares and anxieties. I am now enabled to give them up to my Saviour altogether, and great peace has followed my doing so.

But the chief and overpowering blessing connected with my visit to Oxford was the baptism of the Holy Ghost. There was such a solemn sense then given me of close communion with the Trinity in Unity as words fail to describe; and there has been a new and abiding realisation of the presence and love of Christ ever since such as I have never known before.

I can but describe it as the Holy Ghost taking of the things [illegible] various speakers imparted to me, and showing them to me.

To Him be blessing and glory.

IX.

The Manor Lodge, Harrow,
September 25th, 1874.

Through the ministrations of the Rev. C. H. Morgan and the Rev. W. Haslam I was brought, in the spring of this year, to a full realisation of the Lord Jesus as my Saviour. He brought me to His feet for pardon, and it was unmistakably vouchsafed. I can tell you the day, hour, and place.

Ever since this I have passed for a very good and happy Christian away from home, and people said they envied me my happy frame of mind; but within there was the conviction of inconsistency. At home the idea prevailed that, although I was no doubt converted, there was very little difference in my daily life.

In this unsatisfactory condition, to which I seemed perfectly reconciled, at the request of the Rev. W. Hay Chapman, I went to Oxford, and at one of the later meetings, presided over by the Rev. W. E. Boardman, stated my case. He addressed me most kindly, and assured me that mine would not *always* be a divided household—my life would not *always* be an inconsistent one. On the very next day the Lord enabled me to gladly testify, in the Corn Exchange, that I had entered the Rest of Faith.

Mr. Pearsall Smith said "If you want to know whether you have entered upon the Rest of Faith ask your wife, family, and servants." I am delighted to say that I can now fearlessly make the appeal suggested. It is impossible for me to describe the joy I date from this Oxford Meeting. . . .

Yours faithfully,

A. TRULOVE COX.

I have not the slightest objection to the publication of this letter.

X.

My object in testifying of the blessing I received at Oxford will be to glorify Him who has freely given us all things. . . .

I had attended several consecration meetings in London, but the truth known in my head was not yet in my heart. In June last I gave up all to Him who gave up all for me, and expected in return to receive the blessing I longed for, but in vain.

Two months of this restless life were spent, until arriving at Oxford, where all mists were cleared away; there the Lord showed me that having consecrated myself *to Him was not* enough, I was to give up my will as well as all sinful habits, and that He would work that will for me. He further showed me that He was my "Keeper," which truth came as a message of love in the promise, "I the Lord do keep it (thee). I will water it (thee) every moment, lest any hurt it (thee). I will keep it (thee) night and day."

I always thought this a beautiful promise; but it came to me as from His own lips, and I believed it.

Another truth revealed to me was that my great enemy Satan, whose darts had so often wounded me before, has been defeated by Him who is now my "Keeper;" (Heb. ii. 14), and that, by trusting only to His power, sin should not have dominion over me; that I was to rise in the morning, not to look forward to defeat, but to expect victory, and henceforth to look upon Satan as the defeated enemy. These were the three great truths which were so much blessed to me.

Oh! what a life mine has been since then! Instead of anxiety and striving—rest and trusting.

My past experience was, that after a meeting where I had received blessing, my joy and peace would last a certain time and then come to an end, the period of its duration being according to the measure of blessing received. This I see now was trusting to feeling. My present life is so different. It is the fulfilment of the promise, "Thy peace shall flow as a river." I do not expect that river to run dry, for its waters are "life," and its source is "the Fountain of Life;" and instead of trusting to feeling He has brought me to trust in His word, "which liveth and abideth for ever."

It may be well to mention before closing that I am a young man, holding a prominent position in a wholesale house in the City. I find this truth makes my business life the same life of rest. Testimony for the Master is easier, business temptations all fall under the mighty hand of my "Keeper;" and I look forward to winning my business companions for Christ, not by word only, but by their seeing that a Christian life is a happy one, and that the joy of the Lord eclipses all the joys of the world.

I pray that all who know the Lord Jesus as their Saviour may honour His word by believing His promises and accepting the fulness of His salvation.

F. Aldous.

XI.

29th September, 1874.

For some years I have been gradually led from doctrines to a living Jesus, until I "found in Him my Sun," my Lord, my all; but it was in Oxford that I saw unmistakably proved, that for the Holy Spirit's power to be manifested Jesus alone must be exalted, "in whom dwelleth all the fulness of the Godhead bodily." We too often try, as it were, to catch sunbeams—praying for the Spirit, and seeking to honour Him apart from Jesus, forgetting who it was that said, "He shall testify of 'Me.'" Truly we proved during these ten days the felt presence of our risen Lord (in the Father and the Father in Him), when the Holy Spirit came with His reproving (convincing) power, as searching fire, and then as the Comforter, filling the soul "with joy unspeakable and full of glory."

My own Oxford experience was not of any sudden ecstasy, yet I can say, the Lord taught me there, more than ever to surrender myself, my all, to Jesus; that "all things are possible to him that believeth," to love His precepts as well as His promises, and to take the word of Christ as daily speaking to me whilst I "try and prove" it as I never did before. . . .

For myself I can tell of sweet fruit our Joshua—Jesus—daily brings; and with the eye fixed on Him alone, with a living patriarch I must declare, "My sun doth no more go down, neither doth my moon withdraw itself. The Lord," [Jehovah-Jesus] "is *now* mine everlasting light, and the days of my mourning are ended."

SPENCER J. COMPTON,
Vicar of Hanford, near Stoke-on-Trent.

XII.

Hanford Vicarage, near Stoke-on-Trent,
September 30th.

I desire to send, in a very few words, a statement of the blessing I have received at Oxford.

It was certainly not the "rest of faith," nor victory over sin, which for the last three years has been my almost continued experience; but I think I may say that the Lord *shone in*, *dis*covering so much that I thought was gone, that I felt nothing would do but a new surrender to Himself of self in its full meaning.

I did yield Him all, and especially *my will*, and since that blessed Saturday night He has, I believe, come in to abide, and His will is becoming to me "the sweetest pillow I find to rest on."

The last six months of my Christian life has been almost "Heaven," and now, in His continual presence, it is as though Heaven had begun; only the occasional attempt of self to reassert its dominion, reminds me that it is still the "valley of blessing."

CECILIA J. COMPTON.

XIII.

Bury St. Edmunds,
September 25th, 1874.

Three of our party had entered into the "rest of faith" previous to the Oxford visit; but we all received such a baptism of the Spirit as we never experienced before. We could not refrain from singing all the way from Oxford to Cambridge. . . . .

On the journey we had opportunities of speaking concerning the great salvation, and I have reason to believe that through what was said one young man (a Wesleyan), who came with us part of the way, entered into a full trust in Jesus for everything. Several weeks have passed and we are all full of the joy that remains.

I am the minister of a Baptist church, numbering five hundred members. I never had such power for service in my *life* (I have been a minister about fourteen years), and the effect is seen in the increased life of the Church, and in the conversion of souls. . . . .

M. S. RIDLEY.

XIV.

Harrow,
October 3rd, 1874.

. . . .

I feel that it is my duty and privilege to send my testimony *to* the wonderful blessing I received at Oxford.

I was, I believe, converted some two and a half years ago, and since that time led very much a "life of ups and downs," spiritually, though, alas! the "downs" greatly preponderated, I fear.

I knew that the promise, "Sin shall not have dominion over you," was not at all fulfilled in my life; and when I took the matter to the Lord to know the reason, my heart told me plainly enough, "you are not *wholly* consecrated."

In months past I had known of two things, which it seemed as though I could not give up, and yet I knew that unless these were yielded to the Lord, I could not possibly walk in unclouded communion with Him and constant victory over sin. True I had with full sincerity of heart taken them to the Lord, but I had never *left* them with Him. I had in a manner given them over to Him, but I did so merely because I wanted to have the rest and joy of an unbroken walk with Him, and in doing this I was conscious I did not obey His most definite command of all; I did not with them give my *heart;* I was constantly looking at them and wanting them for my own again.

I was led to the Oxford Conference "by a way that I knew not," and there I was, by God's grace, brought to a stand, and was enabled to give up, I trust, *heartily* and *for ever*, everything I was conscious of in the least holding back, and to say with my whole soul, "Yes, all for Jesus!" I have now definitely and for ever laid "my all upon the altar;" and once having done so, I know it is holy to the Lord, sanctified by the altar, and now I think I can truly trust *heartily* and *for ever*, everything. I would not, even if I dared, take back the least from what I have given.

And now, too, though not without conscious failure, I am yet beginning to realise more and more the wonderful blessedness of the promise, "Sin shall not have dominion over you." I cannot say I experience the exquisite joy which so many testify to possessing, and I fear that my experience is below that of most, through the weakness of my faith; but having given my *all* to the Lord, I have given my *joy* to Him, and I know He gives me just as much as is best, and knowing this I find a rest and freedom from care such as I never knew before. . . .

My heart is very full of gratitude and praise to God for His unspeakable mercies to me at the Oxford Conference. Although *my* parents were both, to their deep regret, unavoidably prevented from attending, two very dear boy-friends of mine were able to come, and both found *the* blessing.

I am particularly thankful also for having found "such a blessing" at this time, as I am going up to Cambridge on the 13th inst., and whereas I was in some anxiety before about my life there, I have been enabled to cast it all upon the Lord.

Believe me,

Yours very sincerely,

F. M. H.

XV.

Lyllington Road,
Leamington.

A HIGH CHURCH lady, formerly prejudiced against Low Church and Dissent, writes: "I do feel very thankful for the guiding love that led me to Oxford. I did not expect to like the meetings.

"I think no sadder heart than mine was there; strange though it may seem to say so, I do not think any one went away more comforted, consoled, peaceful, joyful. I can truly say that I felt that 'the power of the Lord was present to *heal*,' and I have had such peaceful happiness since that I am often saying, with an old writer, '*Thou* givest much quietness of heart and *peace* and festive joy.' I am ashamed to have been so faithless, so forgetful of the great love that has guided me all the time. I do long that the remembrance of those solemn hours may not pass away; that we all may hold fast the gift of blessings that were so richly bestowed upon us."

XVI.

Upper Brook Street, London.
October 21st, 1874.

The Lord brought me to Oxford, to lead me in the *paths* of righteousness for His name's sake, He Himself *being* the way.

I had been present at many meetings during the year,

and I had experienced a deep longing for a holy walk and rest in Jesus.

I sought *it* earnestly for some months, then the Lord showed me I was seeking a *thing*, and turning from Jesus Himself.

I found I had only been looking for what He would give me, and expected a sudden power to come upon me in answer to my prayer. I then turned only to delight myself in Him, feeling sure that at the right time He would give me the desire of my heart. A great trial came to me; but Jesus enabled me to say at once, "Thy will be done."

From that moment I am sure I trusted with my all, and, unconsciously almost, entered the sweet rest in Him I had so long been seeking.

Jesus became to me my personal friend, and my communion became far deeper and more intimate than before, and my life a different thing to me. Still, when asked if I had entered upon the Higher Christian Life, my answer was, "No; I wish I could say I had."

The Oxford Conference taught me boldly to put in my claim as a believer for this blessing, trusting Jesus as implicitly with my walk as I had with my soul, looking to Him as the Finisher as well as Author of my faith.

M. Monod's words on "Have I been so long time with you and yet hast Thou not known me?" came right home to my heart; then and there I told the Lord that I knew Him, and His intense love and patience with me, and I would never distrust Him again. I knew He could not have brought me thus far to put me to shame.

Without waiting to feel the least more free from sin, I thanked Him for deliverance from its power, and boldly confessed to all the great things the Lord had done for my soul. Full assurance of faith came to me at once with the confession of my Saviour's power in me.

Sweetly He has kept me, often in weak health and trying circumstances, in perfect peace, trusting in Him. I can now trust Him to keep me trusting. It does not matter whether the road is rough or smooth, Jesus is living out my life in me, and it is no longer "What can I?" but "What cannot He do!"

I know in whom I have believed, and I am persuaded He is able to keep that which I have committed to Him.

Oh! that my life may be one Alleluia song to Him for

all His goodness to me, one of His weakest ones; but truly all the power and the glory is in His kingdom having come in us and His will done in us.

These words are sent in answer to the request put in the *Pathway of Power*, from one whose heart is full of thanksgiving for the Oxford Conference, as a thank-offering, to be used or not, as the Lord may direct.

XVII.

The Arboretum, Leamington,
Sept. 29th, 1874.

. . . . I wish also to add my testimony to that of many others, and acknowledge the great happiness and blessing I received at the Oxford Meeting. The two days I spent there were certainly the happiest I remember to have spent in my life, and I shall always look back to them with the greatest pleasure.

I was enabled to give myself up to God more entirely than I had expected, but was for some time tempted to expect greater joy and feeling in the matter than I afterwards did, but then I saw that faith in Christ alone was necessary.

But I want more joy and pleasure in His service, and faith in His power to use me for His glory.

Still what I have already received has made my life very different to myself, and I am enabled to live day by day by faith in Christ.

I have only made a beginning, but I trust God to make my spiritual life one of growth from this time forward, and to increase in the knowledge and love of God.

I trust that the Oxford Conference will only be the beginning of glorious showers of blessing for the people of God, and hope that its example may be followed up in many other places.

I think such a series of meetings would be greatly blessed in the places where the great revival has brought so many thousands to Christ.

I desire to praise God for His great goodness to me through the influence of the late meetings at Oxford.

I remain, yours very respectfully,
W. H. Maberly.

XVIII.

Bonner Terrace, Bonner Road, E.,
Sept. 29th, 1874.

. . . . On the 23rd of December last, in conversation and prayer with Dr. Boardman, who has several times previously visited at my house, and preached to my congregation, I made a full surrender of myself to Christ, and realised a power which no words can possibly describe. It was the rest of faith.

After this I had many conflicts, and sometimes almost lost my confidence in my precious Saviour; but at the Oxford Conference it was greatly strengthened and confirmed, and the joy I experienced there was "unspeakable and full of glory."

The meetings to me became better and better, and I returned home consecrated for service, and in the full rest of faith.

On Sunday, Sept. 6th, I preached and spoke to my own people, telling them what I had heard, and seen, and experienced at Oxford, and the day was a very delightful and hallowed one to many. I have not been without severe temptations since, but I hold my ground, and intend to hold it by the grace of God. I am abased; He is exalted. I am nothing; He is all in all. As a minister I have known the *theory* of Christian holiness for many years, but I never experienced it before. . . . .

THORNLEY SMITH.

XIX.

18, Cunningham Place, N.W.,
Oct. 3rd, 1874.

Words cannot express the blessing I realised at Oxford. Through the tender mercy of the Lord I had some months previously been led to make a full surrender of myself to God, and found a new experience of joy resulting; but the added blessedness given at Oxford no tongue can utter, it was and is "unspeakable and full of glory." Never was sin so hateful, never was Jesus so precious to me, as now, and never was labour for Him so sweet and so easy.

I trust the publication of what God has wrought will

lead many of His people to seek and find the fulness of the blessing of the Gospel.

Yours very sincerely,
THOMAS D. MARSHALL.

XX.

Starcross, Devon.

I have not doubted my salvation for the last twenty years. For some time before the Oxford meetings I was conscious of distance from the Lord, and of repeated failures in many ways. A few days before the meetings the Lord gave me a marked quietness of spirit, and enabled me to expect blessing at Oxford.

When Mr. S. told of his conversation with an active Christian, and of the latter's reply to the question, "Do you believe when you pray, 'Deliver me from evil,' that the Lord will do it?" and the reply was, "Of course not," I felt then that I too had often practically said, "Of course my prayer will not be answered."

On Tuesday three consecration speakers pressed us *much* to believe God's promises; and one brother told of two who, looking to Jesus, were saved from their most besetting sin.

After this meeting I went home, and, alone with the Lord, by His grace, then and there, and on the strength of such words as, "My grace is sufficient for thee;" "I can do *all* things through Christ who strengtheneth me;" I was taken away from self, and enabled to trust only on the promises.

The thought was, God's word will be the same to-morrow, next week, &c., and so the Lord made that Tuesday the acceptable time for me.

Since that ever to be remembered day I have experienced such a fulness in God, and such a quiet joy and communion, as never before; and the thought often comes to me when walking, Oh, what a blessing have I received since I last passed this spot!

And now I am expecting and believing that my spiritual experience will be like what we read in Ps. civ. 15—"It is better on before."

Yours, with Christian regards,

H. T.

XXI.

I must tell you of one fruit of the blessed Oxford Meetings. My housemaid called on a friend of hers, and found with her two young women, engaged in a warehouse in London. They were wanting to know what "being converted" meant; for their employer had been to Oxford and "got converted," and he had gone through his entire business establishment and rearranged everything. All was to be done for Jesus now; and he was so altered himself—like a different man—ever so much better a master—the girls thought it must be something worth seeking for—this change that affected, not only the man's conduct, but all he had control over. I think he must surely have found a twofold blessing—conversion and consecration. So that it reminded me of Mr. Smith's words, "If you don't know whether you are consecrated, ask your clerks and servants: *they know!*"

XXII.

When my way was unexpectedly opened to go to Oxford, I went *expecting great help*, and the whole series of meetings seemed like the gate of heaven. After the Thursday forenoon meeting, when all who wished to give themselves up "body, soul, and spirit" were asked to stand up, *I did*, and then went home and fell down before God, and asked him earnestly to "take me," and do what He liked with me, and mould me as the potter the clay.

I believe *I did* give all into His hands, even to my "will," which I could not understand before. He did take me, and I resolved, in the words of one of the ministers: "Emotion or no emotion, feeling or no feeling, *not to take myself back*." But I fear I did not look up "moment by moment," as by the Sunday evening I got much discouraged at finding the old "self" not dead. It seemed to have been very lively all day. Still, "though faint," I had no wish to take the gift off the altar. I had had too great peace and rest, unknown before, to do that. So I cried to Jesus, and He answered my cry; for the next morning, while waiting for the meeting to begin, He gave me this text (1 Sam. ix. 24), " And Samuel said, Behold that which is left (reserved), set it before thee and *eat;* for unto this time hath it been kept for thee, since I said I have invited the people." I can indeed say, since then, " He hath put a new song in my mouth." Home never looked so bright and happy before. A calm and beautiful feeling that God appoints the daily event, and that I may just look up continually and say, " Lord Jesus, what wouldest thou have me to do?" " Lord Jesus help me!" seems to raise me above the little anxieties and worries. I have never in my life spent so happy a three weeks, and I hope others around me are happier in consequence; for " we must live this life at home," and " I trust," for the future. I may just add that I am so afraid of grieving Jesus and losing my peace that I feel the need of watching and praying more than ever, and am constrained by the *love* of Jesus to love Him more than ever. I see as I never did before what Jesus *is* to me. I believe, for God is unchangeable, that I shall have reason to bless God to all eternity for letting me attend those happy meetings at Oxford. I see that " self," however, is not to be killed *all at once;* but that as each fresh bit crops up I must go on taking it to Jesus, and " He accepts all we give Him, and returns to us only peace and joy."

On the Lord's day, September 6th, I believe hundreds entered into the spiritual Canaan of rest, and trusted a living Saviour for everything. At dinner on that day my companion and I could not eat. We had to fall down on our knees constrained by the love of Christ, to give thanks for His marvellous manifestation of Himself to each of us.

Some weeks have passed away since then. Those sweet meetings are now over, and I write not from the mountain, but from the plain; but I can testify that in the cares and crosses of business life, in temptation, in service, and in joy, " Jesus saves me all the day."

His presence has not left me; but when failure comes (alas, it does still!) the practical truth I learnt at Oxford was instant confession and restored communion.

The Bible is now my delight, and prayer a reality, as, looking forward, I have faith given me to say, " I shall yet praise Him more and more."

H. F.

XXIII.

Last week's *Christian* tells me that I may write *privately* about the Oxford Conference and its shower of blessings. Words utterly fail me. I can only thank God I was there. Who can tell the noble acts of the Lord, or show forth all His praise? Bless the Lord, O my soul, and forget not all His benefits. As long as *I live* I shall feel grateful to the channels of blessing and comfort during my stay at Oxford.

Long ago, indeed, I knew that my sins were all forgiven, washed in the precious blood of Jesus; the burden of them had been intolerable. I had sought to find peace in Him which none but His loved ones know. Yet for years what a gulf between my knowledge and my life! How cold and dull my prayers, how worldly my thoughts! The sorrows of life seemed beyond my strength. The gold had become dim and the fine gold changed. My sins had taken such hold on me that I was not able to look up. I was always thinking of them, always feeling how little I did for Christ. In this state of mind I heard of the Oxford meetings. To be able to cast *all* my burden *on* Jesus—to realize His abiding presence—to look away from self and say, not I, but the grace of God within me—to pray and long for the baptism of the Holy Ghost, the Comforter—to believe that one so vile as I could become His living temple;—all this and more was joy unspeakable, and peace such as the world can neither give nor take away. Earnestly did I wish to surrender *all:* to give myself wholly to the Lord.

I am not conscious of wilfully keeping anything back, and yet I know that the heart is "deceitful above all things" and even in its regenerate state, "desperately wicked." I feel much *happier* since I have been at Oxford, and though I never asked to be included in the prayers of God's people there, I have real need of them, and would ask them now, and pray that, in His own good time, He would remove my earthly anxieties and sorrows, and sanctify me wholly, body, soul and spirit, so that I may be preserved *blameless* unto the coming of our Lord Jesus Christ.

XXIV.

For three or four weeks before the Conference I had asked the Lord to allow me to go if it was according to His will, as I felt a great need for this higher Christian life, and an overpowering sense of my sins, and constant falls made me utterly wretched.

I had known Jesus as my Saviour for eight years, for I found peace when fourteen years old, and about two years ago I thought I had entered into this rest of faith, but I was trusting to my *emotions*, and when they failed I gave it all up, and thought I must have made a mistake. But this slight foretaste of a closer union to Christ left "an aching void."

In spite of many difficulties and drawbacks, God led me to Oxford in a wonderfully plain and decided way. Jesus enabled me when there to give up *my* will entirely, and accept instead *His* most blessed will.

I cannot describe the rest it is to my spirit, soul and body. I am full of joy and comfort. My whole life is now peaceful, and I *do* realize a power and victory over sin, I had not before.

I know not how to praise Him enough. I realise more and more " He is *altogether lovely. This* is my Beloved, and this is my Friend." And I fully believe that daily, monthly, yearly, I shall know more and more of Him and of the blessedness of this glorious union with Jesus.

XXV.

I have great pleasure in testifying of the blessings received at Oxford. I do trust and believe I have given up my will and entered on this life of blessed consecration. Up to the present my life as a Christian has been one miserable failure in fighting with unsubdued inward corruption, but now I see clearly that all self-trust must be given up, and that I must trust my Saviour for salvation from the power of sin as I did at conversion from the guilt of sin.

XXVI.

In myself, I feel that I have received a distinct blessing from the meetings at Oxford. It is now about a year since, at the time of my mother's death, I was enabled to trust Christ with *myself* as never before, and to "enter into rest."

My one longing and desire in going to Oxford was that I might know by experience what was meant by the "baptism of the Holy Ghost." I hardly knew what I was expecting; I think it must have been some wonderful, overpowering emotion, and a stock of realized *power*, upon which I could draw at pleasure.

I trust God has satisfied the desire, but it has been in His way, not in mine, and there still remains a "thirst for ever ardent, yet evermore content."

I had been asking for many days at Oxford that Jesus would let His own will be done perfectly with me and in me, if only He would fill me with Himself.

He took me at my word, and instead of letting me be present at the Saturday night meeting, when so many of His children experienced the outpouring of His Spirit in such a marvellous degree, He laid me aside to suffer, and then, in the midst of intense pain, He came to me, and made His abode with me, filling me so full of His own Presence, that even the friends who were standing round, doing all in their power to alleviate the suffering, seemed far off and distant compared with Him.

He just took my will so completely out of the way that I knew what it was to "lie passive in His hands, and know *no will* but *His*." I had known before what it was to say from my heart "Not my will, but Thine be done," but now it was something more than this; for the words "*not* my will, *but* Thine," imply the existence of two separate wills, His and mine, even when I can chose His; but there seemed to be no longer two wills, but one, and that equally His and mine, whatever it might be, not so much by the blending of the two together, as by the utter absorption of the one in the other; and then how gloriously He manifested Himself. Not as my Father, as I had so long known Him, but as "*My Beloved*," whose desire was toward me. Oh! it was glorious just to lie still, with His left hand under my head, and His right hand embracing me. Was not this the bap tism of the Spirit, as the Revealer of Jesus? I know that many Christians are afraid of what God may do with them if they really surrender themselves utterly to His will, but, for the help of such, I can testify from experience that, even should His will be affliction, whether mental or bodily (which of course does not necessarily follow), He can so cause the consolation to abound that we are enabled not only to be perfectly submissive, but to "*glory* in tribulations also, that the power of Christ may rest upon (us)." You are at liberty to make what use you like of this, if you think it will be helpful to any.

XXVII.

I write to acknowledge with great thankfulness the blessing the Lord gave me, in His love, at Oxford. He showed me there that I had not fully yielded myself up to Him; one after another He showed me things I had kept back; and when the last was given to Him, oh! what joy He poured into my soul! He gave me at that time, and has continued to me ever since, power to speak in His name, and I see that the words spoken for Him take effect now. It is, I think, because now I only desire that *He should speak through me*, whereas before I was always thinking what *I* had to say. The Lord has graciously given me almost continuous joy and communion with Himself ever since Oxford. I cannot express half the good things He has given me, but I must say that I find a delight in prayer and the reading of His Word I never had before, and it is the greatest joy I have to tell others of His love. May the Lord cause me to bring forth much fruit to His glory. "His service is perfect freedom." "Bless the Lord, O! my soul, and all that is within me bless His holy name."

XXVIII.

All are invited to send you a thank-offering, in the shape of a letter, for blessing received at Oxford. I only arrived there mid-day Thursday, but I felt a blessed outpouring of God's Spirit into my soul, from the marvellous, simple way, in which Pastor Monod preached on the Sunday. I thought I was resting and trusting fully, but He showed me very quickly I was not; for while we have a care, or worry, we are *not* resting. First, I received a great help from Mr. Smith speaking of discouragement being the devil's work, *never* God's gentle, loving Spirit. I saw Satan uses this more than anything to stay God's work, and I resolved in God's strength never to allow Satan to discourage me again.

I can't tell you half the blessing I received, but I simply learned Jesus is *the* Way, the Only Way, and the Whole Way, and I love to call this holy, happy, blessed rest, *rest* in Jesus. Now I really am resting, moment by moment, in His dear arms, and I find His will "as soft as downy pillows are." I can now talk of this to dear Christians who cannot enter into full possession; and one dear friend, on my return, fully agreed with me because I said it was simply *knowing and trusting* our loved Jesus more,—who could not talk about this rest before, nor did she like to hear others.

I praise my God for taking me in a singular way to Oxford; every meeting seemed to lift me nearer to God, nearer heaven.

XXIX.

Those blessed Oxford days! Shall we *ever* forget them? Not even, I think, amid the songs of Heaven; the recollection is so sweet. And how many homes and churches must now be filled with the savour of that ointment! Like the early disciples, "scattered abroad," who "went everywhere preaching the Word," and bearing testimony, like precious fragrance, to their Master's name. And so will it surely be now. My dear brother at Nottingham, who was with us, writes, of the week following: "I think I can say, without hesitation, that the last week has been the very happiest of my life. The week at Oxford was happy, but it was the happiness of hope; this has been the happiness of *Rest.* I know entirely now by experience the meaning of that word. 'We who have believed do enter into rest.' Instead of losing, as you know I feared I might, the joy of those days, it has been grace for grace.

"*I never* believed it possible that I should ever walk

with God, but now the 'glorious Lord' is to me 'a place of broad rivers and streams.'"

Hundreds of the King's children will be bearing a similar testimony.

XXX.

In compliance with a notice in the *Pathway of Power*, I send you a few lines to express how I felt a day at the Oxford meetings like a week of common life, and the few days there like a month; yet each day seemed to pass only too quickly.

XXXI.

I am thankful to be able to send a thank-offering to "tell what the Lord has done for my soul." He hath put into my mouth a new song, so that I can say, "O sing unto the Lord a new song, for He hath done marvellous things; His right hand and His holy arm hath gotten Him the victory."

I can never thank the Lord enough for taking me to Oxford, and sharing in the rich feast He prepared for His people there. I went with expectations, but the Lord has given me even more than I was able to ask or think.

He has shown me what a full Saviour I have in Jesus, and that it is in a perfect simple trust in Him, moment by moment, that He supplies *all our needs;* and that this "rest of faith" is not a hard doctrinal statement, which one has to strive and labour for, but a simple giving up of *self* unto *Christ*, letting Him be all and everything in us. Indeed I can only say, "The Lord hath done great things for us, whereof we are glad."

It was such a joy to me in leaving Oxford to know that I was not leaving the blessing behind, but taking that away, and realising "'Tis better farther on."

XXXII.

Some years ago, though I knew Jesus as my Saviour, I became very unhappy; feeling terribly the want of constant communion with God, as I felt that Christians ought to have this; but whenever I mentioned the subject, those around me told me my feelings arose entirely from ill-health.

In my misery God sent an old friend to me, who said, "Ask God, Himself, to open your eyes!" That was all, and I did so. I was then in great distress, and while I prayed came such a revelation of Jesus as my complete Saviour that He seemed to be *everything* in me and for me, and my will so blended into His that I *myself* had no will or care left.

But after some months I began to lose this, and I went mourning, all my friends telling me that these feelings were ideas of my own, and that they were wrong. *But to me the Bible was full of them.* Lately I became very unhappy again and could not sleep, when it was again put down to ill-health; and now, to finish, I went with my husband to Oxford and found, before many days, that *every word* I heard there I had before *experienced.* Praise God for it! And though I have not yet re-entered into the same full communion again, I can say, with Isaiah, "The days of my mourning *are* ended."

XXXIII.

It is the joy of my life to know, as I do, that Jesus is mine and I am His. I went to Oxford decided for Jesus, but not satisfied; longing after more peace and rest, which I seemed to feel must only be attained in heaven. During my stay there it came to me, and my joy was such that during the night I felt I must get up and sing "Praise God from whom all blessings flow," &c.

I look back upon that week as the one in which, through grace, I was enabled to "lay aside the sin which doth so easily beset us" (unbelief), and I can now "*run* with patience the race set before me, looking unto Jesus the author and finisher of our faith."

Life is all joy and rejoicing; I have no anxious care, for I have cast it all on Jesus, and I realize that He *does* care for me. I stand upon the Rock, and Jesus holds me there; no confidence in self, no strength of my own. I am nothing, and because of that Jesus is everything to me, and I believe "*He will* never leave me nor forsake me."

XXXIV.

Oxford has indeed become to me an endeared name. It has, with its new blessed associations, much blotted out the old ones, that I do not now very well remember what they were.

My conversion, twelve years since, gave me a very full and unwavering satisfaction in Christ as a Saviour from the guilt of sin, but only now have I learnt all He is to us for victory over it also. Two great events, and the last is simply second in importance. It certainly also magnifies the first, and I wonder how I so long missed seeing it.

Now I desire to urge it on all Christians, and to insist that they do not starve in the Christian life, surrounded, as they are, with such abundance. I grieve for having turned so constantly from the One whom I sought only to assist, instead of letting Him do all for me.

Of course there was a peace and rest (as having been delivered from death, and being born into the family of God), but not *the* measure and amount that I believed one ought to have.

I have been interested in this "Higher Christian Life" literature for years. Its teaching commended itself to my understanding, and I strove for its realization, and sometimes thought I had laid hold of it; but not so, the power and communion did not abide.

Then came the announcement for meetings at Oxford, and how heartily did my desire respond to go, in spite of all scarcity of means and time from business.

Well, bless God! I went, not for *a* blessing, but *the* blessing, and I found it; and now, after three weeks of such trust and abiding, I feel as if (God willing) I would rather die than return to the old dishonouring way of Christ and myself instead of Jesus only.

In common, of course, with all others who find this fuller baptism of the Spirit, the Bible is an altered book. I am reading books in it that I think I scarcely read before. All are profitable, and I am much wondering.

In many years I have been wearied with the wilderness warfare, and have often said I should prefer to die, if God *so willed* it. I did not know—as so many do not—that to *get out* of it we need not die. And now I am asking God *to let* me live a few years to learn more about Him, believing that I shall learn, as I am seeking to do now, what the anointing means—the anointing for service.

My tears flow freely now, and oh! what a falling of these there was in those dear rooms of mine at Oxford, and at the meetings too; but they were all of joy and wonder—wonder that such an one as I could attain to such things. How much there is to say! and all of praise and thanksgiving!

Of course God, in revealing Himself, is also showing me myself, and this last gives much grief as being so humbling, for the flesh does not like it. Only it must be so, if I am to learn the full lesson of entire obedience; must it not?

XXXV.

I am glad to testify to the blessing received while attending the meetings lately held at Oxford.

I was led there with little hope of receiving the peace, and abiding in Jesus. I had been praying and struggling for over twelve years. When there, at my wits' end, and in much sadness and hopelessness at past failures, I was led to see that what was needed, together with no reserve on my part, was continuing trust in Jesus; *not trusting only whilst feeling lasted, but after and in spite of no feeling.*

This giving up and trust was followed by a very decided and blessed experience, certainly (in my case) as decided as when first I knew the Lord.

Since leaving Oxford the experience has been somewhat tried, but I find now a great difference from my former Christian life, and am assured there never can be again the uncertainties, or experiments, or round-about ways of trying to gain what must be received by submissive faith alone.

XXXVI.

I would take this opportunity of thankfully acknowledging the *rich blessing* which I received at Oxford, and in doing so I find it difficult to express shortly what the blessing *to my soul* was,—the manifestation of Jesus to my soul was so wonderful, so varied. But perhaps the best description would be to say, that everything in this Higher Life has become to me a greater *reality*.

I knew a great deal *intellectually* which has now become true to my inner consciousness; and though I had known something, before going up to Oxford, of this complete salvation experimentally, I realised there, as never before, the transforming power of a manifested Christ.

I determined when I went to open my mouth wide, and I *expected* to be filled; but He enlarged my capacities for receiving, and filled them to overflowing, far beyond all I could have asked or thought; not according to *my desires*, but according to the riches of His grace in Christ Jesus.

XXXVII.

I went to the Oxford Conference expecting spiritual refreshment and a blessing, but little thought *how* great that blessing would be.

For the last year or two I have thought and read a great deal on the subject of "holiness of life," but am thankful to say, very much that I only knew in theory before I now know as a reality.

The reason is soon explained; I did not *fully* believe in the promises, and had not given up my will to the Lord. I knew I had not, and for at least a year kept it back because I *felt* I could not give it up, and because I feared I should not be able to stand in such a position.

Now that I have surrendered my will, and abandoned self to the Lord in return, He has given me joy, peace, and rest. The wondrous depths of each no words can tell: and I know now what it is to trust Him entirely, in simple faith for all things, and not to doubt His power. In so doing He will give the victory; Christ's all-sufficiency meets my nothingness. "I can do all things through Christ which strengtheneth me." (Phil. iv. 13.) "My grace is sufficient for thee." (2 Cor. xii. 9.)

The assurance of my salvation has been a joy to me for *many* years, and now I have to thank the Lord for a *further joy*, in opening my eyes to see the assurance of present *rest* in Him. My wilful desires have all vanished in a [illegible]y, and having no will but the Lord's, is like [illegible] a disease. I need no longer say,—

"[illegible] weary in spirit, I am restless in will;"

[illegible]

"Jesus saves me all the time."

My desires after more truth and light seem unsatiable, [illegible] are the promises to accept and believe: "Delight thyself also in the Lord, and He shall give thee the [illegible] thine heart"—(Psa. xxxvii. 4)—and "He will [illegible] of them that fear Him." (Psa. cxlv. 19.) [illegible] of Scripture which I thought I had realised [illegible], and which had even proved watchwords, now [illegible] such a new light, as though I had never read [illegible] before. What only glittered like silver, now shines like gold. My difficulty now seems how to praise the Lord sufficiently for all His goodness. "If we live in the Spirit, let us also walk in the Spirit" (Gal. v. 25); then Christ will be so reflected through us, that He may be made manifest in our daily life, to those around, and prove that the happy meetings at Oxford are a lasting reality.

XXXVIII.

I cannot forbear calling on those around to hear, and I will tell what the Lord has done for my soul, through His precious Gospel, while at Oxford. I have known the Lord for more than forty years, and have engaged in His work with much gladness as He has given me opportunity, but *not* with that abiding power which I knew was for me in my Lord. For some time past I have suffered much from sore temptations, through an infirmity of the flesh (my nerves), which I have wrestled and contended with, thinking that it would become worse and worse if not striven against, at the same time realizing the strife becoming stronger and stronger, with much distress and fear. I was beaten again and again, till I became so worn with faintness of heart, and my health was suffering from such hard conflict. I thought (though the effort was very great in such a beaten state) that I would go to Oxford. That which the Lord taught me there, and led me into, was entire trust—a perfect Rest in Jesus; after so much battling with *myself*, a quietness of soul in "Him."

Every meeting which I attended seemed to have a succession of messages from the Lord to me through His servants, so that I could only look up with astonishment and gratitude, and exclaim, "It is the Lord's doing, and marvellous in my eyes!"

I became so rich, so strong, so much at ease in Him; and now—thanks be unto His blessed name—when assailed by old feelings and Satan's fiery darts, it is no longer by might and by power, but by His Spirit. I well knew this before, but with this exception, that *I* must do something, and the Lord will help me; but now the Lord is mighty *in me*, and when I only call, "Jesus, Jesus, Jesus!" He is near that justifieth me, and I am not confounded or faint-hearted. "Bless the Lord, O my soul, and all that is within me, bless His holy name!"

Be encouraged, you who suffer as I did, and let Jesus take your whole will, body, soul, and memory; and He will do for you marvellously and abundantly above all you can either ask or think. May the Lord multiply such happy, glorious meetings, and grant more and more of His Holy Spirit!

XXXIX.

I feel that I owe boundless thanks to the Lord for the privilege of attending a part of the meetings at Oxford. I went there hungry for good things. I had been made by God's Spirit to know that my only really safe way was to say sincerely, "Thy will be done" in everything, and I had prayed that He would work in my inmost being, and make all His own; but I thought that the surrender of will must be made on each occasion, and I knew that there were some things that I would not do, even if God showed them to be His will for me.

At Mrs. Smith's ladies' meeting—the first I attended—she asked those who could make the *full* surrender, *once and for ever*, to stand up. This was a new idea, and I was about to rise, when all the hard things I might have to do came into my mind, and I fancied that, if once I gave myself up to God, He would take the first opportunity to give me something unpleasant to do.

Shortly after this, Mr. Smith, in his address, said that *if God* wants fully consecrated Christians to do anything

He will first make us want to do it, and will also make the way plain before us; for "He worketh in us both *to will* and to do of His good pleasure," and "When He putteth forth His own sheep He goeth before them." Next time the full surrender was asked for, I could with joy, though with trembling, put myself over on the Lord's side, trusting Jesus for the future. Nearly four weeks of that future are now past, and I can say He has been exceedingly faithful.

XL.

I write to tell the depth of blessing God gave me at Oxford. He led me last January to full rest in Jesus, and I went to Oxford with the one longing—to receive the baptism of the Holy Ghost. This longing was deepening every day I was there till, on the Friday and Saturday, it was almost more than I could bear. It was on the Sunday morning, at the Holy Communion at St. Aldate's Church, that it came. I hardly know how to put into words what it was—such an overpowering sense of God's presence that all outward things seemed unreal and far away, and it seemed almost impossible to move. I do not think this intensity lasted long, but it passed into a sense of being flung right back into the arms of Jesus, and resting there like a dead weight in a way I had never known before. Ever since then peace has been like a river, and speaking of Him all round has been no longer an effort of trust, but just pure joy. And He has been giving me such glimpses of what is on before me, that I cannot help thanking Him even more for what He will do than for what He has done. "I will yet hope continually, and will yet praise Thee more and more."

XLI.

I have been a Christian thirty-three years; was brought to Jesus in early youth; the daughter of parents of no common piety. At first it was a life of great joy and gladness in Jesus—soon of much conflict. From the miserable, wretched life of failure I lived, I lost all hope that I was God's child, and others told me that their experience was like mine, as to failure. Not being able to reconcile this with the love and promises of God, I doubted the truth of the Gospel, and lived thus for the greater part of a year. "As with a sword in my bones" was the word by which I again found peace, and saw the perfect, finished work of salvation which Jesus has wrought out for us. I never again doubted my acceptance with God. This greatly quickened my intense longings for holiness, while my life continued to be frequent and often utter failures, with times of victory, and then such untold joy and gladness, that it seemed impossible that sin should ever overcome again.

I see now it was the same power, the power of Jesus, but I was not brought to see it constantly exercised for me, nor my own utter helplessness either, to will and to do what is well pleasing in God's sight.

The increasing knowledge of the love and tenderness of our God and Father, our blessed union with Jesus, and the work of the Holy Spirit, made the galling bondage of sin unspeakably bitter. Sometimes I had felt it was possible for God to do all things, that I dared to hope I might find the secret; it was so unlike His love to leave us to fail thus.

After many years of waiting, the desire of my heart was granted—to devote myself to mission work. Now, I hoped, having given up all, as I thought, for Jesus, I should live more as I longed to do. God was with me in my work; but the great sorrow was still the being overcome by sin; no rest of heart, often unable to speak for God for very shame at the thought of the sin that dwelt within. This, added to the sin all around me, led me to see the great need of holiness of heart, as power for work.

Just at this time the subject of "holiness by faith" was taken up in *The Christian.* I eagerly read the letters, and besought God to teach me the truth. I experienced in some measure the victory, and the consequent giving up of will, and consecrating all to Him. I was so backward to confess it, and did not do so, although the Spirit urged me to do so—and I lost the blessing from that time. I did not keep it many days; this was a year ago. The conflict was now greater than ever. I knew the remedy, yet was helpless to obtain it, and I had never spoken to any one who had experienced the blessing, and often longed to write to some of them.

With what joy I saw the invitation to Oxford I cannot

tell. Earnestly I besought the Lord to let me go. He graciously opened the way. I went with the promise, Psalm xxiv. 3–5, as mine. At first I was brought very low, and could not hope to attain to this rest, it seemed so much greater and more full when I heard the living testimony of witnesses.

I was much cheered by Heb. x. 19-23, and again, the next night, Isa. liv. 11-14. The next morning (Thursday) during the silence, the text Isa. xxvii. 3, came to me with power as the word of Jehovah : I saw the victory of which I had heard so much, and felt myself to be sweetly taken into the everlasting arms for ever, for everything, and I was led to consecrate myself to God in the power of the Spirit, not of my will and energy only. I had never been consecrated to God by Himself before. Oh, the blessed resting of one's whole being in the triune God! I can find no words to describe the triumphant joy and gladness of the time at Oxford after Thursday, especially the early morning meetings of Sunday, Monday, and Tuesday. The Bible is a new book ; the promises are every letter true—doubled to me, and daily done for me ; especially Jer. xxxi. 10-14, 25. My mouth is opened to speak for the Lord, my work is indeed a joy. He has used my testimony here, and inclined the hearts of Christians who had not before known of this to send for some friends to hold meetings here. A general interest in the subject, and an awakening seems at hand where such meetings have not been held before.

Praise the Lord. Sing unto Him a new song. Alleluia!

XLII.

It was not my privilege to be able to attend those blessed meetings (for so they have proved to me), at Oxford. But in reading the accounts in detail as they appeared in *The Christian*, they have been the means in the Lord's hands of strengthening my faith and imparting further light, and filling my soul with much joy. I could plainly see that it was a practical illustration of truth, which, alas! to too many appears new, when at the same time it is only *the* truth—good old truth, shall I say?—revived.

So great was the blessing I experienced, I could but weep

for joy in seeing the truth of entire consecration so blessedly brought out. It was not new to me, but *increased* light and joy was given me; and, though being at home, I was enabled to "*divide the spoil.*" To the Lord be all the praise!

XLIII.

I am a Christian business man. The blessing I received at Oxford was a real and definite one. More conscious to me than my conversion, which I cannot remember. I have known the Lord for more than twenty years, and have tried *so hard* to serve Him! My servitude was as long as Jacob's, and with spiritual poverty and effort; outwardly I passed as a faithful steward—many years a deacon—prayed in public—taught the Scriptures—tithed myself—prospered in business, and was able to give hundreds a-year away; but all these things were done as DUTIES, including reading the Scriptures and private prayer.

The Lord led me to Oxford, and there opened my prison-door. First He showed me during those earlier meetings, so searching in their teachings, the evils of my own heart. Oh! the corruption His candle revealed there! The coldness, the pride, the unbelief!

At my lodgings I wept for hours like one utterly heartbroken. I fell on my knees and prayed the Lord to take everything, not a tenth only, but *all*, including my wretched *self*, if only that I might trust Him now. "If it be Thou, Lord, bid me come to Thee on the water." My wounded heart was healed again. I waited another day or two in faith. I heard Mr. Smith's address on the baptism of the Holy Spirit, and then, oh! how shall I describe the flood of joy and peace that filled me? The Saviour was so *near* and *real*, it was, indeed, "the vision beautiful." The true Sabbath morn dawned upon my soul, "Rest in Jesus." "And let them sacrifice the sacrifices of thanksgiving, and declare His works with rejoicing."—(Psalm cvii. 22.)

XLIV.

In answer to the invitation I gladly record the wonderful way in which God met me at Oxford, and gave me what I had longed for as they that wait for the morning. I came expecting to receive "the baptism of His Spirit." Filled with this I was filled with love and joy, rest and faith, and I knew that all was well. I could leave the affairs of my soul and attend to those of others; for these I had now power with God by the prayer of faith. My hunger and thirst after righteousness were satisfied. I found power was now mine, prayer was easy, complaint impossible, holy emotions coming naturally from the indwelling Spirit.

I had heard of this by the hearing of the ear and believed it, but now I saw God in His living presence in the heart. The blessing has continued since, indeed it increased, and the Holy Spirit has wonderfully witnessed to my witnessing to Him.

My soul doth magnify the Lord, and my spirit doth rejoice in God my Saviour, who daily teacheth me of His law and loadeth me with benefits.

XLV.

It was my privilege to spend three days at Oxford, and I hesitate not to say I never spent three happier days. During some of the meetings Mr. Smith requested the audience to sing the Doxology *twice;* he wished first that those who had entered into definite rest of soul in Jesus should stand up and sing it, then those who had found refreshing.

I was among the latter, but the meetings were greatly blessed to my soul, and when I returned home I *did* find that sweet rest in Jesus, and it does continually act as oil to all the frictions of life. One thing I felt impelled to do—to destroy all my old sermons, not because they did not contain clear statements of Gospel truth, but because they were not sufficiently experimental.

I have been raised to a sweet assurance of salvation, and I went before my people and was able, through grace, to say with more definiteness than *ever before,* "The Lord my light," &c.

My first week-evening text after my return from Oxford was, "That which we have seen and heard declare we unto you, that ye also may have fellowship with us; and truly *our* fellowship is with the Father and with His Son Jesus Christ.

I have been a Christian for about thirty years, but have walked so much in my own shadow.

The leaders of the Oxford meeting will ever have a *very* warm place in my heart, as having been used by God in bringing Jesus so very near to my soul. I am a Congregational minister, with a very small charge, but it is such joy to preach even to a few, and to take the sweet name of Jesus from house to house. I now find myself strengthened to speak for Christ to persons with whom I have previously been silent.

I find in public print objections, but they proceed from those who were not present, and my earnest desire and prayer is, that my own life, without any argument, may silence the objections of all amongst whom my lot is cast. I am resting in Jesus on behalf of each member of our very small church, fully believing they will all come into the one glorious secret of peace in the soul, and power in service, by committing themselves in a perpetual consecration to Jesus.

Surrender of my will in all things to Jesus, and trust in Him, moment by moment, for all,—these are my watchwords.

XXXVI.

In early life I was converted to God, and lasted the joys of the new birth, and for fifty years I have been seeking and trying to walk circumspectly in the way of life, so as to please the Lord. The more I planned and struggled, the more I felt and discovered my insufficiency, and that in my flesh dwelleth no good thing. For a long time I had despaired as to myself, apart from Jesus, and I asked the Lord to go with me to Oxford; and I went in the hope of hearing of and getting into the higher life in Jesus. And oh! the joy, when I found that it was to be received by giving up my whole self, and all I have, to Jesus. I at once, then and there, made the willing surrender, being thankful to give and resign my old life, that had troubled and worried me so long, and had always failed me.

And now, I bless the Lord, I live in a new atmosphere of being, looking to Jesus only, enjoying a calm trust, and rest in His doing all for me, and working in me to will and do of His good pleasure. Though in my seventieth year of age, *this* has given me such a lift heavenward that I seem years younger, and more able to bear afflictions and pain as light things. Do pray that I may be a useful light in imparting to others the inner life of love!

XLVII.

The following is translated from the letter of a German Christian:—

Although brought up by Christian parents, and happily blessed with decidedly believing grandparents, I only, for the first time, on May 1st, 1873, knew Christianity, and understood that, until that period (I was then an officer), I had lived for twenty-five years to myself and the world, and I determined that I must and would live to my God and for His honour. I knew my guilt in the holy light of God, yet only by degrees could I be assured of the Gospel, and believe in the forgiveness of sins. I had peace with God, and often joyfully gave thanks that I had a reconciled Father in Christ Jesus. I was permitted to have much experience of the faithfulness and goodness of my Jesus, often of a very wonderful nature.

I had much grace in my home and calling (the Colportage Society), and I was allowed to see much fruit of my work; yet all the time, with all this, something was perceptibly wanting to me; in particular there were some sins which I could not mortify, which caused me much trouble and distress.

What I received, at Oxford, and still more afterwards, and which I had before experienced, either interruptedly or but very feebly, is this. Now, I have in my peace a living joy in Jesus—such a firm and sweet rest as I had not known before—because Christ has undertaken to guide and to guard me. At the same time I perceive in myself not only sin but also utter weakness; and in all my works and conflicts it is Jesus alone who does all. "To be in Jesus" has for me a new and hitherto unknown meaning—a new joy, a new rest, a new strength, a full satisfaction. I feel an unbounded desire step by step to trust in Jesus—to surrender myself to Him who has bought me for His possession with His holy blood, and given me such a sense being near and dear to the Father, and the Father to m as I before only feebly knew. He shows me nothing b goodness and kindness; and since I placed Jesus betwe myself and men and circumstances, everything around r has quite a different appearance.

Jesus Christ is now to me a subduing and a freei strength, so that I dare to sing—

> "Where Jesus is the way
> It is brighter every day."

His word—especially "God manifest in the flesh," al in me—becomes always clearer to me through the Ho Ghost, to the praise and Glory of the blessed name Jesus.

May He daily "be formed in me," through the power the Holy Ghost! Amen.

Julius Baron von Gemmingen.

Barrett, Sons & Co., Crown Printing Works, Seething Lane.